Then she looked at Iolyn, whose face was emotionless despite his close call. But underneath the calm facade roiled a combustible mix of potent feelings, of which the uppermost was fear—for her.

Bria appreciated the sentiment, since she'd felt an equal amount of fear for his well-being as the assassin had taken aim. If Iolyn hadn't ducked, if she'd missed her throw, then he and his brother could've died.

Her heart still skipped a beat at the thought. So, she'd give him his fear for a second or so, but there was no danger now. He needed to get over it.

His forehead creased and his full lips thinned. She mentally smacked her head. Telepathy. She'd forgotten the damn telepathy. He'd just followed her every thought.

Pissed at herself for forgetting what Nadia had told her and at him for not letting her know he was reading her mind, she fluttered her hand at him like a princess to a peon. "Carry on, *gemat*. Your battle-mate has your ass covered."

Iolyn's eyes widened. *Battle-mate?*

His mental voice was a decadent surprise. It was low and husky—and if it had a taste, it would be the darkest and richest chocolate. Its timbre was a sensual caress over her mind. It filled her and made her happy—until she read his thoughts. He was worried. He thought her weak and helpless because of her upbringing and profession. To him, she was a fragile female he had to protect, especially now, after she'd deliberately placed herself in unnecessary danger. It was the Prime male's job to protect his mate, not the other way around.

What a load of crap.

PRIME IMPERATIVE

BOOK 3
THE PRIME CHRONICLES SERIES

MONETTE MICHAELS

ISBN-13: 978-0-9862730-2-5
ISBN-10: 0986273023

E-Book, Published by Liquid Silver Books, imprint of Atlantic Bridge Publishing, 2014.

Editor: Terri Schaefer
Cover Artist: April Martinez

DEDICATION

To my Prime fans—thanks for loving this series and talking it up. Because of you, there will be more books set in the Prime world.

ACKNOWLEDGEMENTS

Thanks to my fan, Margaret Sneyd, for naming my little alien creature. She not only named it—*Wefiantooth,* more commonly known as Ragbag—but also created a whole background for it.

As always, thanks and much love must go to my fan beta readers, Debbie Kline and Cheryl Pringle, for reading an early version and pointing out any series continuity errors. Just getting their positive feedback sustained me through the final revising process.

Mega-thanks and love go to Cherise Sinclair for her insightful and detailed critique of an early partial and then the first draft of this book. She always makes me take that extra step, and my books are always better for it.

And to Ezra Solomon for his meticulous line editing and his gentle nudges in his comments.

Thanks to April Martinez for taking the images I like and making them into a beautiful cover.

And, finally, to my editor Terri Schaefer, who always spots that one overused word and always makes me look good.

A SHORT HISTORY OF THE PRIME

I n the Perseus arm of the Milky Way lay the Cejuru solar system, home to the Prime, the oldest known hominid species in the galaxy.

After millennia of galactic exploration and colonization, the Prime became isolationists as other Milky Way populations initiated their own space explorations and migrated to uninhabited planets.

The Prime did not seek membership in the Galactic Alliance formed by the new explorers, but still felt duty-bound to protect the Milky Way from the Antareans, an ancient enemy from the Andromeda Galaxy. The Antareans were a militaristic, pseudo-reptilian species, and their all-consuming goal was to eliminate every hominid species.

The Antarean invasion of the Milky Way was held at bay for more than a thousand years. But this feat was accomplished at great cost to the Prime.

The Prime female population was targeted by the Antareans during frequent enemy raids, and many women were murdered or abducted to be used as sex slaves. During a particularly fierce siege, the Prime Elder Council ordered the evacuation of the majority of the women and children.

The Prime dealt the Antareans a severe blow and forced them back to Andromeda, but many ships carrying the evacuated women and children never returned.

The missing were referred to as the Lost Ones.

With the loss of so much of the female population, many Prime males could not find and "mark" their optimal mate. This mating mark was an unusual genetic adaptation that allowed Prime men and women to find the mate with whom they would have the best chance of producing healthy children.

When this marking process first appeared in Prime culture is unknown, but the cultural significance could not be denied. *Men and women who did not mark did not mate.*

After the last Antarean siege, the remaining Prime females began to experience low fertility and higher incidences of miscarriage. The cause was unknown. The women who managed to become pregnant and carry to term produced a disproportionate number of male offspring. A girl child was a rarity and considered a great blessing.

With the loss of so many women and children, plus the drastic decrease in birth rate, the Prime faced the reality of extinction for their species.

The Prime Elder Council voted, by a narrow majority, to join the Galactic Alliance. The Council's reasons for abandoning the Prime's isolationist policy were twofold:

One, to join forces with the powerful Galactic Alliance military to address the Antarean threat. The enemy had recovered from the last conflict and now ventured farther into the more populated arms of the Milky Way; and,

Two, to locate compatible females with whom their males could mate.

Though the marking ritual was ingrained in the fabric of Prime society, biologically the Prime had mated with non-Prime hominids in the past during the time of space colonization. The theory was they could do so again.

But a small, vocal minority didn't wish to pollute Prime bloodlines with the DNA of other hominids. This contentious rebel faction, calling themselves "Pure Blood," wreaked havoc on the Prime home planet—and in space.

Shortly after the Prime became a part of the Galactic Alliance, a miracle occurred. One of the Lost Ones was found.

Captain Melina Dmitros, the sole survivor of one of the ships bearing the lost women and children, was found to have a *gemate* mark. Her *gemat* was Captain Wulf Caradoc, the heir of the Prime leader.

Adding to the miracle, Melina brought with her data on altered routes the Prime ships had taken to escape the pursuing Antareans—routes none of the Prime had known about.

The information gave hope to another Prime male with no mate—Huw Caradoc, Wulf's brother. Huw now had a chance to find his Prime mate still alive.

The search for other surviving Lost Ones had been fruitless, but a monumental discovery was made: Cmdr. Nadia Petrovich, a Terran and the Science Officer on the Alliance Starship *Galanti*, carried Prime genetics within her DNA and was marked as Huw Caradoc's true *gemate*.

With Huw and Nadia's mating, and the evidence of other male Prime/female non-Prime matings, the Prime race's bold move to find mates outside their solar system was proven a prescient one.

But the issue of Prime low population growth still needed to be studied. Why did Prime females have trouble conceiving and carrying babies to term? Could Prime women who'd lost their *gemats,* or never had one, mate with non-Prime males? Why did some Terrans and Volusian women mark when mating with Prime males and some did not? And the most radical question of all...were the mating markings even necessary to finding a mate with whom to have children?

Dr. Brianna Martin of the Galactic Alliance Astrobiological Research Laboratory was the leading researcher seeking answers for those questions and more.

The *Galanti*'s next mission would be to venture to the planet Oz in the Tau Ceti system to pick up Dr. Martin and her team and bring them back to Cejuru Prime to assist the Prime scientists in finding answers. But before the *Galanti*'s crew could do so, Dr. Martin issued an SOS call to the Galactic Alliance. She was in danger...and she was a marked Lost One. She asked the Alliance to come get her and tell her *gemat* she needed him.

Her *gemat* was Iolyn Caradoc, the brother of Wulf and Huw and son of the Prime's leader.

And so, Iolyn and Brianna's story began...

CHAPTER 1

"Our leave is canceled." Iolyn Caradoc strode toward his brothers, Wulf and Huw, and their mates, plus Joen Dakkin and his mate Lia, as they lounged around the resort pool. Tor Maren, the Prime ambassador to the Galactic Alliance, barely kept pace with him. "The *Galanti* needs to leave space dock as soon as possible," Iolyn said. "I've recalled the crew."

"What happened?" Wulf had his arm around Mel's shoulder as if he anticipated an attack.

Huw did the same with Nadia.

Iolyn sat, picked up Wulf's whiskey and finished it in one gulp, then picked up Huw's and did the same. He knew he was putting off battle vibes, but he couldn't help it. He'd never felt such fear before and wasn't handling it well.

Tor, who was like a second father to him and his brothers, sat and told the hovering waiter, "Gliesian white wine for me and the ladies. Whiskey for the men." The waiter hurried off. "Since Iolyn is attempting to get drunk, I'll relay what has happened."

Iolyn snarled, grabbed Joen's almost-empty glass and tossed it back.

"I received word from Admiral Nelson at Alliance Command that Dr. Brianna Martin has been threatened...a man stalking her attempted to kidnap her," Tor said. "She managed to escape and put a call out to the Alliance to rescue her."

"That's terrible. Of course we'll go get her and ensure she arrives at Cejuru Prime safely," Wulf said. "But why is Iolyn attempting to get drunk?"

Tor sighed and shook his head. "Dr. Martin is a Lost One. And she is..."

"My mate!" Iolyn pounded his fist on the table. "She sent an image of her marking to the Alliance and Prime Commands, asking that her mate be found and told. She asked, if possible, that he come and get her." He stood and paced angrily around the table. "I'm clear across the fucking galaxy while my mate had to fight off an attack." He threw his head back and roared the Caradoc battle cry to the skies.

Huw and Wulf rounded the table and held onto him until he quit shouting. *Diew*, he was in full-blown *batel rabia*, the Prime battle rage, and would experience lesser stages of it until he had Brianna in his arms.

Nadia joined them and placed her hand on Iolyn's shoulder. "How can we help?"

Mel also joined the huddle, lending her support. Their combined presence calmed him a bit. He wasn't alone in this; his brothers and their mates would see him through the horrible hours until he could be with his *gemate*, the mate fate and the One had chosen for him.

Tor, Joen, and Lia used their bodies to ward off the curious glances of the understandably shaken bystanders. The Caradoc battle cry had turned many an enemy's bowels to water.

"We get to Brianna as quickly as possible," Iolyn growled.

36 Standard Hours earlier
Galactic Alliance Astrobiological Research Lab
Planet Oz, Tau Ceti system

DR. BRIANNA MARTIN EYED HER target and took careful aim. She nailed the male figure right between the eyes.

"Yay! See if you can beat that, my friend." Bria happy-danced her way toward the life-sized, pseudo-reptilian male anatomy chart and pulled her scalpel from the kill zone in the frontal lobe. "Did I forget to mention I was med school scalpel-throwing champion three years in a row? Looks like you get to buy dinner."

There was no response from her research assistant Cheri Stafford. Instead she heard a gasp and the sound of Cheri moving quickly away from their impromptu contest venue.

Primordial instincts Bria rarely had to rely upon in the medical world went on alert, sharpening her empathic abilities. Something dangerous headed their way. It smelled like a hot, fierce wind off a desert. She tasted the dustiness of it on her tongue and felt it flaying her skin. She hurried toward her friend, who stood in the entrance to the lab. "Cheri? What's wrong?"

"Red alert!" Her friend growled the words as she made a move to cut off whoever approached.

Bria peered around her friend and saw her nemesis, Jotak M'tali.

Jotak, the chief of security for the research facility, strode down the long corridor in his ruler-of-the-planet, owner-of-all-he-surveyed mode.

"Really? Now? Doesn't that...that..." *freaking, scary, creep-a-zoid* "...man understand the meaning of the word *no*?" As in never, no way, no how, ever in the infinite future of possibilities.

Cheri paused outside the doorway and threw a commiserating grimace over her shoulder. "I'll venture a guess and say *not*. He hasn't seen you yet. So hide. I'll get rid of the slime-sucking bottom-feeder. He won't get a chance to touch you again."

"No!" Bria grabbed the arm of her loyal and well-meaning friend, the sister Bria had never had because she'd been adopted into a family with six boys. She pulled Cheri back and whispered, "He can smell me. He knows I'm here. Go...get help. Preferably someone who isn't susceptible to his Dornian hypnotic abilities."

"But...but...he hurt you last time." Cheri's eyes filled with angry tears. "And no one did anything about it."

The incident Cheri referred to had occurred about a standard week ago. Jotak, tired of her holding him at arm's length, had become more aggressive in his pursuit. He'd cornered her in the research facility's storeroom, forced a kiss on her...then attempted to rape her.

Bria shuddered and swallowed hard against the sickness threatening to erupt. She still bore bruises and claw marks from his rough handling. If a janitor hadn't happened by, Jotak would've succeeded in assaulting her. Her rudimentary self-defense skills hadn't even made a dent against Jotak's superior strength and training.

The janitor had backed her story when she'd filed the complaint with local authorities, but then the poor man had gone missing. Using his mesmeric abilities, Jotak had persuaded the local law officers that the alleged attack had been a mere lovers' tiff. Her bruises were ignored.

So, until she had security footage of an attack or eyewitnesses who couldn't be *persuaded* to say otherwise—or she was severely injured enough for medical treatment—no one would believe the Chief of Security was stalking and threatening her.

"If he smells you, he smells both of us," Cheri hissed as she reversed Bria's grip and held onto Bria's arm. "Come with me. We can both get away."

"No, he'll hunt us down." And he'd hurt Cheri, because he had no use for her. "Dornians love nothing more than to chase prey." And to kill them. Killing and hiding a body were as easy for a Dornian as putting on clothing in the morning. "It's me he wants."

And he wouldn't kill Bria. He wanted to breed with her.

Not. Gonna. Happen.

Bria gave her friend an urgent shove. "Go out the back. Now." Her friend hesitated. "Cheri, please go...and hurry! Bring back help."

Cheri cast one last angry, fear-filled glance at the six-and-a-half-foot pseudo-reptilian stalking toward the lab and then ran out the back exit.

Bria turned and blocked the lab's main entrance, giving Cheri extra time to make her escape. Realizing she still held a scalpel, she placed the hand holding the lethally sharp instrument alongside her leg. If he got too close, she knew just where to cut him, to force him to take the time and energy to heal himself as his kind did. She might've been raised by pacifists on a communal farming planet and was, by choice, a healer, but she believed in self-defense.

"Brianna! What is-s-s this-s-s I hear?" His low voice carried down the hallway as he decreased the space between them. His voice had an eerie, sibilant hiss due to his genetics and made the hairs on her body stand on end. She shivered and tried to ignore the primitive response of prey. "You will *not* leave Oz. This-s-s-s I will not permit."

Jotak had no rights over her, no matter what he thought in his screwed up, alpha-dominant, narcissistic brain. She'd made the point clear many times...and would again and again until he processed the truth—she'd never be with him.

"Good afternoon to you, too, Jotak." Despite her vow to remain calm and in control, her voice trembled from fear and all the adrenaline speeding through her system.

Of course, her subtly sarcastic reprimand on his lack of manners swept over his head like a solar wind.

"Explain, woman." Jotak loomed over her in full alpha-male-intimidation mode with his fists on his hips and a frown on his practically lipless mouth. Some women might find his six-foot six-inch muscular body, pale green skin, dark-green, almost-black hair, and golden eyes attractive in an exotic way.

Bria found him irritating and very, very menacing.

"We had this discussion almost s-s-six weeks ago. We agreed you were not going to Cejuru Prime."

Jotak spoke the name of the home planet of the Prime race, a recent addition to the Galactic Alliance, as if it produced a foul taste in his mouth. His Dornian race, a nomadic people that ran con games and hired out as mercenaries to the highest bidder, was a distant cousin to the Antareans, the Prime's archenemy for millennia. The antipathy must have been bred into their pseudo-reptilian genes.

While choosing to work within the structure of the Galactic Alliance had made Jotak an outlier within his race, he was no less criminal or less dangerous. The Dornian heritage which made him a good con man and warrior were lousy for just about everything else, including his current job providing security for a bunch of brainiac research scientists.

Whoever had hired and then promoted the man should be shot.

"*You* said I wasn't going," Bria pointed out with a calmness she didn't feel. The raw energy coming off the large and powerful male frame had her hominid primitive brain urging her to run—and another little used and more violent part of her congenital makeup urged her to fight.

For the moment, she chose a higher brain response and attempted to reason with him. If that tack didn't work, she'd use the scalpel on a vital artery and then run like hell.

"If you recall, I didn't agree." Slowly, she moved sideways, further away from his body, toward the rear exit of the lab. Just in case diplomacy didn't work.

During a normal encounter, Jotak had absolutely zero respect for personal space, but his current maneuver of crowding her was aimed at bullying her into submitting to his will.

Bria wouldn't succumb, but that didn't mean she didn't feel threatened...because she did. She'd had up close and personal experience with how quickly Jotak went from a simmering anger to a roiling rage.

For now, Jotak mirrored her movements, stalking her like the predator he was, while closing any gap she created. Then he stopped. His head swept from side to side as his split-tongue tasted the air. His slitted yellow eyes flared. He'd noted Cheri's lingering scent.

Thank the One, her friend was long gone, out of Jotak's reach.

"Someone is-s-s here?" He pinned her with his basilisk stare.

It didn't work on her.

"We're alone." Bria placed her workstation between her and the large male. "Now, say what you have to say and then go. I have work to do before I can leave for the day."

He flicked his tongue, quickly tasting the air once more, and then emitted an almost orgasmic guttural sound. His body seemed to grow another inch in height and breadth. His thin lips twisted upward. If she were brave enough to look, she knew she'd find evidence of his arousal. He was feeding on the smell of her fear, and like the apex predator he was, he liked it.

Why had she ever thought she could be "just friends" with this man? She must've been nuts.

"If you wish to leave Oz, Brianna, I will take you wherever you wish to go. We can join my parent's space caravan."

"I am leaving Oz to do my job. I have no desire to wander the universe—"

She left "with you" unsaid.

"Wrong ans-s-swer," he hissed.

Her gut told her an attack was imminent. How long had it been since Cheri left? Five standard minutes or less? It seemed like hours.

Hurry, hurry, hurry.

Bria held her ground and watched Jotak pace back and forth, his movements sinuous and a lure to the unwary. His hungry stare never left her as he moved ever closer to her position, closer to when she'd have to use the weapon in her hand.

"You can't mesmerize me," she reminded him. "You tried when you attempted to rape me."

"Yes-s-s-s. You got away...and I caught you." He laughed. "That was fun. Run, little Brianna. Go ahead. I will catch you. Make you mine. No one will believe your stories. The local law officers *are* susceptible to my stare."

And he was right, damn him.

Bria gripped her scalpel even more tightly. Looked as if she wouldn't be able to avoid injuring the slime-sucking bastard.

Cut off his head and end the problem forever.

This primal, more bloodthirsty part of her had only awakened recently—right after she'd discovered and accepted she was a mated Prime female. A *gemate*. A Lost One. And a battle-mate.

Bria didn't know the first thing on how to be a battle-mate. And even if she did, she didn't think she could kill any creature, even Jotak. Injure to defend? Maybe. Kill? No. She was a doctor. She'd also been raised by her adoptive parents' people to seek peaceful resolutions to conflict.

Nurture, in this instance, would trump Nature.

"Brianna..." Jotak growled, "you are mine. I have claimed you. I will not let you leave me."

She held her weaponless hand in front of her, palm up, in the universal body language of pleading. "Jotak, please. I'm not yours. I haven't agreed. I'll be leaving with my team when the *Galanti* comes to pick us up."

"No!" Jotak lunged and ripped her microscope from its locked-down position on the metal work station and threw the heavy scope against the wall as if it weighed nothing.

She gasped and jumped backwards. Then he ripped apart her station to get to her. Frozen in place from shock, she barely avoided being hit by debris. His next move was a blur.

Before she could even think about running, he grabbed her arms and shook her. "You are mine."

She couldn't move...couldn't scream and could barely breathe as her mind flashed back to the last time he'd put his hands on her. The room spun around her and spots floated across her vision. As she began to fall into an infinitely dark pit, a surge of energy built within her.

Then the violence-hungry part of her screamed: *Use the scalpel. Cut him. Now.*

Yet she couldn't make herself do it.

"Tell me you belong to me." His fingers dug into her arms so cruelly his sharp nails drew blood.

The pain ramped up her body's fight-or-flight response. But she couldn't flee.

She had to fight.

Hormones poured into her bloodstream. Her heart beat fast and loud in her ears. All her senses became hyper-alert—and her body felt stronger as it prepared to fight.

After which, she'd run like hell for the safest place she could find.

With his eyes slitted like a snake's and his tongue flicking over her face like a small, slippery whip, he roared and shook her until she swore she could hear her bones rattling. "Say it!"

"Enough!" she screamed, shocking him, shocking her.

Then, with every bit of anger-fueled strength she could muster, she kneed him in the balls.

Jotak howled and released his hold on her to cup himself.

Her arms freed, she slashed the main artery to his brain, letting loose a spurting fountain of putrid green blood. And even while Jotak cursed and promised to make her regret her actions, he began to heal.

Bria ran out of the lab as fast as her shaky legs could handle. She'd seen enough pseudo-reptilians heal to know it wouldn't take him long to come after her. She sprinted down the corridor. Her heart threatened to beat its way out of her chest. Her breathing was harsh and raspy, and she was close to hyperventilating.

When she ran into Cheri and two strangers dressed in Alliance military uniforms, she went limp with relief. The soldiers had the light blue skin of Volusians. Volusians were impervious to pseudo-reptilian mesmerism and toxins, thank the One.

"Are you okay?" Cheri placed an arm around Bria's waist and provided much-needed support as Bria's legs threatened to give out. "What did the bastard do to you?"

Before Bria could catch her breath to reassure her friend she was fine, the Volusians growled and placed their very large muscular bodies between the two women and a furious Jotak who sped toward them.

"Dr. Martin," one of the Volusians spoke in a low, terse voice, "tell us. Did the split-tongued bastard harm you?"

Leaning against Cheri, Bria rasped out, "No."

Her friend snorted. "You said that the last time. But I saw the bruises he gave you. This time, your shirt is shredded. You have claw marks on your arms. You're bleeding. That's called being harmed."

The soldier who asked the question nodded his approval of Cheri's words. "Dr. Martin, did he inject any toxins? If so, we must act quickly. My blood is an antidote."

"No...he grabbed and shook me—and yelled. I'm fine. Really."

Cheri didn't look as if she believed Bria's words. Neither did the Volusians.

"He scared me. I kneed him in the balls and followed up by using my scalpel," she held up the bloody instrument still clutched in her shaky right hand, "to cut his main brain artery. Then I got away."

The soldiers grunted. The sound was one of approval. Glad someone approved. She wasn't sure she did. Violence went against everything she'd ever been taught.

*But pacifism will not keep me—or my warrior-*gemat*—alive.*

She understood things would be different in the future. And she was willing to learn how to defend herself and her unknown mate. But, bless the One, she hoped fighting wouldn't be a routine activity.

Bria couldn't imagine feeling as she did now too often. She was extremely wobbly from the flood of stress hormones. She wanted to throw up and lie down with the covers pulled over her head—at the same time. She had a feeling her *gemat* wouldn't be pleased with a notably wussy battle-mate.

"Cursed Volusians!" Jotak's roaring bounced off the titanium walls of the narrow corridor. The ringing sound added to her pounding headache. "Stand down. This does not concern you."

Jotak stopped about a meter away from the two Volusians and glowered at them. His hands were up, and his claws dripped a yellow-tinged, viscous neurotoxin. "That is-s-s an order."

Bria and Cheri held onto each other. Who was holding whom up at this point was a toss up. They both shook so hard it was amazing the floors weren't vibrating.

If Jotak scratched Cheri, she'd be paralyzed, at a minimum, or dead if a large enough amount got into her bloodstream—even with an antidote available.

Bria didn't have a clue what might or might not happen if Jotak's toxin entered her bloodstream. The Prime had been isolationists until recently. The only things she knew about the peculiarities of their—her—anatomy and physiology were what she'd gleaned from working with Dr. Lia Morgan-Dakkin of the Alliance Starship *Galanti*, and those tests had been centered on reproductive biology.

She still hadn't gotten over the mind-numbing shock of finding out she was Prime and not Terran. It had been less than two standard months since that discovery, and she was still coming to terms with the truth. She had a huge learning curve to surmount concerning her true biology.

"Brianna!" Jotak's shout reverberated through her very bones. Cheri made a tiny squeaking noise and held onto Bria harder. Bria wasn't ashamed to admit she held back just as hard. "Pay attention, woman."

Her demented stalker swept a sneering, slitted glare over the two Volusians who'd drawn their battle-blades to defend her and Cheri. "I s-s-said stand down."

The lead soldier shook his head. "We will not." He thrust his blade forward. "You won't heal if I behead you. I suggest *you* stand down."

"You threaten me? I am your s-s-superior officer. I am in charge of all security personnel in this laboratory facility."

The two Volusians laughed. "You are not in charge of us. We are Alliance Military and were assigned by Alliance Command to protect Dr. Martin and her team. Your assault of Dr. Martin will be reported to our superiors—who are also your superiors. Now go, my blade wishes to taste Dornian blood."

"Report me. The Alliance will do nothing." Jotak hissed and glared at the Volusians, then fixed his angry gaze on Bria.

If looks could kill, well—

"We will discuss-s-s this-s-s issue...later...over dinner. I expect you to be more receptive to my wishes by then. I will pick you up at 1800 hours. Do not make me s-s-search for you, *mehina*."

What the hell? He expected her to...the man was as dense as the granite that made up Oz. And like hell she was *his woman*. Well, he'd be forced to come look for her, because she didn't plan to be anywhere near her apartment at 1800 hours.

Since the reply she wanted to give his outrageous demands would only escalate the tense situation, she said nothing, merely inclined her head as he stalked past them. She didn't want the injury—or death—of Cheri and the two soldiers on her conscience.

Once Jotak was out of sight and hearing, she turned to the two men who'd stood for her and Cheri. "I'd avoid him for the next few days if I were you. He won't like that you came to my defense. And just why were you—I'm sorry I don't know your names—assigned to my team?"

"I am V'niko. My comrade is A'nan. The Alliance has heard rumors of threats against you and your team by the Prime rebel faction, Pure Blood," V'niko said as the four of them walked back to the lab. "And be assured, we are not afraid of Jotak M'tali. We will report this incident to the proper authorities in the Alliance Command. You ladies will need to make statements tomorrow at the Alliance Military offices."

V'niko stood in the doorway of the lab and frowned when he spotted the broken microscope and her destroyed workstation. "You are not strong enough to have created such destruction. We will record the scene and the bloody marks on your arm to document M'tali's attack."

"Do what you need to do," Bria said. "But as Jotak said, nothing will come of it. He'll use his mesmerism abilities to make the problem go away. Then he'll kill you and hide the bodies. I suspect he's already killed one witness, an Obam male janitor who was also not susceptible to his hypnotic powers."

V'niko smiled, and it wasn't a nice one. "A'nan and I are not easy to kill. Plus the reports will also go to Tooh 10 to our superiors. M'tali is not as powerful as he thinks he is. You and your people will be safe in our care until the *Galanti* arrives to take over."

"You have to sleep sometime," Cheri pointed out.

"Yes, which is why you will be moved to a hotel and registered under assumed names. A'nan and I will take turns guarding you there...and here as you do your work." V'niko gestured to the lab. "Do you have anything else you need to work on tonight? Or, shall we escort you to your residences to pack enough clothing to get you through the next few nights?"

"The *Galanti* will arrive that soon?" Bria frowned. "I was told maybe another three standard weeks before they could make it. The crew is supposed to be on leave after a mission."

A'nan answered, "Three weeks is still the *Galanti*'s estimated arrival time. If we can't get M'tali relieved of his post and transferred to Tooh 10 to appear before a tribunal for his assault on you, we will guard you as long as necessary."

"Mere words aren't adequate to express my gratitude." Bria managed to conjure up a smile for the two men.

"You were very brave to stand up to him and fight, Dr. Martin," V'niko said. "But let A'nan and I do the fighting in the future."

"I'm *so* all over that sentiment." Bria's breathing hitched. "I couldn't...couldn't stand him touching me again." She wrapped her arms around her middle and hugged herself. She was so cold she thought she'd shiver apart. "I can't ever let him get me alone again. Ever."

Because, today, she'd tipped her hand and made a grievous error—she'd fought back. In the past, she'd escaped his attentions through guile, quick thinking, and just plain dumb luck. In this attack, she'd demonstrated she wasn't a timid plains hopper, had proven she could physically hurt him.

Jotak wouldn't underestimate her again.

"Maybe you shouldn't come into the lab at all. The team and I, with V'niko's and A'nan's protection, can continue to run experiments and get things packed up for the trip to Cejuru Prime. Find a good hiding place," Cheri urged. "If we need input, telecommute. Stay out of Jotak's sight. Once on Cejuru Prime, you'll be out of his reach forever and have other protection."

The other protection Cheri referred to was Bria's *gemat*. Only Cheri knew Bria was Prime. She'd confided in her friend when she'd first become aware what her marking meant. She then had Cheri rerun all the tests on Bria's DNA and document the *gemate* marking. The results had been too important to be tainted by Bria's self-interest.

Before Bria revealed to anyone else about being a Lost One, she wanted to attempt to locate and meet her *gemat*—if he was even alive. She'd seen enough newsfeeds on Melina Dmitros-Caradoc's story to know another Lost One appearing would be big news. She was also aware she would immediately become a target for enemies of the Prime. Although it sounded as if the Pure Blood terrorists had already focused on her because of her research.

She touched the area above her right ovary where her marking lay. It was silly, but she sensed the quiescent mark was impatiently waiting for the perfect neurochemical signature of her *gemat* to awaken it fully, just as real danger had roused what she suspected was her battle-mate nature.

Growing up on a communal farm on the planet Gliese 581C, she'd always known the marking made her different. Unique. Special. She just hadn't realized how much.

Now that she did, she was eager to learn about her birth parents' heritage, anxious to meet her *gemat* and come together with him. Then and only then, she'd be where she truly belonged.

CHAPTER 2

That evening

After V'niko and A'nan escorted her and Cheri to their respective apartments to pack bags, the two men took them to a hotel catering to visiting dignitaries and businessmen near the Alliance Military's compound.

V'niko followed through on his promise and filed a report on Jotak's attack, along with images of her destroyed lab equipment and the claw marks on her arms. The stalwart Volusian had also informed her that after she and Cheri filed their statements, the Alliance Military would send the military police to arrest Jotak.

Bria had been so happy to hear the news she'd cried.

"So?" Cheri relaxed into the padded banquette seating in the hotel dining room and took a sip of the light white wine the waiter had recommended to complement their seafood entrees. "Jotak's ass will soon be taken care of. Let's turn to the more important issue in your life: How are you going to go about finding your *gemat*?"

Bria sipped her wine. It was one made from grapes her adoptive Terran family grew on Gliese 581C. The crisp taste evoked a brief longing for the simpler life she'd led there, but it quickly dissipated. She wasn't Terran. She was Prime. The discovery of her heritage promised an exciting and challenging future. She'd always liked challenges, which was why she'd left the farming commune to attend college in the Tau Ceti system. Her departure had been against the wishes of her parents and five of her six brothers.

Only Damon, the black sheep brother, the wild one, had supported her need to spread her wings. Which was why he was her favorite sibling.

"Bria? Cheri to Bria." Her friend snapped her fingers in front of Bria's face. "What's wrong? You spaced out on me. Are you still worrying about Jotak?"

"Just thinking the wine was probably made from my family's grapes." Her lips twisted slightly. "Was homesick for a second."

Bria frowned and considered her friend's question. Was part of her distraction centered on her scary stalker? Yes—it was. A constant niggling in the part of her she now recognized as Prime was telling her the only good Dornian was a dead Dornian—because then, and only then, would she be safe.

"Bria?" Cheri reached to touch her arm. "I don't like that look. What's wrong?"

"Jotak *will* continue to be a problem."

"You can't know that," Cheri quite logically pointed out. "V'niko sounded certain the Alliance Military would ship him to Tooh 10 for trial."

"But he isn't gone...yet." Bria shivered and immediately thought of the ancient Terran saying about a goose walking over a person's grave. Graves, not a good thought. "I'll feel better tomorrow after we give our statements and he is arrested."

She picked up her fork and began to eat the seafood risotto she'd ordered. "As for your other question? Lia told me the Prime have a detailed bond mark database only accessible to Prime researchers and certain members of the Elder Council.

Once we're on Prime soil, I should have access to the database for our research. I'll run my marking to find my match."

"And what if your *gemat* died during the siege of the planet?" Cheri's voice was soft as she asked the question which, at one time, had haunted Bria.

But Bria *knew* he was alive—and had no logical way to explain that certainty to Cheri or even herself.

"Then I'll mourn the man I never knew. Find my birth father and my *gemat*'s birth parents, if they are alive, and add them to my extended family. And..." She looked Cheri in the eye. "...go on to prove that a Prime woman who has lost a mate—or one who has never been marked—is still a woman who can have a full family life with a husband and children."

"Oh boy," Cheri murmured and took a large gulp of her wine. "The Prime are never gonna know what hit them, are they?"

"No. I plan to set years of myopic cultural precedent on its ear." She picked up a flaky dinner roll, buttered it, and then took a decisive bite. "The era of a paternalistic council of elders dictating who can mate with whom due to some neurochemical, adaptive markings is over. The Prime can't afford to keep any fertile Prime male or female from breeding with other Prime—or with other compatible hominids."

"I hope the lab on Cejuru Prime has good security," muttered Cheri as she fiddled with her silverware. "Remember the saying about 'killing the messenger?'"

"Yeah, I know." She shoved her fingers through her hair. "But they have no choice—the Prime race is dying. They've had less than zero population growth for the last decade according to the statistical reports. Their population is aging, and the men and women who are young enough to have children aren't allowed to do so unless they have compatible markings. And all that is on top of the fertility and miscarriage issues with mated Prime women, which might be the easier issue to fix in the short term. But long term—"

"They'll still lose ground unless they mate outside the marking," Cheri completed the thought.

Bria and her team had had this same conversation many, many times since the Prime joined the Alliance and Bria's team had been assigned to help the Prime solve their population growth issues. The fact there were still some Luddites among the Prime population—the most dangerous among them, the Pure Blood faction—wouldn't stop Bria from doing her job.

In an unspoken agreement, the two shifted topics and discussed anything but Jotak, Pure Bloods, Prime population growth, or Bria's *gemat,* while they enjoyed the rest of their meal.

It was only later, as Bria tossed and turned in the unfamiliar bed, that her thoughts turned once again toward her mate.

This wasn't the first time her sleep had been disturbed with thoughts of her unknown *gemat,* and it probably wouldn't be the last. Because it was dark and quiet, with no one around and nothing to distract her, she wondered: Was he a scientist like her, or a warrior who'd appreciate his *gemate* being a battle-mate? Would she be a disappointment to him with her lack of fighting skills?

Most importantly—would he love her?

Because she knew she would love him. He would be her heart's desire, the one man who'd make her heart sing and her soul melt.

When she'd first discovered she was Prime and had somewhat gotten over the initial shock, it was as if a light had turned on inside her. She *knew* her *gemat* was alive and somewhere in the galaxy.

This knowledge defied all her training as a scientist, as a doctor. While she could explain the *gemat-gemate* marking as a biological adaptive response to supremely compatible body chemistries and would in time explain why the markings first appeared, there was also—all scientific logic aside—

an inexplicable spiritual aspect involved with the mating bond. She *knew* this because she'd experienced it...was still experiencing it.

The Terrans called such spiritual bonding between a man and a woman, soul mates.

Neither concept—the *gemat-gemate* spiritual bonding or Terran soul mates—could be isolated, weighed, measured, or replicated. They just were. And even with all her scientific knowledge, she could still accept that—sometimes, certain things must be accepted on faith.

Soon, she would meet her *gemat*. She hoped he liked her.

CHAPTER 3

The next morning

Her statement to the Alliance authorities completed, Bria cut across the platform of the commuter shuttle station on her way back to the hotel.

As V'niko had predicted, an immediate arrest warrant had been issued for Jotak. V'niko, along with two military police officers, went to the laboratory to take Jotak into custody. A'nan had accompanied Cheri to the lab so she could inform the rest of their team what had happened and to carry on until it was safe for Bria to join them.

Bria had wanted to go with A'nan and Cheri, but V'niko put his foot down. When she'd worried aloud that Cheri could be in danger until Jotak was in custody, V'niko had said, "You are his primary target. Cheri is less than nothing to him, a minor irritant. You are his obsession. Your presence endangers anyone and everyone around you. I will come for you when he can no longer harm you."

So, here she was, wending her way through hundreds of people as they waited for commuter trains. The place was noisy and alive with conversations and the rumbling of the trains. With so many people surrounding her, her empathic abilities went on overload. To alleviate a suddenly pounding headache, she put up the mental shields she'd taught herself at an early age.

Because of the shields, the attack came as a surprise.

Strong arms surrounded her from behind. Her first thought was—*How did Jotak find me?* Her second was—*Oh shit.*

Her third was to struggle against his cruel grip. His arms tightened like a boa constrictor until she couldn't breathe, until her bones threatened to break. Yet she still tried to free herself, kicking at his legs and clawing at his forearms.

Jotak shook her. "You made a bad mistake last night, *mehina.*" His words were a low snarl against her ear.

With a vicious tug, he pulled her against his body and rubbed his erection over her bottom. She stilled and barely breathed, afraid of exciting him even more.

To the other commuters, they would appear to be lovers. But if anyone looked closely, they'd find otherwise. She had to look terrified, because she was. She inhaled deeply, opened her mouth, then—

"If you scream, I will kill that little girl." He lifted one hand and pointed to a blonde-haired cherub with a backpack who held her mother's hand. "Nod if you understand."

Bria complied. She couldn't allow him to harm innocents. V'niko's assessment that Jotak would harm others to attain his target had been one hundred percent correct. She hoped she'd live long enough to tell him so.

Jotak shifted her to his left side, his arm around her shoulders in a vice-like hold, pinning her to him. His right hand hovered over his sidearm.

Bria rapidly examined and rejected maneuvers that would allow her to escape without resulting in harm to others. There weren't any. She'd have to allow him to lead her away from the crowded train platform to a more isolated area.

Once away from the crowds, she'd do her best to get away, even if she died doing so.

"Don't try anything. It would be very foolish, *mehina*." He murmured the words over her ear, then lightly bit the lobe and licked away the blood he'd drawn with his fang-like teeth.

Everything in her cringed at his touch. She pulled her head away from his mouth, afraid he'd bite her again, and this time inject a light dose of his neurotoxin in order to paralyze her.

"And never, ever, move away from my touch. Soon, I will kiss and bite every creamy, golden millimeter of your body. I will build your immunity to my toxins. Once you are resistant to the side effects, I will plant my seed in you." He nuzzled her neck, inhaled, then shuddered with pleasure against her. "You are ripe. My seed will take. You will give me strong sons."

Never. She gulped, swallowing the sickness threatening to come up her throat.

Dig deep. Unleash the battle-mate power.

She was stronger than she thought—and always had been—but had been too scared of the power to use it, even when she hadn't known what it was. It made her "different." She'd inadvertently tapped into the deep, dark energy well as a young adult—to horrible results. She'd broken a taunting playmate's bones and, another time, gave Damon a concussion when he ordered her not to date a boy she liked. Terrified of her aberrant power, she built thick walls to contain the energy, walls very similar to the shields she erected to keep others' emotions and feelings out of her mind. And even then, she hoped and prayed she'd never, ever have to call upon it.

Yesterday, she hadn't tapped into what she'd always thought of as her dark side to escape Jotak, hadn't even thought about it. But that was then. Today, the will to survive flooded her mind and body as the walls around her latent core of strength cracked.

As Jotak led her into a less crowded area of the station plaza, her more primitive side took control. The power surged forth as if it were happy to be free. It bubbled through her blood, warming her, giving her the strength and courage to take matters into her own hands. And as it warmed her from the inside out, she recognized it for what it was. Her innate Prime DNA was coming to the fore. She was becoming a battle-mate.

She'd feel more confident of success if she had some fighting skills or a weapon—a knife or even the scalpel she'd used against Jotak yesterday in the lab. But as a doctor, she usually didn't go about armed in public.

Her Prime genetics dictated she was meant to be a warrior. But she didn't feel like one. Hadn't been trained to be one. And now was probably not the best time to figure out how to be one—or, more importantly, how to balance her warrior nature with her profession.

"Good, Brianna." Jotak's purr of pleasure at her seeming acquiescence pissed her off.

Her primal energy pushed and shoved, wanting to explode, to blast the smug asshole. It was getting harder and harder to keep the almost sentient energy under control.

Patience. One thing Bria was sure of, if she acted too soon, she could fail. The element of surprise—and her intelligence—were her best assets at this point.

The pressure to act backed off. Well, at least, she had control over her power, that had to account for something. That way, she wouldn't shoot her energy wad too soon.

As they traveled further away from the commuter station, she scanned the area, looking for the best spot to make her move. If her memory was correct, there was a local law enforcement facility about five hundred meters east of their current position. If she could break away at the right moment and make it there, she'd be safe. She'd make sure the locals knew there was a warrant out for Jotak's arrest. He couldn't mesmerize a whole station of police officers.

With a course of action set in her mind, Bria forced herself to relax even more within Jotak's hold.

In response, he loosened his painful grip on her shoulder. Her lips twisted with satisfaction. He thought she'd bowed to his will. *Sucker.*

She bided her time as they ate up the meters toward her goal. Her body hummed with pent-up energy. She took deep, slow breaths, oxygenating her blood for the fight. Her senses were alert to Jotak's every move, every breath, every noise.

When he turned to move in the opposite direction from the precinct building, she acted. She weakened her knees. As she became dead weight, Jotak's arm fell away from her shoulders completely.

Before he could even growl or grab her, she whirled away from him.

Damn, she'd moved too far. His body was angled in such a way that his balls were out of the reach of her knee and even her foot.

With no time to think, and fearing she couldn't outrun him, she resorted to her knowledge of Dornian anatomy. When he tried to grab her with his dominant hand, she leaned in—surprising him—grabbed his elbow and pinched a nerve, causing his arm to go numb so he couldn't take hold of her. She kicked his knee and then spun out of reach once more.

He roared. The noise stabbed at her senses like a thousand needles.

Shit, all she'd done was piss him off worse. She kept moving backward. Her gaze never left his angry face, even though all she wanted to do was drop to the ground, curl into a ball, and moan at the pain caused by his sounds of rage.

If he caught her now, he'd hurt her, but he wouldn't kill her. He wanted her alive.

Jotak growled. "Come here. Now." He followed his order by limping toward her as she continued to back away.

And that was his mistake.

She lunged at him and led with a punch to the sensitive space between his slitty eyes, the sweet spot where his reptile-like brain's motor skills and respiratory functions were centered. With him temporarily stunned, she followed up with a solid kick to his balls.

Jotak fell to the ground like a shuttlecraft losing power in heavy air.

Then Bria turned and, pulling on her battle-mate side, raced toward the security facility.

Jotak's gasping cries of pain and outrage echoed off the buildings. The thudding of his uneven gait seemed to shake the ground. His recovery had been too damn fast. A knife would've done a better job in slowing him down.

A knife would've done a better job of killing him.

Bria shook her head in denial. Internal philosophical debates on the ethics of taking a life would have to wait for a better time. The sound of Jotak's wheezing breaths came ever closer.

"Brianna! Stop. You cannot escape me."

She was sure going to try. But it would be close. She could almost feel his breath on her neck.

Then the most chilling, most beautiful sound she'd ever heard filled the air.

A Volusian battle cry.

"Keep running, Dr. Martin," V'niko yelled and then ululated his warrior's call to fight once more.

Bria did as she was told, but chanced a look over her shoulder as she reached the steps of the precinct building.

V'niko had tackled Jotak to the ground. Jotak tried to use his laser pistol on the Volusian, but V'niko disarmed him and threw the weapon out of Jotak's reach. The two resorted to hand-to-hand and the use of blades. They looked to be equally matched in size and skills.

The only sure ways to kill a Dornian were cutting off his head, skewering his frontal lobe, or poisoning. Lasers didn't penetrate the pseudo-reptile's skin. So, V'niko was doing his best to behead Jotak. But if Jotak managed to get his hands on his laser, V'niko could be hurt seriously or killed. The only thing she could do to aid V'niko was to get him backup.

So, she turned and barreled through the front door of the precinct. Bending over, she panted and pointed out the doorway. "Help...the...Volusian."

Several uniformed officers ran out the door as a female officer came around the desk and helped Bria to a seat. "Are you hurt, madam?"

Bria shook her head and concentrated on slowing her breathing and getting her thundering heart rate under control. Her power retreated to its reservoir, where it would lay until it was called upon again. She'd proven she could summon, control, and put it away. She just needed to learn some skills on how to use it more effectively, other than girly self-defense maneuvers and running.

Several minutes later, V'niko strode into the station, followed by two of the uniforms who'd rushed out to assist him. But there was no Jotak, shackled and under arrest.

Her heart leapt into her throat. "What happened?" Her voice was still husky from her exertions.

Then she took a better look at V'niko. He was a mess. He had bruises and claw marks on his torso and face. A gash on his thickly muscled thigh. He was bleeding blue, but, thank the One, not in spurts.

Bria rose to meet him halfway, shouting over her shoulder, "Get me a medical kit."

"I'm sorry, Doctor." V'niko's face was a darker shade than his normal pale blue. She let down her mental shields and read his mood as embarrassed. "The bastard got away. The other officers are tracking him now."

Bria fought off a moment of dizziness, an after-effect of the earlier adrenaline rush and, she'd admit it, of fear. She took the kit the female officer handed her. "Sit down, V'niko, before you fall down. I need to clean your wounds. Dornian claws are filthy, even with your immunity to the toxins."

"I will be fine, Doctor." As if sensing her own weakness, V'niko braced her by holding onto her arm.

"Call me Bria." She looked at his face. He projected an almost eerie sense of calm and no pain. "How are you feeling?"

V'niko smiled. "I'm fine. Do not worry."

"Please, let me treat your wounds," she said. "It's the least I can do. You saved me once again."

V'niko's lips twisted into a charming smile as he sat on the edge of a desk. "And I will continue to protect you as long as you need me. I asked for this duty. You, Dr. Bria Martin, are the only reason my lovely Terran wife and I have two children. You are special."

"Thank you." Bria blushed. It was nice to hear her hard work had made people happy. It was why she'd gone into medical research rather than direct patient care. She could help more people that way.

In a companionable silence, she cleaned and examined each of V'niko's gouges and scratches thoroughly. She hummed with satisfaction when she found no cell death. His body was healing itself. She didn't even need to use the medi-laser on the gash in his thigh. Amazing.

"How did you know I was in trouble?" She looked up and frowned. "Were you following me?"

His expression went from calmly blank to grim. "I called ahead to the laboratory and discovered M'tali had not come into work. I feared he might have managed to track you down. I got off the train at the next stop and circled back to make sure you were okay. I picked up your scent and his and followed them. I thank the One I made it in time."

"Amen," she muttered.

"I arrived as you made your move. You have the makings of a good warrior. Just need some hand-to-hand training and a nice battle-blade."

Bria mentally sighed. Her battle-mate side both thrilled and frightened her. She'd like to believe she couldn't ever kill a sentient being, but was honest enough to acknowledge she would've tried to kill Jotak to keep him from hurting the little girl on the platform.

Thus, V'niko's assessment concurred with her own—she needed to train. So, until she had some fight training, obtaining a battle-blade and some other nicely sharp throwing knives were a priority. Her knife-throwing ability was her best offensive tool for now. But even after physical training, she'd make it her life's goal never to find herself in any position where she'd have to use lethal force.

"Just added sharp weapons and fight training to my to-do list as soon as I get to Cejuru Prime." She shuddered once more at how close Jotak had been to taking her away. "And thanks for the compliment, but I was really scared. I was very lucky."

"Scared is good. It keeps you sharp as long as you don't let the fear paralyze you. And, Bria, you didn't." He shook his head, a glimmer of respect gleamed in his silver-blue eyes. "You made your move, got away, and then you ran like the wind."

"Yes, I did." She preened, pleased by V'niko's words of praise. "So? What do I do now? My presence *is* obviously a danger to others. I'm worried about my team. Jotak could use them to force me out of hiding."

"A'nan and I will protect you and your team until the *Galanti* arrives."

"V'niko—" Bria placed a hand on his arm. "Jotak will not stop. He's obsessed. He threatened a little girl on the platform to make me go with him."

V'niko's face turned grim. "Ahh, he has escalated. He is operating on territorial instincts now. If you are not on Oz, his primary urge will be to leave the others alone and pursue you. You need to get off-planet. You will need military protection. You must leave today. I will make the arrangements."

Bria nodded. "I agree. But I'll make the arrangements. I have connections you don't."

She would contact the Alliance—and the Prime—Military Commands. She would reveal her Prime heritage, show them her marking as proof, and then ask them to find her *gemat*. More importantly, she'd ask for even more protection for her team and a place off-planet for her to hide from Jotak.

This wasn't how she'd wanted to reveal her Prime heritage—or announce her existence to her *gemat*—but it was the smarter move.

"Good. Have Command send your personal protection team to the orbiting Oz space port. Jotak can't get onto the orbiting station without being captured. I will accompany you and wait until your protection arrives." He took her hand and squeezed. "I won't let anything happen to you."

"I know." Bria squeezed back. "Thank you."

"It's the least I can do for the woman who indirectly gave me my children."

Bria laughed. "Um, I know what you mean, but that sounds sort of illicit. How old are the children and what are their names?"

V'niko grinned. "We have three-standard-year-old fraternal twins. My daughter is called Br'anna." Bria gasped and tears wet her cheeks. "And my son's name is M'atin. Those were the closest equivalents in my language to your given names."

Bria smiled at the suddenly very blurred image of her champion and savior. "I'm honored."

CHAPTER 4

Hours later, the orbiting Oz Space Port

Bria woke suddenly, her heart pounding. Eyes widened from the rude awakening, she scanned every corner of the sleeping cubicle travelers often rented while waiting for their flights. The space, smaller than her apartment's galley kitchen, was empty. What had awakened her?

Thud, thud, thud.

"Bria! Bria!" V'niko's voice filtered through the locked metal door. He sounded anxious. He must've been trying to awaken her for a while. "Are you all right? Answer me."

"I fell asleep. I'm fine."

Leaving the narrow bed, she walked a mere four steps to the door and used the security monitor. V'niko's worried face stared into the camera. She unlocked the door, let it slide into the wall, and stepped back so the large Volusian could enter the room.

His presence made the place seem even more claustrophobic than before. She forced herself to remember there was more than enough air. Her adoptive parents had told her she'd been trapped in the escape pod that crash-landed on Gliese 581C. Small spaces tended to trigger panic attacks.

"What's wrong?" she asked after several deep, calming breaths. Her panic didn't ease. Something still caused her gut to churn and her lungs to seize. Opening her shields wider, she inhaled sharply. Something evil was very near, and it was fixated on her. "Tell me." She grabbed V'niko's forearm and squeezed. "Is it my team? Cheri? Has Jotak hurt them? Is he...here?"

"No, no, be calm, Bria." V'niko rubbed a hand up and down her arm. "Jotak has vanished. A'nan has checked in and assured me your team is fine and all is quiet in the lab."

"Then why do I feel as if impending doom is just around the corner?" She let go of his arm and stepped away from his touch. It wasn't uncomfortable, but it wasn't "right." No man's touch had ever been the "right" one. Her discovery she was bond-mated to a Prime had finally clarified that particular peculiarity.

"Ah, *doom*." He closed his eyes as if searching for a memory. "An impending terrible fate. An apt description." His eyes darkened to the deepest blue of an Oz winter night. "The Alliance Military security detail is here. Two men. Proper uniforms. Proper identification." He shook his head. "I do not like their looks. Your feelings have underlined my fear that they are not who or what they seem. I cannot allow you to leave with these men."

Bria had to laugh. V'niko acted like a father vetting a daughter's new boyfriend. She appreciated his protective nature. Their guts were working in tandem. She would know what was in the men's hearts merely by *looking* at them. But she couldn't explain how to V'niko without revealing her Prime heritage, and she was reluctant to do so, unless it was a true emergency. It wasn't that she didn't trust him—she did— but she wanted to make the public announcement with her mate by her side.

"Will you stay with me while I speak with them?"

"Try and keep me away," he muttered. "What is our backup plan? You can't stay on Oz or the space port, neither location is secure enough while Jotak is at large."

She thought for a second. "How about we do this? If, after speaking with the men, I feel it isn't safe for me to go with them, I'll ask you to escort me to this cubicle to get my things"—of which there were none besides the tote bag she'd packed for her stay in the hotel, and she'd be carrying that—"but instead you'll take me to the departure area where I'll make a com call to make other arrangements to get me out of the Tau Ceti system. I'll give you my com unit, and you can place it on a shuttle going to Earth to leave a false trail. Does that sound like a good plan?"

V'niko looked even grimmer if that were possible. "You would be alone."

"Yes. But anyone trying to track me will most likely follow my com unit."

He thought a second and then nodded. "And your destination? Is it safe?"

"Oh yeah." She chuckled. "No one would ever think of it. I'd tell you, but there are species with truth sense. I want anyone asking you questions to sense you're telling the truth when you tell them you don't know."

He placed his hands on her shoulders and squeezed. "You'll let me know when you are safe?"

"Yes, I'll get you a message. At that point, I dare anyone to try to get to me." She leaned into his body and gave him a quick hug. "I'll thank you in advance for all you've done and will do. Please take care of Cheri and my team."

"I will." He bowed his head and placed his hand over his heart. A Volusian warrior's gesture of fealty. "A'nan and I have requested to be permanently assigned as security for your team. You will see us again."

"That's wonderful." She winked at him. "I want to meet my namesakes."

"That will happen. Let us hope sooner, rather than later."

Bria picked up her bag. "Okay, let's go meet my *security* detail." But she already knew she'd be leaving the space port soon...and alone. Her empathic abilities wide open, she could taste the bitterness of the men's deceit even through the titanium steel walls.

"V'niko?" She paused at the still-closed door to her sleeping cubicle.

He looked down at her, an eyebrow arched. "Yes, Bria?"

"Should we even do this? The danger...um, what if—"

"I can protect us both." His lips twisted into a grin of anticipation. "Plus, we might learn who has sent them and why."

"There is that." She blew out a breath. "Let's do this."

V'niko palmed the door control. She followed him out and then walked beside him to the waiting area.

The two alleged Alliance soldiers were large. One was Terran. The other was a hybrid species. Her trained eye detected Terran, Obam, and a hint of Cetan. They wore the uniform of the Alliance Military Police, but their demeanor—all smugness and barely restrained violence—was all wrong. They were wrong.

She'd been told during her call with Captain Linnea Sinclair of the Alliance Military Command that one of her security team would be Prime. The Prime Military Command had insisted upon that detail after her Prime heritage had been confirmed.

Even now the search for her *gemat* was underway. There was no way she'd let these imposters take her away. She had a mate to meet.

The Terran stepped forward. He looked her up and down. "You are Dr. Brianna Martin?"

"Yes."

"We are your escort. I am Sergeant Holtsclaw, and this is Sergeant Joelo." He gestured to the hybrid male. "We've been instructed to take you to Command headquarters on Tooh 10. We must leave now."

Bria stepped closer to V'niko, who growled subvocally and moved his hand to rest on his laser sidearm. "I was told I'd be taken to the Alliance Military space station orbiting Oz's largest moon."

Tooh 10 was the location of the Galactic Alliance Military Command headquarters. But Tooh 10 was nowhere near the Tau Ceti system where Oz was located. Captain Sinclair had clearly stated the Alliance and Prime wanted Bria near Oz when the *Galanti* arrived.

"Alliance Command...um...changed our orders." Holtsclaw stumbled over the words. He acted shocked she hadn't instantly agreed with his instructions. "We must leave now. It isn't safe here."

And that last statement was the only one she found truthful since she'd entered the lobby.

They had to be mercenaries working for an as-yet unknown enemy.

Jotak would never have hired strangers to kidnap her. His race was nomadic and trusted no one other than another of their particular family unit. For Dornians as a whole, every other species was either a mark or prey. While Jotak had broken away from his family unit to work for the Alliance, which made him an anomaly, his nature and nurture still wouldn't allow him to trust anyone else to retrieve her. He'd claimed her; she was his—and his alone.

"Okay, sure." It was time for Bria's exit strategy. "Could you gentlemen give me a moment to get my other bag?" She moved toward the hallway where her sleeping cubicle was located. V'niko covered her retreat.

Holtsclaw hurried to cut off their exit. "I will get the bag. Give me the room code."

She stopped, turned, and pasted what she hoped was a coy smile on her face when all she wanted to do was scream.

"Please, wait here. V'niko will help me." She lowered her eyes as if she were embarrassed. "We'd like to say our good-byes... in private."

V'niko picked up his cue and placed his arm around her waist, then kissed the top of her head. She forced herself to stay within his protective embrace. And, blessed One, she hated to admit she needed it. The imposters' need to hurt her made her sick to her stomach and her knees weak.

"Go, but do not tarry," Holtsclaw said. He and his friend obviously didn't want to create a scene. "Our ship is ready and waiting."

Bria nodded and allowed V'niko to hurry her out of the lobby.

"Definitely bad guys. Tooh 10 clinched it even if they hadn't been throwing off evil vibes like a solar flare," Bria whispered as they moved swiftly past her former cubicle and exited at the other end of the hallway into a cavernous mall-like area of the space port. "I need to make my calls."

"Of course. I will shield you." V'niko ushered her into a small, dark corner and behind some exotic plantings, out of the way of foot traffic. Facing outward, he placed his body between her and any danger that might approach. His hand was on his weapon. His body, alert. He'd hear her calls, hear words that would reveal her true heritage, but it was now an emergency and she trusted V'niko to keep her secrets. He'd proven his honor time and time again over the last twenty-four standard hours.

Her first call was to her ultimate destination. To her black sheep brother Damon, the only other of her adoptive family who'd left the commune. Anyone in her family would've protected her, but she refused to take this kind of trouble to a planet of pacifists.

"Damon?"

"Bria?" Damon's handsome face filled the small com unit screen. His sky blue eyes lit with pleasure at seeing her. He was at work. She could see the bustle of activity behind him and hear the noises of *Hades*, the popular dive bar and sex club he owned on Jump Station Charybdis. "You still on Oz? Or, have you made the move to Cejuru Prime?"

"Oz, but there's a problem." She inhaled and let out the breath to rid her voice of fear and tension.

Damon's eyes narrowed and darkened to stormy blue. He growled. "Where are you? Do I need to come get you?"

Filial love consumed her. She'd known he'd have her back, no questions asked.

Damon, approximately ten years her senior, was the one who'd found her and gotten her out of the escape pod before it exploded. From then on, she'd been his constant shadow, and he, her protector and champion.

When she discovered her Prime heritage, she'd wondered if there had been something in the pod which identified her as Prime. Then she'd instantly rejected such a notion. Her family had never hidden how she'd come to be part of their family. They would've told her; there had been no reason to lie about her Prime heritage.

"What kind of problem?" His voice was low, calm, but there was worry and fear underlying his tone.

"I have a stalker."

Rage colored his high cheekbones red. He opened his mouth.

She cut him off before he could speak. "And now I have someone else, someone even more powerful after me...someone who has ears and eyes in Alliance Military Command...and the upper reaches of Prime Command."

At the mention of Prime Command, there was a flash of knowledge—and guilt—in Damon's eyes. She would've missed it if she hadn't known him so well.

Damon knew—had always known—what she was. A flash of hurt, then anger, swept through her body. She didn't have time to process his betrayal now. Later, once she was safely within the protection of his small fiefdom, she'd ask him why he'd kept such a secret from her.

"A stalker? Someone else is after you? Traitors in the Alliance and Prime Commands?" Damon went silent, and it was an ominous pause of several nano-seconds before he roared, "What the fuck, Bria?"

Bria had to smile, despite her upset. The reaction was typical Damon. He'd always been the least peaceful member of the family.

"This is nothing to smile about. Are you safe, princess?"

His use of the pet name he'd given her when she was a little girl brought tears to her eyes. Maybe he and the family had good reasons to hide her Prime nature. She'd keep an open mind. She couldn't forget the good times.

"Bria," Damon growled like a testy bear, "answer me."

"Yes, I'm safe. I have someone I trust guarding me, but he has a wife and children. I need to get far away from him and my team, so my enemy won't hurt them to get to me."

"What can I do to help?"

No hesitation in his offer at all. He might have hidden things from her, but he was still her protective big brother. He would bend time for her, if needed.

"I need a place to hide, off the grid, until the Alliance sends someone I know I can trust to get me. I'm at the Oz Space Port. I can easily catch a ride to your jump station."

Besides the dive bar and sex club, Damon was also half-owner of the Jump Station Charybdis. The station had a rough reputation. It was frequented by off-duty crews of freighters docking there, mercenaries, disenfranchised citizens of various solar systems, con artists, and others waiting for clearance to enter one of the most volatile and erratic jump gates in the Milky Way.

"Which carriers should I try first?" She had one in mind, but Damon would know the safest ones. Some of the carriers were nothing more than glorified smugglers.

"Catch a ride with either one of Mason's or Brewster's supply ships."

"I'd planned on using Mason." She grinned. "But thanks for confirming my choice was a good one."

He muttered and rubbed a hand over his ever-present beard stubble. "I'll make the necessary calls to pave your way..."

She read that to mean he'd make sure all the Mason freighter captains in Oz Space Port would be ready for her. She also imagined he'd threaten them with bodily harm if anything happened to her on the way to the jump station.

"...lock yourself in the captain's quarters and don't come out until you get to the station. If..." he choked on the word, "...something changes, and you need to get off at a stop on the way, call me. I'll come get you no matter where you're at. If nothing changes..."

Damon gave her his patented don't-mess-with-me-or-pay-the-consequences look he'd aimed at her a lot as she'd grown up and tested her boundaries.

"...do not leave the freighter docking area once you get to Charybdis. Have the captain page me. I'll come get you. And, Bria...for the sake of all that is sacred and my sanity, don't attempt to come to my quarters by yourself."

Damon's quarters, and in fact, all the jump station employees' living quarters, were on the level connected to the bar. The bar/sex club was a well-defended fortress within the huge no-man's land, or more specifically the no-female-was-safe-land, of the jump station...it even had an artificial moat. Not that she'd ever seen any of it.

Bria had only visited Jump Station Charybdis once on a break from college classes. She'd never made it to *Hades*. In fact, she'd been lucky not to be raped, kidnapped, or killed as soon as she'd stepped off the freighter she'd hitched a ride on. Luckily, Damon had intercepted her before she'd made it much farther than her docking tube. It had taken some fast-talking to keep him from blistering her butt for being there at all.

"I'm not stupid or suicidal, Damon."

His only response was a snort that clearly indicated disbelief.

"See you soon." She touched the screen. "Love you, big brother."

"Love you more, princess." His voice was husky, and the heated, raw emotion in his eyes disturbed her.

Damon's feelings for her seemed to have changed, grown...more sexual. Damn, she didn't need this now. He was her brother, and she loved him, but not in a sexual way. She had a mate, one she'd instinctively sought in every man she'd met since leaving Gliese 581C. She had to tell him, prepare him for the reality. Let him get used to the idea before she set foot on the station. Even though she suspected he knew she was Prime, he might not know about her mate.

"Damon"—she hesitated and worry instantly filled his eyes at her tone—"I'm Prime."

And there was the flash again, confirming his knowledge.

"I have a bonded mate, a *gemat*..."

And now he grimaced. Well, shit, he'd also known she was a *gemate*.

"...the Prime are looking for him."

A look of devastation crossed his face.

Like a coward, she closed down the call before she lost it and yelled at him for lying all these years—before the tears in her eyes streamed down her cheeks. She prayed he and the family had damn good reasons for hiding everything from her, because if not, her heart would surely break.

She wiped the tears from her face on her sleeve and then took a couple of breaths to calm herself...to keep from throwing herself into V'niko's arms and bawling her grief and sense of betrayal into the stalwart Volusian's shirtfront. He wouldn't allow her to leave if he felt she was too fragile.

"Are you okay, Bria?" V'niko looked over his shoulder. "You sounded distressed at the end."

"My brother..." She shook her head and gave V'niko a reassuring smile that must've fallen far short of the mark since he frowned even more. "He knew I was..."

"Prime?" V'niko asked.

"Yes. He and the family hid it from me all these years."

V'niko nodded, his face solemn. "Maybe they had a good reason. I could tell from his voice he loves you, wants to protect you. You will be safe with him."

"Yes. But I can't love him the way he wants. To me, he's the brother who cleaned my scraped knees and stopped the bullies from taunting me. I have a mate, one I've searched for without knowing it all my life." She'd never, in her wildest dreams, thought of Damon in a sexual way.

"Yes, I heard that is the way with Prime bond-mates. Bria..." V'niko swept a lone tear off her cheek. "...if your brother loves you, he will wish you to be happy, yes?"

"I hope so, V'niko, I really do." But she doubted it.

After taking a few seconds to pull herself together, Bria placed her next call—to the only person in the Alliance Military she trusted one hundred percent. Since her last call to the Alliance Command seemed to have been intercepted by an enemy to the Prime, she couldn't trust that a second call would bring any better results. Someone had ordered her kidnapping, for what ultimate purposes only Holtsclaw, Joelo, and their employer knew.

This call would go directly to Dr. Lia Morgan-Dakkin, her contact on the *Galanti*. The Alliance starship could swing by Jump Station Charybdis and pick her up. She'd then ride with them back to Oz to get her team.

The call wasn't answered. She was switched to Lia's message box. Bria left a brief video message outlining what had happened, what she needed, and where she'd be.

"Let's go, V'niko." Her gut—or her Prime battle-mate instincts—urged her to move. She pictured Holtsclaw and

Joelo tearing up the hostelry to find her. By now, they could even be searching the central mall, which, thank the One, was huge and crowded. It would take them some time to search all the private and public areas between the hostelry and the passenger departure area.

But the imposters wouldn't think of looking at the freighter docks which was where she now headed. V'niko once again covered her back.

No woman in her right mind traveled on freighters alone, especially ships traveling to Jump Station Charybdis. That would be what allowed her to get away without a trace.

When they arrived at the entrance to the freighter docks, V'niko held out his hand. "Your com unit?"

She handed it to him.

"Buy a new one as soon as you can," he ordered. "Call me when you arrive at your brother's." He hesitated, then added, "Bria, I hope all goes well between you and your brother."

"Me, too. I'll call as soon as I can." She touched his arm and squeezed it. "Thank you for everything."

"It has been my honor. I will see you when you return to Oz. A'nan and I will take good care of your people."

"I know you will."

He nodded then left. She almost called him back. His hyper-alertness, his kindness, and big male frame made her feel safe and cared for.

She shook off the momentary weakness. She needed to stay alert—and, somehow, obtain a weapon.

Weapon buying was out, for now, but staying alert was something she could do. Bria concentrated and found she could read the auras of the people closest to her without interference from the massive amount of other people. It was tiring, but she didn't want anyone sneaking up on her as Jotak had.

With her psychic abilities at full force, she made her way to the Mason Freight Company offices on the lowest level of the docks. She ignored the looks of interest colored with a healthy dose of lust and paid a deaf ear to the lewd suggestions on how she could make some extra money.

Bria didn't relax her guard until she was on a Mason ship heading to resupply Jump Station Charybdis. Damon had come through. The captain had been watching for her. He sneaked her aboard, gave her a choice of weapons from his own cache—she chose a slender knife akin to a Terran stiletto with a sheath she could strap to her thigh—and then gave her sole possession of his cabin. The door was locked with a guard stationed in the hallway.

As safe as she could be, she lay down. Exhausted, she fell into a restless sleep. Her dreams were alternately filled with images of Jotak chasing her with the help of Holtsclaw and Joelo and those of Damon and a faceless Prime male fighting, the winner claiming her as his own.

CHAPTER 5

Iolyn tore off his sweaty clothing and tossed it into the cleaning unit. Naked, he stalked to the bar in his quarters and poured himself a shot of Valerian whiskey and drank it in one long gulp. Then he poured another. Maybe getting drunk would help haze the morass of fury, fear, and frustration boiling in his gut—in his head.

Almost twelve standard hours had passed since they'd left Tooh 2 where he'd learned of his precious *gemate* Brianna's existence—and of her danger. It felt like a lifetime.

He snarled and slammed the half-empty glass on the counter. *Ansu bhau!* He was tens of thousands of light years away and could do nothing to protect her. The inability to act threatened to drive him crazy. Every primitive instinct urged him to seek out the stalker threatening his mate and tear the *apayebo* apart. Then he'd take Brianna in his arms and shelter her from all peril.

But he could do nothing because he was—Too. Far. Away.

So, instead of being a man and protecting his mate, he'd spent the last few hours, ripping apart his quarters and

56

putting them back together in preparation for her arrival. His quarters hadn't been all that bad, but his brothers' *gemates*, Mel and Nadia, had insisted upon the thorough cleaning and redecoration. It was their way of distracting him—and siphoning off some of his rampant energy.

The distraction had worked, but only for a short time.

Iolyn clenched his fists and paced like a wild animal in a cage. He needed action. If he didn't release some of his pent-up emotions, he could inadvertently hurt someone. He would have to take his brothers up on their offer of hand-to-hand combat before he escalated into full-blown *batel rabia*—the Prime battle rage. *Batel rabia* plus close quarters equaled extreme bodily damage. Good for fighting enemies, and men who threatened a man's mate, but bad for fellow crew members.

He took in a frustrated breath and noted he stank of anger, fear, and his earlier physical labor. This was something he had control over.

Entering the shower, he turned on the jets. As the hot water pummeled his aching muscles, he used a mind-over-matter exercise taught to all Prime warriors and forced himself to relax—muscle by muscle, beginning with his neck all the way to his toes.

While his body loosened up, he couldn't shut down his mind. His mind's eye created all sorts of horrible images and worst-case-scenarios concerning his little mate.

His lips twisted in a self-deprecatory grin. Now he knew how his brother Wulf had felt when first learning of Mel; she'd also been a Lost One and was now the co-captain of the *Galanti*. He could especially relate to his brother Huw's extreme turmoil over mating with Nadia, a Terran who had the latent DNA to be marked by a Prime. Both women had been exposed to peril, and his brothers reacted just as he did now.

Mating was a Prime imperative and had never been taken lightly by their society. Finding a compatible female with whom to mate was even more crucial now with a negative population growth. A Prime's *gemate* was the center of his personal universe. Danger to such a precious being wasn't taken lightly.

Iolyn rubbed a soapy hand over the faded mating mark on his chest. He'd received the mark during a particularly vicious siege of the Cejuru solar system by the Antareans. Under a dire state of emergency, the Elder Council had made the extreme decision to expose all unmarked males and females, no matter their age, to one another. The bond mark wasn't determined by sex hormones, but instead was initiated by an olfactory neuro-chemical reaction when a male was exposed to the scent of his perfect genetic mate. After the bonding ceremony, all the women and children were sent away so they wouldn't be killed during the conflagration.

Iolyn had been one-standard-year-old at the time. He never knew the name of the child with whom he'd bonded.

As one of the heirs of the leader of the Prime, he wasn't sent away. He, his brothers, and mother had been hidden away on Cejuru Borus, an isolated planetoid in the Cejuru system. The Antareans totally bypassed what they saw as a desolate, uninhabitable rock.

After the Antareans had been defeated and driven back into Andromeda Galaxy, the women and children began coming home. But Brianna hadn't. She, and dozens of other women and children, had become the Lost Ones.

After the *Galanti*'s last mission failed to find any surviving Lost Ones, Iolyn had been on the cusp of making the decision to search for a non-Prime mate, one he could mark and mate as Huw had with Nadia, something which had been previously inconceivable.

He was relieved he hadn't begun that search. Brianna would complete the mind-body-soul trinity with him. He'd be whole for the first time in his life. His *gemat* marking would again bloom with color and vitality.

"Thanks and blessed be the One," he murmured. "Protect Brianna until I can do so myself." And then he planned to protect, cherish, and love her for the rest of their lives and beyond.

After drying off and getting dressed, he sat at his desk and pulled up the official Alliance files on Dr. Brianna Martin on the monitor.

The three-dimensional color image was lifelike. He traced her features with a shaking finger and imagined how soft and warm her creamy golden skin would be.

Her pillowy lips were unsmiling, but her amber eyes sparked with humor and joy. Her glossy, dark hair was twisted on top of her head. A couple of wavy tresses had escaped and framed her oval-shaped face. He'd wager her hair was thick and silky in texture. He could almost feel the long curls caressing his naked chest, brushing over his *gemat* marking, and inciting him to a state of painful arousal as he held her close in their bed.

He groaned and shuddered—was forced to adjust his cock as it hardened at the thought of having her beneath him, taking him deeply inside her sex. "*Diew,* torture yourself, why don't you?" he muttered.

Soon. Patience. It will happen.

His *gemate* was a very beautiful woman. An intelligent one. She was a woman any man would wish to claim as his own.

He fisted his hands. No, he couldn't...wouldn't think about any other males she might have been with. He couldn't expect her to be a virgin. She was raised as a Terran. She would have dated, experimented sexually. He growled and could feel his rage heating once more. He took several deep breaths and beat his anger back.

He'd be surprised if she were very experienced, though. His sister-kin Mel had told him once that intimacy with other men had been doable, but felt wrong, uncomfortable.

Nadia had admitted the same once she met Huw and began to bond to him. And Nadia was a Terran with latent Prime DNA.

Once Iolyn had completed the final physical bonding with Brianna, she'd be his and no other would dare touch her ever again.

"Brianna." He liked the sound of her name on his lips. He'd looked up the origins of the name. It was Terran Irish and meant "strong."

And she would've had to have been. At the tender age of one-standard-year, she'd survived an evacuation in a time of war, pursuit by the enemy, and a crash landing, according to the records the Alliance had eventually found once they knew where to look, and who knew what other dangers as she'd grown.

Her Terran parents had named her well. He would tell them so when he took Brianna home to visit the people who'd nurtured her, kept her safe...for him.

Brianna's official file didn't contain much about her life before she left Gliese 581C, a farming planet. Her adoptive parents, John and Mary Martin, were descendants of farmers who'd emigrated from Earth to the water planets of the Gliese system and tilled the scattered, fertile land masses.

He imagined his *gemate* must've lived an idyllic childhood before she went off-planet to attend university and achieved multiple degrees with highest honors. His mate's research in hominid species genetics, in particular cross-hominid fertility, was cutting edge. This would make her a target of the Pure Bloods and any hominid-hating race such as the Antareans, even if she hadn't been his mate. Being his *gemate* just placed a bigger target on her back.

This worried him. Brianna wouldn't have the training to protect herself as Mel had as an Alliance military officer. Brianna would need him to protect her—and for the moment, he couldn't.

As his worries and fear about what could be happening to his mate took over his mind once more, his com unit beeped.

"Yes?" The word barely escaped past the tension-tightened muscles of his throat.

"Iolyn..." Wulf's voice was low and filled with an emotion that had dread settling in Iolyn's gut and raising the hairs on the nape of his neck. "...come to the Captain's Board Room. We have news."

Iolyn surged from his chair, knocking it over. He grabbed his com unit and ran from his quarters.

"What happened? Is Brianna all right?" He couldn't keep the panic out of his voice. He slammed his palm on the elevator pad and grunted his relief when the door opened immediately. "Command Deck," he ordered even before the doors had closed.

"Lia has received a secure and scrambled video transmission from Brianna. You need to see it. Out."

Soon he'd see...hear his *gemate* for the first time. Just the sound of her voice would call to the bond between them. The result would be both pleasure and pain as his heart, body, and mind would demand the final step to complete the *gemat-gemate* bond.

At this point, he'd take anything of his mate he could get.

Iolyn raced from the elevator and cut across the Command Deck. He was vaguely aware that every soldier and officer on duty stared after him. They knew—and cared—about his good fortune. The unmated Prime males among them envied him the blessed gift of a *gemate*.

As he ran into the Captain's Board Room, the occupants turned to face him. He ignored them. Ignored the tension in the air. His attention was fixed on the large video screen over Wulf's shoulder.

There she was, his Brianna, frozen in Pause mode. She was beautiful—but fear darkened her amber eyes and worry etched creases on her pale forehead.

"What happened? Why did she call Lia?" Iolyn walked to the screen and traced the tense muscles lining her throat. He swore he could almost feel her pulse pounding against the fragile skin over her carotid as her body processed stress hormones. His eyes narrowed as he assimilated the rest of the image. "She's in a public place. Not under guard. Why isn't she under guard? The Alliance Military was to send her one. Captain Sinclair told Tor so."

"She has a guard. A Volusian who'd been sent to protect her and her lab team before we knew she was a Lost One. As for the other guards...the ones Admiral Nelson ordered... well, you'll see and hear," Wulf said. "Please, brother...come... sit next to me. We'll play the whole call. You *need* to hear her voice."

His older brother approached and touched his arm, then lowered his voice, "I remember what Mel's voice did for me. It will bring you some relief for a short while."

It also would be torture. His body's neurochemistry would awaken his mating urges. He wouldn't be quite sane until he had her in his arms.

"Sit. Listen," Wulf said. "You'll tune in to her feelings better than we can."

"I don't need to hear her voice to recognize she's frightened." Iolyn moved to a seat to the left of Wulf's at the head of the long steel-and-stone conference table. He turned to look at the others present—Wulf's mate Mel sat to Wulf's right, his other brother Huw and his mate Nadia sat next to Mel, and Dr. Lia Morgan and her mate Joen Dakkin were next to him.

Lia's gaze was filled with understanding. "Iolyn..."

The doctor would try to reassure him, and he wasn't having any platitudes. He cut her off. "She needs me." The words were a low growl.

I need her.

"Tone it down, Iolyn," Lia's mate warned.

"Joen, please, you're not helping, love." Lia stroked Joen's face, then smiled at Iolyn. "We understand what you're going through, Iolyn. Yes, she's scared. She has a right to be, but she has also made all the right moves to put distance between her and danger. She's safe for the moment and will remain so until we get to her. Believe in that."

Lia spoke in what Iolyn thought of as her doctor voice. He could've been bleeding out, seconds away from death, and she'd use that same tone of voice to make his last moments calmer.

Nadia chimed in. "Iolyn, Brianna's smart. She called Lia as soon as she realized the danger had escalated beyond the original stalker creep."

"Escalated?" The dark fire of his rage came up his throat and escaped as a buzz-saw growl which was soon echoed by the other three men in the room—and every Prime male within one deck. The floor began to shake and objects vibrated on solid surfaces.

"Stop it!" Mel ordered. "Now isn't the time to go bat-shit crazy with all the growling and snarling. Save the *batel rabia* for when you really need it."

Iolyn closed his eyes and willed his fury back inside until it boiled and popped under his skin. He knew he and the other Prime who'd joined in the buildup had succeeded in dampening the effects of their battle rage when the three women sighed their relief. As battle-mates, they fed and built on the emotions of *batel rabia* also.

Iolyn turned toward Wulf and said, his voice harsh from unspent anger, "No one answered my question—where are the military guards? One Volusian isn't doing it for me. What in Balcon's Balls name happened?"

Wulf grimaced. "It's on her message. But the short version is two men showed up. Brianna and the Volusian protecting her determined they were imposters."

Iolyn cursed.

"There has to be a leak at the highest Command levels.

The word of Brianna's existence was either sold or given to one of our enemies as soon as Brianna contacted Alliance Command the first time," Mel said. "Brianna's existence was marked as need-to-know."

"The Prime Elder Council would also have been informed," Huw added. "All Lost Ones are reported to the Council for verification since the Council keeps the database of the *gemate* markings."

Iolyn's stomach lurched. "So, it could be any of the Prime's enemies or the rebels."

"Or someone totally new," Wulf added.

"Great." Iolyn grunted. "You mentioned a Volusian protecting her..." He should be protecting her, not some stranger.

"The Volusian," Wulf said, a wry twist to his mouth, "is V'niko, a former member of the Volusian Special Forces. He's also Commander A'tem's cousin. V'niko requested the assignment to protect Brianna and her lab team because she is the reason he has twins with his Terran wife."

Iolyn let out a breath and muttered, "That's a *bakking* relief."

"Yes." Wulf gripped his brother's arm and squeezed. "Now, listen to Brianna's message." He hit the Play mode.

"Lia..." Brianna's voice was low and melodious despite the tension in her voice. The sound shot straight to his heart and then hit his groin—hard.

Iolyn almost moaned out loud as something buried deep inside him surged forward and filled him from head to toe with a life force he could only have felt once before—when he'd marked Brianna as his mate. He massaged his mark as it tingled and itched and...burned.

His brothers chuckled at his gesture and Joen smiled. They must've had the same reaction to their mates.

"...the man stalking me, a Dornian by the name of Jotak M'tali, tried to kidnap me after I reported him to the Alliance Military."

"*Ansu bhau! Ne! Ne!*" Iolyn surged from his seat and stormed around the room.

A cursed Dornian. A nomadic species and weaker cousins to the Antareans and Erians. Thieves. Liars. Con men. Mercenaries. Kidnappers of women.

"A *bakking* Dornian. How did he get near my mate?" He glared at Wulf.

"He was the Chief of Security for the research laboratory," Wulf said.

"How in Balcon's Balls did he get hired by the Alliance?" Iolyn raged.

"That's being looked into by Admiral Nelson," Wulf said. "The Alliance Military Police stationed on Oz are tracking him now. M'tali might already be off-planet and heading for his family caravan. Now, sit down, Iolyn."

Iolyn looked at the video monitor. Wulf had stopped the call playback at the beginning of Iolyn's loss of control, freezing his precious, fragile Brianna's image once more. Her eyes pleaded for help.

I'm sorry. So sorry I'm not there.

"She's safe, brother," Wulf said. "Your mate has shown herself to be strong and resourceful."

For now, she's safe. But for how long?

Mel rose and walked to his side. She took his arm and pulled him back toward his seat next to Wulf. "Trust in Brianna's intelligence. Listen to the rest of the call. Then we'll make plans."

Iolyn allowed himself to be led. Once seated, he placed his fisted hands on the table and took several deep breaths until he no longer saw red and could speak without choking on his fear. "I'm fine, Mel. Thanks." Maybe if he said it enough, he'd believe it. "Brother, please play the rest of the call."

Wulf, after exchanging a sharp glance with Huw, unpaused the call. Iolyn almost laughed. His brothers would have him tranquilized if he went ballistic—and he wouldn't blame them. He wasn't himself. He'd always been called the calm Caradoc brother.

Not today.

"...V'niko," the camera panned to a tall Volusian with his broad back to her, guarding her, "and his friend A'nan assisted me in getting away from Jotak. My call to the Alliance Command..."

Iolyn leaned forward. The tension in her voice had escalated.

"...brought two imposters masquerading as Alliance guards."

Iolyn fumed and made a vow to seek out the two *apayebote* and break their fucking necks.

"...V'niko helped me escape again."

He owed A'tem's cousin a great debt.

Brianna took a deep breath which hitched with what might've been a sob. Yet, she shed no tears. His mate was mentally and emotionally strong, but physically she was no match for mercenaries and stalking Dornians.

"...I only trust you, Lia—and your shipmates. Come get me." Brianna paused and the camera panned down her torso where she lowered her waistband and revealed her marking. He covered his mark in response. "I have a favor. I asked the Alliance Command to request the Prime to find my mate. If there's a traitor, as I suspect, then my request might not have gotten to the proper authorities. I worry that my *gemat* might also be in danger. I beg you, please ask Wulf Caradoc to contact his father and find my *gemat*..."

Her initial request had found its way to the proper person, thank the One. After that, who knew where the information had leaked? That, while dealing with her own safety and fears, she'd reached out to Lia to seek protection for him spoke to her generous nature. He was so blessed.

His gaze devoured the image of her faded marking and followed her finger as she traced the design. He could imagine the ecstasy he'd feel, then share with her, as she traced his marking as they made love. Any lingering doubts he might've buried deep inside about a misidentification of her mark were put to rest by the visual evidence. The mark was an identical match to his.

His soul sang. She was his, and he, hers.

"...tell my *gemat* I can't wait to meet him." Her full, lush lips twisted into a slight grin. "I bet he'll be as shocked as I was about all this."

Then Brianna's lips turned downward, and her voice filled with what he read as disgust. "Jotak wanted to force me to breed with him. He won't stop pursuing me. Dornians are persistent to the point of compulsion."

The Dornian was a dead man. Iolyn would see to the deed personally.

"...the fake escort." Brianna shrugged. "I assume they were ordered to kidnap me, then maybe kill me for whatever crazy reasons their employer might have. My enemies won't get their wish. Once you find him, tell my *gemat* not to worry. I promise I'll stay safe until we can be together."

She'd better remain safe. If she were hurt or taken by the *bak* M'tali, Iolyn's rage would be unlike anything the galaxy had seen in a millennia. To forestall another Galactic war, he needed to get to her as quickly as possible.

"...go to Jump Station Charybdis. When you arrive, ask for Damon Martin. He's my eldest brother, and he co-owns the station and operates *Hades*." Brianna stopped talking and looked around before gazing intently into the camera. "Got to go. My skin is itching. Trouble's coming. Hurry, Lia!"

The screen went black. Then what she'd said sank in.

"*Hades*!" Iolyn roared. "That den of iniquity! She thinks she'll be safe there? *Ansu bhau*. She needs a keeper!"

Hades was infamous across the galaxy. It was a very, very bad place on an equally notorious jump station located in the isolated region on the outer edges of the Milky Way where the Perseus arm merged with the Cygnus-Orion arm. The bar was a dive with live sex acts on stage and private sex rooms. *Hades'* claim to fame was that it featured real sex with real women, not just sex sims or sex androids, though those were also available. The roughest element in the galaxy—pirates, mercenaries, shady freighter captains, con artists, thieves, and murderers—used *Hades* as a place to let off steam before entering the most dangerous jump gate in the Milky Way: the Charybdis Gate, a frequently treacherous whirlpool of a shortcut to the other side of the Cygnus-Orion arm. Only those who had Obam navigators could use it safely. The benefits were worth the risk by providing shorter travel times and increased profits for the freighters that used it.

Decent people like his *gemate* weren't safe on Jump Station Charybdis, let alone in *Hades*.

"Iolyn," Lia called to him, "she trusts her brother to keep her safe."

"How do you know that?" Iolyn looked up from his fisted hands with their white knuckles.

"She told me about her family once." Lia chuckled. "She has a great affection for all six of her brothers, but especially Damon. She called him the black sheep since he didn't want to be a peaceful farmer."

"Six brothers?" Iolyn thought of his precious mate growing up around six other males, not of her blood, and snarled.

"Yeah." Lia smiled at his snarl as if she knew where his mind had gone. "She always knew she was adopted, but that didn't stop her from loving them as if they were blood. She had a good life on Gliese 581C due to the Martin family, so you'd better get it in your head to like them and trust them with Brianna's safety and happiness."

"But they weren't her real brothers." Iolyn was angry and, yes, jealous. "They could've—"

"Don't complete that thought. They didn't. She's unattached and wants you..." Huw snorted. "...if you can believe that."

Iolyn turned and glared at Huw. "Shut up."

"Iolyn," Wulf said, "we have to trust in Brianna's faith in her family. Keep in mind, she asked the Alliance, and then Lia, to find you. It's obvious she wants the bond."

"Yes." That was the only thing keeping him halfway sane at the moment. But it was a short moment, a mere nanosecond, before his fears and worries surged to prominence once more.

"This is a good start to your relationship, Iolyn," Mel said with a smile. "Remember? I ran from Wulf. At least Brianna is keeping herself safe the only way she knows how...for you."

Iolyn looked at Wulf. "How soon can we get to the jump station?"

"A lot faster than we could to Oz. A slight backtrack and then use the Andromeda Jump Gate which will dump us close to Jump Station Charybdis. This will cut our travel time by a quarter."

Maybe another twelve hours until I see her, can hold her in my arms.

Iolyn nodded. "Good. But I need to let off some energy now. Cleaning and redecorating my quarters didn't hack it." Mel and Nadia laughed. "I don't want to scare my *gemate*."

Especially since I'll have to lecture her about hiding in a den of iniquity. I need to be calm, reasonable, and not yell.

Besides not wanting to frighten Brianna, he wanted to make love to her as soon as humanly possible. The way he felt right now, he'd physically hurt her without meaning to.

"Who's up for some hand-to-hand?" Iolyn asked.

Huw had come to stand behind his chair. "I'll fight you." He slapped Iolyn on the shoulder. "I still owe you for a few dirty moves you used on me when I was out of my mind over Nadia."

Nadia giggled as did Lia and Mel, who added, "Wulf can help. I'll command the ship while you boys beat the crap out of each other."

Joen stood. "I'll referee. I might even join in. I haven't had the chance to beat on a Caradoc for a while. Need to keep my skills up. Who knows?—We might have to wade into a bar fight to get Brianna out of *Hades*."

"Joen," hissed Lia.

"What?" her mate replied.

"Iolyn didn't need to hear that last bit." Lia turned to Iolyn. "I'm sure Brianna will be kept safely hidden away from the bar patrons. Her brother wouldn't expose her to any overt danger."

The image of his beautiful, fragile, and unworldly scientist mate sitting in a raunchy sex bar among the dregs of the galaxy and the women who catered to them threatened to fray his last bit of control on his *batel rabia*.

Iolyn vocalized his displeasure at the images in his head. The agitated rumbling rattled the commendations on the walls of the boardroom.

"*Ansu bhau*. Can you just stop it, please?" Mel glared at Iolyn and the other males who'd once again chimed in. "Wulf, do something. And do it off my Command Deck."

"Huw, push your engines." Wulf stood and dragged Iolyn from his seat and shoved him toward the doorway. "We need to get to Brianna as fast as we can."

"You got it, brother. Don't start pounding on Iolyn until I get there."

As Iolyn left the room, he heard the women laughing and placing bets on who'd win the battle of the Caradocs.

There was no doubt he would. The way he felt right now, he could take on every Prime male on the ship without breaking a sweat—and still have enough energy to take down Jotak M'tali, the two fake soldiers, and his beloved *gemate*'s big brother, just because.

CHAPTER 6

Jump Station Charybdis

Bria walked through the decontamination chamber and into the docking tube which connected the Mason freighter to the supply docks of the jump station. The Mason freighter captain was right on her heels. She'd wanted to remain on board until Damon could come get her, but station rules stated that all living creatures on a docked ship must go through decontamination and then disembark while the ship was unloaded and then sanitized.

Feeling as if she were a tremendous burden for the captain, she looked over her shoulder and said, "I'll be fine now. Damon will come for me."

"Your brother said he'd have my balls for breakfast if I let you out of my sight." The man's lips twisted into a grimace. "I've seen what he's done to men who've crossed him. I'll stay with you until he gets here."

Bria was somewhat shocked to hear the fear in the captain's voice. Yes, Damon had always been assertive and more alpha-dominant than her other brothers, but she'd never thought he was scary.

But then, she hadn't really seen all that much of Damon since he'd left home. And judging by their earlier conversation, maybe she never really knew him as well as she thought she had.

She stepped out of the docking tube onto the docks and stopped as if she'd slammed into a wall.

The noises hit her first, like the percussion from an explosion. The high-pitched whine from auto-loaders. The shouts from numerous males of all species. The rumbling of ship engines as they docked and departed. And underlying it all, the throbbing sound of the massive air compressors which provided life-sustaining oxygen to the busiest area of the jump station.

The cacophony made her head pound and her stomach churn.

Then the smells struck, adding to her nausea. A potpourri of exotic spices, male sweat, decaying produce, engine lubricants, and the sour tang of reprocessed air.

While she might've forgotten the noise and smells from the one time she'd been here, the supply dock itself hadn't changed visually at all. The metallic platform was various shades of black and gray and seemed to curve toward infinity in each direction. In reality, the platform completed a 360-degree circumvention of the lowest level of the circular jump station with dozens of docks. The ceilings were high and crisscrossed by numerous pipes for heat, air, and other mechanicals.

The freighter captain ran into her still form. He caught her arm before she could fall into the path of an auto-loader pulling a pallet filled with large metal conduits.

"You okay, missy?" The captain's normally fluid Obam accent sounded harsh to her ears. Her hearing might never recover from the overwhelming racket.

"Yes, fine." Bria waved him off with her free hand. "Just forgot what it was like."

Bria was glad for the captain's presence. Even now, dozens of men's stares had singled her out and a rustling of voices passed the word down the dock in both directions that a woman had invaded the harsh, all-male territory.

"Ahh. The noise. Yes. Very loud." The captain's brow creased into numerous deep wrinkles, creating dark rust tunnels on his normally pale orange visage. He pulled a pair of what looked to be ear buds from his pocket and offered them to her. "Here. Try these. Sound suppressors."

Bria took them and popped them into her ears. "Thanks."

The relief from the din was immediate. But nothing could stop the males in the vicinity from eyeing her as if she were a full-service cafeteria—or stop the resulting creepy-crawly feeling on her skin.

Bria had a feeling nothing good could happen from her being on the docks, with or without a guard.

The captain's instincts seemed to run parallel to hers. "Many bad men. Stay behind me. Do not meet their eyes." He took a position in front of her, placing his thin, wiry frame between her and the danger on the dock platform. The captain's hand hovered over his laser blaster. From what she could see of his face, he glowered at any male who dared to look her way.

As she and the captain waited for Damon to appear, her gaze was caught by a large pile of rags near the Mason freighter's dock. She could've sworn they hadn't been there when she'd first debarked. When the rags moved and moaned, she realized the pile was alive. Was someone buried under all the ragged clothing? Were they hurt? She moved away from the captain and started to bend over, her hand extended toward the outer layer of cloth.

"Don't touch." The Mason freighter captain turned, grabbed her arm, and pulled her out of the way of the shifting mound of fabric. His move nearly had them colliding with another robotic unloader. He dragged her to a rusted steel pillar far away from the shuffling pile, pushed her against it, and growled, "Stay away from the Ragbag. Has teeth and is poisonous."

Angry shouts from the back of his ship drew the captain's attention. He was clearly torn between guarding her and responding to what looked to be a major brawl between his men and some nasty-looking Terrans and Erians.

His crew was getting the worst of it.

"Go," she urged. "I'll stay right here. My back against the pillar. You can see me from there."

The captain shook his head, but then the sound of laser fire decided the matter for him.

"Here." He handed her his sidearm, leaving him with his blaster and a long battle-blade. "Don't move." He jabbed his finger at her face. "Don't attract attention. Don't get raped or killed. Anyone comes near. Shoot to kill."

Then he ran to enter the fray, his blaster spitting wide sweeps of stun-level blasts and his battle-blade slashing at the Erians.

Bria placed herself as close to the pillar as she could while keeping the captain within sight. To give the man credit, he looked her way frequently even while shooting and slashing. Damon must have a horrific reputation to make the captain that attentive even as he fought for his and his men's lives.

She shuddered as a feeling of deep dread piled on top of her sensory overload. The walls shielding her empathic senses cracked under a bombardment of dozens of angry and lascivious male emotions. Her heart pounded and her fight-or-flight instinct raised its hackles. Loss of hearing and nauseating smells were now the least of her worries.

There was danger here—and the darkest was focused on her.

Bria checked the settings on the laser pistol with trembling fingers. She shoved it to high stun. While she wasn't comfortable shooting a laser pistol, she knew enough to point and shoot, if needed. With her dominant hand, she drew her knife from the sheath strapped to her thigh. This weapon, she was far more comfortable with—if she could get up the nerve to kill someone.

Find the nerve.

Yeah, well, until the captain came back or Damon came to fetch her, she planned to follow the gruff freighter captain's advice and not attract undue attention.

Unfortunately, her sensible plan of action failed almost immediately.

Danger sought her out in the form of one male. His emotions, his intent, read more hungry greed than murderous or sexual. He moved away from a small pack who'd stayed behind to leer at her rather than watch the fight. The male was pseudo-reptilian, probably Erian since Antareans didn't normally venture this far into the Milky Way. He looked too reptilian to be a Dornian. Dornians had more humanoid attributes than their distant cousins.

His movement toward her was sinuous and slow in an attempt to lull her into a false sense of safety. But he wasn't at all safe. He could strike quickly and inject her with a toxin very similar to his pseudo-reptilian cousins, the Antareans and Dornians.

From his lipless mouth, his tongue flicked in and out in a rapid fluttering motion. He was tasting the air, scenting her.

Erians liked to terrorize and *play* with their prey. Many were mercenaries and traffickers of anything they could sell to make a profit including women and children. Had this man been sent to kill her? Or was she a convenient target for a fun time and then potential profit?

She guessed the latter. No one knew she was coming to Jump Station Charybdis but Lia—and she trusted Lia as much as she trusted her family.

The Erian's narrow-eyed glances up and down her body repulsed...frightened her. His intent had turned more sexual.

Recalling what passed for the sexual act in his species, Bria shuddered. Adrenaline poured into her bloodstream, and her body readied itself for flight or fight. Her heartbeat sounded too loud and fast in her ears. Her breathing threatened to tumble out of control.

Think. Think! What were her options?

She could scream for help.

But the captain was still fighting further down the docking area and wouldn't be able to hear her above the noise of the fight and all the other dock noises.

She could run, but the Erian and the men who'd stayed behind to leer at her had her paths to the freighter and the exits from the dock platform cut off. If the Erian didn't catch her, some other equally dangerous man or men would.

For the time being, she couldn't flee. She refused to give in to the fear threatening to fracture her self-control. The Erian wanted her afraid. He wanted her to lie down, belly up, and present her neck in submission. *Not gonna happen.*

Preparing to defend her position, Bria called up her battle-mate energy from deep within. It filled her with invigorating warmth, cleared her mind, and bolstered her resolve to stand strong. While she was still wary, she was no longer frightened to the point of paralysis. If she went down, she'd go down fighting.

The best defense is a strong offense.

But she wasn't a trained warrior, so she'd be less successful at going on offense in a physical way. Using her brain was her strong point. She needed to outthink and outmaneuver the enemy.

In the current situation, the laser pistol was no protection against the Erian, whose thick skin would deflect the laser stream, even at kill levels. She shoved the laser in the back of her waistband. Her knife would be the better defensive weapon. She palmed it and held it against her thigh, out of the Erian's line of sight. She needed to damage a vital area so he'd have to take time to regenerate. Then she could escape the box the Erian had placed her in and run toward the captain for help or even back onto the ship.

"Prime female. Here. Alone." The Erian's automatic translator labored slowly in Galactic Standard. He looked her up and down and then attempted a smile which came across as more of a leer. "Need protection. I give."

Protect, my ass.

His emotions bombarded her psyche until images of what he wanted to do to her threatened the calm facade she'd adopted. He saw her as a weak vessel for his lust and a rare commodity to sell. She hated it when she was right.

But the Erian underestimated her fortitude and her brains—and that gave her an advantage.

Taking a deep breath and letting it out slowly, she forced a slight smile on her lips. "I'm waiting for someone. But thank you for offering."

After a short pause for the translation, he laughed. The sound slithered along her spine like a river of acid. She shivered, swallowed hard, and rubbed her thumb over the hilt of her knife, then adjusted her grip.

Patience. In this game, she'd only have one chance to take him down.

"He fool. Not protect. I take." The male nodded.

He moved forward once more. His body swayed with each step. Her hindbrain shouted "danger." He was attempting to mesmerize her with his movements. He was close to the do-not-cross line she'd chosen. At that point, she'd have no choice but to escalate the confrontation.

Her muscles tightened and prepared to fight. She raised the hand holding the knife and waved it in a back-and-forth motion, drawing her opponent's attention to the fact she wasn't totally helpless.

She focused her gaze on her target—the spot above the Erian's nasal slits and between his eyes. The target was small, about the size of a peanut. She was sure she could hit it with a scalpel, but the knife she held was still unfamiliar. But even a less-than-perfect hit would cause enough damage to allow her to get at least into the docking tube and back to the freighter.

Then the noise on the docks lowered what seemed like a decibel or two. In her peripheral vision, she noticed the fight at the back of the Mason freighter had ended. But it was too late. Even if the freighter captain spotted her danger, he wouldn't be able to get to her in time.

The Erian's energy had changed, heightened until he almost vibrated. He was about to attack.

"Little knife. Ha. Puny female. Not harm me." The Erian closed the gap, edging ever closer to her breaking point. He stopped, postured, thumping his chest. His tongue darted out and tasted the air again. "You ripe."

Okay, well, that was disgusting and terrifying...and grated on her last fricking nerve. Anger unlike any she'd ever felt before roared through her body like wildfire. She'd had it up to her eyeballs with pseudo-reptilians telling her she was fertile.

"Back off, you split-tongued slimeball...or I'll use the knife." Bria took several slow, calming breaths. Muscle memory from all the years of scalpel-throwing challenges was her best ally at the moment—once she stopped her hand from trembling from the overabundance of adrenaline and battle-mate energy. "I can take you down with one throw...then take your head."

That last part was a bare-faced lie. She wouldn't know if she could kill the Erian until she was confronted with the actual decision. But Damon had always told her, "When you bluff, bluff big." Of course, that had been when they'd played cards. She was fairly sure he hadn't ever meant for her to face down a full-grown Erian mercenary with one small knife.

Happily, she didn't have to prove her boast or make the choice.

A roar of pure masculine rage echoed throughout the cavernous dock area. She knew that bellow, having been at the receiving end of it many times over the years.

Damon had arrived. His call to battle would've done an ancient Terran Viking warrior proud.

The stupid Erian was on the ground, bleeding out from a battle-blade cut to his brain's major artery, before Bria could even blink.

Her knees went as limp as wilted lettuce. She moved to lean against the pillar at her back and barely missed tripping over the Ragbag.

She looked down at the quivering pile and muttered, "You were no help. You could've bit him."

The Ragbag uttered some high-pitched gibberish, then swirled away in a cloud of dust and moved toward the Erian.

"Bria!" Chest heaving, Damon stood over the Erian as he looked her way. A muscle in her brother's jaw pulsed, and he clenched and unclenched the hand fisted around his weapon.

"I'm fine"—she stared at the downed, bleeding male who'd already begun to heal—"that was too close."

The Erian growled something Bria couldn't quite catch, but it had to have been nasty, because Damon slashed the man's carotid artery again. "Don't even think of getting up, fucker." Then her brother placed the tip of his battle-blade between the Erian's slitted eyes. "And keep your filthy snake mouth shut or chance losing your head."

Damon turned his head and smiled at her. "Never a dull moment around you, is there?"

"Guess not." She tried to smile, but failed miserably. Instead her lower lip trembled and tears welled in her eyes. All she wanted to do now was throw herself in her big brother's arms, bawl her eyes out, and let him comfort her as he used to do when she was a little girl.

What a loser of a battle-mate she was turning out to be.

"Bria...princess...look at me." Damon's voice was soft, but commanding.

She opened her eyes which she hadn't even realized she'd closed and looked up. Her brother's blue eyes glittered with rage. His need to kill the Erian for threatening her safety poured off him in violent waves. His anger was so hot, so turbulent that she was forced to raise her mental shields against the pounding heat.

Damon's fiery gaze checked her thoroughly, from top to bottom—twice. "He touch you?" The guttural voice was almost unrecognizable as his.

"No." She took a wide path around the jittery pile of rags and the glaring Erian to stand by Damon's side. She touched his arm. His muscles were so tense they felt like titanium steel cables. "You don't need to kill him. He won't bother me again. He knows I have protection now."

"Bria—"

"Damon, please. I couldn't handle it if you killed someone for me." She patted his arm. "You're the law here. Can't you kick him off the station or something?"

Damon used the thumb of his free hand to swipe away the wetness on her cheeks. "He made you cry. I could kill him for that alone."

"You and the other brothers made me cry a lot when we were growing up, and no one killed you." She squeezed his hand. "It's just salty water, Damon. I'm fine."

Damon growled "fuck" under his breath and then shoved her behind him. Then with his blade once again at the Erian's neck, he leaned down and whispered something to the mercenary.

The Erian's emotions became so chaotic she couldn't get a reading on them even when she lowered her mental shields. After several seconds, the injured male nodded. His gesture might've shown acquiescence, but his emotions told another story. The chaos had crystallized into rage and retribution.

Maybe Damon should kill... No, she wouldn't be able to live with such an act on her conscience, even if Damon could.

Besides, she'd be safe within the perimeter of *Hades*. Damon would see to it.

After Damon had turned the Erian over to station security, he turned to her. He grasped her arm and pulled her toward the exit to the central part of the station. "Let's go. It's not safe in any of the public areas for you."

Before they'd moved five steps, the Mason freighter captain approached. He was out of breath, his pale orange skin streaked with blood and purpling bruises from the fight.

"Is missy okay?" He cast a fearful look, first at her and then at Damon. He shot an angry glance at the back of the Erian as he was led away. "That one paid to create a disturbance."

"He specifically targeted my sister?" Damon growled and turned with his battle-blade at ready. "He's a fucking dead man."

Bria pulled on his arm. "Stop. You've hurt him. You're kicking him off the station. It's over."

Damon glowered. "He's going to detention until I determine what to do with him. I'll also be checking to see if there are any outstanding Alliance warrants against him. Bria...he's a criminal. I can't let him go."

"Okay. I can see that. But you can't kill him. It's not how we were raised. Press charges and turn him over to the Alliance and let them punish him. Now, may we go? I'm dirty and tired and hungry."

The captain grunted. "I will be happy to swear out a complaint against the Erian. His actions lost me two crewmen and damaged my cargo."

Damon grunted. "Good. But why didn't you assign a guard to watch over Bria?"

"Damon, he did the best he could in a bad situation. I should've insisted I stay on the ship despite *your* stupid station rules." Bria turned to look at the freighter captain. "Thank you for your care on the trip here. I'm sorry you were injured because of me."

"No problem, missy. You go now." The captain bobbed his head rapidly. "Damon protect you now."

Her brother snorted and muttered, "Damn right I will." Then he steered her around the bundle-of-clothing creature, which had slid to where the Erian's blood pooled on the deck. A slurping sound had her stomach clenching.

"Um, Damon, is that Ragbag creature licking—"

"Yes. It's a Wefiantooth or Weaver Tooth in Standard. Ragbag is a nickname. It's a plant-spider hybrid from the Mu Arae system, a scavenger. The little buggers keep the docks clean." He aimed a stern look her way. "Don't ever come between one and its meal. Don't ever touch one. They bite."

"So the captain informed me." She looked around as they walked into the central core of the station. "Are they all over the place?"

"No. If they come above dock levels, the security guards shoot them." He touched the weapon at her back. "Your laser pistol will kill them. Full stream into the center of mass. Don't hesitate and get all girly. Just shoot to kill."

Bria planned on staying out of the creature's way. She didn't think she could kill one for merely being hungry and acting on instinct.

Damon, it seemed, had no issues with killing...in the heat of battle or otherwise. There was no doubt in her mind if she'd answered "yes" to his earlier question, Damon would've finished off the Erian without a blink. It was a side of him she'd never seen before and she wondered if their parents knew how much Damon had changed since leaving home.

Obviously, the Viking warrior genes of his Terran ancestors were strong in him. He even looked like one—tall, broad muscular shoulders, narrow hips, blue eyes, long blond hair. All he needed to finish the picture was a Viking ship and a crew to pillage the galaxies.

Bria wasn't sure if Damon's ease with violence and killing made her feel safe or scared. Probably a little bit of both.

As they wended their way through the station, taking multiple lifts and skywalks, she observed the bustling activity on the most dangerous jump station in the galaxy. So far she hadn't seen a single female in the public areas.

Damon's club, *Hades*, employed the vast majority of women living on the station—prostitutes, dancers, and barmaids. The remaining women were the wives and girlfriends of jump station employees. Her brother had once told her that every single woman on the station lived within the highly secured perimeter on the *Hades* level.

Bria did feel safe with Damon by her side. Still she kept her hand close to her knife after they left the docks...just in case.

"We're here, princess." Damon smiled. "You can take your hand off your weapon."

"Okay." She examined the entrance to *Hades* and grinned. She'd only seen images of it in news vids about the notorious club. "Very tacky, big brother."

And it was.

For the entrance, he'd taken a page from ancient Terran Greek myths and called the artificial river flowing around the curved building, the River Styx. There was no boat and no Charon, the boatman. There was, however, a retractable bridge over the recirculating waters. Flames shot out of the moat, and moans and groans from what she presumed to be lost souls peppered the air.

Damon smiled, but it wasn't a nice one. "The water has its purpose. I throw drunk and disorderly patrons into it." He guided her across the bridge. "Don't ever put your hand or toes in the moat."

She looked at the Stygian waters more closely. When a flame lit up an area close to them, she spotted movement below the surface. "What's down there?"

"Man-eating *Gigantor* pirana from the Amazonian basin on Earth." Damon swept a finger over her lips. "Very aggressive suckers. So, no swimming or wading."

"Damon, you don't—"

He brushed a light kiss over her forehead and whispered, "Yes, princess, I do. This isn't Gliese 581C or one of the Alliance-protected planets where civil law rules. Here a man survives on his willingness to defend what's his. *Hades,* this jump station, and *you* are mine to protect. Live with it."

"I'm sorry, Damon." She hugged him. "I didn't mean to bring trouble to your station."

"It's okay. I'm glad you came to me." He kissed the top of her head. "I can handle the Erian's kind of trouble. We do it here every damn day." He rubbed her back. "Let's get you settled in your room. You can have a bath, change your clothes, and then I'll come and eat with you. We'll talk about all the other trouble following you then. Okay?"

"Sure." She paused, bit her lip, then added, "And we'll also be talking about why you hid my Prime heritage and didn't tell me about my mate marking."

Damon's face turned grim, the frown lines on his forehead deepened, and his lips thinned. He said nothing, merely stared at her for a few seconds. He nodded and then escorted her to her suite of rooms and left without saying another word.

Long after he'd gone, the heat of his desire for her lingered on the air. His anger also remained, a heavy pall in the suite. Damon was pissed. He didn't want the talk. Tough. Her heart hurt. She wasn't looking forward to it either, because it might very well mean the end of her relationship with her brother—and the entire Martin family.

CHAPTER 7

Damon left Bria in the suite of rooms connected to his. *Dammit all to hell and back.*

Somehow she'd figured out he and the family had lied to her. The discovery had hurt her—hurt her more deeply than he'd ever expected. There had been logical reasons to keep the knowledge from her, but in hindsight, they sucked—all of them.

The initial decision to keep her heritage from her had been his parents', since Damon had only been eleven when he discovered the crashed escape pod with an injured Bria inside. At the time, their reasoning to hide her Prime origins had been valid. The Prime hadn't interacted with other populations in the galaxy for many generations, so there was no way to contact anyone in the Cejuru system to report the crash and one little survivor.

But later, when Bria turned eighteen, it had been his call to continue to keep the secret—and the family had reluctantly agreed.

His business partner Borac, a self-exiled Prime, had visited Gliese 581C with him for Bria's eighteenth birthday celebration. When he met Bria, Borac had instantly recognized her as Prime and began asking Damon pointed questions. It had been his partner who'd told him the mark on Bria's body was a mating mark. Borac had gone on to explain how the presence of the mark might affect Bria as she matured.

For Damon, the news she *might* have a mate had been a non-issue. He didn't believe Borac about the significance of the mark. And even if he had, the Prime were still isolationists at the time and still unreachable.

Damon's call not to tell her about her Prime nature had been totally a selfish one. He was in love with Bria and had loved her since she'd turned sixteen. He'd waited for her to turn eighteen, so he could court her and make her fall in love with him.

But Bria had wanted to go to medical school. Damon had loved her enough to help convince his parents that going away to school would be good for her. He'd kept in constant touch with her and waited patiently for her to see him as marriage material. But the timing had never been right. She'd continued on and gotten a fellowship. He and Borac had taken over the jump station and had worked hard to make it as safe—and profitable—as possible.

Then the fucking Prime joined the Alliance, and Bria began working with Prime DNA. He guessed it was inevitable that his very smart Bria would figure out what she was.

And she had—and the time had come for him to pay the consequences for his, and his family's, lies of omission.

He wasn't looking forward to their "talk."

How could he admit the main reason he'd kept silent was because he wanted her for himself? That made him sound like a selfish bastard. He really wished she hadn't intuited that he'd lied. Now, she'd hate him and never want to see him again—and that would hurt the worst of all. Anger riding his heels, he sought Tomas, one of his most trusted security people. Bria was on his station and in danger. No one—not a mercenary Erian nor a lusty bar patron nor her stalker nor a Prime or Alliance traitor—would harm her while she was under his care.

Bria was still his to protect until her fucking Prime mate came to claim her.

If her mate claims her. He could be dead.

Now, wouldn't that be nice?

If her mate were dead, he'd stake his own claim and win her love.

Borac's union with a Terran woman had proven Prime could mate outside their own species, despite Borac's earlier claims of Prime mating supremacy. Borac's wife, Cissy, now carried their second child—a feat that was supposed to be impossible according to what Borac had been taught during his childhood on Cejuru Prime.

Damon found Tomas at the guard station located at the back entrance to the bar, which connected directly into the corridor leading to the employees' quarters.

"Hey, boss. Your sister okay? Heard what happened." Tomas shook his head. "Fucking Erians."

"She's fine." Thank God, or there would've been a lot more blood on the docks to clean up. "Get one of the other guards to take over here. You're on Bria guard duty. No one goes in her quarters," Damon growled. "And she doesn't come out unless a guard is with her. Understood?"

"Got it. Sweet thing like her doesn't need to be anywhere outside the employees' quarters." Tomas frowned. "What the fuck's she doing here anyway?"

"She has people after her. They're not gonna get her." Then he stalked off.

With Tomas on his way to guard Bria, Damon stepped into the main bar area. He automatically noted the place was packed, and the men present included the crew of the Mason freighter which had brought Bria to the station. While a little worse for the wear after their fight, the freighter crew was loud, noisy, and drunkenly appreciative of the live sex shows going on in the alcoves around the seating area.

One of *Hades'* best strippers was on the main stage, making love alternately to her stripper pole and a boa constrictor. Three mercenaries who used the Charybdis gate routinely were all but leaning on the stage, calling out lewd suggestions of what to do with the snake. With good humor and an eye for larger tips, the dancer was obliging them with pleasurable results for all concerned. One of his bouncers was nearby to make sure the men didn't climb on the stage and participate.

Damon had private sex rooms for that kind of activity.

All in all, it was a typical scene for the bar that stayed open around the clock.

He scanned the circular room, looking for Borac.

"She here?" Borac spoke from behind him.

Damon turned. "Yes. And she almost got snatched off the docks by an Erian mercenary and his pals. Not sure if he wanted her for himself or to sell her. But he knows she's Prime. He scented her."

"*Ansu bhau.* He won't stop now that he has her scent." Borac kicked a stool. "She needs to stay hidden until the Alliance and her *gemat* gets here."

"I had security lock up the Erian. That takes care of that problem." Damon sat on a bar stool and looked his friend in the eyes. "Who says the Alliance will bring her mate when they come to get her? Her *gemat* could be dead, you know."

Borac frowned. "Damon, my friend, it is very likely—"

"—he's still alive and on his way. I know. I know." Damon swore under his breath. "Whatever happens, we need to keep her safe. Bria's the curious sort. Nothing keeps her down for long. She'll want to come out of the secured area and talk to people."

"We can't allow that." Borac's words echoed Damon's earlier thoughts. "She is only safe inside the security perimeter."

Borac had personally trained the security personnel for the employees' quarters. He'd wanted nothing to harm his wife or their child.

"Cissy will visit her," Borac continued. "Or Bria can visit our suite. Tomas will guard them both. That should be enough socialization for your sister." He smiled. "Bria will be interested in the miracle of Cissy having given birth to a Prime-Terran child and being pregnant with another."

If Borac had buttons on his uniform, he would've been busting them. The man was extremely proud of fathering two children.

"Borac," Damon smiled, "Bria will be interested in your children, but she won't be surprised. It's her area of research and the reason why she's going to your home planet. She wants to show your people—"

"And her people," interjected Borac.

Damon grunted and continued, "—that they can have children outside the Prime race and that the fertility issues have to have something to do with the planet's environment." Bria had talked his ear off after she found out she was going to the Cejuru system. She'd been thrilled to get the invitation— and that was before she'd concluded she was Prime. He bet she was more excited now.

His little sister would turn the Prime's cultural concepts upside down.

"The old ones won't like that." Borac stated flatly. "Let's hope her mate is politically connected, because she'll need all the power behind her she can muster to change centuries of cultural beliefs."

"Her mate better be strong, period," Damon huffed, "or I won't let him take her off station. I'll hide her first."

Prime bond, be damned.

Borac shook his head and slapped Damon on the back. "Word of advice, old friend. Don't come between a Prime male and his marked mate. All Prime males are warriors.

They connect empathically during times of Prime battle rage. You mess with one, you mess with them all. Not even I would be able to resist the call of *batel rabia*."

"You'd take me down?"

Borac nodded. "In an instant."

"Bria's too gentle to live with a warrior."

"Oh, Damon..." Borac shook his head and laughed. "...your little sister will rise to her greatest potential with her *gemat*. Living with Terrans, she sublimated her Prime nature. I know you don't believe in the bond, but listen to me and believe my words—meeting her mate will awaken her latent abilities, and she'll become one with her man. One perfect loving unit. It is a wondrous thing to see. My parents had that."

Borac's sigh sounded sad. His parents had died in the last Antarean onslaught. The one which had sent Bria to Gliese 581C and his family.

"Well, I'll believe the perfect loving unit crap when I see it." Changing the subject, Damon said, "I want our Volusian guards on the doors to the employees' quarters and at the front and back doors to *Hades*. We can shift the non-Volusians to the other areas of the jump station."

The Volusians were a warrior race and fought fiercely. Damon didn't know who'd targeted Bria, but he wasn't taking any chances with her safety. He wanted his fiercest security people on alert while she was on-station. "No days off for any guard until my sister is off-station. All lasers are to be on maximum stun, and everyone carries a battle-blade."

"I concur." The large Prime almost vibrated with excitement over the possibility of a fight. Running a jump station and a dive bar and sex entertainment club was fairly tame for a man trained to be a warrior.

"I also need to find out who's stalking Bria so we can be better prepared."

"Let me know," Borac said. "So I can see to rearranging the duty roster and adding more men, if needed."

"Thanks, old friend." Damon stood, slapped Borac on the back, and then left the bar to have his "talk" with Bria.

CHAPTER 8

The next day, Jump Station Charybdis

After what seemed like an endless decontamination process, Iolyn jogged through the connecting tube and then onto the jump station's main passenger dock.

His battle-ready senses were at their optimal levels and bordering on dangerous as he scanned the crowded dock. Even four strenuous hand-to-hand sessions with his brothers and several other members of the *Galanti* crew during the interminable flight had barely taken the edge off his frustration and fears. He wouldn't calm down until Brianna was safe in his arms.

His first view of the station did nothing to allay his turbulent emotions. The passenger shuttle docks were old and gritty-looking. The metal walls were corroded and needed a paint job. On some of the surfaces, there were amorphous spots that glowed from some variety of microbe or alien life forms. So much for the decontamination chamber's efficacy. And the air was stale and stank like sweaty socks and rotting meat.

Worse was the drubbing his empathic senses took from the hostile, chaotic atmosphere created by the sentient life forms populating the busy dock platform. Mercenaries, pirates, plus assorted thieves and con men loitered in the open, dimly lit areas, and even darker corners. The one hundred percent male crowd wheeled-and-dealed, fought, and caroused as they waited for their shuttle crafts' departure times back to their larger ships, which waited their turn to use the erratic jump gate.

Iolyn's hand itched as it hovered over his laser pistol. Had his sweet Brianna run the gauntlet of the dregs of the galaxy to get to her brother's bar? Every Prime instinct rebelled at the thought. If she had been so much as touched, harmed, he'd—

Suddenly, the clamor on the docks quieted to the skittering and rustling of the smaller, less deadly males as they fled the danger zone. The remaining badasses focused their less than congenial gazes on him and his fellow shipmates. All it would take to ignite the current combustible aura of fear, hate, and murderous and larcenous intent was one wrong move from either side.

Iolyn pulled his laser pistol. The weapon felt good in his hand. With his other hand, he made sure the sheath for his battle-blade was open for an easy pull. Without turning his head, he spoke to Huw on his left flank. "Keep Nadia close, brother. I don't like the feel of this place."

Wulf, on his right flank, mumbled, "Neither do I. *Ansu bhau*. We should have left Nadia with Melina."

"Wulf. Iolyn. Don't make me hurt you." Nadia elbowed Huw out of the way and moved to Iolyn's side at the end of their assigned docking tube. One hand hovered over her laser pistol, and she had her battle-blade in her other hand. "I can take care of myself."

Huw grabbed Nadia around the waist and pulled her to his side. "Stay close and behave, she-cat." Then Huw belied the stern order by brushing a kiss over Nadia's cheek.

For a single, distracting second, Iolyn envied Huw. He wanted Brianna anchored to his side...now. He snarled with frustration. Sensitive to his emotions, Huw and Wulf echoed the sound, along with the other Prime males in the landing party.

The atmosphere in the dock area heated up another notch as if the surly mob recognized the danger the *Galanti* landing party represented had just escalated.

"Boys, cool it," Nadia hissed. "We're here to pick up Brianna, not to start a galactic war on this dump."

With great difficulty, Iolyn harnessed his erratic emotions and the other Prime males followed suit. The dock area seemed to sigh with relief—or maybe that had been Nadia.

"Can you sense her yet, Iolyn?" Huw murmured.

"No." Despite the futility of it, Iolyn opened his senses wider, leaving him vulnerable to the odd psychic attack from any alien who had the ability. But there were too many other strong emotions bombarding his psychic sense, and the bond connection he shared with Brianna at this point was one-sided: he'd heard her, but she hadn't heard or sensed him in any way.

Iolyn needed Brianna's scent, her intimate touch, in order to develop the more solid emotional link which connected all *gemat-gemate* couples. He'd have the full sensory contact soon, and then he'd always know when she was near and how she felt.

"Wulf..." Iolyn turned his head slightly toward his brother. "This place—"

"Yes. Not at all safe. I've set the guards for the shuttle." Wulf's face was grim and his gaze alert. "Once we've found Brianna, we'll signal the men guarding the shuttle and have them get the craft ready for quick departure. I don't want to remain here any longer than is necessary."

Wulf swept the landing party with a piercing look. "Highest stun on all lasers. Battle-blades close to hand. There are too many damn criminals here for my tastes."

"Mel needs to know. The ships in the jump gate holding pattern might be a danger to the *Galanti*," Huw said. "I see several groups of what look like Rim pirates."

Most pirates had no allies, only enemies and prey. The Rim pirates or RimPz as they were called, were different and operated in what they called family groups. Family being a loose term, mostly defined by sharing common criminal objectives. RimPz tended to prey on the less-populated solar systems in the outer rims of the galaxy. Iolyn and his brothers had fought the RimPz to protect Prime territory long before the Prime had joined the Galactic Alliance.

"Mel already knows," Wulf said, his voice low. "We studied the ships on long-range sensors before we dropped into orbit. I recognized the markings on some of the ships. There are two RimPz families represented and several known mercenary groups. She's already alerted the Alliance Security Forces for this region and the Alliance Command. I updated her mentally on the interior situation as soon as we cleared the end of the tube."

"Heads up, team," Wulf said. "A Code 99 will bring all *Galanti* weapons to battle alert. Mel will then send several security teams to this station to extract us. Don't use the code unless it's truly a life-or-death situation."

Nice to know his brother wasn't taking the jump station's bad reputation lightly. But no matter what happened, Iolyn wasn't leaving without Brianna. He shuddered to think of her in the hands of any of the men on this dock. Every single one he'd seen so far would rape her first and sell her into slavery afterward. Women were a rare commodity in the rim worlds.

Huw grunted, drawing Iolyn away from his dark thoughts. He noted the threatening look Huw gave a scraggly Terran wearing a RimPz patch. The man had stared at Nadia a tad too long and lustily for his brother's peace of mind.

"I think a mostly Prime landing party can handle this bunch." Huw's voice was loud and echoed off the metal walls on the mostly silent dock.

Iolyn snorted at his brother's bravado. But he, too, sensed the lust in the crowd aimed at his six-foot-plus, blonde sister-kin. She was a prize worthy of taking on a Prime landing party. His lips twisted in a wry grin. He'd seen Nadia fight. The man or men who tried to capture her would soon rue the mistake. Of course, first, they'd have to get past the men in the landing party.

As they made their way onto the platform, the crowd lingering at the end of their docking tube parted—not for them, but for someone else.

Wulf growled and every man plus Nadia went on alert, pistols raised.

Two very tall males walked through the crowd as if they were the kings of all they surveyed. One was a Prime, which in and of itself was highly unusual. Not many Prime voluntarily lived outside the Cejuru solar system.

The other man was Terran, and tall was an inadequate term to describe him. He towered over any of the Prime in the landing party and was extremely broad in the shoulders. His body tapered down to muscled hips and legs that looked as if they'd hold up a shuttlecraft all by themselves. His long blond hair and sharply sculpted face covered in a darker beard scruff gave him an edgy, dangerous look. The expression on his face and in his piercing blue eyes said he didn't want them here.

This had to be Brianna's brother, Damon Martin. Iolyn hated him on sight.

The Prime male stepped forward and bowed his head in the traditional manner. He offered his arm for a traditional warrior's greeting, which Wulf accepted with a bow of his head.

"Welcome, brothers," he said in Prime, then switched to Galactic Standard. "I am Borac, co-owner of this station. My friend," he waved the Terran forward, "is Damon Martin, my partner, and the adoptive brother of Dr. Brianna Martin." He scanned the landing party casually as the man at his side frowned and did the same. "Were you able to bring Bria's *gemat* with you? She is anxious to meet him."

Iolyn read Borac as truly happy to see them and his statement about Brianna rang true. But Brianna's brother was angry and—*ansu bhau*—jealous.

"I'm Brianna's *gemat*." Iolyn stepped forward and inclined his head.

"And your name..." Borac asked, one dark brow raised, as he looked Iolyn over from head to toe and back, "...Lt. Commander?"

"Iolyn Caradoc, son of Premier Ilar Caradoc." Iolyn was pleased to see the shock on both men's faces. "Where is Brianna? Is she well? We came as soon as we heard she was in danger."

"Bria's in the employees' quarters. She's safe." Damon's voice was low and harsh and just this side of rude. His posture was stiff, but underneath the outward calm, his core was hot and churning with turmoil—and, if Iolyn were reading him correctly, hurt. "I'll take you to her."

Damon turned to lead them away from the docks and the interested onlookers. Once they were out of earshot of the crowd, Brianna's brother stopped and turned to face them.

"Bria only leaves this station once I'm satisfied she'll be safe with you." His voice was filled with an icy-hot threat.

"Damon. We've already had this discussion." Borac's tone was admonishing. He turned to address Iolyn. "Bria is looking forward to meeting you and going to Cejuru Prime. She has told both myself and Damon that."

"Yeah, but I haven't approved any of this yet," snarled Damon. "And I don't fucking care if he's your people's version of fucking royalty. He could still be a fucking abusive bastard."

Damon scowled at his partner, glared at Iolyn, and then turned his back on all of them and stalked away.

Iolyn clenched his fists. A more primitive part of him wanted to chase the bastard down and gut him on the spot. It was obvious Damon had attempted to convince his sister to stay away from her *gemat*.

Huw must have read Iolyn's fury because his brother laid a hand on Iolyn's arm and muttered, "Calm down, brother. You don't want to meet your *gemate* with the blood of her brother on your hands."

Yes, he did. No man comes between a Prime male and his mate. None, not even a much-loved brother.

"Mr. Martin..." Nadia spoke loudly and clearly as they followed Damon and Borac. "I am Nadia, Huw Caradoc's *gemate*. You need to understand that once a Prime male is mated, they're over-protective and loving in the extreme. Brianna will be in safe hands with Iolyn."

Borac shot her an approving glance. "I know this, Commander Nadia, and have told the thick-headed mule that many times in the last standard day." A speculative gleam glimmered in his golden eyes. "But how can you be termed a *gemate*? You are Terran. I have a Terran mate, but she is not a *gemate*."

"Nadia carries Prime DNA in her blood, a result of our planet's imperialist era," Huw answered. "We now have many Prime male/non-Prime female mate bonds among our crew. This is, after all, why the Prime joined the Alliance—to find mates and save our race from totally dying out."

Borac hummed his approval. "I applaud our Elder Council's decision. I left the home planet to seek my lost *gemate*. Instead, I found Cissy and am very happy. We have been blessed with one child and another is on the way. Do you think I would be allowed home now in order to take my family to visit my relatives?"

"Our father would welcome you. But expect a lot of notoriety," Wulf said. "Both good and bad."

"I'd heard there was unrest about the Council's decision to join the Alliance and seek mates outside of the Prime culture." Borac grimaced. "Is it true? Prime are turning against Prime?"

Damon had said nothing during this exchange. But from his alert posture and the intent look on his face, he was listening and not liking what he heard. The man would use any ammunition he could to convince Brianna to stay away from Iolyn and her people.

"The unrest is small. We have already rooted out some of the traitors," Iolyn said. "And we will find the rest."

"They'll come after Bria. Several have already tried to kidnap her, masquerading as Alliance soldiers." Damon stopped and glared. "Her research will make her a target for the fanatics. Why should I let her go into such danger?"

Iolyn stepped forward until he was toe-to-toe with Damon. The man's emotions were loud and clear. He loved his sister, and not just in a brotherly way. The two types of love were so intertwined in the man it was hard to figure out exactly which love reigned supreme. Damon was conflicted about her mating, but underlying the man's agitation was the fact—he'd die to protect his sister.

So, instead of punching Damon in the face, Iolyn made him a promise. "I'd die before I let anything happen to Brianna. She is a gift I will cherish, protect, and love for the rest of my life. And if something should happen to me, she will have the protection of the Caradoc family. It is the Prime way."

Iolyn didn't know how long he and Damon stood, staring at one another, reading each other, testing the other man's mettle. But it couldn't have been more than a minute or so when Nadia's humor-filled voice broke the tense standoff. "Mr. Martin—"

"Damon." The word came out rough.

Nadia smiled. "Damon, then. Have you ever seen Prime warriors in full *batel rabia*?"

"No." Damon shifted his attention to Nadia. Iolyn stepped back and let his sister-kin charm the man. "Borac has spoken of such, but it sounded like an exaggeration."

"Well, I have. And let me tell you, it's a fearsome thing to behold. I'm Siberian with Hunnish bloodlines and thought my relatives were fierce berserkers. Prime warriors are much, much more feral."

Borac laughed and slapped Damon on the back. "I told you so, my friend. This is why the Antareans haven't taken over the Milky Way. My people have stopped them time and time again."

"And almost caused the end of our people in the process," Wulf added. "But we are still strong in spirit, if not in numbers, and with the Alliance partnership, we'll continue to protect the galaxy—and your sister. My sister-kin."

Damon grunted, obviously not convinced. "Bria's suite is through here. We'll avoid the bar area. I'm not sure my patrons would like to see all those Alliance uniforms parading through."

Borac choked on his laughter. "*Diew*, it would be a mass exodus."

Iolyn could care less about the bar or whoever populated it. He wanted to see and touch his mate, take in her unique scent—and then whisk her away to the *Galanti* where he could begin the more intimate aspects of their bonding.

He rubbed his *gemat* mark. It had begun burning as they'd gotten farther from the passenger docks and closer to *Hades*. Her scent had lingered in the air in just enough quantities to trigger the neurochemical response in his brain. If he exposed the mark, he'd see the colors getting richer.

He inhaled deeply. She was so close now he could barely contain his need.

Iolyn and the others followed Damon down a plain hallway and then into a nicely appointed suite. Here, her scent was fresh and undiluted. He almost moaned at the richness of her essence. She smelled like exotic flowers found only in the Cejuru Prime rain forests, crisp ocean air, and her personal, intoxicating feminine musk.

His loins throbbed, his mark pulsed, as his body anticipated the final step of the mating bond.

But where was she? The place was quiet and had an empty feel. He glanced around, then moved to look in the other rooms. She wasn't here.

Damon had come to the same conclusion, because he threw back his head and roared, "Bria! Goddammit!"

Iolyn grabbed the man and shouted, "Where is she?"

"Calm down, both of you," Borac ordered. "She's probably with Cissy. Remember, Damon? She said something about wanting to do a physical and take some samples for her research in Prime/non-Prime fertility."

Borac touched Iolyn's arm to tug him away from Damon.

Iolyn shrugged off the other man's touch. The pain was unbearable now, whereas it had only been irritating after he'd first heard Brianna's voice.

"Sorry," Borac said. "Forgot. Her scent must be driving you mad."

"What does that mean?" growled Damon, looking between the two of them.

Borac shot a look filled with exasperation at his friend. "I explained the mating bond to you. Brianna confirmed all I said—and still you don't comprehend?"

Damon shook his head.

Borac sighed. "Until Iolyn and Bria mate fully for the first time, they will suffer pain and need."

"That's crap. She's had that mark since I found her in the pod. She was fine growing up." Damon had a bullish look on his face. "She hugged us all the time. She had no pain."

"The young age at which she received the marking has a lot to do with that," Wulf explained. "My *gemate* was a Lost One. She led a fairly normal life. But, when we first heard, then scented one another, there was never any chance she could ever be with another man again. It would hurt too much. We suffered greatly until we came together."

"Jesus," muttered Damon. "I thought it was all cultural bullshit. Bria said a lot of the stigma was misplaced."

"And that may also be so. My having children with Cissy proves that one of the Elder Council's edicts was wrong." Borac moved to look his friend in his face. "Iolyn and Brianna have no choice. Your sister, a very intelligent and logical person, has accepted the parameters of the bond even while she is debunking a lot of the old dogma."

Damon's expression was still mulish, but Iolyn sensed a shift in his emotions from anger and hurt toward grief.

Borac shook his head at the look on Damon's face and then turned to the others. "Come with me. My family's quarters are this way."

They followed Borac out of Brianna's rooms and down a long corridor. There was excellent security on all the marked exits. It would take laser blasters or explosives to get through the doors, or inside help.

When Borac opened the door into his suite, Iolyn spotted a pretty, petite, dark-haired Terran with a toddler on her lap. Her pregnancy was obvious. She looked as if she would explode any second.

"Cissy, *lubha*." Borac's voice was filled with love and adoration for his woman. "Where's Bria?"

"She was here for a while." Cissy smiled. "She'll be back soon. There was a medical emergency in the bar. A knife fight. Dozer said one of the dancers was hurt and a patron was severely injured in an attempt to protect her. The station paramedics were already dealing with another emergency. So, Bria went with Tomas to care for the injured."

When Iolyn growled and Damon cursed, Cissy frowned. "Was that wrong? Tomas and Dozer will be by her side the whole time. She should be safe."

"Fuck." Damon hit the wall by the door with his fist. Then barreled out of the room.

Iolyn followed on Damon's heels with the rest following both of them.

Borac shouted as he moved to catch up with his friend, "Damon, calm down. Brianna is a doctor. She did what she felt was necessary. Cissy is correct. Tomas and Dozer will protect her." He then looked at Iolyn. "Be assured. Your *gemate* is safe."

Iolyn nodded as he listened to Damon speak into his com unit. "Tomas, please tell me Bria is with you and safe."

Damon's face grew dark, and his emotions raged higher and higher.

Iolyn's stomach clenched as his battle rage rose once more in response to the Terran's chaotic emotions. What was wrong?

"Stay put. Call in more security. No one gets near her other than the patients she's treating. Understood?" Damon snarled. "We're coming. I've got her mate with me. Out."

Iolyn asked, "Is Brianna safe?"

Damon looked at him. "On a normal day, the bar could erupt into an all-out brawl. Today isn't normal. Tomas has... concerns. So, no...Bria is not safe, since she's in a dangerous place."

Iolyn paced Damon as he began to run. "You really didn't answer my question. Is Brianna all right?" He'd heard some really bad stories about bar fights in *Hades* from some Volusians now stationed on the *Galanti*. He didn't want her caught in the middle of a drunken riot.

Damon growled. "Bria's fine...She is triaging and treating patients on the fucking bar floor. Tomas, Dozer, and the bartender have created a ring of protection around her. But the status could change in an instant." He shoved his hand on a security plate and let them into a kitchen area. "Most of my patrons know the rules. But we have some real bad asses on the station right now who don't think the rules apply to them."

"Bad asses?" Iolyn growled. "Like the RimPz we saw on the passenger docks?"

"Yeah." Damon threw him a dark look as he led them through the maze of the kitchen area. "There are also some mercenaries on station led by an Erian who took one look at Bria and decided he wanted her. I locked his ass up after he tried to take her off the freighter dock."

Iolyn's blood began to boil. "Take her?"

"Yeah. But I cut his throat before he even touched her."

He owed this man for keeping Brianna safe. So he'd cut Damon some slack for having sexual fantasies about his *gemate*. At the end of the day, she would leave with him.

"If the Erian is locked up, why do you still seem so worried?" Nadia asked Damon.

Bria's brother looked at her and said, "Was locked up. Tomas just told me. The Erian's friends helped him escape. My security people are looking for them now."

Ice-cold fear swept through Iolyn's body and settled in his gut. "Get us moving, Damon," Iolyn growled out. "Get us to Brianna. Once we're sure she's safe, get out of the way so I can go after the *bak* who threatened her." His hands fisted. "And if she's been harmed in any way, you'd better hide until I calm down, because I'll want to skin you with my battle-blade—after I've covered it in the blood of any man who dared touch her."

"Fucking hell." Damon, reluctant respect in his eyes, opened the door into the main bar area. "Can't say I'd blame you."

Once inside, all Iolyn could see was a massive crowd making a lot of noise. No fighting. The all-male crowd seemed to be entranced by the various sex acts. The largest crowd seemed to have fixed their attention on what appeared to be the main stage.

Obviously, someone had gotten the idea of taming the majority of the savage beasts with something more interesting—group sex, with five men taking on one naked woman. Her screams and moans could've been anything between ecstasy and pain.

Searching the area, he couldn't see a dark-haired woman treating any injured. But the place was huge, with multiple stages, dozens and dozens of tables, and more than one bar set up. And lots and lots of big, rough males.

"Is it always this crowded?" Wulf asked.

"Yes." Damon pulled a passing barmaid to him. "Where's my sister?"

"At the second-stage bar with Tomas and Dozer." The woman cast a curious, appraising look over the landing party before scurrying off with a tray of empty glasses.

Iolyn shoved past Damon and moved through the crowd in the direction the barmaid had indicated. Whatever had happened to injure two people to the point of requiring medical attention hadn't seemed to slow down the bar's main activities of serving drinks and entertainment. Besides the action on the main stage, there were sex vignettes, including several of the sado-masochistic bent, going on in alcoves around the edges of the room.

He punched Damon on the arm. "You let your sister be exposed to this?" He waved a hand at the five-on-one action. While Iolyn was no prude and actually quite dominant in his sexual proclivities, he believed sex was meant to be private, not shared with hundreds of drunk, lusty, rough men.

"No. I told her to stay out of the bar no matter what happened." Damon stopped, shoved back a freighter captain who looked as if he was going to join the on-stage action, and then proceeded to walk toward what looked to be the main entrance to the bar. "She doesn't listen. Good luck with that, by the way."

"You're going the wrong way." Iolyn pulled on Damon's sleeve. "Brianna is that way."

Iolyn pointed toward a stage which was empty and the bar serving the area. The crowd was lighter in that area of the room, and he spotted several large and armed Volusians dressed in the station's security uniform.

Even with all the noise and odor of over-ripe males, spilled alcohol, and greasy food, his ramped up senses told him Brianna was within the protective cordon—and that she wasn't afraid for her safety. His tension calmed somewhat, but for some reason, Damon's had racheted upwards.

"Bria is safe. But remember the Erian I spoke of?"

Iolyn would never forget and even now mentally plotted all the ways he'd hurt the *apayebo* before he beheaded him.

His brothers, Nadia, and the rest of the landing party surrounded the two of them, both to provide protection from the unruly bar crowd and to hear what Damon had to say.

"Yes," Iolyn answered. "What of him?"

"He and his buddies just entered the bar. To get inside, they had to get past the Volusian guard I had on the door." Damon's voice and gaze were frigid. "They're armed and heading for Bria. So, go to Bria. I've got some killing to do."

Iolyn let loose with the Caradoc battle cry as his *batel rabia* broke loose of the chains he'd placed around it. It echoed off the high ceiling of the large barroom. His brothers' rage aligned with his, creating a wave which pulled in the other Prime in the landing party along with Borac.

Nadia muttered, "Damn, I'll never get used to that."

Damon, eyes widened in shock, looked at Borac. "What the fuck was that? It's like the atmosphere heated up."

Borac answered, "That's the Prime battle rage I told you about. Feels wonderful."

"Well, hell—" Damon shrugged. "Whatever." He headed for the Erian and his men as they pushed through the bar crowd and moved toward Bria's location.

Iolyn thrust his arm across Damon's chest. "No. The Erian is mine." He angled his head. "Huw. Nadia. Take the others and guard Brianna."

"You've got it," said Huw. Then he and Nadia sliced through the crowd, taking the other three landing party members with them.

"I want the Erian." Damon had pulled a large knife and held it in a tightly clenched fist. "I saw him first."

"Brother-kin, I sense Brianna would be very upset with me if you were hurt." Iolyn pulled his much larger weapon, a battle-blade. "Plus, you already got to make him bleed once. He's mine now."

"Fair enough." Damon grunted. "I will keep the others off your ass."

"That would be good. Wulf will assist you. Won't you, brother?"

Wulf laughed and brandished his battle-blade. "I live to assist."

Iolyn laughed and noted Damon cracked a smile and shook his head.

"Let's go get these *baks*," Iolyn muttered.

The three moved quickly to intercept the Erian and his mercenaries. When they were about four meters in front of the Erian's path, they stopped.

"Leave. Now," Iolyn shouted. Rules of engagement always provided for a chance to retreat. He also wouldn't want his *gemate*, raised on a pacifist planet, to think him a blood-thirsty barbarian.

His roar effectively silenced the bar patrons standing nearby and startled the Erian and his gang into halting their forward progress.

"This is your only warning." One which he knew the Erian would ignore.

In fact, he was counting on it.

CHAPTER 9

Minutes earlier, Hades

"**B**ria, please go back to your quarters." Tomas's voice cracked with tension, and his head was in constant motion as he scanned the dimly lit and smoky bar. "You've done enough. The security guards have basic emergency medical training."

"No." She continued to check over the male victim on the floor beside her for indications of why he was unresponsive. "This man's in shock, and his life signs are decreasing. The dancer's leg is still bleeding. I don't have the equipment I need to stabilize either patient quickly, not even a medi-laser, so I'm forced to do things the old-fashioned way...hands-on care. My hands. You want me to leave? Get me gurneys...now. I can treat these people more effectively in the medica."

"*Madre de dios*, Bria." Tomas tore at his hair. "You aren't safe here. The sharks are circling. Your brother is gonna have my balls for breakfast for exposing you to danger and"—he swept his arm to include the stage shows and the smaller sex vignettes—"things a proper lady like you should never see."

Until Tomas had mentioned it, she'd managed to ignore the live sex shows to her right and left, because she had patients to triage. Now, she looked up and was amazed that the violence and its bloody aftermath had barely fazed the performers and their rapt audience.

Emotions still ran hot in the large barroom. Most of the tension in the air was sexual. Yet, there were toxic threads of violence interwoven in the lust. The same kind of violence that had one lusty patron attacking one of the dancers. The injured man she now examined had pulled the bastard off the woman.

Things could easily explode again with the right spark. The sooner her patients were stabilized and out of here, the better. She didn't like the feel of the atmosphere.

Bria continued her examination of the male victim. "Tomas, I can't leave my patients. Just can't. And as for the sex acts...doesn't bother me. So get over it."

Well, she might have lied a tinge. She'd studied sex in medical school, the biology and psychology of it. She worked in research where the sex act was often discussed, but in a clinical fashion. She'd also had sex. But nothing within her experience resembled what was going on around her.

A thought struck her. Would her *gemat* expect some of these acts? She'd heard from Lia that Prime males were very alpha-dominant. She shuddered—with excitement or dread—she wasn't sure which.

Tomas opened his mouth, probably to plead with her to leave once again when a security guard tapped him on the shoulder. The two men huddled. Their auras flamed with anger and fear. She was about to ask Tomas what was wrong when—

"Doctor..." The security guard attending to Siri, the dancer whose leg had been slashed, pulled her back to the here and now. She'd worry about sex, and what it would entail with her Prime mate, when she'd found him.

"Yes, Dozer?"

"Siri's bleeding isn't slowing. What am I doing wrong?"

Blood flowed freely through the guard's hands as he put pressure over Siri's wound. The dancer's eyes were glazed with pain and her already pale skin was almost translucent.

"Press harder. You're being too gentle," she told Dozer. "Tomas..." Bria glanced up and found Tomas blocking her view of the room at large, his body posture on guard, his weapon drawn. "...are the gurneys coming from the next galaxy? If I don't have transportation in the next few minutes, then we'll have to draft help and carry the patients to the medica on tabletops."

"I'll call again." Tomas looked harried and more worried than her request required. "The paramedics have their hands full with multiple injuries elsewhere on the station. I sent one of the door guards to the medica to get a gurney. You need to leave. Now."

She glared at him and didn't answer. Her response hadn't changed since the last two times he'd told her.

"*Ai yi yi*, Bria...*por el amor de Dios*—" Tomas's plea was cut off by the sound of his com unit. "What!" he shouted into the unit.

Bria listened to his side of the conversation with half her attention as she felt for fractures or wounds on the male victim. She checked Dozer and nodded with approval as Siri's bleeding was under control.

"She's here." Tomas spoke into the com device, but his narrowed gaze continued to sweep the area around them. His grip tightened around his laser weapon. "Damon, even if I told her about the Erian's escape, she wouldn't budge."

The Erian mercenary had escaped? A twinge of fear shot down her spine. Then she looked at her nearly dead patient and muttered, "Damn right, I won't."

Dozer choked back a laugh.

Tomas glared at her. "Fucking come and get her yourself, *¡Cabrón!*" He snarled. "I hate to say it, but I agree with her. She needs to stay. The guy's really white. He looks dead."

"And that's what he'll be permanently"—she paused to take the man's pulse—"if I don't get him to higher level of care and soon."

Tomas glowered and then hissed into his com unit, "She's more effin' stubborn than you. *Ai yi yi. Pinche puto pendejo baboso!*" Tomas's anger ran so high he'd devolved into gutter Spanish. "Yeah, yeah, I'm not going anywhere. Roger that. Fuckin' out."

"Where is he?" she asked after Tomas shoved his com unit into a pocket and grumbled in Spanish under his breath.

"Borac's suite. The *Galanti* is in jump station space. The landing party's with him...including your *gemat*."

Her gemat? *Here?*

"Really?" When he nodded, joy and anticipation at meeting her mate...mixed with worry he'd be disappointed. The opposing emotions swirled in her stomach, making her feel sick.

"Bria?" Tomas's voice had gentled as if he were afraid of scaring her. "You okay? You look sort of...green."

God, did she look that bad? Probably. She felt light-headed like some too-stupid-to-live heroine in the romance novels she read. She finally remembered to breathe and then attempted to reassure Tomas she was okay. "Yes. No. Hell, I don't know."

Bria shook off the weakness and forced herself to concentrate on her patients. As long as she focused on what she knew and did best—caring for others—she'd be fine. Just fine...for now. So, she'd occupy her mind with what was in front of her.

The question uppermost in her mind: What had she missed on this patient?

She'd finished the pat down on the man. Nothing broken. No contusions on his head. Unconscious, but breathing shallowly. Lying on his back. No blood on his front. No blood pool under him.

She shook her head. "Fuck this. I need to turn him."

A couple of the lookee-loo bar patrons came forward while Tomas yelled into his com unit about the gurney.

"Gently now," Bria urged the men as they turned the patient onto his stomach and peeled off his torn shirt which got hung up on something on his lower back.

"Well, hell," she said.

The man had been stabbed. His back was one huge bruise of pooled blood. He had a knife tip stuck in his back over his left kidney, which had effectively plugged the hole. The knife must've broken off sometime during the fight or the man's fall to the ground. "This man needs surgery and now."

"Tomas—" she called out.

But before he could respond, the crowd parted and two men brought in a gurney.

"Thank the stars. Get this man to the medica. Put him on a regen bed face down and find me one of the damn station paramedics. I need him to assist me with both patients. Someone needs to carry Siri to the medica and put her on a regen bed also. Now, people."

As men scurried to do her bidding, she supervised, but all the while, at the edges of her consciousness, she fretted over the upcoming meeting with her *gemat*.

"Go. Don't wait on me. Get them to the medica." Bria picked up the injured man's laser pistol which had fallen out of his waistband after they'd stripped off his shirt. She made sure it was locked and then stuck it in her back waistband so it wouldn't go missing.

Once her patients were on their way, Bria began to follow when an abrupt and uncomfortable silence settled over the bar. The silence seemed even more ominous considering that Siri's stabbing and its aftermath had only caused a hiccup in the bar's activity.

Then Bria scented something on the air, something addictive that negated the odor of blood, sweat, booze, stale sex, and smoke. An aroma which made her forget where she was and what she had to do. She had a sudden intense urge to seek out and then cover herself in the luscious scent.

She took another deep breath and sighed. The aroma brought to mind a deep, dark woods in the heat of the day. All rich smoky resins and musk. She took another breath, and a tingling began in the skin over her right ovary. Her breath hitched, and the bottom seemed to drop out of her stomach.

Her mark! Something was happening to her *gemate* mark.

Bria gently touched the area. Heat burned through the material of her pants. The mark throbbed with a delicious pain that also pulsed in her sex.

Using Tomas's big body to block out curious gazes, she turned her back to the room and gingerly peeled down the waistband just enough to uncover the mark.

"Oh my God." Her mark had come alive. Where before the pattern had been pale, now it bloomed with vibrant color. She traced the swirls of color and gasped as her sex contracted and her clit ached. "I didn't believe it."

Lia had told her about Mel Dmitros-Caradoc's bond mark reaction when first exposed to her *gemat* Wulf after twenty-seven years of separation, but Bria had been skeptical...until now.

"What is it, Bria?" Tomas nudged her toward the bar, keeping his body between her and the room. "Pull up your pants," he hissed. "*Dios*! There are men here who would take that much skin as an invitation to fuck you blind."

"Tomas, you're in my way." She turned and craned her neck to see if she could spot the only man who could've made her mark react with merely his scent. But there were too many bodies, too close together. "I need to find my brother. My *gemat* is with him."

"Yeah, I told you that, remember?"

"You told me he was on-station. Now, he's *in* the room. I scented him." She tried to move Tomas out of her way, but he was too big. When she tried to go around him, he countered her every move. *Infuriating, over-protective male.* "Move it, Tomas."

"No. Something's wrong. Stay put." Tomas turned his back to her and scanned the room. "Oh shit. Well someone's here and heading straight for you." He pulled his weapon and stepped forward as if to confront whoever had put that harsh, angry growl in his tone. "And it ain't your *gemat*, that's for damned sure."

Now that his back was turned, Bria managed to wiggle away from the bar and step to Tomas's side. She followed his narrow-eyed gaze and— "Oh shit is right."

The Erian mercenary and a bunch of ugly characters were headed straight for her. But then the crowd shifted and revealed Damon and two tall, dark-haired, brutally handsome males in Alliance uniforms. Several other soldiers and a tall blonde woman, also in an Alliance uniform, stood off to the side. Her brother and the two men with him moved quickly to cut off the Erian and his gang.

Everything in her body sat up, panted, salivated, and yearned. One of the unfamiliar males was the source of the wonderful smell that had jump-started her dormant libido. He was her *gemat,* and he acted to protect her before he'd even met her.

Bria's mate was also off-the-scales furious. She could almost taste his fury. Her *gemat's* rage glimmered in a dark aura all around him, singling him out from all others. His erotic scent had turned hot and smelled like burning embers. A low, buzz-saw growl emanated from deep within his throat and vibrated throughout the room and raced over her skin like an approaching electrical storm. A storm that would protect her with its ferocity, while sheltering her from its harsh side effects.

The furious rumbling crescendoed as it was echoed by the other Prime males in the landing party.

The need to growl swept over Bria. She touched her throat, soothing the tight muscles as the guttural sound fought to get out. As the Prime males' rumbling increased, the noise swallowed all other sound in the room.

Intellectually, Bria had known the physical attraction would be strong between them because of the potent pheromones which had created the mating mark all those years ago. But she'd never realized how much her heart and soul would be involved...until now. Or, that in an instant, she'd fall head over heels in love with her mate.

The urge to rush to his side was strong, but a vicious battle waged within. She had a duty to see to her patients, but her instincts were to stay and defend her mate.

This time, nature beat out nurture and training. She'd stabilized the patients the best she could, and the paramedic would keep the male alive in stasis on the regen bed until she got there. She'd be damned if her *gemat* was hurt, or worse, before she even met him.

Bria pulled her knife from her boot and waited. For what? She didn't know.

Then she did.

Damon, her *gemat*, and the other Prime male were focused on the Erian and his men. So focused, they might not have felt the other evil in the room—it was a sly, secretive evil wearing the face of an ally.

Bria scanned the room, clearing it section by section. So far she found no one acting hostile, but the feeling was present and growing stronger. She'd stand back and let the men handle the obvious danger, but was poised to act to cover their asses, if need be.

And from what she could see, her *gemat* had a very fine ass.

"Bria, what are you doing? Damon will kill me. All of the Prime look as if they could eat titanium hulls for breakfast. One of those big-ass bastards is your mate, and he'll kill me, if Damon doesn't," Tomas said. "We need to get you out of here."

"Brianna needs to stay. She has us to protect her." The tall, blonde woman in the Alliance uniform and another Prime male came to stand by them. Three other Alliance-uniformed soldiers formed a protective perimeter while giving Bria a view of the center of the room where the confrontation was still at the verbal stage.

"The man next to Brianna's brother is my brother Iolyn Caradoc." The Prime male told Tomas. "You try to take his *gemate* from this room, he'll get distracted. That would make this an even bigger clusterfuck than we have now."

The blonde woman smiled and inclined her head in greeting. "Brianna, I'm Nadia and this"—she indicated the man who'd addressed Tomas—"is my *gemat* Huw. Wulf, the oldest Caradoc brother, is backing up your brother and Iolyn."

"Brianna, is any of that blood yours?" Huw frowned. "Iolyn will go even more berserk—and he is already as unhinged as I have ever seen him."

"*Sladkie*, he's been ready to boil over ever since he knew Brianna was in danger." Nadia leaned into Huw, who rubbed his chin over her shoulder.

"Not my blood." Bria turned her gaze away from the obvious love and affection the couple felt and wondered if she and Iolyn would be that way. She hoped so.

She focused on the action in the middle of the room. The other evil in the room was still at the intent stage, and how she knew that, she didn't know. Her empathic abilities seemed to have increased a hundredfold since Iolyn came into the room.

"Brianna—" Nadia murmured. "Are you okay? You look... lost."

"Call me Bria. I'm...I'm not sure what I'm feeling. Is the reaction to a *gemat* always this intense at first?"

Who'd be better to ask than another *gemate* who'd gone through similar feelings, right?

"I'm not Prime, obviously, so my road to mating was a little different as I'm sure Lia told you. So, describe *intense*."

Nadia also turned to monitor the situation in the middle of the huge barroom.

"I...I..." she turned her head toward Nadia and waited until the other woman looked away from the preliminaries to the inevitable fight.

The Erian wouldn't back down. Bria easily read his determination to kill anyone who tried to stop him from kidnapping her. He had plans to make a lot of money on her. And how could she know that? Was she going crazy?

She found an amused understanding in the other woman's icy blue eyes. "Go on, Bria. We're all friends here. We'll understand."

"I need him. I smell him. I-I-I feel his rage, and his intense, bordering on scary, need to protect me. His growls prick my skin and...and I want to growl, too. Is that part of being a *gemate*—or does the battle-mate allele have something to do with the feelings?"

"You have the allele?" At Bria's nod, Nadia's beautiful face glowed. "It's both. Isn't it amazing?"

"You're a battle-mate?" Huw's voice was filled with shock and happiness. "*Ansu bhau*. We Caradocs are truly blessed."

"Can you read Iolyn's thoughts?" Nadia leaned into Bria and whispered, "You should have enough of a sensory impact now to do so. It's just a higher form of the empathy I sense in you."

The nearness of Nadia's body, even the slight wisp of her breath, made Bria cringe away. Her skin had become extremely hypersensitive since she'd scented Iolyn.

"Are you feeling—being drawn to—an outside source of energy? It will feel strong and masculine and comforting," Nadia said. "It's Iolyn's energy, and you'll be able to draw from it."

Bria's brow creased in confusion. "I have my own energy well. Why would I need Iolyn's?"

Her own power had served her satisfactorily. And with time and training, she imagined she could become a formidable opponent—if she could get past the teachings of her childhood and her profession of doing no harm.

Nadia nodded. "All battle-mates have their own well of energy as warrioresses. But there should be a connection to Iolyn's. I could connect to Huw's even before we physically joined for the first time. Visualize it"—Nadia closed her eyes and Bria could feel electricity in the air and knew the woman was connecting to Huw—"as a life-line connecting the two of you. Huw's and mine is like a faintly glowing rope in my mind's eye, which grows brighter when our energy wells connect. Seek it now."

Bria closed her eyes. Seeking deeply within, she found a phantasmal connection that might have been there before, but now glimmered—and it led to Iolyn. His power source was super-bright. It roiled and bubbled, held in only by Iolyn's stronger will. "I see it. I feel Iolyn's energy. He's readying for battle."

Nadia smiled. "Yes. You can draw on it whenever you need, just as he'll be able to draw upon your energy when he has need."

Bria couldn't imagine the vigorous energy well she'd touched ever being depleted, didn't want to think about how badly hurt Iolyn would have to be to draw upon hers. The idea of her warrior-*gemat* drained of his animal vitality to the point of death had her ready to scream her outrage to the galaxy.

"Send him a thought—now." Nadia's urgent tone brooked no argument. "He heard your voice on the message you sent Lia. He scented you as he entered the room, and, I can tell you from experience, the need to be with you is driving him crazy. But most of all, he needs to know you are safe."

The tall blonde leaned in closer and murmured in such a low tone Bria knew no one else could overhear. "And save yourself the aggravation and accept the gifts of the bonding sooner, rather than later. Fighting it doesn't help."

"Why would I fight the bond?" Bria asked out loud, drawing Huw's attention. "I've waited for the one man who'd make me feel alive all my life. I just don't want to let him down."

Growing up on Gliese 581C, she'd known instinctively there was only one man for her in the universe. She'd left home not only to obtain an education, but also in the hopes she'd find the "one." The men she'd met, dated—and the few she'd had sex with—had left her feeling cold...disappointed.

With one mere breath of Iolyn, her whole body, soul, and heart had come alive. Fight against the bond? Never. She'd grab onto it, fight for it, and never, ever let it go.

"Don't worry. You can't disappoint him," Huw said. "Trust me on that. Iolyn wants you with every breath he takes."

"Good." Bria turned to face Iolyn as he, his brother, and Damon stood between her and the danger of the Erian and his men.

Both sides growled and postured. The barroom crowd had moved away, clearing a large space, and then watched in a hushed, hungry-for-a-fight silence.

And then there *IT* was again. The sly evil. The elusive trickster. Its focus was on Iolyn and Wulf. Why didn't Huw or Nadia sense it?

Bria turned to ask and noticed the attention of Nadia and the others was riveted on the center of the room and the standoff. Nadia and Huw seemed especially attuned to Iolyn and Wulf. There was a mental energy wave flowing among the four that beckoned, but she didn't know how to attach herself without losing her sense of the other evil in the room.

In her gut, she knew the sneaky evil was more dangerous to the Caradocs and Nadia, than the Erian was to her.

"Nadia!"

The blonde woman turned, noted the look on Bria's face, and touched her arm. "What is it?"

"Can you feel it?" Bria lifted her head and sniffed the air to see if the danger had a scent. It did. Decayed vegetation and rotten meat. "Smell it?"

"What?" Nadia looked around and took a few deep breaths.

"A crazy, deluded evil." When Nadia said nothing, Bria continued, "Not the greedy wickedness coming off the Erian and his men. This evil hides and then attacks from behind."

Nadia closed her eyes. "There's something. But I can't get a fix. I'm riding the *batel rabia* wave, and it's very strong and concentrated on the Erian. Can you show me the danger?"

Bria followed the sensory impressions that kept digging at her brain. This evil was the most foul she'd ever sensed. It sickened her with its fanatical hatred of her mate and his brothers, but she persevered until she found its location.

She opened her eyes. The man—just one, thank the One—was on the periphery of the crowd. He moved among the bar crowd like a shark cutting through the ocean, weaving back and forth, coming ever closer to his targeted prey. Iolyn was his first goal. Then Wulf. Then Huw.

He was an assassin with a rabid focus which promised death.

But why? And why here and now?

Her empathy had its limits. They'd have to ask the man once he was captured.

"The assassin...is coming in from our right, behind Iolyn and the others."

Nadia murmured something to Huw who drew his weapon and alerted the other Alliance soldiers. Nadia then moved closer to Bria and began to scan the crowd slightly behind Iolyn and Wulf.

Bria could see him more clearly now. He was large, tough-looking like many of the men populating the jump station, and was alone. The assassin lifted his arm. In his hand was a laser pistol. He aimed at Iolyn. There was no time to show Nadia or Huw. Only time to act.

"Iolyn. Down. Now," Bria screamed.

The urgency in her voice did the trick. Iolyn dove for the ground. Damon, Wulf, and station security, weapons drawn, moved to surround the Erian and his men, who'd been distracted by her scream.

Stopping the assassin was up to Bria.

In the second or two after her shout, Bria ignored heated demands for information from Huw and Nadia and one overwrought male voice inside her head. She kept her eyes on her target. As the assassin switched from the now inaccessible Iolyn to the easier target, Wulf, she stepped forward and threw the knife still clutched in her fingers.

Her aim was true. She hit the assassin in the upper chest as she'd done countless times in throwing contests in the lab. The wound was in his left shoulder. He was down and bleeding, but remained conscious, armed, and still dangerous.

Before anyone could move to contain him, she pulled the laser weapon she'd placed in her waistband and stunned the assassin for good measure. His hand went lax and his pistol fell to the floor. A jump station security guard picked it up and stood guard over the downed man.

Bria closed her eyes as her knees threatened to give way and the room spun around her. Blessed be the One. She'd stopped the man and hadn't had to kill him. But she could have. Easily. She swallowed hard against the bile threatening to come up her throat.

When she was sure she wouldn't vomit or fall down, she opened her eyes. It seemed as if every gaze in the room was on her. But she only had eyes for her *gemat,* who looked taken aback. She tore her gaze away from his shocked one and looked at her brother.

Damon was pissed.

Wulf Caradoc saluted her with an approving smile on his handsome face.

And the Erian and his crew looked intrigued and even more interested in her than before. They'd been disarmed and were surrounded by station security.

"Good job, Bria." Nadia moved to her side. "Where'd you learn to throw knives? We heard you weren't trained as a fighter."

"Thanks." Bria shoved the borrowed laser back in her waistband. "Medical school. Scalpel-throwing champion three years in a row. That hit would've garnered me 250 points."

Nadia grinned. "We'll have to have a match some time."

"I'd like that." Bria smiled and knew she'd made a new friend.

Huw moved to her other side. "Welcome to the family, sister-kin. Would you like another knife?" Bria nodded. "Take mine." He handed her a finely balanced throwing knife.

Bria took it, moved forward a couple of steps toward the center of the room, and then spoke in a loud and what she hoped was threatening tone, "Anyone else who tries to harm my man or his people will answer to me."

She was fairly certain the would-be assassin had acted alone, but just in case, wanted to warn anyone else who might be foolish enough to take a shot at the landing party. Then she looked at Iolyn, whose face was emotionless despite his close call. But underneath the calm facade roiled a combustible mix of potent feelings, of which the uppermost was fear—for her.

Bria appreciated the sentiment, since she'd felt an equal amount of fear for his well-being as the assassin had taken aim. If Iolyn hadn't ducked, if she'd missed her throw, then he and his brother could've died.

Her heart still skipped a beat at the thought. So, she'd give him his fear for a second or so, but there was no danger now. He needed to get over it.

His forehead creased and his full lips thinned. She mentally smacked her head. Telepathy. She'd forgotten the damn telepathy. He'd just followed her every thought.

Pissed at herself for forgetting what Nadia had told her and at him for not letting her know he was reading her mind, she fluttered her hand at him like a princess to a peon. "Carry on, *gemat*. Your battle-mate has your ass covered."

Iolyn's eyes widened. *Battle-mate?*

His mental voice was a decadent surprise. It was low and husky—and if it had a taste, it would be the darkest and richest chocolate. Its timbre was a sensual caress over her mind. It filled her and made her happy—until she read his thoughts. He was worried. He thought her weak and helpless because of her upbringing and profession. To him, she was a fragile female he had to protect, especially now, after she'd deliberately placed herself in unnecessary danger. It was the Prime male's job to protect his mate, not the other way around.

What a load of crap.

You are precious to me. You're beautiful and recklessly fearless, gemate lubha. *But you aren't a warrior. You are all that is good—and a healer. I want you away from here. Now.*

She liked hearing the precious and beautiful parts, but the recklessly fearless, not so much. She also didn't want to be sent away like a small child. So she made her position clear.

I downed the assassin who'd targeted you and your brothers. I was the only one who sensed him. I have enough skill to cover your back—and I can learn more.

Iolyn's eyes narrowed. *Targeted? He wasn't here for you. You're sure?*

He'd neatly ignored her actions in the defense of him and his brothers. *Men!* In her experience, the male of the species tended to see and hear what they wanted and disregarded the rest. Passive-aggressive asses.

Yes, she replied, *I read his intent.* Iolyn's eyes widened with surprise at her words. *The assassin was alone.*

We'll have Lia patch him up. You're never to come near this bak. *My brothers and I will question him on the ship. Now, you must go. Your brother and I must deal with the Erian and his men.* His mental touch stroked her hair and then moved to brush softly across her lips. *You are mine. I have to keep you safe.*

Bria threw up her mental walls and blocked Iolyn from her thoughts—or at least, she hoped she had. She had a feeling her walls would get stronger and stronger while dealing with Iolyn. She'd heard and dealt with attitudes similar to his a lot as she'd grown up with six older brothers who thought they knew best for her. The dominant, alpha-male, I-command-all-I-survey attitude.

Supreme lordliness had never worked on her back then. It wouldn't now.

But dealing with such attitude took skill. Bria didn't know Iolyn well enough yet to determine what tools in her dealing-with-a-stubborn-male skill set she'd need to pull out. Eventually, he'd learn not to underestimate her. She wasn't a weakling just because she was untrained. She was smart—and educable.

His mere presence had already increased her empathic skills and made her feel stronger than she'd ever felt in her life. With some training, their mating could be a partnership as she sensed Nadia and Huw's was.

It would all begin today.

"Brianna, leave." Her mate's growl echoed off the walls and into her very bones. "Go to your quarters. I will come for you soon and then we'll leave this place."

She inclined her head, turned, then stomped out of the bar. Nadia and Huw and the other Alliance males stayed behind. Tomas was on her heels.

As she left the room, Iolyn pounded on her mental walls. She strengthened them and was thrilled to see they held. They'd talk later about his lack of faith in her intelligence and courage.

Right now, she headed for the medica. She had renal surgery to perform.

CHAPTER 10

"*Ansu bhau!*" Iolyn turned and looked at Wulf. "She blocked me."

Without turning his attention from the assassin who'd tried to kill them, Wulf snorted. "Melina did that also. Brianna probably had to develop shields to protect herself as she grew up." He knelt by the man Brianna had knifed, then shot. "This man is Prime. I've seen him somewhere before."

"Cut the chatter," Damon muttered. "We have to deal with the Erian and his pals before we figure out who the guy on the floor is."

Before either Iolyn or Wulf could respond, Huw and Nadia joined them along with the other three *Galanti* crewmen.

"What are you doing, slimeball?" Huw glared at someone over Iolyn's shoulder.

Iolyn turned to see the Erian staring after Brianna. The Erian mercenary's split tongue licked at the air slowly as if savoring it.

"The Prime woman..." the Erian spoke in halting Standard as he shifted his slitted acid-yellow gaze to focus on first Huw, then Iolyn. "She is a battle-mate? She belongs to—"

"Me." Iolyn fisted his hands and stepped forward until he was less than an arm's length away from the slimy bastard who'd targeted his Brianna. "My *gemate*. My battle-mate. Mine."

With each word, his voice got louder, until the last word echoed off the metal rafters. Brianna's brother jerked as if hit by a laser stream, and Iolyn was aware of Damon's fixed stare and the pain—and hopelessness—blasting through the man.

The Erian tasted the air again. "Yes-s-s-s. She smells of you. Wondered."

"Wondered what?" Iolyn stroked a hand over the battle-blade sheathed on his thigh.

"She was-s-s with him." The Erian angled his head toward Damon. "Not smell right. S-s-so—"

"So you thought you could take my sister since she didn't smell like me?" Damon's face flushed with his anger.

The Erian smiled. "Yes-s-s-s. She no belong to you. Need to belong to s-s-somebody."

Brianna's brother flinched, then his blue eyes went cold and empty as a starless night sky. Iolyn sensed the man's reluctant acceptance of the Erian's words.

Damon turned toward Iolyn. "I say we kill him—and his friends. I don't like their looks or attitudes."

The two men would always have this in common—the need to protect Brianna.

"It's my right to kill the slit-lipped *apayebo*. He was going after *my* woman." Iolyn turned toward Wulf. "I want him."

"We aren't the law here, brother. It's the galaxy rim, and martial law applies." Wulf bowed his head to first Damon and then Borac. "These gentlemen have every right to police their station as they see fit. The Erian and his men are their responsibility. I would like to make a request that they allow us to remove the would-be assassin and leave his punishment to Alliance and Prime law."

"Agreed." Damon turned to the Erian. "You'll be placed in detainment until Borac and I decide what your ultimate punishment should be." Damon turned to address the six heavily weaponed station security officers guarding the outlaws. "Take them to the holding cells. Keep them separate. And if any of them escape...heads will roll."

As Damon's security men moved to take charge of the Erian and his crew, the Erian attacked Damon. The station security guards, taken by surprise, were separated from the mercenaries by some less-than-lawful bar patrons.

"I was hoping that would happen," Iolyn heard Damon mutter as Iolyn was forced to engage one of the Erian's men, while Huw and Wulf engaged the other two.

Nadia, armed with her laser in one hand and her battle-blade in the other, stood guard along with Borac who was similarly armed to prevent any more of the barroom crowd from choosing sides and joining in the melee.

It took no time at all for Iolyn to down his man. His brothers also quickly subdued their opponents. The men in their landing party cuffed the three ruffians, all Terrans who hadn't had a chance in hell against the *batel rabia* strength of three pissed-off Prime warriors.

"Should we help Damon?" Nadia moved to stand next to Huw. She placed her arm around her mate's waist and kissed his ear.

Iolyn looked on with an envy that bordered on pain. Soon that would be him. He'd have Brianna by his side, where he could touch and be touched in the affectionate way of bonded couples. But first, the Erian had to be declawed once and for all, and the Prime assassin secured and his injuries stabilized. He would be questioned later. Extensively. Iolyn wouldn't take even an infinitesimal chance with Brianna's safety, even if she didn't seem to believe the assassin had been targeting her.

"Damon seems to be holding his own for a Terran raised in a pacifist society," Wulf commented dryly from behind Iolyn.

"I trained him." Borac stood with them, his narrowed gaze following the fight closely. "He has the soul of a warrior." He smiled at one of Damon's particularly vicious countermoves, which cost the Erian part of his arm. "When I first met Damon, he didn't know how to fight dirty. He learned quickly. We get all sorts of less than law-abiding citizens here. We have to hold onto what's ours."

But Brianna wasn't Damon's. She was Iolyn's.

Borac turned toward Iolyn and inclined his head. "Ah, I sense your concern, son of Caradoc. Yes, Damon does not want you to have Brianna. He loves her. Has loved her for many years."

Iolyn watched as a bloodied Damon beheaded the Erian, admiring the man's fighting ability even as he wanted to kick the man's ass for coveting his *gemate*. "He can't have her."

"Then do not give him a chance to take her." Borac turned away from Damon as the man was surrounded by a swarm of congratulatory bar patrons and said in a low voice, "You need to know that Damon's family hid the truth of her heritage from her. They had an angry discussion about this matter. Brianna made it very clear she has always known there was someone in the galaxy for her—and that it wasn't Damon. She wants you and what the bond promises."

A load of worry and dread was eased by Borac's words. Iolyn had feared Brianna would be torn between the love for the man she'd known for over twenty-seven standard years and him and their bond.

"Damon was hurt by the truth in the Erian's words, Iolyn," Borac's tone held deep concern for his friend and partner. "It is beginning to sink in that the bond is not a fiction. Give him time and distance to come to terms with all this. Take your *gemate* and leave as soon as possible."

Iolyn glanced over and found Damon's blank stare fixed on him and Borac. His emotions were too chaotic to single out. Borac was correct—Damon needed time, and Iolyn needed to put distance between the step-siblings for now. He would discuss with Brianna about how to repair the brother-sister relationship, since underlying all the chaos in Damon's emotions was a solid foundation of love for a little sister.

Borac finished saying good-bye to Iolyn's brothers and Nadia and had turned to join Damon and the crowd of the drunken well-wishers. "Borac…" Iolyn called out.

"Yes?" Borac turned to face him.

"You and your family are welcome to stay with Brianna and me anytime you visit Cejuru Prime." Iolyn offered his hand.

Borac gripped it in a warrior's acknowledgment, hand to forearm. "I would be honored." Borac released his grip on Iolyn's arm. "Go. Be with your *gemate*. We will meet again soon. I have a raging need to see my home planet again."

Once Borac was away, Iolyn turned and addressed Wulf and Nadia. "I'll go to Brianna's quarters, and let her know we're leaving. We'll meet you at the shuttlecraft as soon as she gets her things together."

"Hurry," Wulf said as in the background Huw directed the landing party to take the assassin to the shuttlecraft. "We don't need any more would-be assassins taking a shot at us. Obviously, the rebel faction has long arms. How they knew we were coming here and got an assassin here in time to attack us is a question I want someone in Alliance and Prime Commands to answer."

As he left the bar, he heard Nadia ask Wulf, "Do we have enough time for me to see if the bartender knows how to mix a Black Siberian? I haven't had one of those in a long time."

"A Black Siberian?" Wulf asked. "Let's go see. I wouldn't mind trying one myself."

Iolyn shook his head and smiled as he moved quickly through the bar, retracing the route they'd taken from Brianna's rooms.

Ten standard minutes later, Iolyn stood in the middle of the living area of Brianna's quarters, hands on his hips and a scowl on his face. "Where in Balcon's Balls name is she?"

His words echoed in the empty space. He'd searched all three of the suite's rooms—including every corner and closet—and even under the bed. She wasn't here.

Now that he'd stopped stomping around like an enraged beast, he did what he should've done to begin with—he sought her through their sensory and empathic connections. Yes, she'd blocked their battle-mate telepathy. But he had the *gemat-gemate* bond. He had her voice, her scent, her image imprinted on his brain, all of which would allow him to sense if she were near and provide a general direction to follow.

Once they were completely joined, she'd become part of his soul and have a much harder time blocking any of the aspects of their bond—he hoped. His brothers had confided that their battle-mates could still throw up some damn good walls when the women were mad. Anger made some strong walls, it seemed.

Iolyn tugged on his connection to Brianna. He turned in a circle and stopped when the directional pull was the strongest. *Ahh, there she is.*

One level up. Her shield was still up, but wasn't as strong as when she'd left the bar. He could ride on some surface thoughts now. She seemed to be concentrating on some task. He opened his empathic senses to the bond and nudged with his telepathic link to see if he could figure out exactly what she was doing.

He inhaled sharply. A distinct coppery, earthy smell flooded his olfactory nerves. *Blood!* The odor was so strong he could even taste it. But she wasn't in pain or distressed. *Not her blood, thank the One.*

But she was worried. And then it hit him—she was treating the people's injuries which had drawn her to the bar in the first place. She was in the jump station's medica.

Brianna was safe and saving a life. He admired the strength of her dedication to her profession. His woman was both intelligent and compassionate, but naive about the dangers lurking outside her insular world of medicine, especially on this jump station. While the Erian was dead, he wasn't the only predator in this place.

Concerned for her safety, he'd told her to go to her quarters. She'd deliberately ignored him. He'd read enough of Brianna's thoughts prior to her blocking him to know she was used to taking care of herself.

That was before. Now, she had him to see to her well-being. She couldn't just flit about, even to do her job, without having a care for her safety. His enemies would love to use Brianna to get to him—and by extension, to the Caradoc family.

At least her research could be performed in a highly secured environment on-planet. Unlike his brothers' mates, who put their lives on the line as Alliance officers each and every time they left space dock, Brianna's job was not inherently dangerous. *Thank the One.*

He left Brianna's quarters. The door creaked shut, the sound echoing loudly off the corridor walls. Another door opened down the hallway, and the man called Tomas poked his head out of the door. He nodded at Iolyn and smiled.

"Oh, it's you. Bria's in the medica. The injured man needed some laser surgery on a kidney. Our paramedic needed her assistance. I'll show you the way," Tomas offered.

"No, thank you. I can find her."

And he planned on never losing her again. The concept was unacceptable.

CHAPTER 11

Jump Station Charybdis medica

"There, that should do it." Bria set the surgical laser to the side after sealing the wound entrance. She turned to the paramedic who'd responded to the emergency in the holding area—an emergency that had resulted from the Erian's escape. Darned lizards. "Clean him up. Then watch him for the next few hours. If his blood pressure stays up and he feels like it, release him with standard post-op instructions."

"Yes, Doctor." The paramedic programmed her instructions into the regen bed and started the palliative cycle to speed up the patient's post-op recovery.

Now that her mind and body weren't occupied by caring for her patients, the niggling sensation at the back of her brain came roaring to the front of her consciousness. It seemed to be separation anxiety from her *gemat*—Iolyn—she had to start thinking of him as Iolyn. She felt a strong urge pushing her to get back to his side. Her body ached for him. She wanted to see him, scent him, and most of all to touch him and be touched in return. She needed those sensory inputs as much as she needed her next breath.

She'd heard about these feelings, these urges, from Lia. She never expected them to be so uncomfortable, as if she'd die or go crazy without Iolyn by her side.

Preparing to seek her mate, Bria pulled off her disposable gloves. Then out of the blue, a whoop-whoop-whoop noise startled her. "What's that?"

"An emergency code." The paramedic checked his com unit. "They need me in the bar area."

Someone was injured in the bar area? Fear struck Bria, and she opened her senses and let down her walls enough to touch Iolyn's mind. He was uninjured and hunting for her. She breathed a sigh of relief.

"I have to go. I'm the primary medical until Borac and Damon find a doctor willing to work here." Obviously torn, the paramedic looked at Siri and then at the male patient who was still unconscious. "Doctor..."

Bria needed to be with Iolyn, but the male patient also needed to be watched, as did Siri. Her training, her conscience, urged her to stay. The part of her that clamored for Iolyn's nearness had subsided when she touched his mind and found he was seeking her. There was no doubt in her mind Iolyn would find her, even if he had to tear the jump station apart.

She could let him know her exact location, but that would be too easy. After the way he ordered her to go to her room like a little girl, instead of asking nicely and saying "please," she didn't want to make it easy. The man had to learn she was used to making her own decisions.

Plus, she would've come to the medica even if he'd asked nicely. A life had been at stake.

Bria turned to the paramedic. "Go on. I'll stay here until you get back, or you send someone else."

The paramedic smiled. "Thanks, Doctor." He grabbed his medical kit and ran from the room as if a horde of Antareans were on his heels.

Bria turned back to the male patient. She programmed a change in his oxygen levels and then began to clean up the supplies used during the operation. Once the surgery was spic and span, she dictated her orders into the patient's chart and electronically signed it.

With that chore done, she moved to check on Siri. As she reviewed the dancer's vitals with one part of her brain, she recalled her first impressions of Iolyn with another.

Tall. Broad shoulders. Leanly muscled. Smelled like a forest in summer. Bossy. Over-protective. He was everything she'd expected—and more.

A sharp pang of intense desire threatened to take her to the floor.

Bria hunched over and hugged herself as the mark on her lower abdomen burned with a sharp, stabbing pain that mirrored a clenching in her core and the aching of her clit. Now, this was sexual desire—on steroids. She'd never lusted after any man before and had never imagined it could be this strong. That she'd be so needy.

And for the rest of her life this need, these urges, could only be assuaged by Iolyn's touch.

Instinctively, she searched for the psychic path she'd sought during their first encounter, just a short while ago. She examined the connection. It was saturated with his scent...his voice.

The sensory memories soothed her, allowing her to unbend and take slow, calming breaths.

Now that she'd regained some semblance of control, noises in the corridor grabbed her attention. The squeaking of soft-soled shoes over metal floors made her cringe. The irritating noises approached the medica. There was also a clanking of metal on metal—weapons, someone had a lot of weapons jangling in harnesses.

Danger. Some really bad men were headed her way—and Iolyn was nowhere near. He'd go ballistic that she'd placed herself—albeit inadvertently—in danger once again.

Bria shot into a state of hyper-awareness. Colors were suddenly brighter. Visual details more crisp. Every smell, sharper. Every small sound, louder. Her heart beat more rapidly, an erratic *drub, drub, drub*, as adrenaline and battle-mate hormones flooded her veins. Her well of primal energy surged through her, readying her for battle just as it had on the docks the day she'd arrived and in the barroom earlier.

She reached for the knife Huw had given her and then remembered—per standard protocol, her weapons were locked down in the medica's changing area. Well, hell, if she'd suspected there'd be more trouble, she would've ignored the rules and remained armed.

Iolyn was too far away. There was no one else in the immediate area, other than the volatile males heading her way. She began to assess her situation.

The surgery had only one exit, and it led into the medica, where she saw two men enter the waiting area. She was trapped. And even if she hadn't been, she wouldn't have run. Siri and her rescuer were unconscious and helpless.

The two men stood in the waiting area and watched her like the patient predators they were. Their fixed stares and ugly smiles chilled her skin and raised the hairs on her neck. They definitely weren't here seeking medical care. If their expressions and the aura of danger around them hadn't convinced her, the fact they weren't bleeding and looked fit and strong would've. They were also armed to the teeth with knives, battle-blades, and laser weapons. Their clothing was a mixture of less-than-clean flight uniforms from several different freighter companies. The skin that wasn't covered by hair was decorated in scars, tattoos, and piercings.

The only conclusion? The two were either mercenaries or pirates. It didn't really matter which—they were bad news.

A pregnant silence settled like a lead blanket over the medica.

Bria struggled to handle her fear of the men and the flood of fight-or-flight hormones. Her heartbeat was so rapid she was sure she'd have internal bruises on her chest wall. If she didn't get her breathing under control, she'd either hyperventilate or have a heart attack. Already, her vision dimmed as blackness edged in from the side and streaks of white and yellow dots floated across her visual field.

How in the hell did battle-mates deal with all the stress hormones?

Then she knew.

Bria dug deeply into her energy reserves and found the necessary strength to rein in her breathing. She heaved a silent sigh of relief as her senses once again tuned in to her surroundings.

During her slight panic attack, the two men had moved closer. Much too close.

Weapon. She needed a weapon. Anything sharp or lethal would do.

Without taking her eyes off the men, Bria backed away, slowly, until her bottom hit the surgical laser array she'd shoved against the wall. Beads of sweat formed on her forehead and back, sending chill bumps over her skin.

Sweat, she couldn't control, but she could present a calm face to the enemy—and stall until Iolyn came for her.

One man—she'd call him Asshat—turned to the other—he'd be Rat Bastard—and muttered something she couldn't quite hear. Rat Bastard retreated to cover the medica's main entrance as Asshat moved to the surgery doorway where he stopped and glanced around the suddenly claustrophobic room.

Her throat tightened as her fear of being trapped in a small place won over reason and took control of her mind. A scream rose in her throat which she managed to cut off until all that came out was a strangled gasp.

Asshat smirked, and his dark eyes lit with an unholy gleam at the sound.

Show no fear—and breathe.

She forced herself to take one deep breath, then another as Asshat remained ominously silent and motionless except for his hawk-like gaze which quartered the room.

His stillness was scarier than if he'd spoken or lunged at her.

Bria practically vibrated with the need to do something, anything, to end the standoff.

Once again she was relegated to playing defense, to out-waiting her nemesis, letting him make the first move and hoping he'd make a fatal mistake to give her an advantage.

Asshat and Rat Bastard had already made one huge mistake—they'd given her an opportunity to succeed by dividing themselves.

The seconds ticked by in slow motion. Not that much time had passed since the men had appeared in the medica, but it seemed like forever.

Iolyn was coming. The knowledge was her lifeline. With any luck, he'd arrive before the men made their move—whatever in the hell it was.

Then Asshat grinned, showing unusually bright white teeth against his swarthy beard scruff. The predator knew he scared her. He got off on it.

Bastard! She'd had e-fucking-nough.

Empowering anger swept through her like the wind before a storm. She'd had her fill of big scary men intimidating her... finding her amusing. She didn't need this...this crap. And she wasn't going to wait to be saved. She'd save her own damn self.

Bria stared at Asshat while checking that Rat Bastard was still at the outer entrance. He was, and, oh lucky day, his back was to the surgery. Yet, he was still mere steps away.

Weakening doubt crept in once more. Two, large, heavily armed males could break her into little pieces without breaking a sweat. She shuddered as she heard bones breaking in her head.

Then she recalled Nadia's words about drawing on her mate's power. Maybe Iolyn didn't have to be in the room to help her.

Bria dropped her mental shields and sought the psychic connection she'd visualized earlier and tugged it.

Brianna? You're frightened. What's wrong?

Instantly a surge of masculine power swept across the connection, adding his strength to her own. She was still angry *and* scared. But she wasn't alone any longer.

Come to the medica. I need some backup.

I'm already on my way. What's wrong? Open to me fully.

Bria dropped the partial shields she hadn't even realized she'd kept up.

Iolyn swept in and took in the situation. His growl sent shivers down her spine and made her smile, which wiped the smile off Asshat's face.

As you can see, I'm stalling. But not sure that will last much longer.

How many total?

Two. Heavily armed.

Keep stalling.

I'll try.

Try harder. Her mental snort elicited another growl from her *gemat*. *Stall, my* cwen.

Bria shrugged and slammed up her shields. She didn't need the distraction of Iolyn's worries—or his bossiness.

She stared fiercely at Asshat. "What do you want?" She was proud her voice was calm and strong, showing none of her inner turmoil. Her gaze moved over the man and zeroed in first on his hands, then his expression and posture.

Asshat was relaxed at the moment, not threatened by her at all.

Good. Asshat's guard and that of Rat Bastard would be down. They wouldn't expect her—a woman and a doctor—to defend herself.

"You're coming with us." Asshat took a step into the small surgery.

The room seemed even smaller. The air became thicker, more suffocating.

Bria said—did—nothing in response to his provocative move.

"Did you hear me, woman?" Asshat took another step toward her and held out a large, dirty-looking hand. "Come. We're leaving. I don't want to hurt you. You're worth more alive and undamaged."

Playing dumb, Bria said, "I can't leave. I have patients." She gestured toward the regen beds.

Asshat's gaze shifted toward the two patients. As his attention was diverted elsewhere, Bria reached behind her, feeling for the surgical laser. She grabbed it. Surgical lasers could do a lot of damage to a body, especially thin-skinned hominids like Asshat.

"Leave them. We need *you* to negotiate a deal for us." The leader's gaze was back on her as he moved closer.

Bria resisted the urge to retreat—and scream. She did fully drop her shields. *Iolyn. Hurry.*

Do. Not. Block. Me. Again.

Fine. Just hurry.

Iolyn's response was a loud rumbling that reverberated in her head. A surge of masculine power once again boosted her own, and it was all she could do not to cry out at the intensity of the feeling.

Then Asshat charged her.

Bria brought her arm around. The surgical laser was on and set for cutting bone. She swiped it across her attacker's arm as he grabbed for her.

For a second, maybe two, there was a stunned silence in the surgery and then Asshat screamed. A cuttingly sharp shriek that rattled the glass cabinet doors.

"You bloody bitch." He jumped back. She followed and

swept the active, sizzling laser back and forth in front of her, herding him toward the outer room.

Rat Bastard rushed to stand outside the surgery door at his friend's shout of pain. He blocked her and Asshat's exit.

Okay, that wasn't good. She'd lost the element of surprise. She still had the advantage that Asshat wanted her alive and undamaged, as he'd put it.

Time to stall again.

"Stay back." She waggled the laser in front of her, singeing Asshat's sleeve when he got too close. "I'll kill you."

"You're a fucking healer." Asshat had the audacity to look outraged by her actions.

Bria felt a twinge of guilt for maybe a nanosecond, but just as quickly got over the feeling. "And you're mercenaries threatening me. So the Hippocratic Oath went out the door as soon as you entered. Now, leave before I slice off your penises." She aimed the surgical laser and let loose several short bursts.

"Fuck." Asshat jumped back as the beam set fire to his pants, right above his pubic bone.

Rat Bastard cringed and covered his cock in response. "Man, she's serious."

Of course, Asshat and Rat Bastard didn't need to know she'd have a really hard time following through on her threats.

"Ain't no fucking merc. We're free-traders," snarled Asshat, who remained just out of her and the laser scalpel's reach. "Heard on the docks. The Alliance values you. We need you to get what we want from them. Sort of like bartering."

"You're pirates?" Not men hired to kidnap or kill her. A crime of opportunity and greed, rather than planned. Relief engulfed her at the news that no one had followed her to the jump station. Nevertheless...

Bria snorted. "Mercs. Pirates. Same difference. You're still bad guys."

The men bristled. Their emotions grew darker and more heated. Their patience was running out. She needed a weapon with longer reach.

She blasted another laser stream to draw their attention and force them to move back. She used the distraction to palm a scalpel from the cart behind her. The steel instrument felt good in her hand.

Her *gemat's* shock at her bloodthirsty plan wisped along the surface of her thoughts. He was with her, monitoring the situation—and getting closer with every passing second.

"Fuck, bitch." A dark flush of anger turned Asshat's face beet red. "Ain't never hurt a bargaining chip before, but..." He looked her up and down. An evil gleam entered his dark eyes. "...for you I might make an exception."

Rat Bastard then upped the ante in the game of standoff and aimed a laser pistol at her upper chest and shot.

Bria dove to the side as he'd raised his weapon. The low stun tagged her upper arm. Gasping for breath at the shock to her nervous system, she managed to hang onto the surgical laser as she scrambled to regain her equilibrium. Acting totally on instinct now, she threw the scalpel at Rat Bastard and then sent a laser stream toward Asshat to keep him off-balance.

Rat Bastard dropped his laser weapon with a wounded screech, his hands clasped around the scalpel buried in his throat, just centimeters from his carotid artery.

Dammit, her aim had been thrown off by trying not to fall. Blessed One, she hadn't wanted to kill him, just stop him from shooting her again.

Asshat stared from Rat Bastard to her, shock on his face. Then he roared and charged.

Heart in her throat and her gut churning, Bria stepped forward and kicked Asshat in the balls. Hard. The pirate fell to the floor. Then she kicked him in the diaphragm. The only sounds coming from him were harsh, labored wheezes.

Dropping the surgical laser, Bria sidestepped Asshat and approached Rat Bastard, who was choking on his own blood. He'd pulled out the scalpel—bad move—but, at least, the blood didn't spurt from the wound. She'd missed the artery. He'd live with proper treatment.

Swearing under her breath, she stooped and picked up Rat Bastard's laser, setting it to low stun, and slipped into her waistband. Then she kicked the bloody scalpel under a cabinet.

Grabbing some surgical gauze off a shelf, she knelt and applied pressure to the wound. The gauze was saturated in a mere second, so she tossed it to the side and applied another pad.

From his still-coiled position on the floor, Asshat shot at her. The laser stream flashed across her arm, the arm Rat Bastard had already tagged.

Bria hissed at the pain.

Brianna! Iolyn's mental voice held fear.

She rolled over Rat Bastard, whose body blocked the doorway, and out into the medica waiting area. She took shelter on the other side of the door, out of Asshat's view, fairly sure the bastard had set her on fire, but too busy to worry about it right this second.

Brianna! Answer me.

I'm fine. Sort of busy here.

She rubbed her sleeve against the wall to snuff out the fire. She hissed at the pain and smelled the pungent aroma of singed flesh and cloth. She looked at her arm and let out a breath. She had a second-level laser burn. It hurt like a bitch, but could be easily treated—later.

Later is unacceptable. You're in pain. Warm, soothing energy came across their bond link and calmed the pain in her arm.

She'd find out how he'd done that later. *Are you close?*

The elevators are out. Fires were set in the stairwells.

How in the name of all that's holy was he coming, then? She got an image of closed-in, dark, dirty spaces. Maintenance tubes. He was crawling in them to get to her. Better him than her.

Okay, he was on his way. But she still had a situation that wasn't going to wait on help to arrive. Her empathic ability told her that Rat Bastard was near death. He needed help ASAP.

"Your friend will die if you don't let me help him," she called to Asshat. "Throw your weapon through the doorway, then come out with your hands in the air."

"Fuck you, bitch," he gasped out the words, the kicks to his balls and abdomen still affecting his breathing. She wished she'd kicked him harder. Maybe in the head.

Bria listened carefully for Asshat's next move, because she knew he was stupid enough to make one. Asshat's muttered curse words, the sounds of him dragging himself across the floor, and the noises from the regen beds were the only sounds in the room for the next few seconds. No sound was coming from Rat Bastard, which was troubling. Was he dead? Had she killed him after all?

Then the squeak of the surgical array's cart wheels startled her. The screech was followed by a groan of pain and swear words. She pictured Asshat using the cart to help himself stand.

With his position fixed in her mind, she dove across the doorway and fired Rat Bastard's laser, set on low stun, through the opening at the approximate spot Asshat's torso should be.

He bellowed his pain.

Her weapon readied, she peeked around the corner.

Asshat lay on his back, pale and laboring for each breath. Defanged, for now.

Rat Bastard became her focus. His bleeding was sluggish, an indication his heart had slowed immeasurably.

Bria came around the corner. She knelt, put the weapon in her waistband, and checked Rat Bastard's pulse. It was fast, thready. Breathing, shallow. Color, white. She pulled the surgical laser over from where it had fallen to the floor and sealed the hole in the artery. Now, she needed to get him on a regen bed, pour blood in him, and do a little arterial repair work or he'd die.

Asshat moved. She turned. He aimed his laser pistol in a white-knuckled, shaking grip. The man would just not quit.

Pulling her laser as she rolled to the side, she sent a laser stream, this time on high, into his torso.

Asshat dropped his weapon as her shot knocked him flat on his back—again.

Even if he were still conscious, his nerve endings would be synapsing like crazy. He wouldn't be able to hold a spoon to feed himself, let alone fire a laser, for hours after such a hit.

"Brianna!" Iolyn's voice echoed down the hallway leading to the medica.

Now, she'd get the lecture that even now he rehearsed in his mind about placing herself in a position to be attacked by pirates. He needed to save his breath. She'd do everything she'd done again except the next time she'd remember to arm herself while doing surgery in a place where there was a threat potential. And to always use high stun.

There will be no next time.

Yeah, there would. She was a doctor, and she'd go wherever the patients were. It was her calling.

I'm your calling.

Arrogant ass.

Bria slammed her walls back up and muttered, "We'll just see about that, mate."

"Brianna, stop shutting me out!" Iolyn's roar vibrated over her skin and made her knees shake. He was the epitome of a frustrated, pissed-off male.

Well, she'd had a lot of those in her life. One more would be a no-brainer—but she dropped her shields because there'd been some hurt mixed up in all the alpha-male frustration.

"Bria, goddammit. Talk to us!"

And that was her brother. Guess he'd gotten past the frank "talk" they'd had earlier. She'd forgiven the family and him for keeping her Prime heritage a secret after his very rational explanation. And she couldn't be mad that he loved her, but she was sad he was hurting.

Right now, he was just as pissed-off as her *gemat*. They really were quite a lot alike.

He wouldn't appreciate the comparison, gemate lubha.

Bria couldn't help but grin at Iolyn's wry tone.

"I'm in the surgery," she called out. "Situation is under control..." then Bria muttered, "...as you, *my gemat*, well know."

She stood and on shaky legs walked over to prep the only remaining regen bed for Rat Bastard's surgery. The pounding of heavy feet announced the arrival of her backup.

"I need a little help here." Bria turned. Dirty and disheveled from their journey through the maintenance tunnels, Iolyn and Damon stalked into the medica, with Wulf, Huw, and Nadia, all equally grubby, following on their heels. She smiled at the look of shock on their faces as they took in the bodies. Even Iolyn looked shocked, and he'd been in her mind for most of it.

She turned back to her preparations. "Someone needs to lift Rat Bastard," she gestured toward the prone pirate, "onto this regen bed. He needs surgical repair and lots of blood. Someone else needs to call the paramedic back, because I'll need assistance."

"Don't bother, princess," Damon snarled. "The bastard's a dead man anyway. Both of them will be sentenced to death for this day's work."

"Damon..." She looked at her brother, but was caught by the deadly look Iolyn aimed at both the pirates. Her *gemat* agreed with her brother. She wouldn't waste her breath to argue with them. She'd do what she had to do.

She shrugged. "I'm still stabilizing the bleeding man's condition. What you do to him when I'm gone is on your conscience, big brother—not mine."

"What about this one?" Iolyn growled as he nudged Asshat with his booted foot. "Does he need surgery...before your brother passes judgment?"

"No. I only had to kick and stun him a few times. He'll recover in a few hours. Might have some residual twitching and numbness—and sore testicles."

Nadia choked back what sounded like laughter. Wulf and Huw didn't bother masking their chuckles. Damon and Iolyn had the exact same expression of disbelief on their faces.

Bria smiled at Huw as he laid the limp body of Rat Bastard onto the bed. "Thank you, Huw."

"You're welcome, sister-kin." Huw fingered the hole in her sleeve. "Nasty-looking burn. You okay?"

Bria smiled at her new relation. "Iolyn did something right after it happened"—she looked at her arm and poked gingerly around the blister—"it looks worse than it feels. In fact, it seems as if it's healing super-fast."

Huw grinned and nodded. But it was Nadia who enlightened her. "Yes, Bria, it is. Remember what I said about not fighting the bond? This is one of the reasons why. Warrior-*gemats* can soothe your pain, heal your injuries during battle. If you don't let them, they get anxious and grouchy."

Huw frowned, but didn't contradict his mate. He did add, "It's a Prime imperative to protect one's battle-mate from hurt and fatigue."

Nadia moved to Bria's side. "Go to Iolyn," Nadia muttered, "before he explodes. I can set the regen bed up for surgery. I've had paramedical training."

Bria smiled her thanks and took a step toward Iolyn, who stood and watched her with an unreadable look on his face. She touched his mind—she *had* hurt him by shutting him out.

Iolyn opened his arms. She walked to him and let him enfold her within his embrace.

"Brianna...Bria...you prefer I call you that?" Iolyn pulled her close, took her chin in his hand, and gently tipped her face up until her gaze met his fiery amber one.

"Yes-s-s." She swallowed hard.

One touch, his first touch—and she wanted him to touch her all over with those calloused, but gentle, fingers. She'd never responded this way to any male—ever.

"Please, Bria...*gemate lubha* ...keep your shields down. I didn't intrude when you were fighting the pirates, did I?" Iolyn whispered.

"Yes, you did...but it wasn't that bad. I'm not used to conducting mental conversations and fighting off bad guys at the same time." Her lips twisted into a slight grin. "I don't respond well to orders."

"And that's the truth," Damon grumbled. "She's very independent."

But she sensed with every fiber of her being, Iolyn had wanted to issue commands and take over. That it had almost killed him to hold back and merely give support from a distance as she fought for her life. And that in the future, when he was more sure of her, he'd be his usual autocratic self.

The Prime male instinct to protect one's mate was strong and would never go away. They'd both have to compromise and adapt. They were a team now, not two separate beings.

"We'll learn how to work together." Iolyn swept a thumb over her lower lip, and she felt the touch all the way to her sex. "I promise to try not to take over. I can't guarantee I'll be successful. It goes against every instinct I have."

He closed his eyes and took a deep breath before opening them. Then it was as if he looked straight into her soul when he said, "I can't lose you."

Bria blinked back tears. His need for her was palpable. Her existence was essential to him—like air, water, and sustenance. She'd never been essential to anyone's existence before. Well, she had for patients, but this was different. Not even Damon had shown this kind of emotion when he'd admitted to wanting her as his wife during their talk.

"You won't lose me." She leaned her face into the palm of his hand. All she wanted was to go somewhere private so they could begin their new life together. She sensed he wanted that also—very much.

But she still had a patient to care for. Later...

Later. I will hold you. Love you.

Bria shivered. She turned into his body and leaned her forehead on his chest. *I'll look forward to all of those things... and more.*

"*Gemate lubha,*" Iolyn breathed the words over her cheek before he tilted her chin to brush a kiss over her lips.

Damon hissed.

Bria, startled by the sound, turned, and looked at her brother. His eyes were filled with pain as he stared at her in Iolyn's arms. Despite their conversation earlier that day, it would take a long time before he'd accept Iolyn as her lover, mate, and the future father of her children.

Iolyn placed his arm around her waist and squeezed. The silent support was appreciated. Her mate knew when to talk and when to shut up. Within a little over an hour of meeting her, he already anticipated her emotional needs. She hoped she'd be as supportive of his urge to protect her when it butted up against her desire to make her own decisions.

We'll make adjustments as we go, lubha.

Bria rubbed her cheek against his chest and inhaled his scent. It soothed her as much as his warmth and words.

"Why didn't you just kill them?" Huw asked as he looked at the surgical laser Nadia had sterilized for Rat Bastard's repair work. "You obviously had the upper hand at the end."

"Huw," Iolyn growled, "leave her alone. She doesn't need to relive her experience to satisfy your curiosity." He kissed the top of her head.

Bria sighed and relaxed against his strong body, letting him support her weight for just a few seconds. The paramedic had arrived and took over prepping Rat Bastard for surgery, so she had time to luxuriate in being held. It was nice having someone to lean on. She'd never had that before, never thought she needed it—not even with her family on Gliese 581C.

"But I want to know," Huw said. "If we're in battle, can she kill if needed?"

"Huw..." Iolyn stiffened against her. "Now is not the time for this."

Bria stroked his chest, soothing him as he'd soothed her. "It's okay."

"No, it isn't," Iolyn whispered against her ear. "You don't have to answer."

"I want to answer. You all need to know." Bria glanced at the patients in the regen beds. "I sensed the men would use my patients' lives to force me to go with them. I couldn't let that happen. I was relieved less-than-lethal force stopped them." She shuddered, and Iolyn gathered her closer. She looked at Huw. "But I would've killed the men if I'd had no other way to stop them. Does that answer your question?"

"What about to save your own life?" Wulf asked.

Bria sensed Iolyn's unease at her answer. He hadn't liked that she'd stayed and endangered her own life.

She equivocated. "My life was never in danger." She shivered, and Iolyn ran a soothing hand up and down her back. "I was worth money to them."

Iolyn whispered against her cheek. "I'll protect you in the future."

"You can't protect me from everything," Bria protested.

"I can damn well try." His possessive growl vibrated through his touch into her bones.

Damon cursed and left the medica.

Iolyn's touch, his scent, his emotions combined to send a frisson of awareness down her spine and then into her sex. Her panties got wet, and her *gemate* mark burned.

Bria swallowed a low moan and fought the urge to bite his chest, right on the spot where his mark should be. A dominant-alpha-chest-thumping male had never been attractive to her before today. She'd always made it a rule to challenge and defy such male authority from the time she'd become aware she could solve her own problems.

Bria was at a loss to explain this sudden turn-about. She glanced at Nadia. The tall blonde had a wry twist to her lips. The woman winked at her and mouthed "later," as if Nadia knew exactly what Bria's thoughts were.

Yes, later. She'd ask Nadia, and maybe Mel and Lia, if they'd ever had the same feelings when their mates went all growling male on them.

One thing she was sure of—her response had nothing to do with logic or her past experiences with men. It must have something to do with her Prime nature and the bonding.

Sometimes, even a scientist had to accept that when it came to nature versus nurture, nature refused to be defeated. But, while this supremacy of nature was great for survival, it could play hell on personal, intimate relationships. Her life had just gotten more interesting.

CHAPTER 12

Starship Galanti, Iolyn's Quarters

Iolyn paced the sitting area of his quarters like a caged animal. In a few minutes, he'd enter the bedroom, take Bria to bed, and complete the physical part of the bonding. This was what he'd longed for his whole life, right after he'd realized what the mark on his chest meant.

So...why was he hesitant about opening the door and claiming what was his?

Because, dumb ass, you're afraid you'll overwhelm her with your passion.

Oh, yeah, that was why.

Iolyn stopped and stared into space for a second or so, then turned and recovered his tracks for the tenth or so time. Maybe he and Bria needed to have a conversation about past sexual experience. Hers, not his.

A rumbling started low in his chest and before he could rein it in, he snarled and hissed, the sound akin to a thousand angry stinging insects. He didn't care for the idea that Bria might have been with other males. But she'd been raised as a Terran, and Terrans dated and had sex before settling down.

He understood the reality...but hated it.

And he suspected she might know something about Prime males using sex surrogates from her past conversations with Lia about Prime mating.

Damn it all. Susa.

Bria would eventually meet the sex surrogate who'd taught his brothers and him all about the sexual act. Susa knew things about him that no other knew, not even his family. But she was bound by oath never to tell, and he trusted her.

Bria would learn those things as their sexual relationship matured.

Susa was definitely in the past. Prime males were infinitely faithful once they'd completed the physical bonding.

Still, Iolyn needed to be prepared to address Bria's concerns about his past sexual intimacy with Susa. He didn't want Bria to be ambushed by the knowledge as Nadia had been when Huw had gone to Susa while he and Nadia had danced around their unusual bonding.

At least Bria had wanted to be with him from the moment she knew about him.

Iolyn smiled as he recalled how Bria had melted against him after her altercation in the medica. She'd taken to their telepathic connection with ease. Well, he frowned, except when she threw up those damnably strong mental walls she had. His sister-kin had them also.

Strong women. Strong mental shields. And Bria was a battle-mate just like the other two. But he never wanted to see her in battle. There would be no fighting for his *gemate*. She'd be safe and sound in a research lab on Cejuru Prime with excellent security.

The door to the bedroom swished open. He turned, and his cock grew even harder than it had been since he'd first scented Bria.

The dimmed spotlights over the bed cast an angelic glow around her tall, curvy body as she stood, framed by the doorway. Her long, dark, curly hair was clasped in a loose ponytail, exposing her graceful neck. She wore one of his workout shirts—and nothing else.

She was beautiful.

She was really here.

Iolyn swallowed hard, past the lump of emotion in his throat.

He moved his gaze down her body until it fixed on her long, bare legs. Her skin glowed from the bath oils Nadia and Mel had placed in his bathroom for Bria's arrival. The scent floated across the space between them. She smelled of exotic jungle flowers from Cejuru Prime and her own unique musk, a sort of vanilla sweetness that made him want to lick her from top to bottom.

Without conscious thought, he closed the distance separating them. He stopped, his body so close to hers he felt the moist heat left over from her bath wafting off her skin. He inhaled and groaned low in his throat. She was aroused. Her earthy scent made his groin ache and his heart beat faster.

She wanted him! Thank the One!

And the One knew he wanted her, but how to go about it? He was a bundle of nerves. Afraid to scare her with his strong urges—his *needs*.

"The usual way?" Bria raised a delicately arched dark brow. She had a slight smile on her lips. "Or, do the Prime do sex differently?"

"No," Iolyn's voice came out low and husky, "the usual way works for us also." He gently grasped her upper arms, pulled her against his body, and then kissed the top of her head. She fit him perfectly. He leaned back and smiled down at her. "With variations...at least on my part."

"Vari-..." Bria coughed. "...variations?"

While she'd been open, accepting, and curious to this point, now he sensed nerves...and some fear. Nerves were okay. Fear wasn't. He'd never hurt her.

Bria must've read the promise in his mind, and she relaxed into his hold with a little sigh.

Iolyn brushed a kiss over her lush pink lips. "I promise you'll like my variations." He went back for another taste of her mouth, sucking on her lower lip. "I'll make sure of it."

"You need to know." Bria's cheeks flushed a dark pink as she lowered her head and concentrated on his chest. "I've only had three sexual partners."

He stiffened, a low rumble escaped his chest before he could stop it. He'd known this was a possibility, but now he knew how many. Would she think of them and compare him to them in her mind? It would kill him if she did.

Bria looked up, her eyes widened with distress. She trembled against him. She shook her head, her ponytail flinging wildly from side to side. "No...no, you don't understand..."

Rein in the jealousy, you fool. You're scaring her.

Bria continued, her words stumbling over one another. He'd missed some of her explanation as he tried to dowse the fires of jealousy raging through his mind and body. But when he heard her next words, he relaxed and regained control of the rampant emotions that had scared Bria.

"...only one time with each." She let out a self-deprecating laugh. "I always thought I was defective or something. Then I found out they weren't the right men...only you...have ever, um, made me wet...or ache...merely from scenting you... hearing you."

She moved closer until he felt her from chest to groin, her taut, gently curved stomach trapped his erection between their bodies. Then she stroked his tightly clenched jaw with one silky soft fingertip. "Don't be angry. I didn't enjoy the act with any of them and often wondered what my women friends were gushing about all the time."

"*Diew*, you're sweet. So innocent...but then again not." Iolyn turned her, placed one arm around her back and the other around her legs, and picked her up. "I'll make sure you enjoy every damn second." He brushed a kiss over her forehead. "Then you can gush to your female friends all you want."

"Goody." She gave him a sweetly brilliant smile and snuggled her head against his shoulder. Her warm breath raised chill bumps over his skin and caused his cock to jerk within the increasingly tight confines of his uniform pants.

Her unfettered response made him feel ten feet tall. So much so, he was fairly sure he could defeat the Antarean Fleet single-handedly.

When Bria licked the column of his throat, he inhaled sharply. His cock jerked again and spurted pre-cum. He wasn't sure he'd be able to last long the first time, so he'd better make sure she came first.

"You taste good. Just like you smell. All male woodsy musk." She nipped the underside of his jaw, and he shuddered. "Spicy."

Diew, if just her tongue and a little bite threatened to take him to his knees, he wasn't sure he'd survive anything more intense. He'd have to remember to apologize to his brothers for teasing them about being pussy-whipped. He was fairly certain he'd be a member of that select male group by the time they reached Oz.

"Iolyn?" Bria whispered, her voice soft, filled with concern and something else...fear, again.

He touched her mind and read her worries. The last two lovers hadn't been kind when she hadn't responded the way they felt she should. His little *gemate*, a beautiful, strong, and intelligent woman, had no sexual confidence. Her insecurity made him want to howl, then go find the *apayebote* and beat them into the ground for hurting his mate's tender feelings.

"Don't worry, *lubha*." Iolyn touched his nose to the side of hers. "There's no way in the universe you won't respond. You're already wet for me." He kissed the tip of her nose. "And if you don't respond, that will be my fault...not yours. It is my duty to make sure you are fulfilled when we make love."

"Is it making love," Bria asked, "or is it merely mating?"

"It's always love between Prime bond mates." Iolyn laid her on the bed. He swept his hands over her gentle curves and groaned. "Once we complete the physical joining, we'll be one...mind, body, and soul."

Iolyn straightened and pulled his shirt over his head. Then he traced his bond mark, which was hot to the touch.

Bria gasped and touched her mark through the shirt she wore.

"See? We're already connected partially in body, the sensory part, but with the actual joining of our bodies, culminating in our mutual ecstasy, we'll then be joined in our souls, our hearts," he stressed the last word, "and nothing and no one will ever come between us. We'll be one. If that's not love, well, no mate-bonded Prime couple has ever said differently."

As he stripped off the rest of his clothing, Bria's pupils dilated until only a thin rim of amber showed. Her nipples poked at the thin fabric of her borrowed shirt. She was definitely aroused and liked what she saw.

Iolyn was thrilled she desired him. Now, he'd see if she could handle a dominant Prime male in her bed.

"Take off the shirt, my *gemate*. Show your *gemat* the mark which makes you mine."

Iolyn's low, husky baritone was filled with a masculine authority she'd normally challenge. But that was in the workplace. In this, their bedroom, she found herself hurrying to comply. She sensed it would give him more pleasure for her to strip for him, than for him to tear the shirt off her body—though that image made her wet and her heart skip a beat.

Who knew she'd be sexually excited by a dominant male? That she'd want to please him?

Bria sat up and slowly inched the overly large shirt up her torso, exposing her naked flesh a centimeter at a time. When she uncovered her dark feminine curls, Iolyn groaned and muttered in a raw, raspy tone, "*Diew*, save me."

His obvious arousal at the sight of her pussy made her smile. While Iolyn might be dictating the path to their joining, she was the one in control of his reactions. It was a heady feeling.

After she was naked, she sat, one hand bracing her on the bed and the other covering her *gemate* mark, and waited for his next command.

His molten amber gaze burned her skin as he looked her up and down. "You're very beautiful, *cwen*." He stared at her lower abdomen and the hand she'd placed there. He frowned. "Lie down, *lubha*. Move your hand. I wish to see your *gemate* mark."

Bria lay back. Before she moved her hand, she traced the heated whorls of color. They began to swirl. She gasped as something akin to electricity seemed to flow between her and Iolyn.

Iolyn must've also felt the supercharged current since he swore under his breath. She sought his *gemat* mark. It had grown darker and swirled at the same beat as her heart, her mark, her core. Then she dragged her gaze away from his mark and moved lower. His cock, already hard and pointing straight upward, twitched as if it had palsy. The purpled crown of his erection glistened with pre-cum.

"Stop. Stroking. Your mark," Iolyn gritted out the words even as he took hold of his cock and squeezed the base until his knuckles showed white. "Our marks are directly linked to each other's sexual response. I'll come if you don't stop."

Bria covered her mark, but no longer stroked it. "Really?"

Iolyn's answer was to touch a finger to his mouth, wet it... then he traced the marking on his chest.

Bria gasped, then squeaked as her hips thrust upward. It was as if her sex sought Iolyn's cock. As he continued to stroke his marking, her inner muscles clenched around an all-too-empty space. Her clit engorged to the point of throbbing pain.

If Iolyn didn't stop teasing his mark...she'd come—for the first time in her life without a vibrator.

"No," she cried out, "please, I want you in me when I climax."

Iolyn stopped caressing his mark and joined Bria on the bed. He moved over her, his thighs between her legs, his cock lying over her mound, and his arms braced on each side of her upper body.

He was so much bigger than her. She should've felt threatened, but instead she felt safe, protected.

"I'll be in you many..." He slid his hot, smooth-skinned cock up and down over her moist slit, stopping just short of insertion on each up stroke. "...many times before we reach Oz. The first few times must be for you. If I entered you now, I'd erupt at the first touch of your silken channel."

Bria couldn't help arching into his body. All she could think of was that she wanted...no...needed his cock inside her to ease the ache which threatened to drive her insane.

But her man wasn't budging off the ladies' first notion.

Stubborn, alpha-male, thinking he knows what I need.

What she needed was his cock inside her, filling her achy sex.

Holding back was costing Iolyn, though. His neck muscles were taut, his breathing labored. His heart pounded like a marathon runner's. His emotional aura was flaming hot with desire.

Iolyn's magnificent body shuddered above her and glistened with sweat—as he held back the primitive urges to take her like a rutting bull. And his every thought was about completing the final stage of the bond—the Prime imperative—but only after making sure she was satisfied first.

Bria buried her face against his muscled shoulder, then tempted the beast within her man. She licked and nipped along his shoulder. She moaned. He tasted—yummy. Decadently yummy.

Iolyn groaned. "What are you trying to do to me, *cwen*?"

Cwen meant my woman. Bria had managed to talk just long enough with Nadia on the shuttle from the jump station to the *Galanti* to ask her what the word meant. She liked being his woman, and no other's. It was what she'd wanted as far back as she could remember—to belong to someone and have them belong to her.

"I'm trying to get us both some satisfaction, *gemat*." She traced a pulsing muscle along Iolyn's jaw with her tongue. "You're so tense. I feel your need—and, sweetheart, it feeds mine."

He groaned. "*Lubha*, I'd hurt you if I took you now. I need to prepare you." He took her lips in a deep, carnal kiss. One hand braced his body over her, and the other massaged one of her breasts, his thumb brushing over her nipple until it puckered to the point of pain. Pleasurable pain.

The kiss was unlike any Bria had ever received—and she only had slightly more experience with kissing than with intercourse. Previously, kissing had been, at a minimum, uncomfortable and, at the worst, nauseating.

But Iolyn's kiss was delicious and exciting. His deep tongue thrusts had her wanting his cock in her—hard and deep and rough. And now.

Gripping Iolyn's shaggy-to-the-collar dark hair, and after a temporary moment of distraction over his hair's thick, raw silk texture, she tugged. She'd have enough time later to play, stroke, and pet his hair after the edge of their mutual need had been taken down a notch or two—or three.

When Iolyn didn't take the hint and halt the kiss—which had gone from hot to fissionable and made her break out in a full-body, moist glow—she moaned and pulled on his plentiful locks harder.

Iolyn broke away from the kiss on a low groan. "*Lubha*, was I too rough? Did I scare you?" As he spoke, he peppered sweet kisses over her nose, cheeks, and on a sensitive spot behind her ear. As he did so, he cupped and stroked first one breast, then the other, threatening to drive her crazy with desire.

Scared? *Pfft*. She wasn't scared, she was—what was the Twenty-First Century Earth word?—oh, yeah, horny. She was as horny as hell and needed satisfaction. Now.

"Read me." She slid her hands from his hair to cup his face and then turned it so she could look into his fiery golden eyes. Then she enunciated, slowly, "Read. Me. See—what I need."

Bria dropped the mental shields she'd grown so used to having in place and let him into her mind as deeply as their telepathic connection would allow.

His face lit up as his mind lovingly stroked hers. The sensation was amazing. His mind-touch felt like gossamer threads trailing through her consciousness. She could actually feel his emotions and reactions as he examined and cherished each thought he came across. Felt his excitement as he took in each of her sexual fantasies. She, in turn, read his sexual cravings, of how he wanted to cherish and make love to her.

Now, what she lusted for was Iolyn to take her as wild and hard as he needed. He could be gentle and creative later when both of them were exhausted and sore from the early marathon of *gemat-gemate* bonding sex. Even after the early mating heat was done, Lia had told her bonded mates still craved each other as often as two to three times a day for up to ten standard years. They'd have many opportunities over the coming years to go gentle and slow.

"You're amazing," Iolyn breathed the words with adoration and awe, "but—"

Bria leaned up and covered his lips with hers, swallowing the protest she found in his mind. After several seconds, she pulled away and whispered, "You're worrying too much. Take me. Now."

She followed her words by placing a hand on his tight ass and pulling him against her lower body, forcing his cock to breach her opening. They both inhaled at the sensation of his cockhead stretching her widely.

"*Diew.*" Iolyn closed his eyes as if praying. His body trembled above hers. "So tight. So good."

"Give me more."

Iolyn's eyes flared open. They glowed like a million stars. "Then that's what you'll get." Bracing himself on one arm, he slid his other hand under her bottom, cupped it, and pushed into her with one unrestrained thrust.

Bria grunted. His cock was big and thick and filled her to the point of...pain...then pleasure. Her neck arched. She closed her eyes as she teetered on the verge of a conflagration she might not survive. But she sure wanted to try.

But to get there, Iolyn needed to move his so-fine ass.

"Iolyn," she begged, "please...fuck me."

Her devious lover laughed. "No, you little menace, I control the pacing. Always. Now, be still. You need to adjust to my length and girth before I start pounding away on your sweet body."

"Move it, Caradoc, or—"

"Or what, little *cwen*? You'll make me?" Iolyn chuckled.

Iolyn rotated his hips, grinding against her mons. The pressure on her clit was almost enough to tip her over, but not quite. She mewled her need. "Iolyn-n-n."

He leaned over and licked and nipped a path from her jaw to her ear where he gently bit the lobe then suckled the slight sting. "Not going anywhere."

Bria gasped as heat lightning swept down her spine and targeted her clit. She clenched around his dick.

Iolyn threw back his head and groaned low in his throat. "Taking. My. Time."

His jaw tight, he pulled out slowly and then thrust into her sheath in one quick move. A mini-spasm resulted, and she moaned as pleasure suffused her lower body. It was divine, but not nearly enough.

"Pacing, smacing." Bria lifted her head and placed biting kisses along his jawline across his chin and upward to suck his lower lip between her teeth. She released his lip then laved the redness.

His lusty groan made all her female parts happy. She affected him as much as he did her.

"Make me come..." *my arrogant* gemat, "because..."*mate,*"...I'm about to go out of my ever..." She bit his chin. "...loving..." She teethed his neck. "...mind." She bit his shoulder.

The bite on the shoulder did it.

Iolyn roared. His cock still planted fully in her tight channel, he surged upward, onto his knees. With one hand holding her bottom off the bed, he pulled up one of her legs and braced it on his shoulder. Then he positioned his hands, so one each cupped her ass cheeks and held her in place. Her lower body was going nowhere he didn't want it to go.

"Put your other leg on the opposite shoulder, Bria. Now," he gritted out between clenched teeth as she flexed her vaginal muscles around his cock, testing his control.

When she didn't move fast enough to suit him, he braced her sweet ass with one hand and dragged the other leg onto his shoulder. "Like that, my little menace." Then he rotated his hips, grinding his pubic bone against her clit.

Bria screamed and tried to move away from him.

Too late, peata. *You asked for it...you got it.*

Iolyn continued to rotate and grind, but he didn't thrust. He smiled at the picture she made as she clutched at the bedcovers and tossed her head from side to side as she tried to reach for her pleasure. Her body was under his control, and it would be *his pleasure* to give her what she so desperately needed.

When he pulled his cock out until just the head breached her opening, she moaned, "No-o-o," and reached to hold him to her.

"Put your hands back on the bed, *lubha*."

When she did, he thrust back into her fully. She grunted, and her breasts shook from the momentum. He continued to pull back and then thrust. In. Out. In. Out. In a slow, steady pace that held them both on the edge of a high precipice.

Iolyn turned his head and licked one ankle and then took a small nip of her satin-smooth calf.

Bria shrieked, "Iolyn—" and his cock twitched inside her at the sound.

Her every breath brought a moan or a cute little grunt as he slowly built her pleasure to the tipping point. Her breasts swayed sensuously with the rhythm of his thrusts. In. Out. In. Out.

As sweat poured down his spine and his balls tightened to the point of excruciating pain, he knew he had to bring her off soon or end up losing control over his own orgasm. He moved one hand from holding her ass to rub his thumb through her musky juices then spread them over her engorged clit. Two swipes of his thumb, and Bria screamed her climax. Her pleasure swamped his senses, his mind, saturated his every pore, and fed his need to come.

Holding onto her ass with both hands once more, Iolyn let his fierce control loose and began pounding into her sex so hard and fast that Bria's upper torso moved up and down on the bed. Her breasts bounced wildly now. The only sounds coming out of her were unintelligible grunts and gasps. He touched her mind and found a dreamscape of an infinite universe with billions of exploding stars.

As her body clenched and pulsed around his cock and her sexy little noises made him crazier with lust, he continued to soar until his pleasure-pain reached an apex and then he fell, roaring his orgasm against her neck. His cock fully lodged inside her hot, velvet channel, he held still as he released jet after jet of cum.

Locked together physically, he shared her pleasure and she, his. His mind merged with hers and took flight, leaving the real plane of existence.

Bria's feminine essence twined and curled and tempted his masculine one until his spirit essence took hers into his. Their souls were now one, never to be separated in life or death.

The *gemat-gemate* bond was complete.

As he fell back into his body, he and Bria experienced another powerful joint orgasm, then another, and then another until neither of them could climax any longer.

Iolyn wasn't sure how he managed it, but he pulled his spent cock from an unconscious Bria. He arranged her limp body on the bed. He ran gentle fingers over her sensuous curves with a sense of wonder and again thanked the One for gifting him this special woman. Then, more exhausted than he could ever remember being, he crawled into bed alongside her and pulled the covers over their damp, cooling bodies. He turned onto his side, pulled her sweet bottom against his cock, then placed an arm over her waist and his leg over her legs. He wanted...no, needed her close.

Finally, he planted his face into her sweet-smelling hair and let the welcoming darkness take him.

He was home now...and it felt wonderful.

CHAPTER 13

Bria woke slowly. Stretching, she discovered aches and twinges of pain in muscles and places on her body she was damn sure she'd never used before. She also found she was trapped on her side by a muscled arm around her waist. Her naked body was plastered against her very naked, extremely aroused *gemat*.

She had a full body spasm as Iolyn's long, thick erection slid between the cheeks of her ass, the cockhead nudging at her puckered small opening. She held her breath, then sighed with relief when the tip settled against her lower back.

Some day, lubha. *But not today.*

Her relieved sigh elicited a chuckle and a kiss on her naked shoulder. "How are you feeling?" Iolyn's voice was husky, loving. He massaged her stomach and then worked his hand lower.

How was she feeling?

She looked over her shoulder and found her mate's heavy-lidded gaze on her. He idly caressed her puffy labia with a thick, talented finger, smoothing her sexual fluids over her clit. She inhaled sharply then exhaled on a long, low moan as her inner muscles clenched at her all-too-empty channel.

"You want me again?" she asked, the words coming out on gasping breaths.

"Yes, again. Then again. And then again." He traced her ear with his tongue. "Forget Oz. We may not make it out of our rooms until we reach Cejuru Prime." He nuzzled her cheek. "Now answer my question."

What was the question? She couldn't think. She was distracted by his emotions sweeping over her like a warm, sultry breeze, by his touches exciting little-used nerve endings—by his mental list of what he wanted sexually. It was a very long and decidedly kinky list.

Oh, yeah, the question...how did she feel?

"Needy. Aroused." She angled her head to nip his chin. His low sexy groan made her tingly and happy. She could do that to him with just a small touch. Amazing. "Hungry...for you."

Bria sent him an image of her sucking his cock and him holding her head steady, guiding her movements. An image she'd plucked straight from his head.

Her cheeks flushed, and she lowered her eyes. Her feelings were a mixture of shyness, embarrassment, and excitement. Would he think she was too forward? She'd never been tempted to perform oral sex on a man, but she'd seen how much it would please him, and she wanted to give her mate that.

"Brave, *peata*."

Little pet.

Iolyn moved his hand from her mound and stroked her hip in a soothing motion, allowing her arousal to cool a bit. "I'd love for you to suckle me, but first, I think I'll feed you." He petted her stomach which took that moment to rumble loudly. "Can't have you fainting from hunger."

"I never faint."

"Never?"

She wiggled within his hold, and he loosened his arm enough so she could look him in the eye. "Never," she asserted. "I'm not weak. Just untrained."

As a lover and a fighter. But she was more than eager to learn lessons in both arenas.

Iolyn brushed a kiss over the tip of her nose. "I don't see you as weak, *cwen*. But you don't need training as a fighter. You're a doctor. A researcher. You'll have security to protect you at work and me to protect you at home and when we're out." He grinned and moved his hand to cover her mound once more. "As for sex? I'll teach you everything you need to know."

"I'm sure you will," Bria said, "but I still want warrior training. I want some offensive skills—just in case."

As Iolyn massaged her labia and clit, driving her slowly insane with an increasing need, he frowned and shook his head. "We'll see."

Which meant "no."

Bria's arousal cooled, and she regained control over her body long enough to shove thoughts of what kind of training she wanted and when and how she'd get it into a corner of her mind. Then she built sturdy, thick walls around her plans.

She refused to argue with her *gemat* in bed. There were always ways to get around a stubborn, know-it-all, over-protective male without using sex.

And—she refused to be the weakest link in the bunch.

"Bria?" Iolyn turned her to face him, then rubbed his hands up and down her back. "What's wrong? You seem... distracted."

"Just thinking." She rubbed her cheek over his chest. Time to do some distracting of her own. She placed a tiny, nibbling kiss on his *gemat* mark. It glowed and swirled with colors of red and yellow.

Oh my! She trembled as her mark responded. The connection between them was very strong. Stronger than the first time Iolyn had demonstrated the link between the marks. She bet her mark was also glowing and moving. They were in the early, simmering stages of arousal and a mere wisp of breath or touch on the bond marks seemed to accelerate the race to climax.

Then her stomach growled again, and she realized she was actually low on fuel.

Iolyn chuckled and smoothed his hand over her ass then around to her tummy.

"Food does sound good." She covered his hand with hers, just wanting the connection. "What do we have to eat? Or, do we need to get dressed and eat somewhere on the ship? I've never been on a starship this size before."

"We'll eat here. I want to feed you by my hand...while you're naked." Iolyn lifted her chin and stared into her eyes. She felt him touching her mind, seeking her thoughts. He found only what she wanted him to see—her need for food and him.

Iolyn growled when he bumped up against her solid mental shield. Then shook his head and shot her a smile which held the promise of fulfilling all her hungers. "Little menace, keep your secrets for now. I'll uncover them eventually."

Not if she could help it. She believed in *fait d'accompli*.

Bria relaxed into his hold and kissed the underside of his chin. It was a relief to know that even a completed bond with her warrior-*gemat* couldn't compromise her ability to shield her private thoughts and plans. After all, a girl always had some secrets to keep from her man. She was lucky she'd learned to compartmentalize her thoughts while growing up. There'd been more than Terrans working on the Gliese 581C Alliance farming communes. Plus, the native Gliesians, a pseudo-amphibious species, were known for their psi powers, as were several other species which worked the farms.

Iolyn cupped her bottom and pulled her mound against his cock. "I don't know how you battle-mates do it."

"Do what?" Affecting ignorance, she traced his *gemat* marking with the tip of her index finger. His sharp inhalation had her smiling.

"Don't act as if you don't know what I'm talking about." He nipped her lower lip. "I sense your emotions easily, because of our *gemat-gemate* link. But with us being battle-mates, I should have access to all your thoughts...at all times." He gently tapped the tip of her nose. "But you, like Mel and Nadia, can hide your thoughts. You three are unique."

Bria took his finger, nipped the end of it, and then sucked it into her mouth. Iolyn's eyes darkened to the color of burnt honey. She let his finger slide out, nibbling on the tip once more. "Maybe, Mel, Nadia, and I, because of our personal history, have different strengths than Prime battle-mates of the past."

Something to think about later and do some research on with her team. Now was a time for fun and bonding with her man, not a time to think about work.

"Maybe." Iolyn's breath hitched as she moved to suck on the spot where his neck curved into his shoulder. "*Peata*, if you keep teasing me, you won't be eating *food* anytime soon."

Which implied she could be eating him.

After one long lick from his neck to the top of his shoulder, Bria leaned back, smiled into his fiery eyes, and said, "Goody."

Iolyn's blood heated. While he knew she'd hidden something from him, it had nothing to do with here and now or with the sexual intimacy which grew between them in giant leaps and bounds.

Unlike their first sexual encounter—one which even he admitted had been fraught with his own chaotic emotions—whatever nerves or fears Bria had were now gone, burned away in the heat of their initial joining, in the rightness of their completed bond.

The discovery that his little battle-mate was willing to play games in the bedroom elated him. She was his perfect match.

With her last response—and the fervid emotions and desires her body and mind gave off—his *peata* had sealed her fate. Food and drink would have to wait until his—and her—current sexual appetites abated. Total sexual satiation might not occur for years from his observations of other *gemat-gemate* bond couples.

"I'd like an appetizer before our meal." Iolyn gently pushed Bria onto her back. He then pulled two lengths of silk from behind the headboard; a little addition he'd added after Mel and Nadia had helped him with his redecorating. "Hold onto these. Don't let go. Don't move." He placed a kiss on her rounded mouth as she exhaled an "oh." "You *will* take everything I give you. You'll give me everything I demand. Understood?"

Bria frowned. Her nose scrunched as if she were working on an intricate puzzle. He lightly touched her thoughts which—*thank the One*—were wide open to him. She was excited, but wasn't sure she should be.

He chuckled. "What we do in the bedroom is for us alone. There's nothing wrong with indulging in pleasure."

"O-o-kay," she bit her lip, "but don't you want to tie my wrists? I mean, that's what I've read in some romance novels."

"We can do that." Iolyn brushed some locks of hair off her face and tucked them behind her ear. "But this time, I thought we'd start slowly. By holding onto the silken ties, you are submitting to me, to my will. You won't let go or move, because you want to please me...and want me to please you in return."

The look on her face, a mixture of excitement, trepidation, and curiosity, was so adorable Iolyn couldn't help himself. He leaned down, gently forced her hands to the mattress above her head, and then took her mouth hard and fast until he had her moaning and writhing beneath him.

Breaking off, he left her gasping for breath. His cock had hardened to titanium steel and every casual brush against her body was a painful pleasure he'd willingly endure for the rest of his life.

"Later...once you trust me completely, and I have a better idea of what you like and don't like...I'll bind you and then push your limits."

He took each hand and placed a silken tie into it, then wrapped her fingers around the fabric. As he did so, he sent her images of what he planned to do to her for the next standard hour or so. Of how he'd take claim of every single millimeter of her body. Of how he'd teach her the fine balance between pleasure and pain before he allowed her to come again and again. He planned to make her beg for his cock.

Most people perceived him as the "quiet" Caradoc, the "calm" Caradoc—the "nice" Caradoc. He was all those things, but more. He had an edgy side. Only one person in the galaxy knew of his sexual predilections—Susa—and she'd never tell a soul. Bria would be the second and final person to know his dominant sexual needs.

He kissed her fingers where she held onto the silken ties. "Don't let go, *peata*. You let go. Everything stops, and we eat dinner."

Bria's beautiful eyes glowed like the finest citrines. Her pupils were dilated. She sucked on her lower lip until it was rosy red. Her generously rounded breasts heaved with her rapid breathing. She was in his mind now. He could hide nothing from her, including his past with Susa. She could read his every salacious thought, and she was aroused...and maybe a little bit scared. She wasn't going to let go. She wanted this...wanted what he'd give her, what he'd take.

Good.

But he needed her to agree out loud. Voiced words made it real. She could think she was okay with his sexual predilections, but until she voiced her accord, it was all fantasy.

"Are you afraid of my sexual needs, Bria *lubha*?"

"Yes. No. Maybe...Um, I'm happy to let you lead—in the bedchamber. I trust you to never hurt me, because you can read me and I can read you. So you can bind me now if you want." Without letting go of the ties, she leaned up, sank her teeth into his lower lip, suckled it, then let it go with a sucking *pop*. "But no more Susa. Got it?"

He touched her mind. The evidence of her intense jealousy gave him a spurt of pleasure. She was just as possessive of him as he was of her. Good, that was the way it was supposed to be between bonded mates. He was also shocked at some of the things she'd read in books. Part of her jealousy was based on her sexual inexperience and that she wouldn't be able to meet his needs as Susa had. The rest was based on the fear she'd give him everything, and he'd practice polyamory.

The first fear would fade the more they made love. She'd soon learn that no other woman would ever satisfy him as she could. The latter fear could be taken care of now.

Iolyn gently lowered her head to the bed then cradled her face between his hands. Touching his forehead to hers, he explained why her fears were unfounded. "Susa was the chosen Caradoc family sex surrogate for males with no completed *gemat-gemate* bond. She taught me all I know about making love. Later, I discovered my kinkier needs, and she accommodated them."

Bria's eyes glistened with unshed tears.

"Shh, shh. Don't cry. She's nothing to me now other than a cherished—platonic—family friend." He wiped a tear that slid down Bria's cheeks with his thumb. "Sooner or later, you will meet her. It is unavoidable, because sex surrogates are part of the Prime culture and have been since the *gemat-gemate* bonding first arose. But Susa will never speak of what went on between her and me—and I'll *never* visit her again.

A bonded male has no need, no desire for anyone other than his *gemate*."

Bria sniffed. "I understand, but I can't promise that it won't be awkward the first time I meet her."

He brushed several kisses over her cheeks, forehead, and finally her mouth. She did understand. It was there in her mind. He let out a sigh of relief.

"I understand how you feel," Iolyn whispered. "If I ever met any of the men you had sex with, I would be hard-pressed to be civil." He'd probably beat the shit out of them.

Bria snickered, then laughed. "Big bad Prime male." She turned her head to kiss the palm of one of his hands, then flicked it with her tongue. "So—are you going to get your appetizer? I have a hunger for some Grade A Prime meat once you've finished with your starter on this evening's menu."

Iolyn snorted and pulled her to him. "Ahh, *peata*. You read my plans for you. But nowhere on the menu is my cock. You are every course this evening on the sexual menu. We'll save the education in how to suck a Prime male's erection for later."

"But..."

Iolyn cut off her protest with a hard deep thrust of his tongue. He covered her fisted hands with his own and kneed her thighs apart. She gripped the scarves tighter in response. As he slid his cock over her wet slit, he started to kiss and nibble every millimeter of her skin beginning with her face and lips and downward. He planned on taking his time. He would learn how each part of her tasted and where her hot spots were, then he'd revisit his favorites.

And all the while he'd monitor her mind...because he planned to keep her on edge of her climax for a long, long time. She'd only gain her ultimate pleasure when she begged for his cock—or when he couldn't hold back his need to come any longer.

It was a toss-up on who would give in first.

Bria held onto the silken, now damp with her sweat, ties until her fingers hurt. Her body shook from the need to come.

Iolyn was a beast. He wanted her to beg for his cock, beg him to let her come. But she was too stubborn to give in. He'd come first, or she'd die first—which she just might. She'd tried everything to make him take her. She'd arched her hips against his thick and hard cock, rubbing her mound over his throbbing member. He merely moved out of the way and continued to tease her skin and erogenous zones with his teeth, tongue, and lips.

When he'd let go of her hands to stimulate her nipples and clit, she let go of the ties and tried to pull him into her body. And as he'd promised, everything stopped. He sat back on his heels and glowered at her until she took hold of the ties again.

Alpha-male throwback.

But I'm your alpha-male throwback.

Yes, he was. She sighed.

"Little menace," Iolyn husked, his low tones almost vibrating her bones, "just a few words and I'll take you over the top and give you more pleasure than our first joining."

And that would be saying a lot. Because their first joining had rocked her with the power of several stars going supernova. She wasn't sure she could even handle that kind of pleasure again without dying.

"But what a way to go, *peata*." Iolyn lifted her hips with both hands and began, for the umpteenth time, to nibble, lick, and suck on her labia and clit.

He took her up fast and rough. She was so sensitized now, it didn't take much. As she mewled in half pain, half ecstasy, her hellacious, sweet torturer inserted a finger into her anus. And that was all she wrote.

"Iolyn. *Gemat*. Please...please..." She shuddered and strained for her peak. She wanted to fall over it and into a never-ending spiral so badly, that begging didn't seem so bad.

"Please what, *lubha*? Ask for it." He finger-fucked her ass as he took her clit and sucked...hard. Then stopped.

"Fuck me." She pulled on the silken ties, twisting them with her sore fingers.

"Thank the One," growled Iolyn. "Hold on. This will be rough."

Her tormentor pulled her toward the bottom of the bed, stretching her arms above her to their full length. He placed her legs on his shoulders, notched his pulsing cock at her opening and plunged inside, to the balls, in one hard thrust. Then stopped.

"Sweet, sweet *diew*." Iolyn grunted and panted as if he'd run a gamut of armed warriors.

"Iolyn...move." Bria panted and wiggled. "Please, please, please..."

I'm dying here.

"Yes-s-s." Iolyn growled and began slowly, but soon was pounding into Bria's body so hard and so fast she couldn't get enough breath to make intelligible sounds. All she could do was gasp, grunt, mewl, and feel the pressure mount to the point of no return.

When she reached the top, Iolyn fed her his own feelings of tortured pleasure, which to this point he'd dampened somehow, and snarled, "Come now."

And she did. And he did. And the incendiary result had her screaming soundlessly as she fell into an infinite pool of pleasure that wracked every pore in her body. And just when she thought she might hit bottom, Iolyn stimulated her clit, stuck a finger into her rear opening, and roared, "Again."

And she came again, taking him with her.

She lost count of how many times her loving tormentor made her scale the heights and fall into infinity. More than three times? Four? Who knew? She didn't.

The only thing she could swear to was Iolyn was with her every step of the way, holding her, protecting her, loving her. And she looked forward to another round—after a nap and some food.

CHAPTER 14

A little over two standard days had passed since the *Galanti* left Jump Station Charybdis and picked up Cheri and the rest of Bria's team from Oz. V'niko and A'nan had fulfilled their promise and kept her people safe. The starship was now en route to the Prime home planet.

While Iolyn hadn't let her out of their quarters on the much quicker journey from Jump Station Charybdis to Oz, Bria had argued for more "personal" time on the longer trip to the Cejuru system. Iolyn had reluctantly acquiesced, but only because he agreed she needed a break from the frequent and intense sexual interludes. He also was under the misapprehension that she was using the alone-time to work in the lab with her team and getting some girl-bonding time with the other *gemates* and Cheri.

If he found out she was using part of the free time to learn more offensive and defensive warrior skills, he would've tied her to their bed.

"Bria, keep your guard up!" Mel's voice echoed off the high ceiling of the *Galanti*'s gym as she stood at the side of the thick workout mat.

Bria was attempting to learn a multiple martial arts street-fighting technique perfected by the Alliance Military called *fot-hander-cyllan* or FHC. The Standard translation was foot-hand-kill. The name was totally fitting, because she'd used her hands and feet, and it was killing her.

As Bria's legs were swept out from under her by Nadia—for what seemed to be the hundredth time—Lia and Cheri, who'd decided she also needed more fighting skills, groaned from their positions on the edge of the mat.

Bria shot them an angry look. "Why are you groaning? I'm the one who got put on her ass."

Nadia bent over and offered Bria a hand. "What is it about keeping your guard up you don't understand?"

Bria ignored the hand, rolled over onto her stomach, and lay there in a sweaty, panting mess of sore muscles and bruises. She also concentrated on reinforcing her mental shields since Iolyn could easily sense her exhaustion and pain and, yes, even after days and days of frequent and energetic sex, her horniness.

"Go away, Nadia. Iolyn's getting suspicious. He's pounding on my shields. And I don't know how I'm going to explain the bruises."

"Lie like a used shuttle salesman." Cheri came over and knelt on the mat by her side. "Or rethink all this." She waved a hand around the capacious starship gym with its weight machines, free weights, and sim-rooms for training in simulated, but realistic, battle situations. "If he doesn't want you to be a warrior battle-mate, maybe you should just listen to him and do what you're good at."

Lia had also come to kneel next to Bria, but turned to Cheri and glared. "And that would be what, exactly?"

"Research. She's a damn doctor, not a fighter."

"I'm a damn doctor, and I train and fight by my *gemat*'s side," Lia retorted.

Nadia sat on the mat cross-legged and began to knead Bria's shoulders. How did the woman know where to rub? "That's so good. Thanks, Nadia."

"You're welcome." Nadia continued to massage kinks out of Bria's neck and upper back. "I'm a science officer. I do research. I fight."

"But..." Cheri sputtered. "Iolyn doesn't want her to. Shouldn't she listen to him?"

Mel stood over them all. "My brother-kin is wrong, Cheri. Trust me on this. Bria needs to know how to protect herself and fight by Iolyn's side. While her eye-to-hand coordination on weapons is beyond excellent, she needs the physical training."

"Why, for chrissakes?" Cheri asked.

"Because bad things are already happening on Cejuru Prime, and Bria's research will escalate the rebels' attacks." Mel paused and listened to something no one else could hear. "Wulf can't hold Iolyn back any longer. Yoga positions, ladies. If he asks, we're doing Ashtanga yoga, a particularly strenuous form, and Bria's unfamiliarity caused her to lose balance, thus the bruises."

"And before you go back to your quarters, Bria," Lia whispered. "Come by Sick Bay and I'll treat the bruises with the cold laser. They'll be gone by the time I'm done."

"Bless you, Lia." Bria groaned as she put her sore body into downward dog. "Can I have an energy booster, too? All the sex is tiring me out."

"Wish I had that problem," grumbled Cheri as she scrambled into the transition move essential to most forms of yoga.

Nadia, in position on Bria's other side, shot her a commiserating smile. "Hasn't he done a *gemat* sexual healing on you, yet?"

Cheri looked sideways at Bria. "What's that?"

Bria knew her cheeks were red. "Um, well..."

Mel snorted and answered before Bria could figure out how to answer the question without revealing too many intimate details. "It's the Prime male version of healing with the hair of the dog that bit you."

Cheri's brow creased. "What?"

Bria looked past Nadia and glared at Mel, who winked back. So much for keeping intimate things private.

"That's an old Terran saying. It means..." Bria sighed. "... um, okay, all the mating sex is rough on my more, um, delicate sexual membranes."

Sheesh, she was a damn doctor. Why was this so difficult to explain?

Maybe because I'm not used to discussing my sex life with others?

Hell, she hadn't had a real sex life before meeting Iolyn.

Lia took pity on her and said, "Cheri, her clitoris is sore. Her vaginal membranes are sore. Maybe even her anal membranes are sore."

No maybe about it. Iolyn had placed a small anal plug in her during their morning sex and then healed her sore bottom. He planned to plug her at least once every other day, with increasingly larger plugs, until she could take his cock.

When Nadia hissed, "Lia..."

Lia glared at the blonde and said, "Well, they could be." Then she continued, "All of her sexual tissues are hypersensitive. Intercourse starts to hurt. Couples in the early stages of the *gemat-gemate* mating have sex often... and sometimes it can be rough. The woman has little to no recovery time between intimacy, and so Prime males use the energy connection they have with their mates and a healing agent in their saliva to heal the pain they caused. It's most assuredly an offshoot of a primordial adaptation for survival since frequent sex leads to higher rates of pregnancy. Being battle-mates, our men can also heal more deeply than most *gemats.*"

Cheri gaped at Bria. "You mean, Iolyn heals the results of too much intercourse with oral sex?"

Bria moaned and looked away from her friend's far-too-intrigued expression.

"Yep." Lia laughed. "By the way, it's really good oral sex since it has a full-body energy aspect to it. It feels like an internal warm blanket and a soothing bath in healing salts at the same time as well as providing gentle, continual orgasms that ebb and flow like ocean tides. Very relaxing." She sighed. "I really love it when Joen does it. He takes hours and hours to heal me. It's almost as fun as the sex that led to the need for healing."

Cheri moaned. "Oh, lordy. I think I had a full-body orgasm just hearing about it. I'm really happy we found a decent amount of Prime DNA in my genetics. Do you gals know of any single Prime guys looking for a short, curvy blonde of Terran Scottish lineage with a submissive bent?"

Bria muttered, "I'm sure you'll be very popular once we get to Cejuru Prime."

Her friend had a bouncy, outgoing personality and had always had an active dating life. Cheri's Prime DNA was smaller in amount than Nadia's and Lia's, but more than some of the other Terrans' DNA they'd sampled for the research project after Nadia had marked with Huw.

Cheri might or might not mark.

They had no defined parameters of how much Prime DNA a Terran female needed in order to truly bond. But a bond mark wasn't necessary to procreate. As Borac had proven with Cissy.

Every time Bria thought about the Elder Council holding onto the "must mark to mate" philosophy, her blood boiled. Stupid paternalistic men had sabotaged their own population growth.

"Cheri, Prime males won't have casual sex with anyone other than a sex surrogate." Bria felt her friend needed to be aware of that point.

"I know that, bossy lady." Cheri lifted one hand, and while maintaining a perfect one-handed balance—*show off*—pinched Bria on the arm. "I promise to behave. Besides, I'm ready to settle down. I want a man who'll love only me and give me lots and lots of babies."

"Prime males are good at monogamy, Cheri." Iolyn's low baritone sent shivers along Bria's spine which then affected her sex as little electrical shocks. "We take good care of our mates. Don't we, *peata*?" Iolyn stroked a finger down the middle of her back. "You look wiped. Time to take a nap."

Mel snickered as Bria fell to the mat in a boneless heap. "He calls you *little pet*?"

Bria glared at Iolyn who gathered her into his arms and kissed her sweaty forehead. "I can't believe you said that in front of my friends."

"*Lubha*." Iolyn placed a biting kiss on her lips. "Why are you embarrassed that I think you're as cute and sweet as a little domesticated feline?"

Because...it's private. Do you want me to show you my claws?

Iolyn chuckled. "Say good-bye to the ladies, Bria." He nuzzled her neck and took a lick. "You taste salty and sweet. We're leaving."

"Iolyn!" Bria sank her nails into his shoulder. "We weren't done."

"And now you're done." He whispered loudly enough for the others to hear. "I have another sort of exercise in mind."

Cheri sighed. "I'm so jealous right now I could just spit."

Iolyn smiled at her petite friend. "You might want to meet one of my computer techs. His name is Zaek Magga. He is extremely attracted to you." Iolyn winked. "Extremely."

Bria's lips twitched with amusement at her *gemat's* blatant match-making. "Is that the tech who helped us set up the ancillary lab off the Sick Bay?"

"That's the one." Iolyn chuckled. "Cheri, he's working on interfacing your databases with the ship's medical data bases right now. I'm sure he'd love some company."

Cheri's eyes brightened. "Oh, yum. He was a hunk. I need to get cleaned up and get back to the lab." She sprang to her feet and ran out of the gym.

Bria registered her friend's overweening excitement and then started to worry. "Iolyn—" she whispered, but was cut off by her man's hungry tongue-thrusting kiss which didn't last nearly long enough.

"No worries. I wouldn't have mentioned Zaek if I wasn't sure he was serious." He looked her and then Lia in the eyes. "He's a good man. He's never marked. He was curious about Huw and Nadia's reverse marking. He has some of the same symptoms Huw had. He is open to the mating. He really, *really* likes Cheri. Said she smelled right."

"That was fast. Almost as fast as Joen and me." Lia rose gracefully from the mat. "I'd better get to the lab and start the sampling on those two. Cheri was only exposed to him once she got on ship and for less than an hour."

"I'll come—" Bria really wanted Lia to treat the bruising from the training before Iolyn questioned how yoga could produce such injuries. Plus, she wanted to check this Zaek out again.

Iolyn covered her lips with his fingers. "Lia can handle Cheri and Zaek. You can go to the lab tomorrow. Later, we'll have dinner with my brothers and their mates." He turned to Lia and smiled. "Joen will pick you up for dinner, because you're both invited."

Lia grinned. "Looking forward to it." She looked at Bria. "You'll find a copy of everything on your database after Cheri's new love finishes syncing the systems."

"Thanks, Lia." Bria waved over Iolyn's shoulder as he carried her from the gym, held securely against his chest. "See you all later."

Mel, Nadia, and Lia waved back, identical, knowing smiles on their faces. Lia mouthed "enjoy the sexual healing" and then started laughing like a loon.

"Did you have a nice chat with my sister-kin?"

Bria punched him on the shoulder. "How much did you overhear?"

"I came in when you were explaining to a very interested Cheri about how a Prime male heals his woman." Iolyn shook his head. "I think Zaek is going to have a hellion on his hands."

Bria had to smile. "Yes, she can be a handful. She's also smart and loyal and funny and very, very into dominant alpha-males. I just hope she can stick with one. She's used to a variety."

"She'll be fine." Iolyn rubbed her back where he held her. "You might not have noticed, but when she said she was ready to settle down, she sincerely meant it. And Zaek is like all Prime males—he'll keep her so busy in bed she won't have the time or energy to do anything else but her work and have sex with her mate. And Zaek is interested in working on your databases. I wouldn't be surprised if he didn't ask to be assigned to your research lab."

"That would make it convenient." Bria started to giggle. "I can just see her asking for a sex break."

"I'll be asking for a lot of those too." Iolyn smiled and cuddled her even closer.

———

IOLYN PLACED HIS HAND ON Bria's lower back to guide her to the large booth he'd reserved in the Officer's Lounge for the dinner with his brothers, Joen, and their *gemates*. After two hours of healing Bria, followed by an hour-long power nap, he was energized and ready for more active sex games. Yet, he sensed Bria was still a bit overwhelmed by the frequency of their sexual encounters.

Yes, Bria had a high level of arousal—it vibrated red hot in her aura and the eventual pleasure was uppermost in her mind—but her more puritanical Terran upbringing told her too much indulgence was wrong.

She needed to get past that cultural roadblock in her thinking. Mel, a Prime also raised by Terrans, and Nadia and Lia, Terrans, had all managed to eliminate the prudish mind set fairly quickly.

Iolyn hoped a nice relaxing meal with couples all sharing the same bonding issues would help Bria relax and be more comfortable with the sea change in her sex life. He had no intentions of holding back. He needed her. She needed him. He wouldn't deny that fundamental reality, not even to allay her modesty. Now that he'd had her in his arms, had tasted and touched every satiny inch of her gorgeous body, and had claimed her every way but anally—and that would appear soon on the sexual menu—he couldn't bear to be away from her. He now had much more respect for how the other couples—well, not Huw who'd been an asshole—had handled their bonding in the early weeks.

From his observations, eventually he and Bria would settle into a pattern of having sex three-to-four times a day. Any more and neither of them would get their work done.

Also, he planned on leaving the military and staying with her on-planet. He couldn't envision being away from her on missions for weeks at a time.

Bria, proving she'd gotten more comfortable touching on his uppermost thoughts, turned to him and said, "I'll be going with you on the *Galanti*." She scooted into the banquette.

Iolyn followed. "No. You need your lab and your team. I can do research in my field on-planet."

"Iolyn—" Bria stroked his face and then tapped his chin with an insistent finger. "The lab setup on the ship is fantastic. I can work with Lia and a few of my team can join us when you have missions. The rest of the team can work on-planet, and we'll exchange data just as I did with Lia when I was clear across the galaxy. It will work. You don't have to give up your career for me." She turned her attention to her napkin and placed it on her lap. "I don't intend to give up my career choices for you. It's only fair."

"Bria..." He tried to keep his frustration out of his voice, but knew he'd failed when Wulf, standing by the table chuckled.

"Give it up, brother." Wulf seated Mel and stroked a hand over her hair. "You won't win this fight. Why do you think I proposed the co-captaincy to the Alliance Military?"

"Because my very smart *gemat* knew I'd make his life miserable if I had to sit on-planet while he got to have all the fun." Mel smiled at Wulf, taking his hand and placing a biting kiss over his knuckles.

Mel then turned toward Iolyn. "Trust me, this will work out for the best. Bria will want to see new cultures and take blood samples all over the Milky Way. Prime DNA is potentially everywhere, according to what she told us while we did power yoga earlier."

Bria choked back what Iolyn sensed was a laugh, but when he touched her mind to see what was so funny, he found only her low-level arousal, a need for food, and the anticipation of a nice meal with newfound friends and relatives. Whatever she hid he'd eventually discover. Her walls came down completely during sex, so he'd know every thought, every feeling, every desire in her beautiful mind.

"Are you playing the big bad Prime male card already, brother-kin?" Nadia asked as Huw seated his *gemate* with one last tender, loving sweep of his hand over the nape of her neck.

Huw chuckled. "Of course he is. It's instinctive to order our *gemates* around."

"But it is a battle-mate's prerogative to ignore her warrior-*gemat*." Mel picked up the glass of wine Wulf had poured her and toasted her sister-kin. "To battle-mates."

"I'll drink to that," Lia said as she sat down. "To battle-mates." She picked up the glass Wulf nudged toward her and saluted the other ladies.

Joen sat next to her and shot a smile around the table. "You guys thinking maybe we've bitten off more than we can chew?" He turned a hot gaze on Lia. "I love it, though. Each day brings new discoveries about this very special *gemat-gemate* bond."

Bria stirred next to him, and Iolyn turned to her. "What is it, *peata*?"

As the men chuckled at his use of the endearment, Bria glared at him and hissed, "Stop calling me a *little pet*. I'm not little, nor am I a pet."

You are to me. And no one thinks less of you. I'm sure the others have names for their women.

But they aren't using them in public.

"Would you prefer I call you *little menace*?" Iolyn massaged the back of her neck and despite being mad at him, she sighed with pleasure.

"No." She looked at the other women who had smiles on their faces. "Am I being too sensitive on this endearment thing?"

Nadia laughed. "Huw calls me *she-cat*." She brushed her cheek over Huw's shoulder. "It makes me hot."

"And what makes her hot, makes me hot." Huw placed a nuzzling kiss on Nadia's head as it rested on his shoulder.

Mel nodded. "Yeah. When Wulf calls me *little one* in a certain tone, I melt and want to bite his *gemat* mark."

"Which I love," Wulf winked at Bria, "so I call her *little one* a lot."

Lia smiled and shook her head. "Well, Joen calls me all sorts of things including the usual Prime *lubha* and *cwen*, but then lately he's used a Terran endearment—not sure where he got it from—but I love it. And I love him."

"What?" Bria asked.

Iolyn could tell his sister-kin and Lia had alleviated Bria's embarrassment by making it all normal and fun. Bless them. He'd make sure to do something nice for each of them later. They were working hard to include her in their sisterhood—which could be good and bad, because he was damn sure the yoga sessions were more than just exercise. Bria had bruises in places that even power yoga wouldn't produce.

Lia snickered. "He calls me *pumpkin*."

Everyone laughed. Joen kissed Lia's flushed cheek. "One of the Terran engineers gave me a list of names he uses with his wife. I liked pumpkin." He shrugged. "She's so cute—the word sounds cute. But when I looked it up, I wasn't sure why anyone would want to call their beloved a round, orange vegetable."

Everyone at the table erupted in laughter once again.

Bria wiped tears off her cheeks from giggling so hard. "Okay, if Iolyn has to call me something, then *peata* it is. *Lubha* and *cwen* are okay, too." She poked him in the side. "But I am really not a little menace."

"At times, you are." Iolyn cupped her chin and turned her toward him. He took her lips in a demanding kiss to smother her inevitable protest. His brothers and Joen chuckled.

Bria tasted like wine and sex. A heady combination that went straight to his cock. Everything he did with Bria went straight to his cock, and he liked the feeling. He broke away from their kiss and swept a finger over her heated cheeks. At that moment, he wanted to be in their bed, buried so deeply inside her that he couldn't tell where she began and he left off.

Later.

Yes, later, big bad man.

Bria coughed then looked at the others. "Changing the subject, I've done some reading since I first began working with Lia on Prime DNA and the battle-mate alleles in particular, but I couldn't find much on what battle-mates do. I only found that the genetic markers were in certain bloodlines and that after the Period of Galactic Discovery their roles died out."

Wulf nodded. "I found this lack, also, when I did my reading after we discovered Melina was a battle-mate. So I spoke with my father. I wanted to be able to prepare her for what we could do as a unit. There are some general legends, but most of the last few generations think of them as mythic."

"And they aren't mythic," Bria stated.

"Correct. What Melina and I can do was more than the prevalent myths suggested." Wulf pulled Mel into his side and cuddled her. "My father said we should speak with his brother, my Uncle Tenar. He is the Keeper of the Prime History. He has tomes in his library that the general public, including our medical researchers, have never had access to. Mostly because they are in the ancient Prime language."

"Could I speak with him, do you think?" Bria asked. "Get access to the ancient records? I would need them translated, though." She turned and wrinkled her cute little nose at Iolyn. "I need to learn Prime, don't I?"

Iolyn kissed the tip of her nose. "I'll help you with the texts and documents in the current Prime language. And Uncle Tenar, I'm sure, will be happy to help you by translating the ones in ancient Prime."

"That would be good." Bria turned to look at Lia and the other women. "Would you all want to go with me when I meet with Iolyn's uncle?"

Lia nodded. "Yes. I've always wanted to see the view of the capital and the world ocean from his mountainside ancient Prime fortress. I hear it is amazing."

"Yes, let's all go." Mel smiled. "I liked him much better than some of Wulf's other relatives." She looked at Bria. "But you'll get to meet the whole family at the formal dinner Wulf's parents plan for you and Nadia. Lorinda has also planned for all of us to meet the Prime citizenry. The public festivities and ball which had to be cancelled when we had some back-to-back missions has been rescheduled. Now that all the lineal Caradoc heirs have *gemates*, the Prime public has gone wild and wants to see and bask in this miracle."

"Not all, *lubha*." Wulf kissed Mel's shoulder. "The Pure Bloods have ramped up their terrorist acts, according to the latest reports from home."

"We can't let the fanatics dictate how we live our lives," Huw snapped. "The Alliance and Prime Commands have stepped up security on- and off-planet. The anti-terrorist unit put in place after the attack on Nadia and Lia have routed several more terrorist cells. We're hacking away at the resistance piece by piece."

"I still don't understand why? Why Pure Blood?" Bria said. "Every Prime has strains of other hominid DNA. I've studied several hominid races as I worked on hominid species fertility issues, and now that I know what Prime DNA looks like, I can tell you it's found in varying amounts in all the humanlike species I've studied so far. Your ancient relatives left their DNA all over the galaxy. They also brought their foreign mates and offspring home with them since I find Terran, Volusian, and several other hominid species DNA in those who call themselves pure Prime. This pure blood rebellion makes no sense."

Bria shuddered against Iolyn. He pulled her closer and stroked her arm to soothe her. "No, it doesn't, *peata*. We've always felt the rebellion was more about power and greed than genetics. The fanatics who are true believers are being misled."

"Most likely by your slimy cousin Darga." Mel looked pale.

"Who's Darga?" Bria asked. If the man scared a warrior like Mel, he must be horrific.

"He is our father's cousin," Iolyn explained. "His sons, Donte and Uly, tried to kill Mel."

"That's horrible." Bria shook her head. "Family power struggle?"

"Yes," Huw said. "And our Aunt Beria, our father's sister, also tried to hurt Mel and dragged Nadia into it." Huw growled. "I wanted to strangle the bitch myself."

"What happened to the family traitors?" Bria asked.

"Beria and her husband died in custody, killed by their rebel cohorts, we think," Iolyn said. "Their son-in-law, Regin, is in prison along with Darga's son, Donte. Darga's other son, Uly, died trying to kill Mel."

A dark silence settled over the table for several seconds. Bria took a sip of her wine, then said, "Well, that makes the fights in the Martin family look like nothing." She shook her head, a slight smile on her lips. "The boys used to beat on each other over the silliest things, mostly who got to date which girl and who was the strongest. I really lived an idyllic life, didn't I?"

"You did." Iolyn kissed her cheek. "And I'm on-my-knees grateful they kept you safe and happy. I'll do my best to protect you, *peata*."

Bria turned toward him and placed her hand over his *gemat* mark. "I know you will. I have no fears on that issue. None."

Iolyn covered her hand with his and touched her mind and barely caught her words—*and I'll protect you too.*

Not if he had any say. She was never to be in danger—ever. And anyone who tried to harm her would end up dead.

CHAPTER 15

One standard week later, Cejuru Prime

Bria looked into the eyepiece of her microscope and studied the microbes inhabiting a sample of one woman's uterine tissue. "This is wrong. This is wrong," she said under her breath.

Cheri looked up from the data she was analyzing and frowned. "What are you muttering about?"

"The last woman we artificially inseminated? The one whose body rejected the inseminated egg almost immediately?"

"Yeah, what about her?" Cheri came over and peered into the double-headed scope.

"She's got the same overabundance of the microbe *staphylococcus varia* in her uterus, just like the other ninety-plus women we've examined in the last week. For some reason, Prime women's immune systems aren't producing enough of the good bacteria to keep it in check." Bria leaned back in her chair. "The reason the fertilized eggs don't attach is because the women's uterine environment is hostile to the implantation. This bacteria could also be causing the miscarriages."

"So," Cheri looked up, "you're saying that the Prime women who can't get pregnant or get pregnant but then miscarry all have this microbe in larger than normal amounts?"

"It's a working theory. We'll prove it one way or another." Bria shoved away from her desk. "What I want to know is why the Prime physicians and researchers didn't catch this. It wasn't hard to find once I looked at enough tissue on implantation failures. We haven't seen any miscarriages, yet."

"It's a good question. And from what I can tell from the medical records on the women who've come into our lab, no one has ever tested their uterine tissue or the by-product of miscarriages. In fact, from what I gathered from the women who've come through and have had miscarriages, all the placental tissue and fetuses were cremated immediately after, and no tissue was kept." Cheri frowned. "You'd think the women's physicians would want to find out why their patients couldn't carry to term."

"Yeah, you'd think." Bria hung her lab coat on the hook behind the door. "We can't draw any final conclusions about my theory until we sample a wider spectrum of women to see if they carry the microbe and how much of it they have. Then we can run tests on stored eggs, fertilize them, and implant them in lab-grown tissues containing different amounts of the microbe. This way we'll see how much of the bad bacteria it takes to impede attachment—and if the fertilized eggs do manage to attach, what amount of the harmful microbe it takes to cause the spontaneous abortion."

"After that, we can find a way to suppress the bad flora to below harmful levels," Cheri added.

"Exactly." Bria headed for the back exit to the lab. "I also want to figure out what compromised the Prime women's immune system to allow the imbalance to occur."

"It could be environmental." Cheri followed Bria out the door.

"Or it could be indirectly environmentally induced from something they ate or drank." Followed by her ever-present guards, Bria looked at Cheri as they took a circuitous route through the laboratory wing of the Alliance compound on Cejuru Prime. "Finding the underlying cause will take time. We need to find the patterns. Some of the tissue I've seen has less of the harmful bacteria, which tells me the woman's immune system was not as compromised—either from less exposure to the toxin or from a stronger natural resistance. But if we nail down this bad microbe as the reason the women aren't conceiving or carrying to term, then we can put a Band-Aid on the effect while we search for the underlying causes."

"Bria, I've been thinking...as I sometimes do." Cheri semi-jogged to keep up with Bria's longer legs.

Bria laughed and slowed her pace so her friend wouldn't be out of breath by the time they reached their destination. "Okay, I'll bite. What have you been thinking?"

"God, I wish I had longer legs." Cheri shot an envious look at Bria's. "Okay, back on topic...the medical records I've been reviewing are crap. Plus, even when there's no miscarriage, there's a lack of testing and follow-up when women have gone to their physicians with basic gynecologic complaints. It looks like shoddy medicine for the female portion of the Prime population as a whole when it comes to ob/gyn health issues."

"Then we're thinking along the same lines." Bria made sure her mental walls were up and tight. "But I didn't want to mention it yet. To anyone." Even her *gemat*. "It's too early, and the sampling's too small."

Cheri let out a kittenish growl. "It makes me so mad. The women we've seen are capable of conceiving, every damn one of them. Their ova are healthy. The sperm of their mates is healthy. These are some of the healthiest people I've ever seen. So, if it hadn't been for this microbe you found..."

"Then the *gemat-gemate* couples should be having babies left and right," Bria concluded. "Yeah, that's what I thought also. And to pile on top of the low birth rate, the years of isolation, wars with Antareans, and the edict that only marked couples can mate and procreate, you have the current clusterfuck of negative population growth."

"This isn't just bad medicine, is it?" said Cheri, a frown on her pretty face.

Bria sighed, a sick feeling in her stomach that had begun with her first glance of the poor recordkeeping for women's medical issues and no follow-up on the miscarriages. "No, it's not. Isolationism and war are one thing. I can also somewhat understand how the cultural aspects of the bond-marking became entrenched. Having such a bond, I feel the power of it. But I'd really like to understand why the cultural protocols were put into place. There may have been excellent reasons for those...but I bet the old reasons no longer apply. Ilar has already taken the first steps to eradicate them. What I can't excuse, though, is the lack of medical follow-through."

Cheri looked at Bria, a look of perplexity on her face. "Why didn't the Prime medical profession do their job? Are they all incompetent?" She shook her head and grimaced. "They can't all be stupid. Maybe they were told not to follow-through?"

"I'm leaning toward they were ordered not to. And that would have to come from the highest levels," said Bria. "From the Elder Council. And the only person I'm sure who would *not* have issued such an order is Iolyn's father. The rest of the Council is suspect."

Bria stopped at an elevator furthest from her lab and placed her palm on the pad. The door opened and she entered.

Cheri and the guards shimmied onto the elevator just as the door began to close. "Damn those doors are fast. By the way, where are we going?"

"I needed a break. You tagged along." Bria grinned. "We're going to practice more yoga."

Cheri laughed. "Does Iolyn still believe the story that you're doing Ashtanga yoga on a daily basis?"

"Yes. And my mental shields are holding that secret against his probes." Bria smiled. "I'm that good."

Cheri snorted. "He's not stupid, Bria." She looked at the two guards. "You don't think these guys tell him what you're doing?"

Bria glanced at the guards. Two new ones today. V'niko and A'nan had needed some time to get settled into their new quarters on Cejuru Prime. "Do you tell my *gemat* what I do in the gym?"

One guard looked at her. "Your *gemat* has never asked."

Bria smiled and shot a grin at Cheri. "See?"

"Bria, Bria, Bria…" Cheri sighed and looked at the guard who'd responded. "If her *gemat* did ask, would you tell him?"

"Of course. He is my superior officer, and I do not lie."

Cheri turned a triumphant, smug grin on Bria. "See? So, since Iolyn hasn't asked, I expect he already knows you're training with the gals."

"He doesn't know. I would know." Bria checked her shields. Still up and still strong.

Bria took the underground tunnel to the Alliance gymnasium. The tunnel didn't affect her claustrophobia since it was huge and well lit.

"You know, if Iolyn discovers you're training in FHC, well, I think a hard implement might be used on your so-fine, tiny round butt."

Bria palmed the security pad to open the back entrance to the gym and then looked over her shoulder at her shorter, curvier friend. "Why Cheri, I never knew you loved my ass so much." She cast a glance at the guards. "Lock us in, take a break for an hour, and come back for us then."

The two men saluted and left.

"I don't love your ass," Cheri retorted as she followed Bria into the gym. "But it's attached to the rest of you, and you, I love like a sister."

"I'll be fine." Bria smiled and waved at Mel, Nadia, and Lia. "Let's go kick some ass."

Cheri muttered, "I won't need to. Iolyn will beat yours for sure later."

———

LIA WIPED SWEAT OFF HER forehead with a gym towel. "Well, you're finally getting the hang of it, Bria. You put me on my rump handily that last round."

"I told you she had a killer instinct and the physicality for hand-to-hand." Mel approached them. "We just needed to train her natural abilities a bit."

"I'm still more comfortable with my knives—and now the laser pistol." Bria redid her ponytail to get the damp curls off her equally damp neck. The cool air on her nape made her feel instantly cooler. "My eye-to-hand coordination is still my strength. But, at least, now I'll have some countermoves other than kneeing balls or breaking noses if someone attacks me."

"Hey, kneeing balls and breaking noses are still good maneuvers," Nadia added, joining them after putting Cheri through her paces. "But trained warriors know to defend against such obvious moves from women. You now can use some of your new street-fighting moves, then follow up with a solid kick to their balls."

"And then run like hell for your man." Cheri bent over at the waist and panted a bit. "Nadia, I'm so glad you're on our side. 'Cause, girl, you are one mean bitch." Her friend stood up and ran a shaky hand through her blonde curls. "Zaek is going to have to heal something other than my sexy bits tonight. I love the healing almost as much as the Dom-sub sex."

"Heal you?" Mel looked from Cheri to Bria and back. "Are you mating in the Prime way? When did this happen? Last I heard, he was courting you."

Bria smiled and let Cheri address the questions. After all, it was her friend's news. Bria had run the tests and honored the doctor-patient privilege. Lia had also known, but, obviously, had kept quiet for the same reasons.

Cheri, already red from exertion, turned redder. "Uh, yeah. Already mated. Lots of hot monkey sex on the trip here took care of that. I was waiting to tell everyone. But the news will be out soon since Zaek wants to be reassigned to the lab, whether it's on-planet or on the *Galanti*. He applied for the transfer and is citing the mating so he can be with me. Bria and Lia knew since they ran the tests and certified the markings."

Cheri peeled her yoga pants down and exposed a *gemate* mark. "See? Isn't it gorgeous?"

Mel smiled. "Congratulations. I'll check on the transfer and see if I can expedite it. How's the bonding going for you?"

"Thanks, Mel. And it is going fabulously." Cheri grinned. "I've met my sexual match. And I love him, too. First time that's ever happened. He gets me."

"And she's been gotten a lot." Bria laughed then dodged out of the way of Cheri's towel as her friend snapped it at her. "She was late to work today. Then she took an extra-long mid-morning break and an extended lunch hour."

"Um, kettle meet black." Cheri turned to the other women who were grinning. "Ms. High-and-Mighty there also had a long morning break after I returned. And I caught her and Iolyn coming out of the employee break room. The door had been locked, and sounds of a cat wailing in heat were present prior to their emerging."

"Were you listening at the door?" Bria screeched.

"Um, no, not on purpose anyway. Zaek and I wanted to use the break room." Cheri bit her lower lip. "We ended up in the supply closet. The towels make a really nice bed." She scrunched her nose. "But now we're out of towels since they were, um, used. So we might want to increase the towel supply."

Mel, Nadia, and Lia burst out laughing.

Bria looked at Cheri, then they, too, joined in the laughter. It was nice sharing the mating experience with others who knew what it was like.

"I've been meaning to ask, but hadn't had the opportune moment until now. When...um...when exactly," Bria hitched a breath as a left-over snicker escaped, "is this need for sex going to slow down?"

Before one of the others could answer, the locked door, coded solely to their palm prints for the hour they used the facility, was blown open by a laser blast.

Eight masked and heavily armed men wearing body armor rushed into the room before the smoke had cleared.

Before the men had oriented themselves, Bria and the other women dove for their gym totes and used the lingering echoes of the blast and smoke to hide.

Bria took up a defensive position behind a lats machine and pulled her laser pistol and a knife from her bag. Nadia was behind a chest press machine. She was already armed and had her com unit out, signaling for help. Mel was hunkered down behind the leg press and her gun arm tracked the men as they divided up and began to search the room.

Wherever Lia and Cheri had taken refuge, Bria couldn't see them. With luck, neither would the intruders.

The room was eerily silent. No one called out. Not even the men, who communicated by hand signals.

The atmosphere was laden with the intruders' determination to succeed in their mission—to take the women hostage. They were focused and weren't adverse to using bodily harm to get what they wanted.

In the blasted doorway, Bria could see the bodies of her two guards. They were either dead or severely injured.

Mad. Sick at heart. Bria dropped her shields and found Iolyn's mental path.

Stop. Shutting. Me. Out. Status report.

His fury, combined with gut-wrenching worry, blasted her almost as violently as the explosion that took down the gym door. Obviously, Nadia's call for help had gotten to their men.

I'm fine. Hiding. I think they're here to kidnap us.

His emotions boiled over, and the icy-white-heat of battle rage flowed across their mental connection. Her body responded by producing even more battle-mate hormones as she was pulled into the wave which included Mel, Nadia, and Lia and their *gemats*. The power was invigorating and also scary in a good way.

Show me.

Bria began a visual scan of the room, noting the intruders' positions. She'd showed him five of the intruders when she spotted a man advancing on Mel's position behind the leg press. She took the shot, hitting him with a high stun to his torso. He went down.

The silence ended as the remaining intruders returned fire. Bria scrunched behind her machine. The heat from the laser streams chased away the cold in her bones. The whine and color of the streams registered as low-to-medium-low stuns. This confirmed the intruders wanted hostages and not dead bodies.

Bria! Iolyn growled in her head. He was closer.

"Bria!" Mel yelled as she tagged the man Bria had downed in the head—an insurance shot, Mel had called it in shooting strategy class.

"I'm fine." Bria yelled. She looked around her machine and shot at another intruder, hitting him in the legs.

Mel followed up with another head stun. "Grab onto the *batel rabia*, Bria."

"Did..." She shot another man who got brave and tried to approach Nadia's position.

Nadia hit the man at the same time. Two high stuns to the head. He was definitely dead. Right now, survival, hers and her friends, was uppermost in her mind.

"...my skin itches..." Bria got in a head shot on a man who'd zeroed in on the storage closet. Cheri and Lia had to be hiding in there. "...and my senses seem to be on super-amphetamines."

"You'll get used to it." Mel shot over Bria's shoulder and caught a man in the arm.

The man dropped his weapon, but still managed to lunge at Bria. He knocked her laser weapon from her hand and pulled her to him.

Bria! Fight him.

Bria turned into the man then put into use every move taught her and some she made up. But the man was too strong. She pulled his hood off and found the visage of a pseudo-reptilian. Just her effin' luck. She couldn't beat this man hand-to-hand, and her knife had been knocked to the ground along with her laser weapon.

The gym was loud with the sounds of fighting and laser fire. The other women had their own fights. No help from that quarter.

Her attacker flicked his tongue along her neck. "Tasty. I'll enjoy fucking you, *sued-seuater.*"

Bria renewed her struggles, pulling on the energy that Iolyn blasted across their mating bond. Just when she thought she had an out, the man countered her move with ease. Then he began to drag her to the back entrance to the gym where one of the intruders was waving and yelling, "Grab any of them you can. Move out."

Iolyn growled in her head.

The pseudo-reptilian carried her and another man had Lia. Yet another had Cheri.

Mel and Nadia yelled in the background—then she was torn from the hold of her captor and went flying through the air. An Alliance soldier managed to catch her before she hit the floor. He steadied her. "My orders are to get you away, Doctor."

"No." She turned and watched as Iolyn faced off with her former captor. They were knife-fighting. Fear gripped her until she realized Iolyn was toying with the man. He sliced and slashed and outmaneuvered the man, who she could now see was an Erian.

Mel, Nadia, Cheri, and Lia joined her with guards of their own. Their men, even Zaek, were cleaning up the floor with the remaining intruders. A ring of Alliance soldiers wearing the Gold Squadron uniforms circled the fighting *gemats*, cheering them on.

Bria began to shake, her vision sprouted white and gold lights, and her knees went limp. Post-adrenaline drop. A bad case.

Mel placed an arm around her waist and eased her to the floor. "Hang in there, Bria. You did well. Good shooting." She ordered one of the soldiers guarding them. "Get us some water, please."

The soldier ran off to the storage closet and brought back water for all of the women.

Her gaze on Iolyn who still played with his opponent, Bria took a long drink and almost choked when it wouldn't get past the lump of lingering fear in her throat. When she managed to get it down, she took a few smaller sips, then gasped out, "I...need more fight classes."

"Your men are supposed to take care of you," the Alliance soldier who'd caught her said.

"Well, our men can't be everywhere," Nadia retorted.

Iolyn let out the Caradoc battle cry and took the head of the man who'd threatened Bria. She touched her mate's mind and found it icily calm as he dealt out death. She'd never be able to do that.

But she could do her job. "We need to check on the injured," Bria said to Lia.

Lia nodded and offered her a hand up. "Might as well be useful while our men are doing clean up. There's an emergency med kit in the storage closet. I'll get it."

Bria was happy to find her knees worked and the sick, dizzy feeling had subsided. The energy coming from Iolyn was now warm and revitalizing. He was helping her through the aftermath of riding the *batel rabia* wave.

Iolyn and the others were interrogating the intruders who were less injured. So, she began to move to a downed intruder—one whom she was fairly sure was dead, but she needed to be sure.

"Leave him, *peata*." Iolyn had sensed her intent and cut off her path. "These men would've raped you and the others. I don't want you anywhere near them. Other Alliance medical personnel are on their way."

She looked at her mate, who checked her over with worried eyes and gentle hands. Mel and the others were also being fussed over by their *gemats*, though she was sure the men wouldn't want to have their care called fussing.

Iolyn's touch was soothing. The same hands that had taken on a huge mercenary and slain him, now handled her as if she were as fragile as blown glass. He hissed and snarled at each bruise the Erian had left where he'd grabbed her. He fretted and muttered—and she fell even more in love with him. Yes, he was autocratic and over-protective, but in a good way.

Iolyn. She touched his mind to soothe him back and gasped. Internally, he was a chaotic mass of anger.

Bria frowned and glanced at the men Iolyn and the others had questioned. The attackers must've said something to reignite Iolyn's fury. Whatever he'd heard, he'd hidden it under layers of rage. She shuddered and leaned into him. He instantly wrapped her within his strong embrace.

"I'm fine. It's over." She hugged him tightly around the waist and stroked his back.

"It's not over, not as long as the terrorists are still active." Iolyn's voice was rough, but his hands on her back were gentle as he held her close. A low buzz-saw rumbling vibrated from his body to hers. As the sound crescendoed, the other Prime in the room joined in. The vibrations made her skin itch and her bones ache.

"Oh great," Mel muttered, clasped in Wulf's brawny arms. "It's the so-angry-they-could-eat-a-water-beast-whole growl."

Nadia snickered. She sat on Huw's lap, her head on his shoulder. "Yeah, I hate that one. It makes my nerves go on the fritz."

The men glared at the women and growled even more.

Wulf motioned to a military security unit which had arrived. "Take the attackers still mobile into custody and lock them up in isolation. Take the more severely injured to the lock-down unit in the medica. I want them restrained and under guard at all times. And for the One's sake, make sure they aren't carrying suicide capsules anywhere on their bodies."

The assassin who'd tried to kill Iolyn and Wulf on her brother's jump station had killed himself with just such a capsule before he could be questioned. Wulf obviously wasn't taking any chances this time.

The guards saluted and moved to take control of the prisoners. Other Alliance medical personnel were checking out the injured. Bria's guards were alive, but injured severely enough to need portable regen beds.

Bria moaned under the intensity of the guilt. Tears streaked down her cheek.

"*Diew*, don't cry." Iolyn tipped Bria's chin up and kissed her—a deep tongue thrusting, almost punishing kiss.

I could've lost you.

You didn't.

You could've died.

I didn't.

Breaking off the kiss, he leaned his forehead against hers. "Why weren't your fucking guards in the gym with you?"

His tone was as cutting as a knife, slicing away at her skin, shredding her nerves. His tone had her second-guessing herself. If she had it to do all over again, would she—

"Stop it." She shoved against his chest and could barely budge him an inch. "I was within a secure military facility. The gym was coded to our five handprints only for this hour. I—we should've been safe here—in a locked room. The guards were injured because they did their job trying to protect us. You aren't allowed to be mad at them—or me. Be mad at the attackers and whoever put them up to this."

"She's right, brother," Wulf said. "We need to focus our anger where it belongs. The intruders were well-trained, well-equipped, and had inside information. We need to find out who sold them the information about our *gemates'* whereabouts and then who helped them get inside a secure facility. The terrorist faction of the Pure Blood is upping their game yet again. Father will go ballistic."

Iolyn's lips thinned, and he breathed heavily through his nose. She could visibly see—and when she touched his mind, feel—the strength it took to shove his anger and fear away.

When his mind had become a deep, swirling pool of icy calm, he said, "I'm sorry I yelled at you, *lubha.*" He rubbed his cheek over hers and whispered against her ear, in a mild, somewhat teasing tone, "I guess all those *yoga* practices helped. You fought well. I'm proud of you."

Bria's breath hitched and she looked at his face. "You knew?"

"Almost from the beginning. We'll discuss later why you felt the need to sneak behind my back to get FHC training," he added in an amused tone.

"Who told you?" She raised a brow. Now, she was angry. He'd told her she didn't need warrior training, and now he chided her for going behind his back. Un-unh, he couldn't have it both ways.

"Wulf told me when I asked him. Mel doesn't close her mind," Iolyn snapped against her ear. "Not as you do with me. We'll also discuss that issue—later. It must stop."

"Then, my *gemat*, you need to stop smothering me." She hissed into his ear. "As you saw...I can fight and protect myself and others if I need to. I could do it better with even more training."

"Yes, but you don't understand. You aren't to be in harm's way. Ever." Once again there was both anger and fear in his voice. Iolyn tightened his arms around her. "Which is why I assigned guards to you. If they'd been inside the room, they'd have sent the alarm, fought the invaders, and you could've stayed safely hidden."

"Hidden? Seriously?"

"Safely hidden," he growled.

"Oh lordy," Cheri said from within the circle of Zaek's arms.

Iolyn turned and shot her a sharp look. "What in Balcon's Balls does that mean?"

"It means you need to trust Bria to do what's right in the moment," Cheri shot back.

"Yeah. What she said." Bria jabbed a fist into his side. The cocksure, overprotective S.O.B. didn't even flinch, dammit. But he did loosen his hold enough so she could shove out of his grasp.

Then she stomped toward the blasted-out door where a crowd of interested onlookers had gathered. "I'm going back to the lab. I have a nasty microbe to research. Don't wait up."

Iolyn stood still for several nanoseconds. Okay, he probably could've handled that better. His brothers' grins underlined that thought. But Bria running away from him wouldn't get anything settled. He refused to let the situation fester. Plus, he still wasn't over his fear of losing her, and she, if she would admit it, was still shaking inside at the close call. She needed to let him soothe her—for both their sakes.

He growled and tore after her. His brothers laughed. He gave them both a rude gesture. Grabbing Bria from behind, he turned her to face him and then tossed her over his shoulder in one continuous motion.

"Iolyn!" Bria slapped at his ass. "Put me down. I have to go to work."

"Silence." Iolyn spanked a luscious round ass cheek and did it much harder than she'd hit his. "I love you. You worried me. I *need* you now—and if you'd admit it, you need me."

She wiggled. He spanked her again. "Stop it. I don't want to drop you."

Her "ouch" and resulting squirm—and then a low moan—shot a frisson of sexual awareness straight to his dick. He scented her arousal on the air. He rubbed her bottom and she moaned again. *Diew*, he wanted to fuck her now, even more than before. And it would be fucking—not sweet or nice or fun. She'd frightened him. He was coming down off battle rage and his cock was hard enough to drill holes through the *Galanti*'s outer hull. His *gemate* needed to soothe him in a most elemental way.

"Iolyn..." His name came out sounding somewhere between a testy feline's snarl and the come-hither of a mating purr.

"Little menace," he whispered, "I couldn't get here fast enough." He squeezed her firm butt cheek gently. "You were in danger—again—and I was nowhere near."

Bria relaxed into his hold. He smiled, then frowned as she murmured for his ears alone, "You embarrassed me in front of the others. I won't hide while my guards or Nadia or Mel fight to protect me. I have to know how to defend myself and others—especially since I'm not going out and finding these fights. They're finding me. And I'll try to remember to keep my shields down so you can check in with me. But I also need some part of my mind to be my own, where I can keep others' secrets and maybe even surprise you from time to time."

"You're right." Iolyn swung her off his shoulder then into his arms and cuddled her against his chest. Her golden eyes were drenched in tears. "Don't cry, *peata*." He kissed away the silver drops as they rolled down her cheeks. "You're part of my soul. If I lost you, I'd be less than nothing. You're my reason for living."

"I understand that. I feel the same way about you." She stroked his jaw. "But, we could have had this discussion later, away from the crowd. Instead, you pushed me on the training thing and the shields and I got mad. I figured it would be better to cool down before we discussed those topics. I can't shove my anger into a deep, icy pool of water inside me as you can."

"I'll teach you how to do that." He brushed a kiss over her lips.

"That would be good." She nibbled on his chin. "Because we both are stubborn and have tempers." She looked into his eyes. "What made you throw me over your shoulder all Terran caveman style?"

"You walked away." Iolyn entered the elevator that would take them to his ground transport.

He needed to get her home, strip her down in order to check for any hidden injuries. Then he'd fuck her, first, and later make love to her—join with her mind-body-soul and reaffirm their bond and assure himself she was all right.

"I made you so mad. You threw your mental shields up and left me—and I went all primitive." He rubbed his cheek over the top of her head as she nestled it on his shoulder. "It'll probably happen again. It's just the nature of the *gemat-gemate* bond."

"Iolyn—" Bria's body molded to his and she fingered the hair at the back of his neck. "I would've dropped the shields and checked on you as soon as I got to the lab. One thing you'll learn about me is I don't hold onto anger long. I'm sorry I scared you, too."

"When we get to our rooms, I'll probably scare you a little more." He nuzzled her neck and scented the heat of her arousal coming through her pores. "Or maybe not."

"How?"

He growled. "When Prime warriors come off battle rage, we get very aroused. The sex resulting from that can be rough."

"Uh-huh, that makes sense. High stress hormones and all that." She licked his neck over his pulse point and his cock twitched in the confines of his uniform pants.

Diew. "Bria, if you keep doing that, I'll end up taking you against my ground shuttle." He looked down at the most precious being in the universe. She looked interested. He touched her surface thoughts. She was. "*Lubha*, what I want to do to you should probably be done in the privacy of our bedroom."

"Okay." She scrunched her nose. He had to kiss the tip, she was so cute. "But maybe someday, somewhere isolated we can try the fucking against the ground shuttle thing?"

"I'll add that to my list." He rubbed his nose alongside of hers.

"You have a list?" She touched his mind and even that gossamer sensation had his cock throbbing. "Oh my!" She blushed and coughed and closed her eyes. "Iolyn..."

"Yes, *peata*?" He carried her out of the elevator and into the subterranean garage. He increased his pace.

"If Prime warriors get erections after riding the *batel rabia* wave, what do they do when there are no women around to, um, take care of their needs?"

Iolyn shook his head. Only his little scientist would ask such a question out loud. Other women would just think it. "We suffer or we handle it ourselves. And before you ask, I've done both."

"I'd like to watch you handle it yourself, sometime."

At her words, he stopped in the middle of the garage as a wave of lust threatened to take him to his knees.

"*Diew*, I *bakking* need you more than I need my next breath." He kissed her lips, biting, licking, and sucking at them until the two of them gasped for breath. He broke off and whispered against her now-swollen mouth. "The sex will be rough at first. I'm afraid of hurting you—shocking you."

Bria's essence twined through his thoughts—the ones where he wanted to keep her on the precipice between pain and pleasure for hours...feed on it...and then send it back to her doubled, tripled, until they couldn't handle the sensations any longer and they both exploded, sending them into a spiraling free fall.

"Oh..." She swallowed and looked into his eyes. Her gaze held molten heat, excitement, and desire to match his own. "Yes, I want—no, need you like that, too. So, so much."

She trembled in his arms.

"You scared?" He hurried to his vehicle and placed her gently into the passenger seat, then buckled her in.

"A little. But I trust you." She leaned into him before he backed away to shut the hatch and kissed him, a sweet, hot kiss of sexual hunger that matched his own.

He broke away before he pulled her out of her seat and bumped up sex-against-a-shuttle to number one on his to-do sex list. "I'll never hurt you. Never. I'd kill myself before I hurt you." He caressed her cheek with his hand.

"Well, that might be a bit extreme." She rubbed her cheek against the palm of his hand like a kitten. "Take me home and fuck me, my warrior-*gemat*. You've got me all hot and bothered—and you have to fix it."

———

Several standard hours later, Caradoc Estate

BRIA COULDN'T MOVE EVEN IF she hadn't had Iolyn's weight lying over her. His cock was still inside her, and when it twitched, her vaginal sheath responded with another round of small orgasmic explosions. She moaned. Iolyn bit and then licked her shoulder. She grunted when his actions sent another wave of bliss over her body.

"*Diew, peata.* You're going to kill me," Iolyn muttered against her throat.

"Me?" she gasped out the word. "You...you tortured me with pleasure. I thought I was gonna die from orgasming." She tried to lift an arm to shove him off her body, but couldn't. Her bones had turned liquid. She tried to lick her dry lips, but her mouth was arid like the Great Cetan desert on Oz. She must've sweated off a liter of water. "Off. Please. Heavy. Water."

Iolyn chuckled and rolled to his side taking her with him. They were still joined. His cock pulsed rapidly inside her, and she had yet another mini-climax.

Then he looked into her eyes. "You really scared me today."

And his words filled with fear and his infinite love for her had her eyes tearing up. This man for all his autocratic dominance was a keeper. They were still new as a couple. It would take time, but they'd find their rhythm as partners and mates. It wouldn't be easy, but it would definitely be worth it.

Thank the One, God, and any other deity worshiped in the galaxy, they'd found one another.

"I'm sorry." She kissed his lips gently. "So tired. But I need to work."

"Work tomorrow." He kissed her forehead then pulled out of her body slowly. They both moaned at the loss of intimate contact. "I'll get us both a drink. A cloth to clean you up.

Then we'll nap. Can't have you falling asleep tonight during the family dinner."

She groaned. Damn, how had she forgotten about the ordeal of the meet-the-family—plus the Council Elders—dinner?

Lots of booty-banging sex does that to a gal. And one hell of an erotic spanking. Her ass still burned, but in a way she'd never thought she'd find arousing.

"Yes, a nap would be good." She yawned, closed her eyes, and was half-asleep by the time Iolyn had left the bed.

CHAPTER 16

Later that evening

Bria stood with Iolyn, Wulf, and Mel in the great room of the Caradoc family home. It was still early in the cocktail hour. They probably had another standard hour or so before the evening meal. Guests were still arriving, many more than Iolyn had hinted at. She stiffened her spine at the sight of so many strangers and took another bracing sip of her wine. The light fruity drink wasn't doing it for her. She needed something stronger if she was going to make it through dinner and beyond without succumbing to a crisis of nerves. She hated being on display.

"I think I need to switch to scotch."

"Why?" Mel asked, sipping on a glass of a potent Valerian scotch. "Does the wine taste bad?"

"No." She placed the wine on the tray of a passing waiter.

"What's wrong, *peata*?" Iolyn massaged the skin exposed by her almost backless dress.

She shivered at his touch. His casual caress brought back memories of the hours they'd spent before coming downstairs this evening. She wanted him again. Rough. Gentle. However he wanted to take her. Preferably now, so they could sneak away and she could avoid being the center of attention.

Bria would rather face a horde of space pirates than his relatives—and, it seemed like, half the Prime Elder council members and their *gemates* had decided to accept her in-laws' invitation.

"*Lubha*, what's wrong?" Iolyn asked once more and this time gathered her closer against his firmly muscled, warm body.

She frowned. "What's wrong? Your mother" —Iolyn's mother had asked to be called by her name— "um, Lorinda... has half the capital city here."

An exaggeration but it appeared that way.

"It was bad enough when I was supposed to face all of your relatives, but this..." She waved a hand at the mass of people streaming into the great room which had at one time seemed huge, but now felt smaller because of all the bodies taking up space. "Everyone is staring at me as if I'm some freak."

Iolyn gave her a gentle squeeze, kissed her cheek and then whispered, "Be brave, *peata*. It'll be over soon."

"You're the new Caradoc mate. Of course they want a look." Mel smiled, her expression sympathetic. "I had to do this meet-and-greet, too." Wulf's mate shuddered, and Wulf placed a kiss on her shoulder. "So I understand. Just hold on, you'll be second choice and old news once Nadia gets here. Nadia just commed me. She's not speaking to her mate right now. Huw picked out her dress to make a statement."

Mel pulled her com unit out of her evening bag and showed it to Bria. "See the dress? No one will notice you once she walks in the room."

"As Cheri says 'oh, lordy.'" Bria looked at the others. "The dress has more fabric at the bodice and back than mine, but, wow, Nadia's dress has that huge cut-out at the waist on her right side. It's cut low enough to show the edge of her *gemate* mark."

Mel shook her head with distaste. "I'm sure that was Huw's plan. He's pissed that no one believes he marked his Terran mate. Tonight, he plans to show her off."

Wulf and Iolyn snorted with laughter. Bria elbowed Iolyn in the stomach. Mel scowled at her mate.

Bria rubbed a hand over her marking, which radiated the lingering effects of her and Iolyn's marathon sexfest. "I'm not sure I'd want to show my mark off at a formal sit-down dinner. Poolside? Can't avoid it. Exposed skin is inevitable when swimming and sunning. But here? Not so much." She turned to Iolyn and kissed the edge of his jaw. "Thanks for keeping my mark covered." She shivered. "But next time, I get to pick out my dress. My back is freezing."

Iolyn's response was a sexy grin and pulling her even closer to share his body heat. Yes, he did make a good personal furnace.

"Huw's issues with the doubters are why mother and father expanded the guest list. There's been some raucous dissent in the Elder Council. Father wasn't happy at all and sided with Huw on the dress." Wulf tossed back the rest of his drink. "I wouldn't be surprised if Huw doesn't pull off his shirt to show everyone they have matching marks." He looked at Bria and grinned. "I'm getting another scotch. Do you want me to bring you one?"

"Yes, please." Bria smiled at her brother-kin.

"Little one, do you want some more scotch?" Wulf brushed a kiss over Mel's lips.

"God, yes. It's going to be a long night." Mel traced Wulf's lower lip with her tongue before sinking her teeth into it.

Wulf's low groan and rumbled pleasure incited Iolyn to fondle Bria's bottom.

"Later," Iolyn whispered, "I'm claiming this." He swept a finger along the crease of her ass.

Biting back a low moan, Bria shuddered, whether with excitement or fear, she wasn't sure. She clenched her thighs tightly against the rush of moisture spreading over her labia. Her *gemat* was sex on a stick. And deep inside she had to admit she liked being the sole focus of all that Prime male sexual desire and adoration. She especially liked him taking control in the bedroom. Something, as an independent and highly educated woman, she would've denied vehemently before mating with him.

Iolyn chuckled at her reaction and hugged her. "Trust me, *peata*, you'll love it. I'll make it very...very pleasurable."

Bria moaned at the images she plucked from his mind. She probably would enjoy it, if she didn't die from shock and a surfeit of pleasure first.

Mel must've seen Iolyn's gesture and heard their whispers, because she choked back a laugh. She patted Wulf on his ass. "Hurry back, *gemat*. The only reason some of these people don't approach us and ask rude questions is because you're here glowering at them. And I'm very sure they don't need to be close enough to hear our topics of conversation." She turned and winked at Bria and Iolyn.

"I'll go with my brother, *peata*, and help him carry the drinks." Iolyn leaned over and brushed a kiss over her naked shoulder. She felt the light touch of his lips all the way to her core.

"Looks like dinner might be delayed some. Mother has quite a crush. I'll bring back some finger foods to absorb the alcohol. I don't want you too tipsy for later, and," Iolyn patted her bottom, "I don't want you wasting away to nothing. I think you've lost weight since we mated fully."

Before she could respond to the inanity of his remark, the two men walked away.

Bria turned to Mel. "Was he serious?"

"About what?" Mel laughed. "The anal sex and you liking it? Or you having lost weight?"

"You can't talk about...um," she looked around and seeing no one really close, she whispered, "anal sex here." Her whole body flushed with embarrassment, she added, "I'm not wasting away. I could stand to lose a few pounds. My job is very sedentary, and my bottom is wider than I'd like."

Mel laughed and shook her head. "First, sister-kin, get used to talking about sex. Prime mated couples all have it, a lot of it, and it gets alluded to...often. Second, to our men, we're small, dainty, and helpless. Get used to that idea, too." She finished off her scotch and set the glass on the next tray to pass by. "Yes, it makes no sense since I put Wulf on his ass regularly in hand-to-hand combat, and yet, he insists I need his protection."

"I noticed he was mad at you earlier, almost as mad as Iolyn was with me." Bria spotted Nadia entering the room and waved. "Nadia's here. Oh my, the dress is...um...looks even more drafty in person."

The tall blonde's smile seemed plastered on her face as she hurried to join them. Every person Nadia passed stopped what they were doing and stared after her.

And no wonder. She looked like an ancient Terran Greek goddess in the long, body-hugging column of white, diaphanous silk. The infamous right side cutout was set off with exquisite gold embroidery and sparkling white gemstones, which looked even richer against her naturally golden skin tones. The edge of her mark glowed and swirled in brilliant colors.

Huw must've teased her sexually all the way here. Poor Nadia.

He's teasing her now, peata. *Just like this.*

Bria glanced toward the bar where Iolyn stood with Wulf and Huw, who'd joined his brothers. When Iolyn rubbed a finger over his mark, Bria inhaled sharply and just managed not to cry out. All she wanted to do at that moment was curl into a ball and howl at the tortuous sexual buildup. From her recent and many sexual encounters with her mate, she knew it would take actual intercourse to relieve the sexual tension that stimulating the mark caused.

Well, at least, for her it did.

Mel was correct, sex needed to be discussed if for no other reason than to see what was normal or not. Bria made a mental note to have a *gemate*-day-out, somewhere in private, so she could ask the other women how they reacted when their men stimulated the mark.

She could chalk it up to research, and not being nosy. After all, the marking had been, and still was for now, important culturally in mating, but it was grounded in the neurochemistry of reproductive compatibility. And it was an adaptation, so it made sense that how the mark reacted would change over time and from couple to couple...or at least that was her hypothesis.

Peata, even at a party and sexually aroused, you can't stop being a scientist, eh?

Bria shot her grinning baboon of a mate a nasty look, then fingered her marking through the thin silk of her dress in slow, sensual strokes. She was happy to notice his face flush and him rearranging his cock.

Later, peata, you'll drown in the pleasure I'll give you. His mental voice was the purr of a predator.

"*Ansu bhau*, Nadia." Mel had also noted Nadia's aroused mark. "Huw's making sure everyone knows you're marked and his. Sometimes I think Prime males have more in common with the lower animal life forms than the higher."

Mel touched Nadia's arm lightly and pulled her fingers away when Nadia moaned. "Sorry, forgot how sensitive you still are. It does go away the longer you're mated. How *are* you doing?"

"Don't worry, Mel. Even the silk is irritating since I'm very aroused right now. I'm lucky my legs are holding me up." Nadia shot a glare over her shoulder, aimed at Huw and his brothers. "I told him he'd better get me a double shot of vodka for all this suffering. The perverted ass also promised if I let him demonstrate the mark was real..." Nadia took a shivery breath. "...then we'd go to his old suite of rooms before dinner and take the edge off."

Then Nadia shook her head and snorted. "He's being an idiot. As if I care what some gossipy, skeptical, throw-back-to-the-ancient-times Prime Elders think. We know the truth." Her lips twisted into a sneaky-looking smile. Then as Bria'd just done with Iolyn, Nadia rubbed her finger over her mark.

All three women snickered when Huw's shout of "Nadia!" rang out.

Nadia, her back to the bar, looked at Bria and Mel. "Is Huw adjusting his cock?"

Mel laughed.

Bria nodded and smiled. "Yep. I think you might be taking a nookie break, as Cheri has taken to calling the need for frequent mating sex, sooner than you'd planned."

"That was my objective. I've been at a low simmer since we left the house." Nadia fanned her flushed face. "Two can play at the teasing game. Enough about me, how are you doing, Bria? Iolyn's emotions were really potent in the gym earlier. Even Huw commented on it. Did Iolyn hurt you?"

"No." Bria blushed and waved the two in closer then lowered her voice. She couldn't wait for *gemate*-day-out, she needed to share and get their reaction.

"He spanked me...a lot...and it was more erotic than painful." She blushed, but she couldn't help it. Just recalling how once they'd reached their bedroom, he spanked her bare ass, then stroked her pussy and fingered her asshole had her hotter than a star going super-nova.

Nadia sighed. "I love it when Huw spanks me before sex. Well, I love it during sex and afterward, too."

Mel nodded. "Oh yeah. Go on, Bria, then what? We're all sisters here."

This was what she needed. The confirmation that what she and Iolyn did was natural, and not abnormal.

"After the spanking...oh my stars, it was amazing. He'd build me up and then deny me an orgasm. He did that for an hour. I thought I was going to die." Both women uh-hummed. "And when he finally entered me, I had the longest orgasm on record. I swear I lost touch with reality, had an out-of-body experience, and then sort of floated on the orgiastic waves. It was glorious."

The two women moaned and nodded.

Then Mel muttered, "Sounds like Wulf's *modus operandi*. Wonder if Prime males compare notes?"

Nadia giggled. "Huw likes to prolong sex, too—why do you think I was simmering when we left to come here?" She nudged Bria. "Come on. What happened next?"

Bria inhaled and let out a shaky breath. Just talking about it, made her want to do it all over again.

She shivered and then shared. "He began again, minus the spanking part. This time, he projected his tension—his sexual build-up—over our mind-link. His arousal fed mine and, well, let's just say it was an explosive situation. Then after all that, he took me from behind in the shower and told me later..." Bria looked down at her fingers as she pleated her dress. "...later, he'd take my ass."

"God, when Huw did that the first time..." Nadia waved a hand as if erasing the scene from her mind. "No, I can't think about it, or I'll spontaneously combust right here in front of the upper echelon of Prime society."

Mel nodded, a slight smile and a dreamy look in her eyes. "It's really nice when done right. I'm sure Susa worked with all three on the technique."

"Susa?" Bria licked her lips and checked that her mental shields were up and the men still occupied at the bar. "Is she here tonight?"

Mel looked around while Nadia frowned. Obviously Nadia wasn't a fan of Susa.

Bria's supposition was proven true when Nadia said, "Really, Mel. Do you think Lorinda would insult us that way?

I know the sex surrogates are accepted in the higher levels of society, but the Caradocs are introducing two new *gemates* to their friends and family."

Mel shook her head. "I don't see her. And Nadia, you need to get over Susa. I feel sorry for her. Think of what her life must have been like. No love. No closeness. No chance at children. Just sex with men whom she might or might not have even liked."

"But Mel...Huw..." Nadia started.

Mel cut her off. "Huw was being an ass—and in total, mule-headed denial when he went to her that one time, and I will remind you it was only once. You two didn't know what was happening. You didn't mark first, so Huw, while intensely attracted to you, was confused. Now, we know Terrans, if they mark, bond in reverse. But you two had to go through what you did for us to realize it."

"You're right. But I still don't want to meet the woman face-to-face and picture her doing intimate loving things with my mate." Nadia wrinkled her nose. "It would be icky."

Bria had to laugh. "Icky is a good word. And, I have to say, I feel the same as Nadia. But I also would like to help the sex surrogates find spouses or *gemats*, whichever the case might be. Because I agree with Mel, women like Susa must feel isolated and alone."

'You're both nicer than I am," Nadia said. "But I understand your points."

Bria rubbed her hand over her lower abdomen. "Changing the subject, I think Iolyn and I might also need to sneak out and hit our suite before dinner. I really need him...right now. Is it always like this?"

We will make time, peata. *Just hold on for a few more minutes.*

Obviously, his empathy reading was on high and fine-tuned to her even in this huge crowd. Plus, she'd let her partial shields slip at the end.

Stay fully open, please. Mel was attacked in this very room when she was introduced to the family.

There could be rebels here?

They can be anywhere.

"Bria, that's the way it was—and is—with Wulf and me," Mel said. "He can make love to me for hours and then an hour after the last orgasm, I'm aching for him again. The only way I get any work done is to ignore the need until it's more convenient. It also helps that we work together."

"Cheri and Zaek are sure taking advantage of that workplace proximity," Bria said.

Mel and Nadia laughed.

"I really need to learn how you manage getting things done," Bria continued. "Before our gym session today, I was fairly certain I'd discovered the reason why some Prime women aren't conceiving—and why the ones that do conceive, lose their babies. I need a larger sampling of Prime women from different parts of the Cejuru solar system so I can test my hypothesis. But I can't do my job *and* have sex every time the urge hits."

"It should slow down," Nadia said, then looked at Mel. "Why aren't you slowing down? In fact, I thought you had. Bria's newly mated, so her frequency and the urgency of it makes sense. Huw and I were like that initially, but have tapered off some. Is it the Terran versus Prime thing?"

Mel blushed and shook her head. "Um, I think my hormones are elevated, and Wulf is reacting to the scent."

Bria leaned in and said in a tone that didn't carry beyond the three of them. "Are you pregnant?"

"I think so." Mel briefly touched Bria's arm. "Lia ran a test for me after we left the gym, and it showed positive. Lia was going to tell you tomorrow, so you could look at the test results and see if you saw anything that might cause me to lose the child. I don't want to say anything yet and get anyone's hopes up. I could miscarry."

"You also don't want to paint a bigger target on your back for the fanatics," muttered Nadia.

"That, too," Mel agreed, a look of fear in her green eyes.

"We won't say a word." Bria glanced at Nadia who nodded. "I'm almost one hundred percent sure I know what causes the miscarriages, so I can easily spot that abnormality on any uterine tissue sample. Did Lia take some tissue?

"She did, and enough blood to make me woozy. I want to be there when you look at my tissue sample."

"Fine with me," Bria said.

"I want to be there also." Nadia blushed. "I think I'm pregnant, too."

"I'll run the tests personally," Bria said. "I'm sure you both are fine. You didn't grow up here, nor did I. I haven't found the abnormality in my tissue, and I'm fairly sure it's not in either of yours since I ran tests on you before for Lia. We'll look at new samples just to make sure, though. Okay?"

"Thanks, Bria. I feel better already," Nadia said.

Mel nodded. "Me, too." Then she turned to look at their men approaching. The stalwart starship captain sighed. "Aren't they the most gorgeous creatures you've ever seen in your life?"

"Oh hell, yeah," Nadia breathed softly.

"None better," Bria said. "And I'm a doctor and treated my share of men during my earlier training."

The three Caradoc brothers were definitely sigh-worthy and drool-worthy.

"I haven't told Wulf about the pregnancy, either," Mel said. "He'd try to lock me up until the baby was born. My mind is normally an open book to him, but I've got this knowledge tucked into a corner of my mind with strong shields. We've been together long enough he respects that one corner and doesn't try to break through."

"I get that." Bria smiled at Iolyn who smiled back. Her sexual neediness seemed to lower to a simmer as he neared.

Just the increase in the strength of his scent calmed her down. But she still wanted to fuck his brains out—and soon. "I keep all sorts of things from Iolyn. He has to learn to trust me before I give him free reign in my head. Your secret is locked down in my mental wall safe."

"Thanks." Mel hugged her. "Lia said you'd want to monitor me closely."

"She's right." Bria lowered her voice even more. "I don't know what on-planet is causing Prime women's immune systems to become imbalanced and to allow the harmful bacteria to overwhelm the good. So I'll keep an eye on those of us who haven't lived here to see if whatever caused the damage is still doing so."

"What's that about good bacteria versus bad bacteria?" Iolyn asked. "And damage?"

"My, what big ears you have, my *gemat*." Bria took the glass of scotch he offered and took a hefty sip.

"The better to listen and keep you out of trouble with, little menace." He stroked a hand over her ass and then squeezed. "Now, answer my question."

She wrinkled her nose at him. "Okay, earlier today..."

"Before the attack in the gym?" Iolyn asked.

"Yes, before I went to the gym...where I and two other battle-mates held our own," Bria replied. The other men laughed. Iolyn grinned and shook his head. Mel and Nadia saluted her with their glasses. "Cheri and I made a discovery on what could be the primary cause for the high incidences of infertility and miscarriage in Prime women who've lived on Cejuru Prime—and possibly other planets in this system—all their lives. It's a microbe that lives in most hominid species, but the body's immune system normally keeps it in check with..."

"The good bacteria," Huw interjected with a grin.

"Exactly." Bria grinned back. "Something...be it environmental or in the food chain...has caused Prime women's immune systems to become suppressed. Simply put, the balance has been upset and the bad microbes are winning."

"What do the bad microbes do? Exactly," Wulf asked.

"They keep the fertilized egg from attaching to the uterine wall. In miscarriages, the microbe makes the placenta a deadly environment for the fetus and causes a spontaneous abortion."

"What about the women who do manage to carry to term?" Iolyn asked. "Why are they different?"

"They may not have been exposed to the damaging environmental cause or they have a natural immunity." Bria shrugged. "I won't know until I can run tests on a wider sampling of women from around the system and find patterns. Cheri's *gemat* Zaek is already designing the databases and queries for when I get the actual data."

"Will you be able to help the women even if you don't find the cause right away?" Huw asked.

"Yes." She smiled. "But it would be nice to find the pathogen or poison that is damaging the immune systems. More than women might be affected, you know."

"*Diew*, I'm a lucky man." Iolyn kissed her. "You've been on-planet less than a standard week, most of it in bed with me." He grinned when she poked him in the stomach. "And you're already solving problems our physicians overlooked for years."

Bria frowned. "Have you ever wondered why that is? Cheri and I have." She knew what she and her friend thought, it would be interesting to see what this group thought.

"Stupidity, maybe?" Nadia asked. "Couldn't see the forest for the trees?"

"Maybe." Bria hummed under her breath.

"But you don't think so," Wulf said, his narrowed gaze fixed on her.

"No, I don't. I found it too easily, and let's just say, the women who've volunteered for our research project have brought medical records with them that are less than complete." Bria sighed. "I'll want to question the head researcher at the Prime Reproductive Institute and visit some of the physicians represented in the sampling I have. Lia will help me."

Her brother-kin already suspected a conspiracy. She could tell by how he'd voiced his non-question, from the slight nod of his head, and how his lips twisted into a slight smile of approval. He was his father's heir—she'd bet her life that Ilar had suspicions about the fertility and miscarriage issues and that was why he'd pushed joining the Alliance. He must've told Wulf about them.

She and Cheri were on the right track about a conspiracy. But who was the head conspirator?

"And the *Leonidas*'s chief medical officer, Kerr Lenke, can help," Wulf suggested, though it sounded more like an order. "We'll be in space dock for a while. The rest of Gold can handle policing the rim. Father wants us to stay here and help get to the bottom of who is fomenting rebellion."

"What you mean is Father wants to use us as catalysts to bring things to a boil so it explodes sooner," Iolyn said. "I'm not sure I like Bria being bait."

Huw snarled. "I don't like Nadia being bait, either. You agreed to this, Wulf?"

"Wulf and I put the plan together," Mel said. "We need closure. We need to know we can go about our business, be with our loved ones, enjoy our lives without having guards and worrying about who'll stab or shoot us in the back."

"I agree," Bria said.

Mel and Nadia needed to know they could carry their babies safely and not have to worry about the little ones being hurt or killed.

"I also agree," Nadia said. "We can't hide. We have to face them, call the cowards out into the open—whoever they might be."

"I see one of them right now." Huw growled and the other two men joined in until the air surrounding them sounded and felt like millions of angry bees had entered the room.

"Stop it," hissed Nadia.

Bria nodded. "I hate that specific growl."

Though she liked the one Iolyn emitted when he made love to her—or wanted to make love to her. That low rumbling, like a rough purr, made her pussy melt.

Curious as to who could make them so angry so quickly, she turned to follow the three men's angry gazes. The man at whom they aimed their enmity was tall as all Prime males seemed to be, but he carried more bulk around his middle. His dark hair had strands of silver in it. He wore the regalia of a member of the Prime Elder Council.

"Who is he?" Bria asked.

Iolyn pulled her to his side without taking his eyes off the man in question. "That's Darga Caradoc."

"The one whose sons tried to kill Mel?"

"That's the slime-sucking *apayebo*." Wulf pulled Mel into his arms and kissed the top of her head. His arm cuddled her waist; his hand covered her still-flat abdomen and rubbed it in small circles. "You okay, little one?"

It was in that moment Bria knew Mel hadn't been successful in keeping her secret from her man. Wulf knew about the pregnancy. He looked at Bria and shook his head slightly.

Bria nodded. She'd keep his secret just as she'd continue to keep Mel's.

"If Father tries to introduce Darga to Nadia," Huw snarled. "Then we'll leave."

"I agree," Iolyn stated in a terse tone she had never heard from him before. "I don't want Bria exposed to him, either."

"Well, since Huw and Nadia had already planned to visit his old suite for some," Bria paused and then said, "nookie, I think we should leave also. We can sneak into the dining room in between courses. Lorinda said there would be nine of them. I know I can't eat that much food." She swept a hand over Iolyn's tense back, soothing him, soothing her. "So, what do you say we skip out before your parents come to find us?"

Huw shot Bria a grateful look. "Sister-kin, that is a wonderful idea." He gently nudged Nadia toward a side entrance, which led to the back hallway where there were stairs to the family's quarters.

"I love you, little menace." Iolyn anchored her close to his side and followed Huw and Nadia out the door.

"Keep moving," Wulf urged quietly from behind them. "Mel and I want to visit my old rooms."

Mel's low laugh made Bria smile. It seemed that all the Caradoc brothers' *gemates* were going to get lucky before dinner.

CHAPTER 17

Later that night
Caradoc family home
Iolyn and Bria's suite

Bria sat at the master bathroom vanity and moisturized her face. She massaged the creamy oil into her neck, soothing taut muscles that still hadn't relaxed.

The family dinner had been long and stressful—and considering she'd gone into the dinner with every muscle limp from the sexual interlude she and Iolyn had sneaked in between cocktails and the first course—that was an understatement.

The cause of all the tension was Darga Caradoc.

Iolyn had refused to allow the introduction Darga sought—and Ilar hadn't pressed the issue. But she'd sensed the emotions pouring off Darga clear down the very long table. His emotional aura was a dark and nasty mix of hate, envy, and greed—tinged with mental instability.

She didn't find it hard to picture him as the man behind the rebellion, but proving his role was another matter. Personally, she'd never turn her back on him for fear of getting stabbed.

Iolyn's parents deserved an award for acting since they sat near the man and conversed with him during the early food courses.

By course four, and however many alcoholic beverages he'd consumed, Darga had made clear his opinions about the veracity of Nadia being a *gemate*—she couldn't be, because she was Terran—and about battle-mates' existence—they were merely myths. The insults, both direct and indirect, had continued, and by course five, Ilar had finally had enough.

Darga had been escorted off the estate by security. With his departure, a dark and weighty pall had been removed from the remainder of the dinner.

But Bria's personal tension wasn't as easily lifted—Darga was irrational, delusional, and very, very dangerous. He was a threat to all she had come to hold dear.

Iolyn moved behind her and placed a kiss on the top of her head. He wore only a low-slung pair of loose pants. His skin glowed golden in the lights from the dressing table vanity. His hair glistened with moisture from his shower.

He flicked the straps of her silk night slip off her shoulders and then stripped the garment down her body until it pooled around her waist. "Did you forget the rule about no clothing in our bedchamber?" He leaned over and placed a kiss on her naked shoulder.

She shivered from anticipation, excitement, and some trepidation of what was to come. Her *gemat* was ready to play as he had on-ship during the trip from Oz to Cejuru Prime. With the exception of the spanking after the attack in the gym and the interlude between drinks and dinner, her man had made sweet, sensual love to her many, many times over the last week on-planet, giving her more pleasure than she ever thought she'd know. He'd told her it was a tradition, and that the sexual energy from the sensual mating fed the planet's soul. A very romantic notion.

But tonight Iolyn intended to feed his needs and, thus, hers, since with the *gemat-gemate* bond their needs were one in the same. Or so he said.

Tonight would be all about fucking.

"*Peata*," he murmured into her hair, just above her ear. She shivered as his warm, moist breath tickled the sensitive rim of her ear. "Did you forget the rule?"

"No." She smiled at his image in the mirror.

"Little menace," Iolyn growled. His golden eyes glittered with heat, desire, and the sensual promise of retribution. And her body instantly responded to his look.

Knowing it was a futile exercise, she made her excuse for putting on the dainty slip anyway. "I would've taken it off before I entered the bedroom. I'm not used to sitting around naked."

"Get used to it." His voice was husky. It was the voice he used when he was ready to dominate her...fuck her. His thoughts were all about taking her on any available surface in any position he could. His aura was incendiary and ramping up to explosive.

Yet he restrained himself, made no move to carry her off to their bed, and instead, began to massage her shoulders, digging into her deltoids with his thumbs. "You're tight. What's bothering you?" He followed his question with a bite to the side of her neck, then licked away the sting.

She shuddered under his touch. Damn, she needed him inside her, but she sensed he'd make her wait. He liked to make her wait—and beg for release. She liked the results.

"Bria, *lubha*," he squeezed her shoulders, "are you listening? What's wrong?"

"I want you."

"That's making you tense?" He stiffened and cast her a sharp glance filled with concern.

"No." His body and eyes visibly relaxed, and he resumed kneading the muscles along her shoulder and neck. "That's making me tremble with anticipation," she admitted.

Iolyn smiled and chuckled. "Good. I want you to think of how I'll fuck you, then how I'll make love to you all night long. But, first, I need an answer to my question." He sighed and glared at her in the mirror. "You know...if you kept your mind wholly open to me, I wouldn't have to guess what's wrong."

"Uh-huh. That feels so good." She moaned and let her head fall back against his naked chest where his *gemat* mark swirled and glowed with his arousal.

"*Peata*," Iolyn purred the words against her ear, "tell me, why are you so tense?"

"Dinner."

She was fairly sure he'd catch her meaning; her mind wasn't that closed to him. Plus, she'd had to squeeze his thigh several times during the first five, horribly long courses to halt his subvocal growl—the preliminary, as she'd quickly learned over the course of their trip to Cejuru Prime, to the I-want-to-rip-your-throat-out growl of *batel rabia*.

With so many Prime males in the massive formal dining room, Bria couldn't chance his rage getting out of control. She was almost positive calming her mate to keep him from declaring war during his parents' dinner party was one of her duties as a battle-mate.

"I have more discipline than that, *lubha*." He nibbled down the side of her neck and onto her shoulder. Her skin broke out in chill bumps, and she shivered with a mixture of delight and need. "But I'm happy you have my back. Now, what bothered you, or shall I guess?"

"Oh, please guess." She turned her face and licked a purple-colored swirl on his mark.

His body jerked at her touch. He inhaled sharply, then tilted her head backwards and took her lips in a deep, tongue-thrusting kiss. When he broke off the kiss that had her panting and her clit throbbing, he muttered, "Behave."

Then he kissed the top of her head as he softly touched her mind and stared at her in the mirror. "Darga's insults bothered you."

"Yes, but it was more his tone and the emotions coming off him."

"When he called you, Mel, and Nadia *karotes*..." Iolyn's voice was so gritty it could've shredded paper. "I wanted to cut out his filthy tongue."

"That word means whores, doesn't it?" She watched him nod in the mirror. His eyes sparked with his anger. Figuring he couldn't get any madder—plus, she had to know—she asked, "What does *sued-seuater* mean?"

Iolyn's hands tightened on her shoulders. She inhaled sharply. He immediately loosened his grip and smoothed away the pain. "Where did you hear that word?" His voice shook from the force of his rage.

Okay, he could get madder.

"Is it bad?" He nodded, one short terse nod. She bit her lip, then said, "Um, in the gym. One of the intruders used it. What does it mean?"

"Seed-sucker or cum slut." Iolyn leaned over and placed his face next to hers. "If anyone ever calls you that, I want to know so I can silence the *apayebo*. Understand?"

Bria nodded. "Is that why your father ejected Darga? Because he called us whores."

"Yes. You belong to a Caradoc now. No one insults our women, not even another Caradoc." Iolyn rubbed her shoulders and kissed the top of her head.

"From the stories Mel and Nadia told me, I would've banished Darga a long time ago to one of your tundra planetoids for his sons' attempts to kill Mel." Bria frowned. "Why hasn't your father done something about Darga before now?"

"Wulf thinks Father wants to give Darga enough rope to hang himself and hopes he'll lead us to the other rebels." Iolyn shrugged. "Father couldn't morally or legally blame Darga's sons' bad acts on him. Father had to be fair."

"I like your father." Bria rubbed her cheek against his torso. "I adore your mother. She's going to help me plant gardens like hers on our property when our home is done. But most of all, I love you. I think you need to fuck, then love, all the tension from dinner right out of me."

"My pleasure, *peata*." Iolyn licked down her neck along her shoulder until he reached the ball, then retraced his path until he arrived at the juncture with her neck. He bit her there, just hard enough to leave the light impressions of his teeth.

The sharp twinge of pain shot to her clit and made her already damp folds even wetter.

"It's time, *peata*. Tonight, I'll replace the anal plug with my cock."

Bria tensed then wiggled as the plug shifted in her ass. She'd worn a plug at least once a day, most often during sex, since Iolyn had first introduced her to one on the journey to Cejuru Prime, increasing the plug size every other time.

This evening, Iolyn had placed the largest plug yet into her when they'd taken the sexual edge off between drinks and dinner.

Initially, as with all the other plugs he'd used on her, it had hurt like hell. All she could think of was pushing it out. But his whispered promises of a spanking, first, with his hand, then a leather paddle if she let the plug slip out, had kept her from acting on the impulse. Her ass was still sore from the spanking he'd given her earlier today.

After several hours of too much rich food and drink plus the distraction of all the dark undercurrents floating around the Caradoc table and then the drama with Darga's ejection, she'd forgotten all about the thing in her ass.

Until now. The nasty little sucker seemed huge once more. No pain really, just an uncomfortable fullness.

Iolyn picked her up and carried her into the bedroom. He placed her flat on her back on the bed which had been turned down and had a lot of items laid out upon it. Her man had been a busy bee while she'd taken off her makeup and had a bath.

"Bondage?" She shot him one sidelong look as she took in the softly lined leather cuffs, chains attached to the bed in various places, a black satin blindfold, a huge pump bottle of lube, and other objects she'd only seen once before—in the sex boutique on Jump Station Charybdis. Her brother and Borac sold sex toys such as the ones lying on the huge bed.

"Please tell me you didn't buy those," she swept a hand at the array, "from my brother?" She practically choked on the words and could feel her face turning hot pink at the idea he might have.

Iolyn frowned. "I'd never embarrass you that way. It's none of your brother's business what we do in the privacy of our bedroom."

"Well, that's a relief." Bria rubbed her hot cheeks, then let her hands fall to the bed. "So..." the word came out on a slow exhale, "what's the scene?"

Iolyn chuckled and leaned over her to brush a kiss over her lips. "Have you been reading up on BDSM, little menace?"

"Well," she grumbled. "I thought it might be smart so I'd know what to say *no* to. Right?"

"*Lubha*, if you'd keep your mind completely open, I'll always know when something scares you—and I'll stop. You won't need to say a word." He placed the cuffs on her wrists, tightening them just enough but not too tightly, and then clipped them to chains attached to the bedposts at the head of the bed.

Her breath hitched as she tested the bonds and found she had little to no room to move. Soon her ankles would be similarly restricted. She'd be bound, unable to escape.

Bria moaned. A fluttering of her vaginal muscles indicated she'd had a mini-orgasm at just the thought of being under

Iolyn's mastery. He could sexually tease, sensually torment, and keep her on the sharp cusp of pleasure for hours, as he'd proven on the *Galanti*.

And she wouldn't be able to do one damn thing about it—except keep open lines of communication.

"Okay, fine. I'll open up." She glared at him. "But stay out of the little corner of my mind I've walled up like a maximum security prison. Those secrets aren't my own. They're patients' secrets, and you shouldn't be looking at them. Okay?"

"Yes." He stroked his hands up and down the curves of her torso, soothing her. "I'd never breach your professional confidences."

Bria nodded and let her shields down, all but for the one keeping Mel's and others' secrets.

Iolyn groaned as if a wave of pleasure had hit him. "Your mind is beautiful. You're beautiful. Being inside your head is almost as exciting and sexy as making love to your body."

She reached for his mind and moaned as his strength, his love, his desire filled her thoughts, then reached all the way to her soul. It warmed her throughout, wrapping her in his protective, loving strength. Previously, she'd limited seeking his mind to times of danger and during the final culmination of pleasure during sex. But this complete openness was different and utterly fulfilling.

Now she understood why Mel kept her mind open to Wulf. The telepathic connection was the bedrock of and reinforced the unity of the mating bond. It meant never-ending love, support, and companionship. Mind. Body. Soul.

Iolyn closed his eyes and moaned low in his throat. His thick, dark brown lashes lay like feathers on his stark cheekbones. He looked as if he were having a religious experience.

His mental touch swept through her like a warm, gentle breeze. He was learning her needs and wants even as he cherished her openness.

"You love the idea of being tied and taken." Iolyn looked pleased as he placed a reverent kiss on her mouth. "I promise not to disappoint you, *peata*."

He moved to her ankles and cuffed them. He then ran a soothing finger along the top of each foot before attaching the ankle cuffs to the chains at the bottom corners of the bed. Her legs were now wide open, exposing her sex for whatever Iolyn wished to do.

"What I plan, *peata lubha*, is to give you intense pleasure over and over before fucking your pussy—with the anal plug in place." He swept a hand up the leg closest to him and stopped just short of the juncture of her thigh and pussy. "That, my little menace, will be as close as you ever get to a menage. Prime males don't share their *gemates*."

Bria inhaled sharply and shook her head. "I'm not sure you'll fit."

Her man's cock was thick and long. It already filled her to bursting when they made love.

"I'll fit." He sat on the side of the bed and idly fondled one breast while he used the index finger on his other hand to stroke circles over her mons, just missing her aching clit each and every time.

"And after I come inside your pussy, then I'll start all over, giving you pleasure again and again while my cock recovers."

Her man did love to make her come...and come...and come.

Iolyn leaned over. Leaving his hand covering her mons in place, he moved the hand massaging her breast, which felt swollen and needy. He licked and then suckled a nipple before releasing it with a loud *pop*. "Then next time I come into you"—his breath was warm over her wet, chilled bud—"I'll take your anal virginity, but only after..."

He chuckled and lightly bit the turgid nipple.

"After...what?" Her words came out on a breathy exhale.

"I'll deny your pleasure until you ask for my cock in your ass."

Bria remained silent. She hated it when she was right. Iolyn liked it when she opposed his will for as long as she could. He was the epitome of a predator, and she was his captive prey.

Eventually, she'd submit to his will, but she'd give him the thrill of the "chase."

She'd give in as she had the other times they'd incorporated the D/s dynamic into their sexual play. Iolyn had already proven he was an expert at reading her body language. Now that he was in her head, he'd be able to manipulate her pleasure even more closely.

By allowing him to bind her, to exert his will, she'd already acquiesced to the sexual games her mate liked to play. And she liked the end results.

Bria trusted Iolyn. He wouldn't hurt her.

"I would sooner slit my throat than hurt you." He leaned over and placed a light kiss on her stomach.

"I know." She smiled. "I love you."

"And I love you." He resumed the massage of her breast and mons with an occasional tapping of one finger on the anal plug. "You truly aren't afraid of me fucking your ass."

It wasn't a question. Just a reiteration of what he'd gleaned from her mind.

She shook her head.

"I want to hear the words, Bria," Iolyn said softly. "I want to be absolutely sure this is what you want."

"Do I want it? No. But I'm not afraid." She looked into his eyes and smiled. "I also see in your mind that *you* really want...no, you need this. It seems to be a Prime imperative. A territorial claiming. I'm willing to do this for you—at least once. If I don't like it, you'll know as soon as I do."

"Yes, I will—and I'll stop if your pain is unbearable. But I think you might like it, *peata*." Then Iolyn cupped her face with his hands and took her mouth in a deep, ravenous kiss.

We'll see. She groaned deep in her throat as he slid one, then two fingers into her sex and began to stroke the spongy spot on her vaginal wall that pushed her into a quick, sharp orgasm.

Yes, we will.

Iolyn drove her through six back-to-back orgasms before entering her pussy and taking his own pleasure. Without pausing, he pulled from her and proceeded to give her another orgasm. After checking to make sure she was comfortable, he teased and tormented her, keeping her on edge until he'd recovered fully.

His cock was once again hard, and he ached to bury it in her ass. He touched the surface of her mind. Her thoughts were fixed on her next orgasm. She teetered precariously on the peak of mind-blowing pleasure, just where he needed her so he could take her anal virginity and make it good for her.

Iolyn moved away from suckling her breasts and fingering her clit.

She moaned. "Iolyn...please..."

"Shh. I'll take care of you." He stroked a hand over her sweaty forehead and placed a kiss on her lips. "Just one adjustment then I'll please both of us."

Leaving her on her back, he reconnected her ankle cuffs to the head of the bed and shoved a pillow under her hips.

"Now, I'll claim your ass." He uttered the words. His tone was guttural and raw with primal lust.

Yes, the feelings of what this act meant to him were savage, elemental. The act itself was territorial, yet another physical marking of Bria as his and his alone. The claiming of this last virginal vestige of Bria's body would make up for another male taking her hymen.

Iolyn...

No, lubha. *Say nothing. I know you didn't realize what the* gemate *mark meant. This is just what I need.*

I understand.

"*Gemat*?" Bria's voice was a mere whisper. She sounded tired from the almost three-standard-hour-long session of sex play, strained from her need to come again.

Iolyn grimaced. *Diew,* he was a beast. He'd pushed her limits, but he couldn't stop now...the final act was an imperative he couldn't deny.

But that wasn't completely true...if Bria asked him to stop, he would. Her needs would always come above his—every damn time from now until eternity. He loved her more than his own life and would do anything for her.

"Yes, Bria?"

"Fuck my ass."

Love. Relief. Desire. Adoration. The mix of emotions swept through him, making him harder than he could ever remember.

"With pleasure, *peata*."

With one hand cupping a buttock, he captured her loving gaze with his and then notched his generously lubed cockhead into her rear opening. He fed his painfully hard cock slowly, but steadily, into her tight channel, stopping every couple centimeters to allow her to adjust.

Once his cock was lodged, they sighed as one.

"Are you okay, *lubha*?" He'd touched her mind, but needed her verbal response.

His jaw clenched as he checked the urge to move in and out of her ass. He'd almost come as soon as he'd entered her fully, his aching balls pulsating against her bottom.

"I need..." She frowned and then glared at him. "I need to...come. So...move."

Iolyn groaned. "Yes."

As he began a slow push-pull movement, he watched her face for signs of pain and kept his mind merged with hers. He held her bottom steady for his thrusts with one hand and used the fingers of his other to trace her labia and clit, building her excitement level back to where it had been before he'd entered her ass.

Bria moaned with each retreat of his cock and grunted with each advance. He found no pain in her mind, only her need to climax—and that she also needed...more. More stimulation. More speed. Just more.

Needs he was pleased to fulfill.

Iolyn increased the speed of his hips until he was pistoning his cock into her. The fingers of his one hand were wet with her vaginal juices as he focused on rubbing her clit with his thumb and stroking the spongy erogenous zone inside her pussy with two fingers.

The gasps and guttural sounds coming from Bria heightened his arousal. The sight of her breasts with their jutting rosy nipples swaying and bouncing with each push-pull of his cock made him groan.

Diew, she was a wondrous and beautiful creature. And all his.

As Bria screamed and arched her neck with her orgasm, her tight channel gripped him like a vice. The strength of her climax swept through him physically and over their mind link, sucking him into the maelstrom of her pleasure and igniting his own.

Iolyn's climax tore through him like lightning. He threw his head back and shouted his release to the ceiling. His mind was a chaotic swirl of feelings intertwining and curling with hers, feeding from her pleasure and then returning the same a hundredfold.

As he shot one last spurt of cum inside her tight ass, she moaned and then went boneless under him.

Still connected, breathing heavily, he lowered her hips back to the support pillow and then supported himself on his forearms to lean over her torso and nuzzle along her neck and onto her shoulder. "You're beautiful. Amazing."

"Uh-huh. You, too." She opened her eyes, heavy-lidded with exhaustion. "So tired. Hold me?"

"Always."

He chuckled. She looked so cute. He placed a reverent kiss on her lush lips, then moved off her and unbuckled her cuffs. By the time he'd freed her and massaged her limbs, she was sound asleep.

He straightened the bed, cleaned himself up, wiped a warm cloth over her body with special attention to her bottom, and then slid in next to her. After placing her on her side, he cuddled her ass against his front, placed an arm over her waist, and pulled her into his body. He lightly touched her dreaming mind and found her fantasies now included him taking her ass from behind. He was on board with that position.

Iolyn smiled. His little menace liked what he'd done to her—and the One knew, he liked doing it. Fully sated, as he fell asleep, he planned how he'd awaken her in the morning.

CHAPTER 18

Bria awakened instantly. Something was wrong, but she didn't know what. She turned within Iolyn's arms and found him watching her.

"Do you feel it?" she whispered as she leaned into his warmth and strength and gained comfort from his mere presence.

"Yes." He looked over his shoulder toward the wide expanse of glass doors leading to the balcony off their third-story suite. "Evil. Someone's on the balcony."

"But it's a hundred meter or more drop on this side of the house." She kept her voice low and toneless so it wouldn't carry. They'd left the doors open to the outside to catch the night breezes off the ocean.

"It's an easy climb with the right kind of gear." He pulled away from her body and lifted the covers. Soundlessly, he slid out of the bed and pulled on a pair of loose pants with a drawstring waist to cover his nakedness. He threw her his T-shirt. "Put this on and go into the closet and hide."

Bria caught the shirt and dragged it on, muttering under her breath, "Like hell I'll hide." But Iolyn wasn't close enough to hear her response. He was already at the glass door and slipping outside. His mind was fully occupied with the hunt. She spotted a laser pistol in one of his hands and a battle-blade in the other. She had no clue where he'd found those weapons, but was glad he had them.

Moving away from the bed, she tiptoed to the house com unit and pressed the alarm. It would send a silent signal to the guardhouse, and they'd soon converge on the suite.

A loud crash, roars of outrage, curse words, and then a battle cry sent icy shards down her spine. Iolyn was fighting whoever was out there all by himself. His mind was red-hot mad and edging toward the icy heat of *batel rabia*. His focus was now on the kill.

Pain struck her. Iolyn's pain.

She rubbed the phantom pain on her forearm. She gasped as she smelled, tasted the scent of his blood over their bond. He never slowed, brushed the wound off as negligible, and kept fighting. He was in full-blown battle rage now, and she found herself swept up into the morass of fierce emotions and punches of adrenaline. The other Prime coming to Iolyn's aid had already joined the wave.

Before leaving the bedroom, she checked the outer room of the suite. She saw no one, so she ran across the room in order to open the door to the hallway so Iolyn's backup could get in more quickly.

Almost to the door, she sensed rather than heard another presence in the room—the room which had been empty mere seconds ago. She looked over her shoulder. A man had entered the room through an opening in what had looked to be a solid wall. She froze in place and stared in disbelief.

Soundlessly, the intruder ran toward Bria, his arms reaching for her. Shaking off her momentary stupefaction, she spun out of his reach and executed a sweeping side kick to his knee. Mel and Nadia would've been proud. The intruder's leg went out from under him, and he stumbled away from her long enough so she could get further out of his reach.

"Bitch!" The tall male swore as he regained his balance. As he stalked her, she was happy to see him limping. She also noted he wasn't Prime. She wasn't sure what he was other than some sort of humanoid-looking hybrid—and her enemy.

Keeping a wary eye on him for any sudden moves, Bria searched peripherally for a weapon. Any weapon. She vowed never to be caught weaponless again.

Backing away from the man, she edged toward the kitchen. Lots of nice sharp things in a kitchen. Heavy pans would do in a pinch.

All she had to do was keep him from hurting or taking her. Help was on its way. The wave of *batel-rabia*-roused males was getting closer. What she didn't want to do was distract her warrior-*gemat* while he fought for his life.

She grabbed a nice sharp paring knife from the block by the stove. She threw it a bit wildly, because the man had gotten far too close for comfort. The knife took a chunk of flesh out of his upper arm. Her would-be attacker cried out, stopped, and then stared in shock at the rent in his shirtsleeve and the blood leaking from his arm.

Taking advantage of his momentary stupor, she selected another knife—a butcher knife—and took careful aim. This time, the knife lodged in his shoulder.

This time his roar of "Fucking bitch" attracted Iolyn's attention.

Iolyn shouted, "Bria!" Then his battle cry echoed off the walls. But he couldn't get to her, his way was blocked by the two men he fought.

Bria...you all right?

She sensed him dividing his attention between the two attackers and her.

I'm fine, gemat. *Take care of yourself. I have lots of knives to go through yet.*

As much as she didn't want to take a life, she was done messing around. If she didn't eliminate the danger to her, then Iolyn would get himself killed trying to get to her. That was absolutely unacceptable.

She picked up another, thinner knife. She tested the point. Nice and sharp. With the right force, she could take the man out.

You aren't in the closet. You are so in trouble, lubha.

Whatever. Watch your ass. I like it.

"So not worth it...taking you in alive." The male, whom she could see now had a small amount of reptile in his DNA, uttered. "He'll just have to accept you dead." He raised a laser weapon she hadn't seen—then he fell to the floor with a grunt.

Bria stopped her throwing motion and thanked the One she didn't have to kill anyone. She then grinned at her savior.

Her father-in-law stood in the middle of the suite's living area. Like a dark Viking god, his long hair flowed about his shoulders, and he wore a loose pair of pants similar to Iolyn's—and nothing else. Her geneticist's eye noted the strong musculature for a man his age, while her woman's heart fluttered. Lorinda was a lucky woman. Ilar was one sexy and strong warrior—and his sons hadn't fallen far from that tree at all.

Several of the Caradoc estate guards ran past Ilar and onto the balcony. She touched Iolyn's mind and found him immersed in gruesome satisfaction that he'd dispatched his two opponents.

Ilar, oblivious to her previous and totally inappropriate under the circumstances thoughts, cast a concerned look at her. "Are you all right, daughter-kin?"

"Super." That wasn't completely true. Her knees were shaking. Her throat was so tight it felt as if she was breathing through a glass pipette. However, she was alive and unharmed, so maybe her response wasn't a total lie.

Bria came around the counter, knife in hand, just in case any more intruders popped out of the walls. "Where did they come from? How did they get into the house?" The place was a fortress with sheer cliffs on three sides and a heavily gated and guarded front entrance. "I swear that one," she pointed at the moaning mass on the floor, "came through the wall."

Ilar looked at the wall in question. "There are hidden passages all over the house, built for escape during a siege. They lead to the cave system below the house. You're family now. Iolyn should've shown you the escape routes and safe rooms."

"Well, we've been sort of busy," she muttered. "He will now, for sure."

Ilar's expression darkened. His increasing anger felt like a storm front cutting through the room. She wouldn't have been surprised to see lightning and hear its resulting thunder. She braced a hand on the bar counter separating the kitchen from the sitting area.

"This never should have happened. My security has some explaining to do." Ilar paused and took several deep breaths and then it was as if his emotional tempest had never happened. She really needed to learn how the Prime males did that. "As for how they got in? Someone had to let them in—and I know who."

Ilar pulled a com unit out of his pocket and made a call just as Iolyn strode into the room and said, "It was Darga!" Iolyn spat the name. "The bastard hired these mercenaries. I convinced one of them to give me their employer's name before he died."

Bria wasn't sure how to feel about her bloodthirsty mate bragging about torturing another living being, then he walked into the light and she moaned with concern. Her mate had several gashes on his gorgeous chest and blood oozing from the cut on his arm.

She tossed her knife to the side and ran to him as he came toward her.

He grabbed her by the shoulders and shook her. "What were you thinking? I told you to hide in the closet."

"Dammit! Didn't I tell you to be careful? To pay attention to your fight and not mine?" Bria slid her hands onto his chest and sighed when she realized the gashes were shallow and hadn't damaged his marking. The cut on his arm needed more immediate attention. She covered it with her hand and applied pressure to stop the bleeding.

She didn't get mad at his actions or scolding words, because they came from his deep fear of losing her. But she did need to make something clear once and for all.

"I sounded the alarm and then went to unlock the door. I checked before leaving the bedroom and didn't see anyone in the outer room. I was careful. I didn't know about the secret passages until the man entered the room through one. I defended myself until help arrived." She covered his mouth when he opened it. "And I was about to kill the bastard with a knife to the throat when your father shot him."

"*Lubha*—" Iolyn began.

"No. This battle-mate deal is a two-way street. I refuse to hide if I can do something to keep you safe." She grinned. "Plus, before I put two knives in him, I took out his knee with a nice kick Nadia and Mel taught me."

Iolyn pulled her closer to him and kissed her forehead. "I guess you'll have to continue attending yoga classes with my sister-kin then." She smiled as he brushed a kiss over her lips. "When I knew you were in danger...I couldn't fight hard enough, fast enough to get to you. I was...scared."

Bria licked his lower lip. "I know the feeling. I had to do something to get you help—fast. I knew my coming out onto the balcony to fight by your side would only be a distraction. So, I did what I could do."

"You did the right thing. I'm sorry I yelled at you." He kissed her, a deep kiss with lots of tongue. A kiss of claiming. A kiss of reassurance that both were alive and unharmed.

Ilar got off his com unit and coughed. "Children..."

They broke apart and looked Ilar's way. Bria's face burned at the knowing smile her father-in-law aimed at them. "Daughter-kin, you might want to finish caring for your mate's arm, which is dripping all over his mother's silk carpets."

"I got distracted by his chest..." Iolyn laughed. She glared. "...wounds."

Bria moved away and into the kitchen where she'd seen an emergency medical kit in the pantry. "Sit at the kitchen counter, *gemat*. I'll clean you up and seal the cuts."

"Just clean them up, *peata*. They'll be fine." Iolyn moved to a stool, and his father joined him. Then he turned toward his father. "What are we going to do about Darga?"

"After his increasingly irrational actions and words at dinner this evening, I took the precaution of having him and his home kept under surveillance. I was afraid he would do something rash, but never thought he'd go this far. I took out two assassins in my bedroom before I came to your suite." Ilar rubbed a hand over his forehead as if he had a headache. "The surveillance team is bringing him in right now."

"What about Wulf and Mel...and Huw and Nadia?" Iolyn asked. "Have they been warned?" Bria shivered and moved toward Iolyn, who pulled her into his arms, sharing his strength and warmth.

"I contacted them as I came to your rooms." Ilar sighed. "They had also been attacked."

Bria gasped. "No." Iolyn pulled her even closer into his arms and brushed a kiss over her hair.

Her father-kin turned his heartsick gaze toward her. "They're all right. The only injuries were to the attackers."

"Thank the One," Bria pulled out of Iolyn's arms and walked behind the kitchen bar counter. She couldn't comprehend relatives killing relatives.

Pulling out the bottle of scotch, she poured both men a glass, neat, and placed the drinks on the bar within their reach. Then she poured herself one.

"Thank you, *peata*." Iolyn took a sip and sighed.

His father raised his glass to her in a silent salute and then did the same. It was cute how alike the two men were.

After a nice long drink of her own, she wiped a warm, soapy cloth over Iolyn's chest wounds. They were all but gone, in less than a few minutes. She frowned. "These were deeper when you entered the room. Does the battle-mate healing work that fast? And how did I do it? I just touched you a minute or so ago."

"No need to touch. You began healing Iolyn as soon as he received the wounds," Ilar explained.

"Really? No need to touch. That means it's all about energy and wavelengths." She looked at the two men and they both nodded. "Cool. I'll need to study how that happens on a cellular level. It might be replicable. Maybe I could do a gene-splicing and figure how to add that into other hominid DNA."

Iolyn almost snorted his scotch up his nose and ended up coughing. His father laughed and slapped him on the back. "Watch it, son."

"Only my *gemate* would think about trying to genetically engineer healing energy."

Ilar smiled. "Your *gemate* is brilliant, and I'm betting she could manage it."

"Premier Caradoc, sir!" A soldier dressed in the uniform of the Prime Military ran into the room and saluted.

"Yes, Sergeant?" Ilar stood, looking regal despite his lack of shoes and shirt.

"Darga Caradoc resisted arrest. He and whoever was in his house began firing on the security detail sent to bring him here." Noticeably pale, the soldier paused and gulped audibly. "When the tactical unit arrived and breached his front door, the house exploded. Everyone inside the home is dead, sir. The tactical unit suffered some severe injuries, but are all alive."

Ilar paced and swore under his breath. Then he stopped, pulled himself together, and concentrated on the soldier.

"Was Darga confirmed among the dead? There were escape tunnels in his home."

"He's dead, sir. He was at a window, shooting at the breaching team when the house blew apart. He was expelled from the window. He had injuries from the explosion and others from his landing on the stone courtyard." The soldier shook his head. "We checked the tunnels as soon as we could. His family couldn't have used them. The explosion collapsed them. We have to assume anyone in the house is dead. The forensic teams are on call to begin their search once the hot spots cool."

Ilar returned to his stool and sat. He looked at Iolyn and then Bria. Then he turned to face the soldier once more. "Sergeant, thank you. You may go off duty. I will visit the crime scene tomorrow to hear the forensics team's report."

"Crime scene?" Iolyn asked. "You don't think Darga set the explosion to avoid being caught and questioned as a traitor?"

"My cousin was a narcissistic, power-hungry son of a bitch. He would no more kill himself than I would." Ilar shook his head and sighed. "I have no doubt he was a part of the Pure Blood rebellion for his own personal aggrandizement. But I never really saw him as the leader. More of a scapegoat, like Beria and Luka, for the real power behind the fanatics."

"So, you're saying Darga wanted power, but wasn't a true believer?" Bria asked.

"Exactly, daughter-kin." Ilar patted her hand. "The person running this rebellion has an ulterior motive in spouting the Pure Blood cause. Whatever his reasons, they have their origins in the past. The true believers have been misled and misinformed, are small in number, are fanatically religious, and have been around for a long time. Historically, they have been mostly vocal."

Bria then knew for certain Ilar *did* suspect a conspiracy to sabotage the Prime birthrate. Opening Prime society to the rest of the galaxy had been his countermove to force the saboteurs out of hiding.

"Ilar, Mel pointed me to some treatises on Prime culture written by her parents. I found them very interesting. So much so that Mel introduced me to your brother Tenar at dinner. He invited me, Mel, and Nadia to tea tomorrow afternoon to share some early writings on battle-mates and also on the rise of the *gemat-gemate* marking. I want to learn the history about battle-mates for selfish reasons. But I need to discover when the *gemat-gemate* markings were first documented in Prime history. I have a theory about the bond as a genetic adaptation. I also want to see the progression of the acceptance of the markings as a cultural protocol and how that evolved into edict."

Ilar smiled and exchanged a knowing look with Bria. Then he winked at her.

"Go, enjoy yourself. Learn your people's history from my brother," Ilar said. "I'll be interested if you find anything in the historical documents that could help us defang Pure Blood. Tenar has always kept the more precious tomes close to home. Very few have been privileged to view them. You'll be safe in my brother's mountain aerie. But please take guards with you anyway."

"I don't leave home without guards. My *gemat* doesn't let me." She grinned at Iolyn, who grunted his agreement. Then she bit her lip and looked toward Ilar. "Mel didn't mention a *gemate* or children for Tenar. Did he lose them in the Antarean siege?"

"No, he never marked a woman." Ilar sighed, the sound so heavy it hurt Bria's soul. "He did love one. But she was marked by another."

"That's so sad." Bria sensed an odd tension in Ilar and an emotion that felt like regret. She hesitated before she asked, "Who was the woman?"

"My *gemate*...Lorinda." Bria gasped as Ilar closed his eyes. He looked and sounded so unhappy it made her heart hurt.

"After we marked, became bound as a couple, Tenar retreated to his mountain and didn't speak to either of us until well after Wulf was born. We made up for the sake of our people, to provide a unified family front."

"That must've been very uncomfortable for the family as a whole." *And Lorinda in particular*, Bria thought.

"It was." Ilar's lips thinned. "Tenar is still a healthy, vital male. I pray he finds a mate eventually...marked or unmarked. He needs a family of his own."

"Please, don't mention any of this to Uncle Tenar, *peata*," Iolyn said. "He gets irritable and then withdraws. Wulf used to call it 'Uncle Tenar's grumpy mood' when we were kids. He sort of scared us."

"Iolyn is exaggerating, Bria." Ilar grunted. "But it might be best if you don't let on that you know he loved Iolyn's mother and lost her to me. You may share the information with Nadia and Mel if my sons haven't already told them."

She nodded. "I don't see any reason why Tenar should realize I know."

"Well, if anyone has the knowledge you seek or knows where it is written down, my brother knows. He is the Prime Elder Council Historian," Ilar said. "There has always been a Caradoc in that position."

And Tenar could very well be one of the Elders who feared change. Bria mentally groaned. She'd have to be careful on how she asked for the information. She wasn't ready to share any of her theories. She was still placing and rearranging all the pieces of the puzzle she had.

"Tomorrow should prove to be a very educational day." Bria moved to Iolyn and let him fold her into his arms. "Now, can we go back to bed? Someone tired me out, and I need my sleep."

Iolyn laughed and threw a look over his shoulder. "If you'll excuse us, Father, I need to ensure my *peata* gets a good night's sleep. I'll see you at breakfast, and we can discuss how we are going to handle the terrorists in the Pure Blood faction."

Ilar smiled. "I'll meet you then. I'll let Wulf and Huw know to join us."

CHAPTER 19

The next morning
Alliance Astrobiology Research lab

"Yo, boss lady," Cheri called out. "I have another consult. She asked for you."

That was outside the norm. Intake was usually done by her research assistants. Once the questionnaires were filled out and blood drawn, the rotating team doctors—herself included—would do a physical exam and take uterine tissue samples.

Bria was not on the exam rotation today. She looked up from the electron microscope to find Cheri escorting a very attractive Prime woman into the Scope Room.

Since she and her team had arrived a little over a week ago, she'd met a lot of Prime women—some marked with mates, some marked who'd lost mates, and many more unmarked. All of the women wanted one thing—children. So they braved the loud, but non-violent Pure Blood picketers to participate in the research Bria's team was conducting.

Bria's profession had never been so rewarding before. Yes, she'd had past triumphs and accolades, but what she did now felt ten times better. She was helping her people survive the possibility of extinction and giving hope to women who'd had none.

"Welcome." Bria stood and held out her hand. "I'm Dr. Martin-Caradoc. How may I help you?"

The Prime woman was dressed expensively, and her make-up was artful, but also tasteful. This was a woman who took care of herself.

"I wanted to come in and thank you for helping the women of our planet." She took Bria's hand and clasped it between hers. "I'm Susa."

Bria started and pulled her hand from the woman who'd taught Iolyn everything he knew about sex. Inevitably, her thoughts turned toward comparing herself to Susa. The sex surrogate was everything Bria was not.

Iolyn is mine. She can't have him.

Bria was immediately ashamed of her reaction, even if it was perfectly normal. She and Iolyn were well and truly mated. Susa was no threat to Bria's relationship with Iolyn. The woman's emotional aura read as embarrassed, afraid, and concerned.

Embarrassed, she could understand. Afraid? Concerned? About what? Not of Bria, that was for sure. She'd come here and asked for her specifically.

Obviously, Bria's empathic reading and silence had gone on for too long, because Susa's lips turned down and her glorious golden eyes dimmed.

"Ah, I see Iolyn has spoken of me. If I make you uncomfortable, I'll leave and speak with another doctor on the team. I wanted to help by giving samples of my blood and tissue for your research project before I leave the planet."

"No, please stay, Susa. Thank you for coming." Bria waved a hand at the chair next to the scope table. "Please sit. And call me Bria. I'll be happy to do your intake. You've been a good... um, friend to my *gemat*'s family."

Susa's aura turned even more volatile. Bria read fear, regret, fondness, loneliness, sadness, and a myriad of other contradictory emotions. There was more to Susa's visit than helping out the research project.

"Thank you." Susa sat and then looked around the room, at her lap, anywhere but at Bria.

"Susa," Bria lightly touched the woman's arm, "it's okay. I'm happy you came in and asked for me."

Bria would need to start with an easy question. She wanted Susa to be at ease so the woman would say what she'd come to say. The fear and worry in the woman's aura bothered Bria a lot. "You said you were traveling? Will you be gone long?"

"Um, I don't know." Susa looked at Bria. "I'm visiting my cousin Borac on Jump Station Charybdis. His Terran mate will soon give birth, and he did not want to chance space travel with her so close to her due date."

"I've met Borac and Cissy and their toddler," Bria said. "They're a lovely family."

Susa smiled. "Borac mentioned he had met you. I'm eager to see him and help in any way I can."

"That's so nice of you going all that way to help," said Cheri, who'd taken a seat to the side of Bria's scope table in order to enter the intake data.

Susa smiled at Cheri. "He's my favorite cousin. I don't have much family left because of the Antareans, so I was happy he got in touch with me. I am thrilled he's found a mate and that they've started a family. It gives hope to other Prime who are alone."

Then Susa turned back to Bria. "You just came from the jump station. Do you think I'd like to live there...permanently?"

Bria inhaled sharply and then began choking. Susa moved to thump her on the back. "Do you need water?"

"No, um"—*cough, cough*—"just swallowed wrong." After a couple of deep breaths, she said, "It's a rough place, Susa. I was almost kidnapped twice and also attacked in the short time I was there."

"Borac has his family there. He protects them. He'll protect me."

"Yes, he does, and he will," Bria affirmed. "But Cissy and the child never, and I mean never ever, leave the safety of the secured employees' quarters. And most of the station's regular customers know Borac and his partner, my brother Damon, would deal harshly with anyone harming a woman. But you're single and very attractive and...well, marketable, if you understand what I'm saying. Dangerous passers-through could hear of you and make the extra effort to kidnap you."

"Sex traffickers." Susa nodded. "Borac mentioned I'd be restricted in my movements. He said he wouldn't allow me even to visit the bar because of the rough element, as he called it."

"Did he also tell you the bar has strippers, live sex shows on stage and that some of the entertainers give lap dances and other intimate favors in privacy rooms?" At the shocked look on Susa's face, she guessed not. "Oh, we need to talk before you leave."

"Yes, we *do* need to *talk*."

And Bria read in the woman's tone it was not about Jump Station Charybdis, but about what Susa had really come to tell Bria.

Susa looked at the clock on the wall. "Would you allow me to buy you lunch, Bria?"

The woman had noticeably, but in a nice way, excluded Cheri from this *talk*, which screamed it would be about private Caradoc family matters.

"Sure," said Bria. "Cheri, you can take a break. Maybe Zaek is ready for lunch?"

"I'm sure he is. Thanks." Cheri jumped up and left the room before Bria had even finished her sentence. Susa looked shocked.

"She's not rude. Just newly mated."

Susa laughed and her whole face changed. She wasn't merely beautiful, but downright gorgeous. Maybe Bria had better contact Borac and warn him. He'd have to put a security detail on her around the clock and outside her quarters.

Bria picked up a portable data pad. "I can ask the intake questions while we eat. And about this talk, would it be okay if I have Nadia and Mel join us? Or, would that be uncomfortable? I only ask, because later today we're having tea at Tenar Caradoc's, and they were going to meet me here and do lunch first. I think they'd like to meet you."

At the mention of Tenar's name, a look of panic wiped the smile off Susa's face. The beautiful woman feared him. Hated him. A tingling of awareness pricked Bria's mind. Susa knew something bad about Tenar. Something that streaked Susa's aura with oily black shards. It might not have been the reason she'd sought out Bria, but it would definitely be a topic to address during lunch.

Susa recovered her composure quickly. "I've met Wulf's *gemate*. She was very gracious about meeting the woman who'd had sex with her *gemat*—as were you." Susa stood up. "But I am not sure Huw's *gemate* would be happy to see me. He hurt her feelings by denying their attraction and came to me. If I had known about her, I would've told him to leave that day."

"I know." Bria patted the woman's arm. "I think you should know I can read your emotions. You're very open. Trust me...Nadia will read you just as easily. I'm sure that now she and Huw are fully bonded, there's no problem."

Well, that was a white lie. Nadia still had some issues, but her sister-kin would have to get over it. Susa knew something the Caradoc brothers' *gemates* needed to know.

Bria continued, "Plus, Nadia was with me on Jump Station Charybdis. You'll want to hear her impressions also."

"That would be fine."

They proceeded down a long corridor to the exam room, Bria's Volusian shadows several paces behind them. After Bria performed a physical examination, took tissue samples, and drew blood, she waited outside the room while Susa got dressed.

"Where shall we eat?" Susa asked when she exited the room. "The pickets are loud and rowdy today, but I have transport waiting for me. My driver is armed."

"Because of the pickets, we need to stay within the Alliance complex so Iolyn and the other *gemats* don't have fits." Bria looked over her shoulder at V'niko and A'nan, who grinned at her and made no bones about listening in. "Iolyn also has insisted on me having guards."

Susa turned her head to look back. "Oh my. They do look...competent."

Bria had to choke back a laugh. Susa's words belied her intense sexual reaction to the hunky warriors. Her arousal added hot pink streaks to her aura.

"They are. They saved me back on Oz." The she leaned over and whispered to the beautiful woman. "A'nan is single and looking."

Susa giggled, making her look young. "I'm not in the market...yet. But I'll keep him in mind. Thanks."

"We gals have to take care of our sisters."

"That's nice." Susa sighed. "I haven't felt a part of a sisterhood, outside of the other sex surrogates, in a long time. We are a part of society and yet not."

"Well, the future is yours now. You can have a family, if you wish."

"You believe you can solve the miscarriage issue?" The longing in Susa's voice was potent.

"I know why it happens. So, yes, we can treat the issue with temporary fixes. My team and I can eventually eliminate the problem completely once we find exactly what caused damage to your immune systems. You're young enough, you should be able to have children easily."

"But what about the markings? There are some of us who believe we could've mated and had children without the bond mark. But the Elder Council—" Susa stopped talking and looked around to see who might be listening. "—um, you must know how things stand here."

And there it was—one of the reasons Susa had come to Bria.

"Yes, I do know. You could've mated, but your culture allowed reproduction for only those couples who marked." Since they were alone, but for V'niko and A'nan, she asked, "Why *exactly* did you seek me out?"

Susa bit her lip and replied in a low tone, so low Bria leaned in to hear her. "You know that sex surrogates were given hormone therapy?"

"Yes. You were told it was to prevent pain from the touch of a male who was not your *gemat*. But I've tested it and it is mostly a contraceptive."

"Yes, that is what we were told." Susa looked grim. "About five standard years ago, I and several other sex surrogates agreed to test our suspicions and stopped using the hormone and took other precautions against the possibility we might get pregnant. None of us had pain before or during sex. The only sex surrogates who had pain were the marked women who'd lost their men, and that pain decreased over time without the use of the hormone therapy."

Bria nodded. "That's what I suspected, but thank you for confirming it."

"Why did you suspect such?"

"Because I lived fine with my mark for years without any pain. I asked Mel and so had she. It took our meeting our *gemats* to jump-start that side effect. It's all about neurochemistry. So, why do you think the physicians gave you the hormones and misled you and the public?"

Susa snorted. "Mainly to prevent conception. When we shared our results with the physicians assigned to us, they told us we were not doctors and not to question their expertise. Later, we received visits from some of the Elders who warned us about spreading such heresy, as they called it. The other sex surrogates and I concluded that the Elders did not want the public to realize that unmarked females could have babies or that *gemates* could have babies with another male after losing their *gemat*."

And another piece of the puzzle indicating a conspiracy just dropped into place.

"Elders threatened you?" Bria asked.

"Subtly, but yes. All of us took the warnings as a threat to our safety and livelihood." Susa shuddered. "I was so happy when Premier Caradoc opened our society up to the rest of the galaxy, I cried."

Susa slowed her pace and lowered her voice. "Not all of my peers were treated as well as I was. I had the Premier's family as my clientele. *Most* of them treated me well."

And there was the other reason Susa had come to speak to Bria. Why the woman had projected fear at the sound of Tenar's name.

And then the seeds of a potentially devastating idea took root in Bria's gut, or maybe it had been there all along. Susa's two seemingly unrelated pieces of information added details to the image forming in her mind. Her conspiracy puzzle still missed a few pieces, but she could visualize enough of the picture to guess the rest.

Bria wanted to be incorrect, but her brain and instincts told her she wasn't.

"Which Elder or Elders threatened you?" She held her breath and prayed she was wrong.

When Susa gave her three names, one of them stood out like a solar flare. The key piece to the puzzle had fallen into place. She was right—and she felt no satisfaction in that.

"Tenar Caradoc warned you away from speaking out about the truth of the hormone treatments?" Bria's throat tightened. Ilar would be devastated. He'd shown no hesitation in sending her to Tenar for more information or having his daughter-kin go to tea with the man. He'd never suspected such treachery from his younger brother.

"Yes, in his role as an Elder." Susa paled visibly. "But he always scared me, even before he threatened me." She looked away, shame and pain on her face, in her posture.

"What did he do, Susa?"

"He visited me for sex as many of the unmated Caradoc males did—and some still do." Susa shuddered. "He was cruel, rough. He also used me...frequently. He was just...wrong."

Bria stopped in the middle of the hall and turned toward Susa. She waved V'niko and A'nan back, not wanting them to hear her next query and Susa's answer. "Define 'wrong.'"

Susa's smoky green gaze locked onto Bria's face. "He liked to give pain, and not in an erotic way, if you know what I mean?"

"He hurt you?...Badly?"

Susa nodded, tears formed in her eyes, and she looked at her hands, which were fisted against her abdomen as if she had to hold her emotions inside. "He liked me bleeding, screaming." She looked up, her cheeks glistening.

Bria pulled the trembling woman into her arms and rubbed her back in soothing circular motions. V'niko started forward, concern in his eyes. Bria held up her hand, halting him.

"Thank you, Susa. I know that was hard. Would you... Damn, I hate to ask this, but would you share with Mel and Nadia what you just told me? Answer more of our questions? If you can't, I understand. But it's important. Very important to the Prime people's future."

"I figured such, but didn't trust anyone in the Council after my physician reported me to the Elders." Susa sniffed and pulled away. "I can speak with your sister-kin if I have to...but why can't you tell them what I said?"

"Because they're like me, they need to see and read the truth in your aura. They'll then feel the same urgency I feel so we can make plans about what to do about Tenar."

"Why would you do something about Tenar?" Susa gripped Bria's forearms. "Bria, he was rough...a mean sex partner. His warnings about the hormones were echoed by many of the other Elders. The last I heard, neither of those things are a crime."

Bria leaned in and whispered against Susa's ear. "But trying to kill the main line of the Caradoc family is."

"You think," Susa looked around and lowered her voice, "you think he is behind the rebellion?"

"Yes, and even more heinous acts." Bria took Susa's arm and led the way to the Officer's Lounge in the Alliance complex. "I'm beginning to believe Tenar's perfidy began long before the Antarean siege twenty-seven and a half standard years ago."

"When do you think it began?" Susa breathed out the question.

"When Ilar Caradoc mated with Lorinda."

CHAPTER 20

"That dickless bastard!" Mel fumed. "That fucking, scum-sucking, slime creature's hind end."

Bria had to bite her lip to keep from laughing. Mel did have a unique way with words. But, in truth, there was nothing amusing about this situation. Bria, however, was relieved at how quickly her sister-kin had agreed with Susa's observations and Bria's deductions.

"The *apayebo* made you bleed?" Nadia growled. The Terran blonde's buzz-saw rumblings reminded Bria of Iolyn's and his brothers' at their maddest. Her sister-kin had gotten stuck on the violent sexual abuse Tenar had perpetrated against Susa, while totally ignoring Tenar's—plus any number of unknown accomplices'—other crimes against women, unborn children, his own family, and the Prime people as a whole.

Bria understood and shared Nadia's anger. Men who abused women were pond scum.

Susa looked from Nadia then to Mel and then finally at Bria. "Yes. He also threatened me with worse injuries if I told anyone why I was incapacitated. He always made sure I didn't scar. He didn't want to leave physical evidence."

"Please tell me you documented your injuries in some way," Mel pleaded.

Mel was thinking along the same lines as Bria. They needed some written or visual proof of any of Tenar's bad acts in order to start the dominoes falling and destroy his bigger end game.

Susa went pale and remained silent for so long that Bria answered for her just in case the other two were so involved in their own emotions they hadn't read Susa's. The woman was scared and even more embarrassed, but underlying it all was a sense of vengeful satisfaction.

"Oh, yes, she did." Bria picked up Susa's cold hand from where it lay on the table and gently squeezed it. "What did you do? Did you get someone to take the pictures of the damage to your body?"

Susa nodded. "I also..." She shook her head. "You'll think..."

"Susa," Bria said, "we aren't going to judge you. You did what you did to protect yourself."

"I have videos of him abusing me. He threatened to kill me if I didn't keep my mouth shut about the hormone therapy. And...he called out 'Lorinda' when he climaxed. Every time. I guess I look like her."

"Damn, Iloyn is going to go ballistic," Bria muttered.

"We need to see the videos." Mel's voice was flat and tight as if she had to bottle up some strong emotion. "What else is on them?"

"Just Tenar and me." Susa added quickly, in a pleading tone, "I never took videos of any of your men, or any other man. I swear it."

"We believe you." Mel's voice held relief as she patted the woman's trembling hand.

"If you're embarrassed, ashamed, don't be." Nadia rubbed Susa's shoulder. "I would've done the same thing."

"Really?" Susa asked.

"Well, that and taken his balls off with a rusty, extremely dull battle-blade," Nadia added with a shrug, "but I'm Siberian, and we're mean."

Everyone laughed including Susa.

"So, how did you set this up? Do you have tech expertise?" Mel asked.

"No, but Gillea, one of the sex surrogates, was an IT Security engineer before her *gemat* died. When she chose to have a sex life as a surrogate, she was fired from her job." Susa's lips twisted into a wry smile. "Gillea wired our houses to make them more secure. When she realized what was happening to me and some of the others, she installed video cameras which were voice activated to turn on at the mention of certain phrases. I only used it with my known violent clients. I can't speak for the other women."

"*Known violent clients*?" Nadia's aura flashed red and gold, but her voice and face remained calm. "There were others besides Tenar in the Caradoc family who hurt you?"

Susa nodded. "But they're dead now."

"Darga was one, wasn't he?" Bria strained to keep her voice calm and her face expressionless when all she wanted to do was let loose with the Caradoc battle cry and go after everyone who'd ever harmed Susa.

"Yes, and Luka Nabann, Beria's husband, was the other," Susa said. "He was so dominated at home that he liked to take his anger out on me. He was always sorry afterward."

"Pathetic worm," Mel cursed.

Nadia fisted her hands as if she wanted to choke somebody.

When Bria could trust herself to speak without snarling, she said, "After all you've gone through, I can see why Jump Station Charybdis would seem like an idyllic get-away."

Nadia stiffened and turned shocked eyes toward Susa. "You're going there?" When Susa nodded, Nadia added, "Why, in all that is holy, are you going there?"

"My cousin Borac and his family live there."

Nadia relaxed. "That's okay then. He'll keep you safe. His family is precious." She cast a sly look at Bria. "Bria's brother Damon is a hottie and a half. And if he isn't to your liking, she has five other brothers on Gliese 581C, which is a really nice, peaceful place."

Susa laughed. "Thanks, I'll keep that in mind. Oh, and I'll be sure to tell Bria's brother you thought he was a hottie."

Nadia grinned at Bria's groan.

"Okay, enough gossip and matchmaking," Mel snapped. "What in Balcon's Balls are we going to do about Tenar? Bria, you've put forth a serious...and logical argument in the case against Ilar's brother. But we need proof, not just your deductions and gut instincts."

"I'll be happy to give you the video discs so you can discredit Tenar," Susa said. "I have the originals, verified by both myself and Gillea. They are in a lock box under my bedroom floor."

"I don't want to be in the room when our men see those," muttered Nadia.

Susa nodded, a dark look on her face. "Probably a good plan. The Premier and your men are good men. Honorable men. There are other things Tenar said which I haven't told you, can't say aloud. You have to look your mother-kin in the face. I'm not sure even your men or the Premier want to hear some of the vitriol coming out of Tenar's mouth." She paused and then added, "And Tenar often ranted and raged about topics which now make sense in light of what Bria has conjectured. But you need to see...and hear the videos for yourselves."

Bria leaned over and hugged Susa. "You're very brave to help us. Now, you've had enough emotional turmoil for today. We'll take you home, retrieve the discs, and give them to our security team to take to the Premier. We'll also make sure you have a guard from Gold Squadron until you leave for the jump station. Then we *gemates* will go to have tea at Tenar's home."

This would be war on a different level. A war of wits and truth against deviousness, dark secrets, and lies. With Mel and Nadia by her side, Tenar had no chance.

"We're still going to tea?" Nadia asked.

"Sure. Why not? We have to get a sense of his guilt, don't we?" Bria said. "Plus, I still need the texts he promised me. I think we'll find he redacted and rewrote history since the time of Ilar's ascension to the leadership and maybe even farther back."

Mel added, "We can compare his revisionist writings against those my parents placed into the escape pod with me and to the living memory of Elders who aren't in Tenar's pocket."

"I see tea as a scouting mission, Nadia," Bria explained. "I can ask pointed questions. Then the three of us can testify as to his emotional reactions and his truthfulness."

"That's right," Mel said. "Legally, a battle-mate's testimony is considered admissible even without anything else to back it up but her empathic truth-sense. With three of us reading him, plus what's on Susa's tapes, we can begin to build a circumstantial case. The irony is he doesn't believe in battle-mate telepathy or empathy. And it'll be battle-mates who'll take him down."

"I agree with all that. I wasn't implying I didn't want to go. I do," Nadia said. "But if we're going to send Susa's discs to Ilar with V'niko and A'nan, then what guards are we taking with us? Our men would have a fit if we don't take guards."

"Good point, Nadia. How about the Jod brothers?" Mel suggested and then looked at Bria. "They did a good job when Nadia dealt with mercs on Tarn and a giant worm on Ursa 345."

Nadia visibly shuddered. "Ugh, don't remind me about the giant worms. But I agree, the Jods are a good choice."

"Good, that's settled," Bria said. "Call them now, Mel, and have them meet us at Susa's. We can fine-tune our approach on how to get Tenar to reveal his guilt while we drive."

Bria and the other women stood and walked out of the Officer's Lounge. V'niko and A'nan joined them at the doorway. The large warriors had speculative looks on their faces. Volusians might not have empathic abilities, but they could read body language. With their hands on their weapons and hyper-alertness in their stances, they closed in on their charges.

"Are we keeping our minds open to our men while we're in Tenar's home?" Mel asked.

"Yes," Bria said, "but only *after* we get there. If they touched our minds now, they'd try to stop us. And I don't see any other way to get Tenar to incriminate himself. Plus, he obviously thinks women are lower life forms, so he won't be suspicious and will be more open with us than he would our men or Ilar."

"May I say something?" Susa asked.

"Sure." Bria turned toward her.

"You need to take more guards." Susa looked at the two Volusians, who were now openly listening to the women's conversation. Both men wore grim looks on their rough-hewn faces. "The video evidence has been safely hidden under my floor for years—it can stay hidden for a few more hours. That way you can take these nice big Volusian warriors with you. I know the Jods, and while they are typical Prime warriors, they are not equal to the caliber of the Caradoc men or these two."

V'niko interjected, "I don't know what you are planning, Bria. But this woman makes sense. And I do not want to answer to any of your *gemats*. They made it very clear what they expect of your guards. If you so much as shudder with fear, they will emasculate us."

A'nan nodded, his expression solemn and dark.

Bria looked at Nadia and Mel. "Well, ladies?"

"We'll take V'niko, A'nan, and the three Jods—plus we'll weapon up," Mel said. "We'll still meet at Susa's. I'll have the

Jods bring us laser pistols, battle-blades, and a few other war toys. We'll hide our weapons in tote bags. If Tenar asks us about the totes, we'll say we brought them along to take home some of the books with us to study at our leisure."

"And I will give you one standard hour to get to Tenar's and make nice before I call Wulf and tell him about the video discs, your deductions, and your plans." Susa held up a hand, silencing their protests. "You already agreed to be open to your mates. So, this is just a safety precaution. They'll want to see the discs as soon as possible, and my house is closer to Tenar's than the Alliance buildings and your homes—just in case you need more warrior backup."

"This woman makes much sense," V'niko said. "We do it this way, or A'nan and I will render you unconscious and take you to your men."

A'nan nodded his agreement with his partner's threat.

"Fine. Then it's a plan." Bria looked at everyone. "Let's move. We don't have much time to take Susa home and then get to Tenar's by tea time. I don't want to be fashionably late."

CHAPTER 21

An overlook near Tenar Caradoc's mountain estate

Tenar Caradoc's estate was a formidable fortress. The buildings and the surrounding wall appeared to be part of the mountain upon which it was situated. There were crenellated towers at the four corners and a formidable-looking gate at the entrance to, what looked to be from Bria's vantage point, a stone courtyard.

The location was starkly beautiful. Craggy rocks surrounded the residence. One of the many waterfalls the area was known for flowed from under the fortress's foundations down the side of a sheer vertical mountain wall into a tributary of the main river which flowed to Cejuru Prime's world ocean. The ocean itself could be seen in the distance, a glistening body of turquoise blue.

The extensive gardens found at Ilar's home were missing here. All trees and foliage had been cut away from the area around the battlements encasing Tenar's home. There were no feminine touches anywhere. The atmosphere was of a harsh masculine strength. No softness could survive here. It would be quickly smothered by the weight of the heavy stones and cut to shreds by the sharp angles.

"This reminds me of places found in the wastelands of Siberia," Nadia said in a hushed tone as the three women stood on an overlook about a kilometer away from their destination. V'niko, A'nan, and Bre, Cas, and Cred Jod formed a protective circle around them as they stood between the women and anyone coming up the road behind them. "The same places where we now speculate the Prime landed and made their home on Earth before Terrans fully emerged from their caves and began to build cities."

"What the place is...is bone-chilling." Bria shuddered. "I wonder why everyone thinks it's so beautiful."

"No one said Tenar's home was beautiful," Mel pointed out. "They said his view was beautiful, and it is. But as a soldier, I can appreciate the utilitarian beauty of the design. You could outlast a siege in such a place." She scanned the area. "I imagine early Caradocs gained much power and respect because of such prized properties. The only reason Ilar's current home is so different from Tenar's is because Lorinda made it so."

"And Lorinda is the key to Tenar's treachery," Bria said. "If the mating had gone the other way, his home might also have had gardens and the softness a women brings to her surroundings."

Fanciful as it might seem, Bria could smell the acridity of Tenar's treachery on the air. Feel it in the simmering hatred built into the very walls of his fortress. See it in the cold and utter bleakness of his residence. He had nothing to lose in killing off the Prime hereditary line. Tenar had already lost all that meant anything to him. When he'd lost Lorinda to his older brother, he'd gone quietly mad.

"Tenar's plot reminds me of the plays of the Terran called Shakespeare," whispered Nadia. "Family dynastic tragedies. The villain hides away in his mountain fortress. He plots and plans his revenge. When Ilar gained his first heir, the villain re-entered society, mouthed peace and forgiveness, and put his plans in place, waiting for them to fully blossom."

"Another Terran, Francis Bacon, once said 'revenge is a dish best served cold,'" Bria said. "And, Mel, you were the match to the long-buried fuse of Tenar's revenge. Nadia and I are just extra scoring points." Bria shuddered and turned to look at the other women and the men who'd come to provide backup. "Are we ready?"

"This does not feel right." V'niko's face was cast in grim lines. His pale blue skin had darkened to cobalt over his stark cheekbones, and his eyes were the color of a starless night sky. His narrowed, raptorial gaze searched the area for something, a something that had his aura screaming black and red.

"What is it, V'niko?" Mel and the others began searching the area as if V'niko's dread had infected them.

"This place is evil." V'niko pulled his laser rifle off his shoulder and flicked it to high stun. "It isn't safe for you to visit with your *gemats'* uncle today."

"Places aren't evil. People are." Nadia turned in a circle. "But V'niko is correct. We're being watched. The eyes aren't friendly."

Bria turned to look back, down the twisting, turning mountain road they'd taken to reach this point in their journey. "Maybe we'd better leave. Come back with our *gemats* and Ilar as backup." And a couple of military units.

"Too late. We're caught between whoever is behind us and Tenar's fortress. This was a trap." Mel muttered under her breath, "Wulf is going to spank my ass for this."

Then Mel began issuing orders. "V'niko, you and Cred go and see what's coming up the road. Cas take A'nan, find a higher vantage point, and see if you spot any suspicious movement coming from the fortress. Stay off the road. Tenar might've set up an ambush. Bre, find us a way off this fricking mountain other than the road. If that isn't feasible, find us a damn cave or any hole in the ground to hide in until help arrives."

Finally, Mel looked at her and Nadia. "Battle-mates, time to open up to your men. Tell them where we are, what's happening, and what we suspect. Then weapon up. Keep your eyes peeled for an attack from above, because that's what I'd do."

The five men ran to do her bidding without question.

"I'm going with Bre," Nadia said. "He'll need me to cover his ass from anyone trying to shoot him off the side of the mountain." She snorted. "Huw is going apeshit in my head. But they're already on their way. Susa didn't wait the whole hour. They've seen the videos. Huw is using some Prime swear words I've never heard before."

"So's Wulf." Mel sighed. "Be careful, Nadia. This will soon be a battle zone. Wulf's got *Galanti* soldiers coming up the mountain. Find us a place to get out of the line of fire."

Bria tried to pay attention to Mel's orders and what Nadia said, but was distracted by her own *gemat* going nuts.

Bria...Ansu bhau. If you...get hurt...I'll tie you to our bed for a month.

Well, that's no incentive. I like it when you tie me to the bed.

A reluctant chuckle came over their connection. A non-corporeal hand swept over her hair, down her back, and then swatted her butt.

Peata lubha ...stay alive until I can reach your side.

That's the plan.

Stay open to me...no matter what.

I'll try. I love you.

Don't try...do. I love you, too. Now strip the military vehicles for what you need. There should be climbing gear under the rear seats.

"This is all my fault." Bria moved toward the two vehicles they'd used to travel to Tenar's mountainside trap. "I should've taken my theories and Susa's proof straight to the men. But I never thought Tenar would figure out we suspected him this soon."

"He probably hasn't." Mel paced her to the vehicles. "Most likely, he saw tea with us as a golden opportunity to move his plot forward faster. After all, he's tried to kill or capture all of us and failed several times. So stop blaming yourself. You figured him out before he could succeed in his ultimate revenge." Mel shoved her in one direction. "Get all the weapons and the med kit from the Jods' vehicle. I'll get the same from ours."

"Iolyn said there should be climbing gear in the vehicles." Bria ran to the Jods' transport and pulled out the gear Mel had requested and placed it on the ground by the back wheel, facing away from the fortress. She then checked for the climbing gear. "Yes! We're in business. The gear is under the rear seats just as Iolyn said."

Bria pulled out all the ropes, harnesses, bags of pitons and carabiners, and hammers and laid them next to the other gear.

"Bria—" Mel's voice was tense. "We have company."

Bria scanned the area and found nothing. She turned to look at Mel. "Where?"

"Look up."

She angled her head back and found a hovering air vehicle. It was a cargo drone. The side doors were open, and a man in all-dark livery aimed a laser rifle at them.

He shouted, "Don't move. We are sending a harness down for each of you. You will put it on, and then we will lift you one at a time. If either of you attempts to run, I will kill the other. Understand?"

"Yes. We won't run." Mel signaled for Bria to remain quiet.

Bria had no intention of arguing with the man or running. They had backup on the way, and the others were safe. If she and Mel couldn't survive long enough—or find a way to escape—until help arrived, then they'd better resign as battle-mates.

The harnesses came down. They put them on. This was one time she really wished the telepathy she had with Iolyn also worked with battle-mates.

Wait, maybe it could, in a roundabout way.

*Iolyn...*Her mate was aware of her danger and was beyond pissed. Somehow that made her feel calmer than the situation warranted.

You are doing well, peata. *Don't test these men. We'll be there soon. Follow Mel's lead. I'll let you know what she plans. She and Wulf are having that discussion now.*

Good. We'll be fine. We're battle-mates.

Yes, you are. You're also my heart and my soul. Stay safe.

The sound of laser fire came from behind their position.

Bria froze for a split second and then looked at Mel, who shook her head and mouthed, "Stay alert."

Iolyn...some of our people are under fire.

Fear for her friends chilled her to the bone. V'niko and Cred must be taking on the enemy. They'd be outnumbered. Were they hurt?

We're in communication with them and are almost at their position. They're fine. I'll be with you soon.

And just like that, her fear dissipated and a preternatural calm settled over her. Iolyn was always with her, and he'd do anything to keep her safe.

The person manning the harness pulled Mel up first, then Bria.

Once inside the drone, Bria was shoved onto the floor next to Mel. The door slid shut. The drone made a wide turn and headed toward Tenar's fortress.

Mel lay on her side. Her body limp, her eyes closed.

Ice-cold water ran through Bria's veins. "Mel?" Bria shook her friend's arm. No response. But she was breathing.

As she grasped her friend's lax hand, she glared at their stone-faced captor, who still aimed his laser weapon at them. "What did you do to her?"

Iolyn...Mel is...

Wulf knows. Her life signs are good. We'll find you. Don't do anything to make them hurt you.

"We gave her a sedative, *sued seuater,*" the man said.

Seed sucker? Not ever—or not for him anyway.

Iolyn bristled in her mind. *Look at him,* lubha. *I want to see the face of the man I am going to remove a tongue from.*

Bria stared at the man, who was definitely Prime. His dark uniform had the Caradoc family crest on the shoulder.

"We will render you unconscious also. But first, I have one question for you—Where is Huw Caradoc's *karote*?"

This guy had a death wish. Iolyn's buzz-saw growl reverberated through her whole body and made her skin itch. *Huw will kill this one after I remove his tongue.*

"I don't know." Which was the truth, because she didn't.

"Go to sleep, *sued seuater*." The man used a high-pressure injector and shot her in the arm.

Blackness fell on her like a rock fall.

In the fading distance, Iolyn screamed inside her head.

———

"*Ansu bhau!*" Iolyn kicked at the mercenary lying on the ground who, while not dead, probably wished he were. Then he kicked him again. "Bria is unconscious now."

Wulf grunted and looked as if he'd like to shoot the mercenary he had at his feet.

Huw looked up the road as Cred approached with V'niko. "Where's Nadia?"

"She's with my brother Bre." Cred hooked his com unit on his belt. "They're down on the mountainside, but are climbing back up and will come to this position. Cas and A'nan will also meet us here."

V'niko nodded. "A'nan has reported the drone with Bria and Mel is definitely heading for the fortress."

"Good, at least they aren't heading out to sea or rendezvousing with a larger air vehicle," said Wulf, who then turned to address a specially selected security team from the *Galanti*. "Are we secure here?"

Wulf hadn't trusted the on-planet Home Guard's loyalties in this matter, so he'd pulled in all the personnel he could from their own crew already dirt-side.

"Yes, Captain." Lieutenant Commander Z'es, head of security on the *Galanti*, saluted. "We have loaded those still alive into the vehicles. They will be locked down in the Alliance Military facility."

"Wulf."

Iolyn turned and saw their father striding up the road, followed by four of his personal security team. "Father, what are you doing here?"

"Father, it isn't safe," Huw added.

"Tenar has your mother." Their father's face looked haggard. "He invited her to take tea with her daughter-kin. We...I...thought nothing of it. Why would I? I trusted him. When you sent me the videos of what he'd done to Susa. When I heard your report on Bria's theories, I couldn't believe them, but..."

"But what, Father?" Wulf asked.

"I should've figured it out." Their father looked older than his years. The weight of his guilt threatened to choke Iolyn.

"Father..." Iolyn hugged his father. "We all knew Tenar well, saw the face he presented to the world. It took Bria and her more objective point of view to see something didn't make sense—that all the Prime's woes began with Mother rejecting Tenar. It all fits and—"

"And his current actions have proven Bria's theories," Wulf finished for Iolyn. "Now, we need a plan to get into the fortress and get our women out safely."

"Nadia and I can help with that." Bre and Nadia, both disheveled, dirty, and breathing hard, jogged to the group. "But we need to go down and across the tributary to get into the mountainside under Tenar's fortress."

Cas and A'nan arrived from a different direction just as Bre spoke. "The cave systems," Cas said. "I forgot about them."

"Yes, the ones we played in as children." Bre turned to Wulf. "The waterfall that flows from under the fortress's foundation has carved out an extensive cave system. There are both natural and man-made tunnels that run upward into the lower levels of the buildings inside the fortress walls. As children, we explored the tunnels until forced to stop by fortified doors."

"Escape tunnels just as we have in our home, Wulf," Ilar said.

Wulf turned to Bre. "Can you get us into Tenar's home without the enemy being aware?"

Bre bowed his head to his captain. "Yes, sir, with luck, care, and some time. Once inside the natural cavern behind the falls, there are multiple tunnels. We'll need to find the correct tunnel to get us into the main residence's lowest level."

"Sons," Ilar said, "let's go get our mates."

"Father, we'll get Mother back," Iolyn said. "You need to go home. Tenar would like nothing more than to kill you—kill all of us—and achieve his ultimate revenge."

"Your mother is in there."

"Father...please." Wulf grasped their father's forearm and squeezed. "My *gemate* is pregnant. I can't worry about *you* and her."

"Nadia will go home with you, Father," Huw said. "She is also pregnant, and I don't want her in danger. Owww!" He turned toward his *gemate*. "Why'd you hit me?"

"I'm a battle-mate. I'm going after my sister-kin and my mother-kin." She turned to the Jods and V'niko and A'nan. "Pick us up some com headsets from Z'es. Bre and I found the climbing tough going. You'll need your hands. Get me some climbing gear from that pile over there. Oh, Cas, make sure you include head lamps, we're not all night-visioned like Bre. Let's get moving, people." The men jogged off to follow Nadia's orders. "Iolyn, you with us?"

"Yes." He moved to get a com headset and weapon up. His *batel rabia* was bubbling and threatened to explode into the molten wrath of an erupting volcano. He still hadn't been able to touch Bria's conscious mind. She was dreaming. Her dreamscape fed on her fear.

"Wulf, stop arguing with Father," Iolyn snapped out. "He can stay here with Z'es and the other *Galanti* soldiers and begin hostage negotiations. That will provide us a distraction at the front gate."

Iolyn joined Nadia, who already strode toward the brush she and Bre had emerged from less than five standard minutes before.

"That's a good idea, Iolyn. Nadia can stay with Father..." Huw paced his mate.

"Shut it, my *gemat*." Nadia's growl was strong and sounded much like Huw's responding snarl. "I'm on this mission. You stay with your father." She never broke stride as she slipped on the com headset and shouldered the laser rifle Bre handed her. "It'll take at least sixty standard minutes to get down the mountain and through some caves on this side of the fork of the river. Bre and I had almost made it to the fork when we heard about the attack. It's a fairly straight downhill shoot once in the caves. Getting across the Category-Four rapids will be the biggest problem."

"No, it won't," Cas spoke up. "I told Z'es we needed the packs with inflatable boats and paddles. He handed me two. Cred and I are carrying them. We've paddled in those rapids before. We know the tributary's tricks."

"Good job." Iolyn looked over his shoulder and was happy to see Wulf, V'niko, and A'nan had joined them. Wulf had picked up some additional climbing gear as had V'niko and A'nan.

As he kept pace with his sister-kin, who seemed to have the stamina of a long-distance runner and the pacing of a sprinter, Iolyn kept touching Bria's mind. Each time he found no sense of awareness, he grew madder until his skin felt as if it would split open from the pressure within. He couldn't let his wrath loose now; he'd need all that unrestrained energy later when he got his hands on the enemy who'd dared to take his mate.

Iolyn finally received something from Bria as he carefully picked his way across a rockslide. Her mind was filled with crazy images of ancient weapons and dwarves. She was barely conscious, but he saw what her unfocused eyes took in around her. Then he recognized where she was in the fortress.

"Bria is starting to wake up. I'm seeing Tenar's library."

Wulf came up on Iolyn's shoulder. "Can you see Melina? My little one is still unconscious. If Bria is rousing, why isn't my *gemate*?"

"I don't see her yet." Iolyn chanced a glance at his older brother. "As soon as Bria responds to me, I'll find out about Mel. They'll be fine." Iolyn's words were more confident than his feelings. He prayed to the One they'd be true.

"Yes." Wulf growled low in his throat, setting off the other Prime in the group. "They have to be. Because if they are not..."

"...death will reign this day," Iolyn completed his brother's thought.

Wulf nodded, then called out, "Nadia."

"Yes, Wulf?"

"Take Huw and scout ahead since you've been this way before. Travel light so you can move faster." Nadia had already begun handing off unnecessary gear to Bre and his brothers. "Huw, report back on alternating Com Code XX 56."

"If we find anyone lying in wait for us?" Huw asked as he too shed gear and handed it off to V'niko who'd moved up to partner Bre.

"Kill them."

Huw nodded and then turned to catch up with Nadia who moved like the wind over the rocky ground, heading for a dark hole in the mountain barely covered by brush.

Iolyn watched as both Huw's and Nadia's headlamps went on just before they disappeared into the black maw leading underground.

CHAPTER 22

Tenar Caradoc's Library

Dwarves? Ancient weapons? And lots of dark wood and a fireplace large enough to roast an ox-steer. Where was she? Middle Earth in a Tolkien adventure? Was she dreaming? She couldn't ever recall dreaming about twentieth century Earth fantasy novels before.

"Bria? Mel?" Her mother-kin's voice called to them. Her voice was strained, filled with exhaustion and...fear.

That was unacceptable. Lorinda should never be afraid. She was Iolyn's honored mother.

"Bria." Lorinda's voice was closer now.

A cool hand soothed Bria's achy head. The motion reminded her of her mother. But her mother was on Gliese 581C, wasn't she?

"I can see your eyes glinting gold between your lashes. Wake up, darling girl. We're in big trouble."

Peata! *Wake up. Now! Tell me you're all right.*

"Iolyn!" Bria sat up on a leather sofa. The room, and Lorinda's face, swirled around her.

I'm fine.

Bria! His sigh was filled with relief. *Finally, you're awake. Where's Mel?*

She looked around and found her friend on a couch across from hers. *Mel is rousing. Your mother's here.*

We know. Is she okay?

"Lorinda, did Tenar kidnap you?" Bria squinted at her mother-kin and found no surface injuries. But the older woman's eyes held despair, sadness, and fear.

Your mother looks unharmed. We're in what appears to be a library.

You are. I recognize it. I'm with you. Just touch my mind when you need to. Stay safe. We're coming.

"Tenar invited me to tea with you girls." Lorinda's eyes filled with tears. "I can't believe he'd do this. He wants revenge, he said, because I marked with Ilar and not him. He told me some horrible things he's done. He's evil to the core."

Bria patted her mother-kin's trembling hand. "I'd already guessed as much."

"No," slurred Mel, "you made brilliant connections and deduced it. But it's always nice to have it proven." She sat up and swayed side-to-side. She braced herself with one hand on a sofa cushion. "*Diew*, if I weren't already sick to my stomach, this room would make me. Where are we?"

"You are in my library, Melina." Tenar walked into the room followed by several dark-uniformed guards armed with lasers and battle-blades. Several other men remained in the shadows just outside the doorway.

Bria's nerves jangled. Something bad was about to happen, not that what had already happened wasn't bad. But this would be something worse. She shot a glance at Mel, who'd also gone hyper-alert. Lorinda looked between the two of them and frowned.

Bria shook her head as her mother-kin opened her mouth to speak.

Lorinda nodded.

"You invited us to tea," Bria said. "Why are you treating us this way?"

"Because Ilar's sons cannot produce any more heirs for the leadership position." Tenar moved to sit in a large wingback chair covered in some animal hide. "I was always meant to rule. Ilar stole that from me. Then he stole the only woman I ever loved." Lorinda inhaled sharply, but said nothing. "He needs to feel pain and then he needs to die. His sons, while good boys, must also go—except Wulf. He's mine, isn't he, Lorinda? Wulf is my son and heir."

The man was bat-shit crazy.

Lorinda's indignant gasp underlined just how delusional Tenar was. Her mother-kin fisted her hands on her lap. Her face, formerly pale, now blazed with anger. As the older woman moved to rise from the sofa, Bria grabbed her arm and held Lorinda back.

Tenar's guards had raised their weapons and had Lorinda in their sights.

"I was a virgin when I mated with Ilar." Lorinda snarled. "You are a liar. A traitor to our people. A murderer of innocent unborn children. And a defiler of our environment."

Tenar's eyes gleamed with a crazy light. "Ah, Lorinda, I am all of those things and more. And it was you who made me."

Lorinda moaned and Bria hugged her mother-kin to her side and muttered under her breath, "He made himself. Don't let him get to you."

Mel snorted loudly. "Well, Bria, the crazy old coot just proved all your deductions were true."

Tenar turned his demented, wrath-filled eyes away from the woman he professed to love and looked at Bria, then Mel. "Explain yourself, Melina."

"Bria figured out you are behind the rebellion, the damage to the Prime women's immune systems which in turn caused the lower birth rate, and the purveyor of misinformation about the *gemat-gemate* bond."

Tenar grunted and bowed his head at Bria. "Very intelligent, aren't you?"

Bria bowed her head. "And you are a sick fuck." The man's foul presence created a bad taste in her mouth. A soothing, minty sensation replaced the funk. Iolyn was with her, caring for her, providing what she needed to get through the ordeal.

Tenar waved his guards back as they moved in Bria's direction. "Most likely."

"You set out to destroy the Prime race because you wanted what your brother had," Bria accused.

"Yes, I did. And I did a very good job, don't you think?" Tenar laughed.

Bria didn't answer, instead, stalling for time, she asked, "Joining the Galactic Alliance and Mel's appearance were the catalysts to accelerate your revenge, weren't they?"

Tenar clapped. "Very good, Doctor. Too bad I have to get rid of you." He looked at Lorinda. "I would have treated you like a queen. Those boys should have been mine."

"You, *apayebo*." Lorinda spat out the word.

Bria squeezed Lorinda's arm and her mother-kin quieted. "So, are you going to kill us?"

"No, no, never." He rose from his chair and gestured toward the doorway in a come-hither motion. "Come in, gentlemen, and meet the merchandise." He turned back to the three women. "I've sold you to these men. It's very expensive running a rebellion, you know. Melina and Lorinda, they plan to use you most cruelly before selling you to a brothel on Mars. As for you, Brianna, one of them has chased clear across the galaxy to find you. He wants to keep you and use you in unspeakable ways, I'm sure."

Tenar smiled, his expression twisted and lascivious.

"Jotak!" Bria inhaled sharply as the large Dornian entered with five other Dornians and another group of men. Two of the latter group looked familiar. For Iolyn's benefit, Bria looked and pointed. "Holtsclaw and Joelo are the men who tried to kidnap me on Oz Space Port."

They're dead men. Iolyn's mental voice sounded as if he were chewing on titanium rivets.

"Yes..." Tenar replied. "They're mercenaries in my employ. I knew if you started digging into the fertility issues on my planet, you'd find a cure. I couldn't have you ruin my revenge, now could I?"

As Bria was about to ask Tenar to explain how he'd compromised the Prime women's immune systems, she was cut off—

"There are supposed to be four women." The merc leader, a rough-looking hominid, probably from Umbraxi solar system, stepped toward Tenar and snarled, "Where is the tall fair-hair you showed us? She would bring lots of money. Much more than these dark-hairs."

"Yes, well, you'll have to wait." Tenar looked at his personal guards, who shook their heads. "My people are searching the mountains for her."

"Then we wait. We aren't leaving without the fair-hair," the Umbraxian merc said, obviously the leader of the motley gang.

Jotak turned to glare at the merc leader. "I want to leave now. We can't take the chance that a rescue might succeed. I must get Brianna away from here."

"Dornian scum," spat the mercenary. "My ship. My rules. We stay."

Bria, there are caves under the house. They're accessed through the basement.

Bria squeezed Lorinda's hand and muttered "get ready to run." She looked at Mel, who nodded and had a slight twist to her lips and a gleam in her eye. Wulf must've fed her the same information.

Their men weren't close enough and the emotions in the room were getting ugly. Fast. If a fight broke out between the mercs and Jotak and his Dornian friends, the women had to get the hell out of there—or take the risk of getting killed in the crossfire.

Weapons. She needed a way to defend herself—and the others. She searched the room for some nice sharp blades she could grab on the way out and saw several in a display case against the far wall. Tenar really wasn't all that smart. For good measure, she slipped a jewel-encrusted ceremonial knife from a side table into her pocket. *Really* not that smart.

Mel watched the arguing men closely. She stiffened, shot Bria a piercing glance, and mouthed, "Ready?"

Bria nodded and showed Mel the knife she'd acquired.

Mel lifted her hand and revealed a short battle-blade slid up her sleeve. Her sister-kin must have had it strapped to her leg under her dressy go-to-tea slacks.

The argument had escalated, and the war of words only needed a small spark to have it explode into a conflagration.

Iolyn's tension had escalated about the same time Mel's had. His "be ready" whispered through her mind.

A man in the uniform of Tenar's private guards appeared at the open doorway. His eyes filled with fear. "Elder, the Alliance Military is at the front gate. Your brother is demanding to speak with his *gemate* and his daughter-kin."

Jotak roared. "See? We should've left as soon as the women were taken." Then he shoved the merc leader.

Crap. Jotak was certifiable, poking a stick at a wild beast.

The merc leader charged Jotak and grabbed him by the throat. The two began to fight. The other mercs rushed the Dornians.

Tenar got out of the fighting men's way and moved toward Bria, Mel, and Lorinda, his guards at his side. But Tenar and his men got caught up in the melee.

Bria, get out of there.

"Now," Mel yelled and threw a glass globe at the head of the guard on Tenar's left. The man staggered and clasped his head.

Bria threw the fancy knife at the guard on Tenar's right, and the finely honed knick-knack lodged in his throat. Blood spurted with each rapid beat of his heart.

At the same time Bria had thrown the knife, she pulled Lorinda off the couch and urged her toward a side doorway which looked to lead to a back hallway.

As Bria hurried after Lorinda, she grabbed the knives she'd spotted earlier, stuffing them in her pockets, and grabbed a mid-length, ancient battle-blade off the wall by the door. Lorinda gathered likely weapons also, muttering under her breath, "Thank the One, Ilar taught me how to knife fight."

Mel snickered at Lorinda's words as she joined the two, and they exited into the hallway. "You two are bloodthirsty. I think you have more knives than there are bad guys."

"You should talk." Bria sniffed. Mel had just as many weapons as she had. "By the way, nice throw with the tchotchke."

Mel grinned as if she were having a grand time. Her sister-kin was nuts.

"Children, are we going out or down?" Lorinda interrupted their byplay.

"Down to the escape tunnels," Mel said. "Do you know the way?"

"Yes. When Tenar, the *bak*, courted me. He gave me a tour." Lorinda's smile was venomous. "Probably the only thing I'll ever be grateful to him for. Go left at the next hallway."

"Is anyone following us?" Bria asked as she jogged to keep up with Mel while at the same time keeping Lorinda between them. She didn't want to slow down to look back.

"Not yet," Mel said. "They're fighting—but that won't last long enough."

Lorinda shoved open a door and descended steps illuminated by lights along the stairwell. "*Diew.*" She panted as she took the steps faster than Bria thought was safe for the older woman. "He did all this because I marked with Ilar. I can't believe it. I told the *bak* I loved Ilar. I loved Ilar even before we marked."

"And so, Tenar plotted and planned." Bria caught at Lorinda's blouse as the older woman stumbled. "Careful, mother-kin... He punished Ilar for stealing you away by striking at the people Ilar was raised to protect. And Tenar's machinations helped tip the Prime people close to extinction."

"Damn good revenge," Mel said. "But crazy."

"Ilar suspected a conspiracy, but couldn't prove anything," Lorinda gasped out and placed a hand on the wall as she quickly descended the stairs.

"So, he shoved the joinder with the Alliance down the Elder Council's throats and forced the traitor's hand." Mel hummed her approval. "My *gemat*'s father is one smart man."

Bria's heart pounded, and she gasped raggedly. The pace Mel set was wicked, but in Bria's head a clock counted down at light speed as she sensed evil was in hot pursuit.

Lorinda, who looked exhausted, muttered "right" and "left" as they ran through narrow hallways, always heading downward.

Finally, they stopped at a closed door. All three of them took the time to catch their breath and listen for the sounds of pursuit. The men chasing them weren't close enough to hear yet, but she and Mel exchanged worried looks. Impending danger hung thickly in the air.

"Are my sons getting closer?" Lorinda asked.

"Yes." Bria's breath hitched. "They just exited a dark pit of hell, Iolyn's words, and are launching small boats to get across some rapids to get to the waterfall. Does that sound right?"

"From what I recall, yes," Lorinda sighed out the word and leaned against the wall as if her legs could no longer hold her upright. "That's where I'm taking us. To the cave behind the waterfall. Beyond that door is a natural cave which leads to several man-made tunnels, one of which will connect to a natural tunnel that ends in the cave behind the waterfall."

"Okay." Mel opened a door, stopped, and held up a hand to halt them. "No lights, dammit. Somewhere, Tenar has to have some lanterns."

They backtracked and began searching along the lower level corridor.

"I found some," Lorinda called from one of the small rooms they'd passed. "Watch..."

Lorinda's words were cut off.

"Come back, girls, or I'll kill her." Tenar's voice echoed off the stone walls of the narrow hallway. Then he yelled, "You, stupid bitch...you bit me!"

Good for Lorinda. Bria looked at Mel and lifted one of her many knives, then mimed throwing. Mel nodded.

"He's alone." Lorinda screamed, then uttered a cry of such pain that Bria felt it to her bones.

Something fierce rose inside Bria, powered from the deep well of her battle-mate energy. Bria growled. She ran back and skidded to a halt. Tenar had his arm around Lorinda's throat. She tore at his forearm with her nails. Her eyes bulged.

"Tenar," Mel yelled as she came abreast of Bria.

The big Prime sneered. "You come any closer, I'll break her neck."

Bria had a shot. Not an easy one, but it might be enough of a distraction for him to let Lorinda go so Mel could get in and finish him off. Tenar was a head taller than Lorinda, plus he'd shifted her head to the side in preparation to break her neck.

Mel looked at Bria and nodded, then moved to attract Tenar's attention. "Tenar, let Lorinda go."

Bria tuned out Mel and Tenar's exchange, took a deep breath, and focused on her target—Tenar's thick neck. With Iolyn's silent encouragement, she raised her arm, and with both her and her warrior-*gemat*'s strength behind it, she threw. The point entered Tenar's throat and slid through his neck like a hot knife through butter.

As Tenar grabbed the blade and staggered back. The gargling sounds he made had her stomach clenching. He expelled a whistling sigh…and then nothing.

Lorinda had fallen to the ground. Her hands were at her throat. Her harsh, wheezing breaths were painful to hear.

Mel went to Tenar. Bria ran to help Lorinda.

The older woman gasped for every breath, a look of panic in her eyes.

"Just take slow, small breaths, mother-kin." Bria gently massaged Lorinda's abused throat muscles as she checked to see if the trachea was intact. "There you go. You don't look so blue anymore."

Lorinda lifted a trembling hand and patted Bria's arm and whispered through her abused throat, "Thank you for my life, darling girl."

Mel knelt next to them and used the edge of her tunic to wipe the tears and blood off Lorinda's cheek. "He's dead." She looked at Bria. "You okay?

Bria nodded. Or she'd be okay once her knees stopped shaking, her stomach calmed down, and she could forget the garbled death sounds Tenar had made. She'd never get comfortable with taking a life, battle-mate or not. The aftermath was a killer.

It was necessary. A phantasmal touch soothed her shoulders and neck while a small spurt of masculine-feeling energy reinforced her knees and calmed her stomach. The sounds, well, there was nothing he could do to erase that memory. *I'll work on that later,* peata. *In our bed.*

Mel examined her closely as if she could read Bria's mind, then shook her head. "No, you're not...but you will be. Also, remind me to never, ever, piss you off when you have something sharp in your hand." Then she added, "I just let Wulf know his mother's fine, Tenar is dead, and we're safe in the basement."

"Yes, I just received instructions to stay the hell put. They're gonna blow the front gate and take out all the unfriendlies. Iolyn doesn't want me to get my butt blown up before he has a chance to spank it." Bria gasped then turned red as she looked at her mother-kin. "Oh, Lorinda..."

Lorinda winked. Her voice still husky and strained, she said, "Ilar...the same. Lovely, isn't it?...Alpha-male posturing when..."

"When they'd sooner stab themselves in the heart than hurt us," Mel finished. She patted Lorinda's shoulder. "Rest your voice. Just breathe."

The three of them smiled at one another, but the smiles quickly died away as they heard a voice echo down the hallway. "Those bitches have to be down here somewhere, Jotak. We'll find them. The old cook said there was an escape tunnel. We sure can't go out the front. The whole damn Alliance Military stationed in this area looks to be out there."

Bria, Mel, and Lorinda didn't linger. They picked up the two lanterns Lorinda had found and ran quickly and quietly for the cave beyond the door.

Iolyn...Jotak...his friends...after us. Going into the tunnels.

We've turned back. We're close to the waterfall. We'll find you. Just stay open to me. Do not engage them.

Not my plan. Hurry.

We are.

CHAPTER 23

Lorinda led the way into the cave.

"Stop a second, mother-kin," Mel said. "Bria and I need to see if we can jam the door from this side. Slow them down a bit."

Lorinda nodded, her face an eerie mask in the light from the lantern.

Bria waved the lantern she held around and didn't see anything they could shove in front of the door. "How, Mel?"

Mel held up a laser pistol. "I took it off Tenar."

"Why not set up an ambush and shoot them?" Bria waved that off. "Forget that. My brain is not working on all synapses." Laser pistols couldn't kill Dornians. Cutting off their heads would work, but most people didn't hold still and allow themselves to be decapitated. A sharp knife to the frontal lobe would work, but was also tricky since the target would be moving. God, she was getting bloodthirsty. Jotak scared the crap out of her. "What are you going to do?"

"I think, using the laser pistol, I can weld the battle-blade I picked up to keep the door from opening."

"Won't they blast through it?" Bria watched Mel heat the iron of the ancient weapon and then affix it across the metal door and frame like a permanent lock.

"Eventually." Mel looked at Bria and winked. "But we could hook up with our men by then."

Bria nodded. *Hurry, Iolyn.*

I am.

The two joined Lorinda, and they moved forward. They were about one hundred meters from the doorway when the sound of loud thuds reached their ears.

"Is there anywhere to hide up ahead?" Mel asked Lorinda.

"No."

They'd come to a spot where three tunnels branched off from the cave.

Lorinda added, "This was only meant as an escape route to the river and then to the ocean. The Caradoc ancestors didn't build any safe rooms."

"Which one do we take?" Mel asked.

Lorinda held up the lantern and swept it from one tunnel to the next and then the last. "The One save me, I can't remember." Tears sounded in her voice and Bria rubbed her back. "I do know not all go to the cave behind the waterfall."

A loud boom then a crash echoed down the tunnel. Angry men's voices rode the underground air currents.

Air currents!

"There's air movement, Mel," Bria said. "They blew the door, and I can feel a slight breeze moving over me from behind. It's moving toward the far right tunnel."

"Good observation, Bria." Mel gently turned Lorinda's shoulders and nudged her to the right. "Move quickly, and don't whisper. Only talk when necessary and use low monotones. They carry less."

Lorinda moved into the tunnel. Mel followed Lorinda. Bria brought up the rear.

This tunnel was smaller. The air was stale and stifling. As Bria moved forward, the stone walls closed in. Panic threatened to steal her breath. The darkness, only broken by the dim lanterns, felt oppressive. Had Lorinda chosen the wrong tunnel? Were they heading for a dead-end?

Breathe, peata. *Don't let your fear rule your mind.*

Bria took several breaths through her tightly constricted throat. Then she realized the breeze was not only still there, but it also seemed to be stronger the further away they moved from the tunnel split. Somewhere ahead was an opening to the outside. She took a deeper breath and let out a wobbly sigh of relief.

Thanks, gemat. *Are you in the cave yet?*

Yes. Bre Jod is leading. If you see a red glow, it is his caving light.

Has Wulf told Mel this?

Yes. We understand you're being followed. We're moving as fast as we can, but the tunnel is very narrow at this end, and it is slow going.

Okay. Be careful.

"I see a light," a low angry male voice echoed down the tunnel. It seemed close, but sounds were deceptive in caves.

They know where we are.

Lorinda was getting weaker and weaker. Mel was pregnant with an heir to the Prime leadership. Bria knew what she had to do and threw up a wall around her mind to keep Iolyn from talking her out of her plan.

Bria tugged on Mel's sleeve. "Go. Take Lorinda. I'll stall Jotak."

"No." Mel's voice held anger, fear. Her face looked almost demonic in the light from the lantern as she turned toward Bria.

Lorinda turned and shook her head. "Stay together."

"That's foolish," Bria muttered. "I can do this. I have to do this."

"I'll stay," Mel offered. "I have more training."

Bria pressed a hand over Mel's still-flat tummy. "Not an option. Jotak is my problem. Not yours."

Mel growled sub-vocally, but nodded. "If they take you—"

Bria cut Mel off. "Then my *gemat* will come get me. Now, move."

Mel thrust several ancient knives carved from animal bone into Bria's hand. "Go for a kill with each and every throw, sister-kin. If you get the chance, cut off their heads."

Bria gulped. "That's the plan." She could do this. Life or death. She wanted to live, so Jotak and the others had to die.

Mel took Lorinda's elbow and soon the light from the one lantern they'd taken and the sound of their soft footfalls were gone.

The only remaining sounds in the dark, narrow tunnel were the shuffling of large feet heading for her position, the *throb, throb, throb* of her rapidly pounding heart in her ears, and the pounding of Iolyn's angry will against her shields.

Quickly, Bria prepared her defense. She placed the lantern on the tunnel floor, a meter from the slight turn in the tunnel where she would hide. She turned up the intensity of the light and aimed it in the direction from which the men would approach. They would be blinded, giving her time to target them. Then she moved back and into the shadows.

She'd start by throwing her sharpest weapons first. With any luck, she'd take down the enemy and then could finish them off before the pseudo-reptilians had a chance to heal themselves. She had very little space in which to maneuver, and now that she'd placed the light closer to the enemy, she had no way of retreating in the inky darkness of the tunnel leading toward the waterfall cave.

To skew the odds in her favor, she'd need help from her warrior-*gemat*. Taking slow, calm breaths, she lowered her mental shields and met a blast of red-hot rage and fear coming across their mate-bond.

Bria! Bria! Answer me!

I'm here. They aren't...yet. Are you going to be a help or a hindrance, gemat?

Iolyn's fear-filled rage chilled to arctic ice temperatures as the frigid calm of full-blown *batel rabia* set in place. Bria felt the other Prime with Iolyn join in, even Nadia. Mel, who could not have met up with the rescue team yet, also rode the wave.

Ride the battle rage, Bria lubha. *We'll be there soon. Do. Not. Get. Hurt.*

Top of my to-do list, warrior-gemat. The enemy was closer now. She swore she could smell their anger as they approached. *Iolyn...I love you. It's time.*

Iolyn's response was to stroke a phantom hand over her hair and then send her a burst of strength to aid her throws as he had earlier. She also sensed the flow of Prime energy building in strength and speed, like an unearthly tsunami, as the rescue team came ever closer.

"The light is stronger ahead," Jotak said. "It is not moving. They must have hit a dead end."

"Or it's a trap," one of the other Dornians said.

Jotak snorted. "Brianna is a doctor. The one woman is old, and the other I scented as with child."

"Tell that to the men they killed," retorted the only Dornian who seemed to have a brain.

"Mere luck, Davi." Then Jotak called out. "Give up, Brianna, and we'll let the other females go. We came only for you."

"Speak for yourself, cousin," replied Davi. "We can sell the others back to the Prime. They have worth to their mates."

Don't they know I can hear them? Dumb-asses.

Iolyn snorted. The sound, both angry and amused, tickled her senses. *Bad battle-mate.*

Aim true, peata. *If you get hurt, I* will *tie you to the bed for a month and make you beg for your release.*

Nasty warrior-gemat. *They're coming.*

"Brianna! Didn't you hear my demand?" Jotak bellowed like a wounded ox-steer.

Bria got ready to throw.

"It's a trap, cousin," Davi said.

"Are you afraid of three small women, cousin?" Jotak's words were met with laughter from the other in Jotak's party. Yes, Davi was the only bright one in the bunch. Too bad he had to die too. He'd be the one to hang back. She'd save a nice sharp blade for him.

Jotak walked into the lantern's beam of light. He stopped and squinted to look beyond the glare. His gaze passed over her hiding place. He turned his head, maybe to speak over his shoulder to the shadowy images of the men who'd come up behind him. His carotid was there. She could see his pulse, almost hear the beating of his heart.

Perfect throw, peata.

I know.

Bria pictured the anatomy chart on her lab wall in her mind. She needed a thousand-point shot to disable Jotak. A preternatural calm settled over her, aided by Iolyn. She inhaled slowly and as she exhaled, she took her throw. The carved animal-bone knife split the skin on Jotak's throat and sliced his carotid open. The instinct to pull the offending object out also worked to her advantage. Jotak could bleed out before he healed.

Holding his throat, blood spewing from his wound, Jotak stumbled and ended up leaning against the stone wall, then sliding down it. This opened up her next target.

She threw her knife as the man stupidly gaped at Jotak's fallen body. She skewered the thin bone of her target's reptile-like, fragile temple. He fell to the stone floor, the knife lodged in his forebrain. He was dead.

The other Dornians hurried away from Bria's position, but not quickly enough. She threw one more knife and hit another man in the ear and into his brain. He went down also.

One, dead. Two were out of commission for the time being. She had bought herself time.

Exactly how many Dornians had been with Jotak?

Six. Mel's here. She said six, including the apayebo, *Jotak. Move back. We'll be there in less than four standard minutes and take out the rest.*

*And finish off all of them so you won't have to—*was left unsaid, but understood.

I can't. It's dark. I could fall. They could get to me then.

Iolyn's curses rang in her head. She'd never heard half those words before. She'd ask Lorinda what they meant once she got out of this mess.

"Brianna!"

She looked toward Jotak, but he lay face down, unmoving, in a pool of blood. It had to be the smart one, Davi, calling to her.

She didn't respond, but readied another knife in her dominant hand, with a backup in her left.

"We wish to get past you and escape from the Alliance Military. We will leave you and your friends alone."

As if she believed that.

This time, she answered, "Sorry. But the Alliance Military is also coming in this way. So you're stuck."

The low rumbling of voices sounded heated. Any words she did hear were in their language. The tone was vicious. They'd try to fight their way out.

Her heart was heavy and her soul, weary. She'd killed Tenar, the one Dornian, and probably the guard in the library. If these three charged her, she'd be forced to defend herself and possibly kill again. She really didn't want to, but—

You will. You will survive. I'm almost there.

Iolyn's iron will bolstered her. She sensed him coming closer and closer. His fear for her was strong and acrid. But it was—*Too late.*

The remaining three Dornians rushed her all at once. They had blades in their hands and laser pistols. Off-balance and panicking, she threw a knife and caught the leading Dornian in the throat. Pure dumb luck. He fell, and the other two leapt over his body and continued coming at her.

The one she assumed was Davi stunned her as she tried to throw another knife. Her legs gave way, and she dropped her weapon. It was a stun meant only to debilitate. It worked. Her limbs were useless.

Bria! The Caradoc battle cry reverberated up the tunnel. The wave of *batel rabia* was so forceful she gasped, but even riding the wave and absorbing her battle-mate's energy couldn't overcome the debilitating effects of a medium stun.

Now, they had a hostage.

As Davi pulled her up against his body, her back to his front, his heavily muscled arm around her waist, Bria, to her amazement, was already healing from the laser blast.

In less than a nanosecond, Iolyn had poured energy across their bond. A stream of what in her mind's eye looked to be white-hot particles flashed around tunnel corners and across the distance between them to reach her. It was as if she were a powerful magnet and the potent stream, a pile of iron filings.

As Iolyn's warrior-energy entered her body, it was ice cold. But as she gained vitality and her limbs awakened, the power morphed and grew warmer until it got so hot it flashed to the icy heat of *batel rabia*.

Iolyn had pulled on the Prime battle rage to help heal her quickly and to prepare her for the next move in the game.

She was so much better she had to remember to act weak so as not to use her newfound advantage too soon.

She sent her love to her *gemat. What's the plan?*

Peata, when Wulf makes his overly arrogant demand for them to surrender, use the extra energy I sent you to throw the bak *off-balance. Then get out of the way. I need a shot at his head.*

Okay.

Bria heard the rescue team coming. She had to stifle a laugh. They were being really loud in their approach. Prime could move as silent as snow touching the ground, if they so wished.

Watch it, gemat. *Davi is not the stupid one.*

Let him think we're clumsy in our haste to get to you. It makes no difference.

Davi stiffened behind her. The only other Dornian who still stood was off to their side and slightly back.

Bria sent Iolyn a mental diagram of who stood where and a warning that the man she'd hit last, lay on the ground at her feet, and still moved. She also suspected the others she'd hit were also healing as time passed.

Don't worry. Just throw off this Davi's shot and get the hell out of the way.

She was on board with all that. She took slow breaths and narrowed her senses until she could pick out where Iolyn was in relation to Wulf. Nadia was there, also, as was Mel.

Where's Huw?

Coming in from behind you.

"Let my sister-kin go," Wulf roared in a tone she'd never heard before. It *was* super-arrogant. Wulf was a lot of things, but he was never super-arrogant in a lord-of-the-manor way.

Now, Bria!

Using the moves she'd learned from Mel and Nadia, Bria snapped her head back and hit Davi's sensitive nose slit, stunning him, then kicked back at his knee so she could twist down and out of her captor's arms. She fell on top of the recovering Dornian. She looked him in his slitty eyes and saw the promise of death. She pulled the knife out of his throat and then used it to slice his neck from ear to ear. His blood spurted over her. Knife in hand, she rolled over onto her knees and faced Davi, who now stood over her.

Stay down!

A battle-blade whirled through the air, close enough that the air displacement ruffled her hair. Iolyn's aim was true, and the blade sliced off Davi's head. Before she could cry out, Iolyn pulled her away from the falling Dornian's torso.

Hyperventilating and weak from the close call—covered in viscous green blood—she buried her head against her man's chest and went limp. She hoped to hell she didn't have to think, move, defend herself, or, the One forbid, kill anyone anytime soon, because she was done.

Iolyn rocked her in his arms, alternately muttering curses and words of love.

She giggled hysterically. If she'd been the first medical on the scene, she would've given her a bolus of tranquilizer. Then someone did exactly that, and the last thing she heard was Iolyn muttering, "...going to tie you to the bed for two months, not one."

CHAPTER 24

Two standard days later
Iolyn and Bria's suite, Caradoc Estate

"Please...please..." Bria arched her hips toward her mate, seeking the one touch which would finally take her over the edge of what would be her sixth orgasm of the afternoon.

Once the danger had passed and Iolyn had her checked out by both Lia and Kerr, he'd taken her home, tied her to the bed as promised, and made love to her as often as possible for forty-eight standard hours—in between a few spankings for putting herself in danger, hand-feeding her, and giving her soothing baths that led to bath-sex.

It had been a wonderful place out of time, but enough was enough. She had a lab to run, research to do, and findings to prepare for the Elder Council. Plus, she was fairly sure she was pregnant, unsurprising since the moment they'd completed the physical mating on the *Galanti*, they'd had a lot of sex and done nothing to prevent conception.

Right this instant, all she wanted was to come, and for Iolyn to be inside her when she did.

"My big strong warrior-*gemat*—" She strained to meet the tip of his tongue as it hovered tantalizingly just out of reach above her swollen-to-the-point-of-pain clit. "I need your cock. Now."

"So demanding for a bad *peata*." Iolyn shifted his head down and to the side to nip the top of her inner thigh.

Bria heaved a frustrated sigh and relaxed into the bed, which was about all the movement she could manage since her wrists were tied to the headboard and Iolyn's body weight had effectively trapped the rest of her.

"I love you, Iolyn. But you'll have to get over what happened."

When he opened his mouth to give her what she was sure would be the same lecture he'd parroted each and every time she asked to be allowed out of their rooms, she talked over him. "I see what's in your head. Deep inside you're impressed about how I handled myself. Amazed at my skill with knives. Proud I worked in tandem with Mel to save your mother. Pissed that I blocked you during part of the ordeal. But you know why I did it now, and so you were mostly over your manly snit a whole day ago."

"Manly snit?" He growled and teethed her clit.

Bria inhaled and mewled with need. "If the boot fits—admit it."

"You're correct, *peata lubha*." Iolyn chuckled and rewarded her with a lick over her clitoral hood with almost, but not quite enough, pressure to get her off.

And he knew it, the bastard. Her loving, sexy bastard. Her man was in her head, had been ever since she'd awakened in the medica after the tranquilizer Nadia had given her in the tunnel. He'd been reading her every mood, thought, and desire since then.

"Are you *one* with me, yet, little menace?" He caressed her hips in long, slow, soothing, and, above all, loving strokes.

"Yeah, I'm with you." She wiggled her butt as much as she could. "I'd like to be with you more—and soon."

She licked her lips.

Iolyn purred low in his throat like a large predatory cat who'd successfully snagged his prey. He liked it when she licked her lips. His brain went straight to the last blowjob she'd given him, which had been an hour or so ago in the shower.

"We will talk about this snit thing, later. But for now, we'll have..." Iolyn rubbed his beard-roughened cheek over her mons and placed a reverent kiss on her rumbling tummy. "...one more orgasm—together—and then I will let you up."

Iolyn licked around her opening. "We'll get dressed..."

He flicked the tip of his tongue lightly over her needy clit. "...then go to the family kitchen..."

Then he nipped the swollen bud. "...and eat a snack to tide you...and our child..." Pride and overwhelming joy flowed from his mind to hers. "...over until dinner."

As his last words died, he moved up her body and thrust into her with one powerful surge of his hips.

"Iolyn!" Bria just managed to get his name out as she exploded into a climax that threatened to send her into orbit around Cejuru Prime. And it only got stronger and better as her mate began to pummel her pussy.

When he reached his climax, he arched his back and shouted her name. With his cock lodged deep within her and flooding her with warmth, his mind sought hers and he stroked the path which connected them, made them one.

The mental touch threw Bria into another explosive orgasm that threatened to tear her apart.

I've got you, Bria. Hold onto me, peata.

As their orgasms swept through their bodies and across their bond, Iolyn released her hands. She placed her arms around his neck and held on for dear life. Her mind automatically sought and burrowed within his. Her safe harbor against a raging storm. As their bodies were buffeted by mutual orgasms and they clung to one another, Iolyn's presence in her mind soothed and cherished her. Her warrior-*gemat* would protect her in all things, even their turbulent lovemaking.

Now, you've got it.

As Bria rode the wild waves of their pleasure, their mind-body-spirit unity became even stronger than before. The *gemat-gemate* bond was something far beyond rational explanation. She was simply happy she had it. And she wouldn't trade her union with Iolyn for all the wealth of the galaxy. She loved this man with everything in her and always would. He was her lover, her protector, her rock.

I adore you, Bria.

I know.

EPILOGUE

"*P*eata, that's a flower, not a weed." Iolyn stood over Bria and shook his head.

"Why is it that I, the biological scientist in this family, know less about plants than the IT engineer?" She angled her head to look up at him.

The disgruntled look on her face made him smile.

"It's because I was raised on Cejuru Prime and know the flora, plus, as a child, I was my mother's gardening assistant." He offered her his hands. "Let me help you up, *lubha*, and you can sit on the lounge chair and supervise. I brought you a snack."

Iolyn lifted her from her kneeling position. She stretched and rubbed at the small of her back. "That reaching and pulling takes a toll on a person."

"Which is why I came out to take over." He kissed her forehead and rubbed a hand over the just-beginning-to-be-noticed baby bump. "How is our son behaving today?"

Bria wrinkled her nose. "Well, he isn't making me heave

309

everything I eat any longer. So, I'd say he's behaving." She looked past him. "What did you bring me?"

"A nice healthy fruit drink with lots of ice and a slice of that whole grain fruit bread you like." He patted her sweet round butt. "Now, go. Sit and rest. You've been weeding for two hours. I'll finish this bed and then trim the bushes."

"Okay, and..." She gave him a sweetly sly smile. "...later my randy, sweaty, alpha-male gardener can make love to the lady of the house."

Iolyn growled. "Yes, this gardener will. Then the lady of the house will get a back rub and take a nap. You've been working too hard. You and the baby need to rest."

He knelt by the flowerbed his mother and Bria had planted right after their narrow escape from Tenar. The gardens were in full bloom by the time he and Bria moved into their new home a standard month ago. The weeding was a daily chore he and Bria shared and argued over. His little menace loved the gardens, adored digging and planting, but she wouldn't know a native weed if it up and bit her on the nose.

Bria stretched out on the lounger and groaned. "*Diew,* my feet hurt." After kicking off her sandals, she took a deep drink of the juice. "Ahh, that's so good." She peeked at him over her sunshades. "By the way, the baby and I are fine. In fact, all the pregnant Prime are doing well. The non-Prime women mated by Prime males who're pregnant are also fine. There's now officially a baby boom coming to Cejuru Prime."

"The majority of the Elder Council thinks the sun rises and sets on you." The ones who didn't were being investigated by a Prime and Alliance joint tribunal for crimes against the Prime people, women in particular. "How are you and your team coming along in narrowing down the cause of the immune suppression?"

"We're getting more women volunteering their tissue and blood." She tapped out a message on her com-tablet. "Zaek's database is getting fuller, and we can now fine-tune our queries as to common denominators among the women who can't get pregnant, the ones who did and miscarried, and the ones who carried to term. I've requested more medical personnel for my team. I can't trust the local physicians, not until..."

She didn't finish her sentence. That happened a lot lately. When it did, he'd often look up and find she'd fallen asleep. He grinned and checked on his adorable, pregnant *peata*. Not sleeping. She was smiling smugly.

"Bria...?"

"Oh, sorry, just got an e-mail from Cissy. She says something is going on between Susa and my brother. She thought I'd want to know." Bria laughed.

"That ought to be fun," muttered Iolyn as he pulled another taper-rooted weed. "What were you saying about the local physicians?"

Bria put her tablet down. "Some of them admitted they were told by Elder Council members to ignore the symptoms or be black-listed. Those physicians are being forced to attend an off-planet refresher program and then will be required to take a licensing exam administered by the Galactic Alliance Health Administration. The ones who are denying all knowledge of wrongdoing will have to go in front of the tribunal and answer some tough questions. The Volusian doctor heading the Alliance side of the tribunal is reputed to be a tough son of a bitch. He'll get answers, or they won't be allowed to practice medicine anywhere in the Alliance."

She frowned. "It makes me sick to think that healers were harming their patients by withholding crucial information and not following up on the obvious reproductive issues."

Iolyn stood and wiped his hands on his pants. Then he went over and picked Bria up and cuddled her against his chest. "I know, *peata*, but you and your team will make it all right. You've already helped so many women become pregnant who had no hope prior to your arrival five months ago."

Bria snuggled her head onto his shoulder as he carried her to large doors leading to their master suite. He inhaled her sweet, and very much aroused, scent. His *gemate* needed him now. He always needed her.

"We'll find the cause for the immune suppression." She licked his throat, and he rumbled his approval. "And then my microbe therapy will be moot."

"I have faith you will." He carried her through the open doors, past the bed, and into the master bath. "But worry about all that later. Now, all you have to worry about is how many times your hunky, randy, alpha-male gardener will make you come. We'll start in the shower and progress to the bed."

"Sounds like a good plan to me." She licked his *gemat* mark as her hand snaked between them to stroke his hard cock.

"Oh, *lubha*," he purred, "that just got you bondage."

"Goody. I so hoped it would."

Iolyn threw back his head and laughed. "I love you, Bria."

"And I, you." She scraped her teeth lightly over the underside of his jaw and squeezed his cock firmly. "Now, make love to me. I need you so, so much."

As he undressed each gorgeous, glowing inch of his precious *gemate*, he thanked the One for giving him the gift of Bria.

THE END

ABOUT THE AUTHOR

Monette Michaels is the pen name for a multi-published author of suspense/thrillers. She's been married to the love of her life for far longer than she cares to remember. Her home is in Central Indiana.